I AM LUNATIC

DI DYLAN MONROE INVESTIGATES: TWO

NETTA NEWBOUND
MARCUS BROWN

Junction Publishing

Copyright © 2022 by Netta Newbound & Marcus Brown

All rights reserved. No part of this publication may be reproduced, distributed or transmitted in any form or by any means, including photocopying, recording, or other electronic or mechanical methods, without the prior written permission of the publisher, except in the case of brief quotations embodied in critical reviews and certain other noncommercial uses permitted by copyright law. For permission requests, write to the publisher, addressed "Attention: Permissions Coordinator," at the address below.

Netta Newbound & Marcus Brown/Junction Publishing United Kingdom

I am LunaTIC - DI Dylan Monroe Investigates: Two

Publisher's Note: This is a work of fiction. Names, characters, places, and incidents are a product of the authors' imaginations. Locales and public names are sometimes used for atmospheric purposes. Any resemblance to actual people, living or dead, or to businesses, companies, events, institutions, or locales is completely coincidental.

IAL - DIDMIT/ Netta Newbound & Marcus Brown – 1st Ed.

To Nick Plumley - wonderful supporter, amazing friend, taken too soon xx

PROLOGUE

"I'm going." I didn't give either of my friends a chance to respond before I disconnected myself from the game and tossed the control pad onto the bed.

Claustrophobia held me in a tight grip, and I needed to escape the confines of the bedroom, head outside, and breathe in some fresh air.

I dragged the black hoodie over my head, slipped my feet into black Nike trainers, then turned off the bedside lamp, allowing the computer screen to cast its dim glow across the room. I was careful not to make a sound.

As I walked into the open plan living room, I realised the television was still on, meaning she was there. I braced myself in preparation for her onslaught, but thankfully she was fast asleep on the sofa.

I noticed the bottle of wine and the empty glass on the coffee table, and hoped she'd drunk herself into oblivion.

Still, I was quiet as a mouse because if she woke and found me gone, another round of endless questions, followed by non-stop nagging, would be fired my way.

As I tip-toed across the room, she mumbled incoherently, startling me. Rooted to the spot, I held my breath and closed my eyes in silent prayer. Only moving again once I heard her familiar soft snores.

Relieved, I proceeded with stealth and, minutes later, I felt the cool night air against my cheeks.

I glanced up at the full moon glowing in the sky and took deep, cleansing breaths.

Almost immediately, freedom enveloped me and I felt invincible.

Moving swiftly, tall trees that masked the glow of the moonlight suddenly surrounded me.

This reminded me of when I used to sneak out after dark and roam the woods close to my old childhood home as though it were my very own domain.

Ever-changing, and dense foliage surrounded me, but I could navigate this space with my eyes closed.

It was of no importance what I looked like, or that people saw me as a freak. I loved the night – when the world and those that inhabited it weren't judging me. In that moment, I was the only one that mattered. It was the only time I felt truly alive. But something about the full moon energised me somehow. It made every single one of my senses pop and tingle.

An owl hooted, shattering the blissful silence.

I scowled, irritated by the intrusion, and looked up hoping to see it, but in the darkness, it was too well hidden within the leaves and branches of the trees.

I wondered if it sensed my intentions or what I was capable of?

"Shut the fuck up," I hissed into the darkness, wishing I could reach up, grab hold, and tear the feathered wings from its body.

Then I saw its eyes staring down, taunting me. I could almost hear its thoughts. *I know what you've done.*

Its presence unnerved me, but I had more important things to take care of and so I took off again, moving fast.

Through the silence, I heard running water in the distance. *It's close*, I thought, transported back to the time I first discovered the place and how magical it felt wandering about without a care in the world.

I'd never feared the dark or who might lurk in the shadows.

Others should fear me instead and, soon enough, they would.

Finally, I was where I needed to be and by the looks of things, it was still there, buried under the pile of stones – its temporary grave.

I knelt and brushed them to the side with my hand, gazing down at the small rotting, once furry body. Last month's kill. I marvelled at the sight of death and it's peaceful transition.

It had been easy to lull it toward me, then one quick snap of its neck was all it took to silence it forever. I bathed in the delight of maiming its corpse, practising for what was coming.

"Poor little kitty," I said. I didn't mean it, but in the still of the night, felt I owed it something.

Another owl hooted high above me.

Once again, I felt its glare. Was this judgement for my actions? I didn't care. It wasn't as if anybody would miss the scraggly looking thing, anyway.

I climbed to my feet, deciding to bequeath the already stinking corpse to the foxes and other wildlife that would take their share.

There was plenty I still needed to do before the sun woke from its slumber.

It was time to make my mark on the world.

I am LunaTIC.

Fear me.

ONE

Jane headed down the back stairs from her office on the third floor of the call centre building, more than a little jittery. During the day, she had no qualms about using the lift, but it gave her the creeps at night when there wasn't the usual hustle and bustle. Her wild imagination always drummed up way-out scenarios that wouldn't be out of place in a slasher movie.

The sound of the fire door swishing open made her jump and drop her files. *Stupid cow!* She wedged her foot in the door and bent to pick them up. With age, she was becoming more irrational and fearful. At this rate, she'd be scared of her own shadow.

"Goodnight," she called out to the lazy, good-for-nothing security guard stationed in reception who wouldn't know chivalry if it bit him on the arse.

The handsome young Pakistani lad stared at the sixty-inch widescreen television on the wall opposite the reception desk and barely acknowledged her. "Yeah, night," he grunted, distractedly, without so much as a glance in her direction. Suddenly, he let out a loud cheer.

Startled, her feet left the floor, and she turned to glower at him. He took no notice, engrossed in *Match of the Day*. "Fucking idiot," she muttered before stomping off through the double doors and into the night.

She hated working the late shift, but needs must. It paid far better than the day shifts did and, right now, she needed all the money she could get. On the upside, once tomorrow was out of the way, she had four days off to look forward to and they couldn't come soon enough.

She walked briskly across the dimly lit and deserted car park glancing at the expensive gold watch on her wrist, the next item she planned to take to the pawnbrokers. Frowning, she picked up her pace, annoyed it was already way past midnight.

She'd done that same walk a thousand times in the past but, having been afraid of the dark since she was a girl, her nerves kicked in as usual. The car park was eerily quiet, and it didn't help that she was the last one to leave the building, or that she'd had to park her car beside the boundary wall leading to the woodland – the only space she could find when she'd started her shift at three that afternoon.

Although her husband, Jeremy, once worked long hours, he'd never earned enough for her to be a lady of leisure, and since his accident, their finances had taken a turn for the worse. She resented the fact her husband was a failure, but she was stuck with him. It wasn't as if she was beating off a queue of eligible bachelors with a stick. Even in her prime she'd struggled to attract the opposite sex, and now, at fifty-five, she knew she'd be hard pushed to find anyone better. The saggy neck and heavy creases between her breasts told a thousand tales, and, despite the amount of make-up she caked on her heavily lined face, she wasn't able to erase the ravages of nature at its cruellest.

If only I could afford that facelift, she thought, getting closer to her car.

The uber-trendy hairstyle she'd paid over a hundred pounds for in what she considered a posh salon did nothing for her. She knew her colleagues took pleasure in ripping her to shreds behind her back.

Mutton Jane, they'd whisper bitchily, any time she crossed the office in designer heels so high she struggled to walk in them.

Jane glanced at her watch again and made a mental note to claim the overtime back. She'd been so busy preparing slides for next week's presentation, she'd lost track of the time. She loved that side of her job. Nothing made her happier than having a captive audience hanging off her every word.

Her eyes darted from dark corner to dark corner as she crossed the main car park. The lights flickered sporadically and hummed, setting her nerves alight. She picked up the pace.

At last, she reached her sporty little red MG and pressed the key-fob in her hand. Then she walked around it and put the files into the boot, eager to get inside, lock the doors and be on her way.

Shards of glass glistening under the lamplight drew her attention. She returned to the front of her car, furious to find her headlights shattered.

"What the hell?" She shook her head, exasperated.

Her mood worsening as the lights flickered again. "Fuck this." She scanned the car park. "How the hell am I supposed to get home now?" Not only that but add taxi fares to and from work on top of the repair costs – she'd be counting the hours until payday.

She reached into her bag for her brand-new *iPhone*, more desperate than ever to get out of there. She hit redial and her daughter answered the call after several rings.

"Hi, Mum." Jessica sounded tired.

"Hi, Jess, can you come and pick me up?"

"Why?"

"Some arsehole has smashed my headlights. I can't drive home, I might get stopped by the police."

"Aw, Mum, I just got into bed," she moaned. "I've got work in the morning. Can't you call a taxi?"

"I haven't got money for a taxi, or I would."

"What about Dad?"

"We're not speaking."

"Again?"

"Don't ask."

"Okay." She huffed. "Give me fifteen minutes and I'll be there."

"Thanks, love. I'll wait at reception." Jane ended the call. She locked the car, then froze, the sound of a low growl behind her rooting her to the spot.

The hairs on her arms stood to attention and goosebumps covered her entire body. Her senses now on high alert, she was too frightened to turn around.

Somebody was behind her – she could feel their warm breath on the back of her neck.

"Who's there?" she whimpered.

Something cold brushed against her bare shoulder. The touch was so light, she could've imagined it, but she knew she hadn't. This was her worst nightmare come to life.

Her teeth chattered, but she couldn't move. Fear had paralysed her entirely.

Her legs shook and threatened to give way.

She felt the breath again.

Another growl.

Jane stiffened. A sniffing sound sent terror darting through her veins. Warm urine ran down her legs and formed into a puddle at her feet.

"Dirty fucking bitch," a gruff male voice snarled.

Her instincts told her to run, but her legs would not respond and no matter how much she wanted to scream, she could make no sound. She prayed the security guard was watching the cameras and would come to her rescue.

"Please, don't hurt me," she croaked as she found her voice again. "I'll do anything, but—"

"Shut up," he hissed. His voice sounded odd – like he had a speech impediment of some sort.

She shuddered as the car park suddenly plunged into total darkness.

He was close – she could hear him breathing. Or was he sniffing her? *What the hell!*

Vice-like fingers gripped her left shoulder just as she felt a sharp jabbing pain under her right ear. Her legs threatened to give way with sheer terror. Then she felt something warm trickling down her neck and realised she was bleeding. Blood ran down past her collarbone and seeped onto her low-cut top.

"What have you done to me?" The chattering sound of her own teeth filled her ears.

"Look up," he said, holding her firmly in place by the left shoulder. "Tell me what you see."

"I don't want to." Her voice quivered.

"Look. Up," he snarled, "I won't tell you again."

Trembling, she did as he demanded. "The sky. I see the sky," she said quickly, hoping it would appease him.

"And what else?"

"Just the sky," she said again.

"Tell me what *else* you see." He sounded angrier with each passing second.

"The moon. I see the moon," she spat out the words, panicking. "I-I can see the full moon."

"Tell me how beautiful it is." There was no mistaking the

sniffing sound this time. It reminded her of the way a dog would sniff and snuffle at a stranger's crotch. His fingers trailed up her neck and raked through her hair, grabbing and pulling at it before letting go.

Flinching at his touch, she looked down and, from the light of the moon, she could make out her top was now soaked in blood. Strangely, she no longer felt any pain. "Please, let me go. I'll forget any of this ever happened. I won't tell a soul—I swear."

As the moon disappeared behind a cloud, he shoved her forwards and she only just put her hands out in time to stop herself face-planting the tarmacked car park. "If you know what's good for you, shut the fuck up," he growled.

She closed her eyes as he knelt beside her, terrified she was going to be raped. "Please, don't do this. I have a husband and daughter at home."

"Tell me how beautiful the full moon is."

"It's just the moon."

"Tell me." He punched her in the centre of her back.

She screamed as he beat her with his fists. Feeling his strength and his rage increase with every strike, she knew she had to do as she was told. She answered, hoping she had done enough for him to let her go. "Big and white. I-I don't know what else to say."

"Turn around," he commanded. "I want to see your face."

"I don't want to." The contents of her bowels turned to molten lava, and it horrified her to discover she had no control of that either.

"Turn around, you rancid cunt." He leaned close to her left ear and hissed. "Don't make me tell you again."

She felt every syllable he spoke.

Then he sniffed her once more.

"Okay," she said, shivering. "But please don't hurt me." She rolled over slowly, her eyes tight shut as she lay flat on her back.

"Lying there in your own mess, just like a dog," he taunted. "Now, open your eyes."

"I'm begging you, don't hurt me."

"Look at me!"

She shook her head as his strong fingers dug deep into her upper arms, forcing her to acquiesce. Her heart hammered in her chest as she opened her eyes.

The man stood above her, shrouded in darkness, until the moon reappeared. "Fear me," he whispered, baring his grotesque teeth.

Her screams were exhilarating, but soon silenced as I slashed her throat. Then transfixed, I watched whilst she clutched at the gaping wound, desperately trying to stem the flow of blood. Nothing would save her now.

"Don't fight it," I cooed. "It's your time to die. Look up at the moon and just let yourself float away." The rasping sounds she made thrilled me, and I awaited the deliciousness of her final gasp before silence took hold forever.

She gurgled, choking on her own blood. Her hands had fallen to her side, devoid of all fight. I took this opportunity to unclasp her watch strap and slip it off her wrist.

I knelt across her, fascinated, as the light faded from her eyes. My breath hitched as I relished every second, wanting to sear the image into my memory. But I wasn't quite finished with her. Not yet.

Picking up a rock from the edge of the car park, I smashed the woman's skull wide open. Then I hit her again and again until her brains resembled a mass of squashed and bloody earthworms.

Moments later, I cut her top and bra open and began slicing into her bare chest.

Looking down, I smiled and admired my handiwork.

LunaTIC

TWO

The alarm sounded, startling me from my slumber. It felt as though I'd hardly slept a wink and, to be fair, I probably hadn't. Every time I opened my eyes, my mind buzzed with what ifs. I was dreading going into the station today.

I hit the snooze button and groaned, before dragging myself out of bed.

"What's wrong?" Steve asked, pushing the covers back.

"Not looking forward to today." It was the first day back since my ex-partner, Layla Monahan's sentencing, "I'll be okay once I get there."

Steve rubbed sleep out of his eyes and squinted at me. "I'm sure the rest of the team will feel the same way. It's only natural. She was one of your own."

"Yeah but having all the details dragged back up has reopened wounds that were only just starting to heal. Things had settled down a little, over the past few months, but I could see it in Joanna's eyes on Friday—they blame me for what happened."

"How can they? It wasn't your fault, Dylan." He sat up and reached for my hand, his auburn hair in a sexy tangle.

Exhausted, I flopped back onto the bed. "I know, but—"

"No buts," he said, interrupting me. "Layla was butchering people long before you two were partnered up."

"And now she's locked up in Rampton Hospital with a load of crazies, probably for the rest of her life."

"What did you expect would happen? They deemed her mentally unfit to stand trial. She was never going to be able to go home."

"I know, but it hurts like hell."

"You did your best for her and in difficult circumstances, too."

"What about Maxine and the kids?" I'd taken the weight of the world on my shoulders, and it was in danger of crushing me.

"Maxine is fine, you know that, and the kids will adapt in time."

"They'll never adapt to having a serial killer for a mother. They don't even have their father anymore, not now that he's fully transitioned."

"That's hardly your fault. At least the kids have another parent, which was nearly not the case, thanks to their crazy mother."

"I know. You're right." But I couldn't shake the feeling of failure that the past week had brought to the fore again. Layla would have killed me given the chance, but I bore no ill will toward her. She was sick, I knew that.

"Nobody could've known what she was doing. She tampered with evidence and had first-hand knowledge of the investigation. Your colleagues should thank their lucky stars you worked it out at all—they didn't."

I loved Steve for trying to make me feel better, but nothing he said made a shred of difference. "Too little, too late," I replied, pushing myself off the bed again. "Anyway, I've gotta get ready and face the music."

"It won't be that bad, babe. They've all had the best part of six months to process what she did. The media hype will die down again and before you know it, the capers of Layla Monahan will be yesterday's news. And, besides, it's not all doom and gloom, isn't Bella back from maternity leave today?"

"Yeah, thank God." It was the small bright spot I'd been clinging on to. "And what a welcome that's gonna be for her, eh?"

"You need to stop moaning and do what you're paid to do." His eyes were tiny slits, and the vein in his temple popped. I knew he'd had enough and would no longer indulge me while I wallowed in self-pity. "You didn't lose your job like you thought you would, so go back in there and make them see you're the best they've got."

"I love the fact you have so much faith in me."

"Yes, I do and, given time, things will return to normal."

"Not for me, not until I can talk to Layla face to face. I need to find out how she is and let her know I didn't betray her."

Steve flung the duvet off him and put his feet on the floor. His expression showed the contempt he felt. "Why on Earth would you want to see her? She almost killed you, for Christ's sake!"

"She was sick, Steve. It wasn't her fault."

"And she still is, so leave the fuck alone."

I didn't appreciate being told what to do, but wasn't about to have this argument again. I grabbed my clothes and stomped to the bathroom.

Half an hour later, I returned, feeling a little calmer, but Steve had already gone. I made my way to the kitchen expecting a note, but there was nothing. Shrugging my shoulders, I tried to convince myself I didn't care. It wouldn't be the first or last time my job came between me and a boyfriend.

A few minutes later, seated at the table with a cup of coffee, I called him – not wanting our row to fester or hang over my head, today of all days.

His phone rang, but it soon diverted me to voicemail. I hung up and tried again a few minutes later. This time, he answered.

"Hello." His mood obviously hadn't lifted, but I wouldn't give up, no matter how glum he sounded.

"Are you okay?"

"I'm fine. Why wouldn't I be?"

"I didn't like leaving things like that."

"Like what?"

"We had a row and you stormed out."

"I did nothing of the sort. You went for a shower, and I had to get ready for work. There was no storming out, not on my part at least."

I wasn't about to start another argument, so decided to back down. "Well, whatever happened, I don't want to fall out with you."

"We haven't fallen out, but it doesn't mean I want to listen to you feeling sorry for yourself every time we see one another."

"I didn't realise that's what I've been doing." I felt hurt by his suggestion.

"All you ever go on about is Layla and, if I'm honest, it's doing my head in."

"I'm sorry you feel like that, but you have to understand where I'm coming from with this. She was my friend and partner—"

"I know that, Dylan, and I understand." He exhaled loudly. "You feel betrayed, hurt, stupid even, but it should be over and done with by now. But no, you want to visit her and that's the part I *don't* understand. Why won't you let it lie?"

"I need to know she's okay."

"But why?"

"I just do. I need answers."

"What about the families of her victims—don't you think they deserve answers?"

"Yeah, they do, but—"

"But, nothing, Dylan. You care for Layla, I get it, but enough is enough."

"What are you trying to say here?"

"I'm trying to tell you, our relationship is no longer fun because you're still fixated on the past and until you find a way to let it go, we can't move forward. Jesus, Dylan, how long has it been since we enjoyed a night out together?"

"What's us not having a social life got to do with Layla?"

Steve exhaled noisily. "Oh, I give up. Do what you like and leave me out of it."

"Don't be like that, Steve."

"I'm not being like anything, but I'm sick and tired of listening to the same old shit about her. So, we'll have to agree to disagree."

"That's easier said than done. It's causing problems between us, and I don't want that."

"Then what's the alternative?" he asked.

"I don't want to split up. I love you."

"And neither do I."

I waited a few seconds for Steve to say he loved me too, but he remained silent. It was a slap in the face. "Are you there?"

"Yeah," he mumbled like a sulky teenager.

"I don't want to argue with you."

"Look, I just pulled up at the office, so I have to go, but I'll stay at home tonight—give us both time to cool off."

"You don't need to."

"I know, but it's what I want." He sounded more certain than I'd ever heard him before. "Anyway, you have a good day and I'll see you soon."

I was about to reply when he hung up without a goodbye or firm plan to see me again.

My anxiety levels soared, and I hadn't even left for work yet.

I cursed myself for calling him and making matters worse. Why couldn't I have just left well alone?

Steve was the only man I'd met who I could envisage a future with and I'd fucked it all up somehow. I felt worse now than I had before speaking to him.

Heading to my car, all I wanted to do was go back into the house, climb into bed and bury my head under the covers, but I had to do what I was paid to do. I had a team to lead and try to get re-focused.

On the way to the office, I found my favourite playlist; my mind transported back to my performances at Dorothy's and, despite the reasons for me being there in the first place, I realised it was the last time I'd felt truly happy – freed from the burden of responsibility. Freed from my role as DI Dylan Monroe.

I'd performed there a few times since Layla's arrest, but that was under sufferance, or so I'd told myself.

Now, there was nowhere else I would rather be.

Adele's *When We Were Young* played, and I found myself listening intently to the lyrics. They resonated and took me back to my carefree childhood days, when times were simpler, and I hadn't witnessed the horror human beings could inflict on one another.

The song summed up how I felt right then, and I decided, if the time came and I returned to Dorothy's, this would be the song that would launch my comeback of sorts.

To my surprise, the memories brought my emotions to the forefront and tears fell – tears I'd held back for months.

I remembered an earlier conversation with Bella. She'd told me in no uncertain terms I was holding everything in, trying too hard to control my emotions. I'd denied it at the time, but she was right, although I'd never admit it.

Trying to pull myself together, I switched the radio off, opened the window for some fresh air and dabbed at my eyes, not wanting the team to see me at my lowest.

THREE

"Oliver Winston Leyland, will you get your lazy bloody backside out of that bed, right now," his mum yelled from the bottom of the stairs. "We're going to be late for your appointment. It'll take the best part of an hour to get there with the roadworks."

He rolled over and pulled the pillow over his face, hating it when she called him by his full title. "Ten, nine, eight, seven," he counted backwards, his words muffled.

"Are you listening to me?" she shrieked. He heard her charging up the stairs before his door flew open, banging against the wardrobe.

He winced at the racket she was making.

"Oliver." She yanked the duvet off him and dropped it to the floor.

He moved the pillow quickly, trying to cover his morning boner. "I heard you the first time, *Emily*," he snarled.

"It's Mum to you, you cheeky swine." Her face had flushed red. "How many times do I have to tell you?"

"Okay, okay, *Mum*." He covered his ears with his hands,

trying to drown out the noise. "There's no need to screech like that."

She blew her cheeks out, then exhaled loudly. "Get out of that bed before I fill a bucket with cold water and drench you with it." She walked back toward the door. "I won't tell you again." She stomped out of the room, muttering profanities to herself. "And get that shit hole you call a bedroom cleaned. Do you hear me?"

"I'm not going," he called after her, sick of the constant bullying. "And I'm not deaf either." His stomach flipped as he heard her stop dead on the stairs, then turn on her heel before flying back into his bedroom.

"You *are* going," she said. "Even if I have to drag you there by your bleedin' hair."

He took a deep breath, sat up in his bed, squaring his shoulders up to her defiantly. "I'm not, and nothing you say will make me. I hate being poked and prodded like some circus freak."

"You ungrateful bastard." She raised a hand and struck him.

"Get off me." He ducked out of her way and rubbed his stinging cheek.

"Do you know how much time and money has gone into your medical care? It isn't up for debate. You're going and that's that."

He softened his voice, attempting to tug at her heartstrings. "But I don't wanna go out today, Mum. I don't feel too good." He knew she would be considered abusive if he confided to the authorities, but she didn't mean it. She loved him. In fact, she was the only person on the planet that did. She was just hot-headed – they both were.

"Maybe if you weren't out all night long, you'd have the energy to get up in the day and do normal things lads your age do."

"I wasn't out *all* night." He bristled, shaking his head.

"I heard you sneak in at four am, so don't dig yourself an even deeper hole by lying about it. Where do you go at that hour of night, anyway?"

"Just out."

"Well, if you're able bodied enough to go roaming about at that time, there's no excuse. You've got your meds. Take one now and by the time we leave, you'll feel less anxious."

"It doesn't work like that—"

She held a hand up to halt him. "Look, Oliver, complain all you like, but you're going for that appointment, end of."

"You can't force me. I'm sixteen and can make my own decisions."

"I don't care how old you are, but I'll tell you something—if you don't move your arse in the next five minutes, you're gonna wish you'd never been born." She turned and marched out of the room.

"I hate you," he roared.

"Good," she shouted back at him. "Now get out of that bed, or else. You're going to see Doctor Walden and if we miss the appointment, I'll still be charged. I'm not made of friggin' money, you know."

Oliver slid off the bed and kicked the door shut.

He looked in the mirror and averted his eyes, detesting the reflection that stared back at him – the translucent skin that revealed dark veins beneath, red-rimmed pale blue eyes, the shock of white hair, eyelashes and brows, belied his mixed-race parentage. And they were only the most obvious things he had wrong with him. He'd been born with several unrelated illnesses, a cleft palate which had since been repaired but had left a deep scar running from his top lip to his right nostril. He'd tried to disguise it with a poor attempt at growing a moustache, but the hair was too fine to cover anything up and it just made him look worse than ever.

He'd also been born with a condition called Albinism, which

meant he had almost no pigment in his eyes, skin, and hair, plus an increased sensitivity to light. As well as ectodermal dysplasia, a genetic disorder inherited from a parent, presumably his father, that involved defects of the hair, nails, teeth, skin and glands. In short, he could well be the unluckiest person alive or a total fucking freak of nature.

His teeth and fingernails were sharp and conical, the stuff nightmares were made of, giving him the appearance of the vampire from *Salem's Lot*. His mum believed that with a bit of dental work, he'd look relatively normal. Yeah right! It would take a lot more than a mouthful of new teeth for him to be accepted. The only time he was comfortable outside was under the cover of darkness. If he had the nerve, he'd put himself out of his misery, but he was too cowardly to even do that. Knowing his luck, he'd fuck it up, leaving himself in an even worse state.

"I don't hear much movement up there, Oliver," his mum yelled from the bottom of the stairs. "Do I need to get you dressed myself?"

He opened his bedroom door and stomped across the landing to the bathroom. "I'm up!" He smashed the flat of his hand on the bathroom door. "Why can't you get off my case for five minutes?"

"If you speak to me like that again you'll have no need for a dentist because I'll knock every last tooth out of your head. Do you hear me?"

"Loud and clear. I might be a retard, but I'm not fucking deaf!" he yelled before kicking the door closed behind him.

FOUR

Here we go, I thought, pushing the doors to the incident room open. *Take a deep breath.* "Morning," I said brightly.

"Morning, boss," Will popped his head up from behind the computer screen. "Did you have a good weekend?"

"A bit shit to be fair. What about you?"

"Much the same. I couldn't stop thinking about Layla."

"Join the club." Joanna stepped into the room with two steaming mugs of coffee. "Want me to make you one, Dylan?"

"Thanks, Jo, you read my mind."

"No worries." She placed a mug down in front of Will.

"Any sign of Bella yet?" I asked.

Joanna sipped her coffee and nodded. "Yeah, she's just gone to the ladies." She placed her mug down on her desk before scooting back out the door.

"Oh, good." I felt relieved Bella hadn't changed her mind, even though I wouldn't have blamed her if she had. Her maternity leave wasn't officially over, but she'd asked to come back early. She reckoned it was because she was bored at home, but I knew her better than that – she was worried about me.

"Oh, you're here are you, Avaline?" Bella breezed into the room. "About time. The morning is almost over."

I rolled my eyes. "Ha, bloody ha." I opened my arms and gave her a squeeze. "I'm so happy you're back."

"Me too," she replied. "Playing mummy bores the arse off me."

"You don't mean that." Will took a sip from his mug.

"Oh yes, I do. I love my children dearly, but I'm not the stay-at-home type and never have been. I've been dying to get back into work and sink my teeth into something that isn't dirty nappies or *Dora the Explore*r."

I laughed.

"Who's looking after them?" Will asked.

"My sister's got them for a couple of weeks until my neighbour gets back from holiday and then she'll take over. She's a godsend and probably wouldn't have gone on holiday if she'd known I was planning to return to work so soon."

"Lucky you," Joanna said, returning with another coffee. She handed the mug to me. "It costs me and my hubby a fortune in childcare, but neither of us can afford to give up work."

"You'd miss this place too much if you gave it up anyway," Bella said.

"I'm not gonna lie, I would." She grinned.

Bella patted me on the back. "It's good to be back, mate. Now, what were you talking about when I walked in?"

"Layla," Joanna said.

"Ugh, no." Bella had that look, like she'd stepped in something nasty. "Do we have to talk about her?"

"Yes, we do." I didn't want to pull rank on the first day, but I would if need be. As a team, we had to come to terms with what had happened in court last Friday. Some might not care, but I knew Will and Joanna did at the very least.

"Fine," she grumbled. "But leave me out of it, please. As far as

I'm concerned, she's a criminal who knew exactly what she was doing and is no better than the rest of them. It's just a shame she'll live a life of luxury in the nuthouse—a swimming pool, en-suite bathroom, access to a library, TV, and all at the taxpayers' expense, I might add."

I was ready to explode, but Will beat me to it.

"You're out of fucking order, Bella." His cheeks had bloomed deep red. "Strolling back in here like you've never been away, acting like the queen bee, and telling us what we should and shouldn't talk about. Piss off back on maternity leave if you don't like what we have to say."

Bella looked mortified. "I-I—"

But Will hadn't finished. "Layla was one of us, and yeah she fucked up big time and people died, but she was off her rocker. You know that already." He took a deep breath, then served another volley of the truth. "It's been in all the papers, which is why she's confined to Rampton Hospital as a mental patient and not locked up in a mainstream prison. You don't like her, we get it, but we don't wanna hear it, okay?"

"You really believe she's got this multiple personality disorder or whatever her quack says? Come off it, she's fooled the lot of ya." She spat her words, knowing they would hit their intended mark – me.

"You're a fucking DS, not a psychologist," Will argued. "So, keep your opinions to yourself."

The wave of animosity towards Bella was almost tangible. Joanna glared at me, her mouth firmly closed. From a professional point of view, this standoff was unacceptable. "Bella, Will, that's enough."

Bella would argue black was white when she felt strongly about something, but one look at my face and she knew I meant business. "Look, guys, I'm really sorry," she said, now close to tears. "I didn't mean to upset anybody, but—"

I jumped in before anything else was said in the heat of the moment. "Come on you two, this won't help anyone. You're mates in and out of this place and, while you might not agree with one another, you need to respect each other's opinions."

"I'm going outside for a fag." Will grabbed his jacket off the back of the chair and, not even looking in Bella's direction, left the room.

"Shit," Joanna said. "He's been trying to give up for ages."

"It's my fault." Bella ran her fingers through her hair.

"Yes, it is." I wasn't about to lie to make her feel better. "But now you know how sensitive people are about the Layla situation, perhaps you'll watch your mouth going forward." I felt awful. Bella and I were best friends, but she had a nasty tongue when angry and I couldn't afford for the team to fall apart now.

"I get it, and I'm sorry, but she hurt you—"

My desk phone rang. I picked it up, leaving Bella making more apologies to Joanna. "DI Monroe."

"Don't you ever answer your mobile?" Lauren Doyle, Forensic Pathologist, sniped. "I've been calling you for the last ten minutes."

"Sorry, I was just dealing with a bit of friction, first day back and all that."

"I can imagine, but there's no rest for the wicked."

"What's up?"

"I'm on my way to a crime scene now—female, badly mutilated from initial reports."

"Shit," I grumbled, not in the mood for this today. "Where?"

"The call centre next to Eastlake Woods."

"Okay, I'll meet you there as soon as I can."

"Great. Uniform are on site and have already secured the scene."

"Somebody is gonna get their arse kicked for not informing me."

"Try answering your phone then," she fired back.

I was livid because she was right. We couldn't afford mistakes. No doubt Arjun Sharma, Police and Crime Commissioner, and the Professional Standards Department would be watching me like a hawk, and I wanted to keep my job. I hung up and turned back to face the room. "Bella, sorry to do this to you on your first day, but we've got a dead body."

"Oh, God, already," she groaned. "Come on, I'll drive."

"Fine by me." I tossed the car keys to her. She was out the door before I had a chance to think about it. "Jo, when Will get's back have a word with him, please. See if you can smooth things over a bit. Bella didn't mean to upset him. And also, tell the rest of the team I want them here at 4pm."

"Yeah, will do. Do you mind me asking why?"

"I want to see how everyone is really feeling regarding the Layla situation. Get it out of the way so it doesn't cause any further drama. I'll also be able to update them on this body that's been found."

"Got it. See you later."

"Thanks, Jo."

I rushed down the corridor and past Janine's office. She waved at me, so I ducked my head in quickly.

"Ah, just the man."

"Sorry, Ma'am. Gotta rush, but I'll catch up with you later."

"Fine," she yelled, as I closed the door. "And stop calling me Ma'am."

I slumped into the passenger seat more than ready for this day to be over and done with.

"Bloody hell. You took your time," Bella said.

"Sorry. Let's go."

She sped from the car park much too fast, but another argument was the last thing I needed today, so I didn't mention it.

"Well, my first day got off to a crappy start."

Even though I'd told myself I wasn't going to, I bit. "What did you expect, Bells?"

She shrugged her shoulders.

"Emotions are raw right now, without you wading in with your big feet, practically suggesting Layla should have met the firing squad at daybreak."

"I can't help how I feel about her, Dylan. And I'm not gonna bullshit people regardless of what you, or they, say."

"I'm not expecting you to do anything of the sort, but consider everyone's feelings or you'll find yourself on the outside looking in." I'd had enough of this subject already. "Now, let's just agree to disagree on this, shall we?" I'd been doing a lot of this today.

"Whatever you say, boss," she muttered under her breath.

I could hear her teeth grinding and knew she had more to say, but I wouldn't engage with her, not right now. She would only latch on to every word and twist it round to suit herself. I knew her too well and the best thing to do was to let her blow her frustrations out in her own time.

FIVE

I was glad to get out of the car. The atmosphere between us was tense. Bella never said another word to me but, as soon as we arrived at the crime scene, the professional in her kicked in. We were partners and nobody would be any the wiser about what had transpired between us.

I stood back and surveyed the scene while Bella spoke to Lauren inside the cordoned-off area of the car park. I noticed the warmth between the two, which didn't surprise me – they had always got along well.

The Scenes of Crime Officers had arrived and were busily donning their PPE. I approached them and scrounged a pair of disposable bootees, slipping them on over my shoes before entering the taped area.

I stepped forward, glanced at the body, and grimaced. The victim had been laid out on the edge of the car park, her clothing ripped apart and chest mutilated, but it was the gaping wound at her throat that made my stomach turn. Upon closer inspection, I almost threw up last night's supper. The victim's head was mush.

I looked at the throng of people vying to get a view of the

body. *Fucking ghouls.* "Keep that lot away from the scene," I yelled to the uniformed officers.

"Yes, sir," a WPC replied. "Come on, you lot, back away now. There's nothing to see."

She was wrong. There was plenty to see.

After my spats with Steve, and then Bella, I was already in a foul mood. I wouldn't usually hold on to anger, but I'd hardly slept, and my nerves were hanging on by a very thin thread. Woe betide the next person who pissed me off today.

I glanced back at the body, repulsed by what I saw. "Were you first on the scene?" I asked the officer guarding the cordon.

"Yes, sir. PC Alan French. I secured the scene as soon as I arrived."

"Do we know the victim's name?"

"Jane Cross," he replied.

"And what time was she discovered?"

"About six-thirty this morning, sir. The security guard came outside for a cigarette and found her. Poor lad's in a terrible state."

"Where is he?" I asked. "And what's his name?"

"Jay Chadha. Twenty-one-years-old. His uncle owns the building by all accounts."

"Yeah, got that." I didn't mean to appear abrupt, but I just wanted answers to my questions. I didn't need superfluous information. "Where is he right now?"

"He's been taken to The Royal. Suffering from shock, I've been told."

I wrote the security guard's name in my notebook. "Thanks. Anything else?"

"We found a rock covered in blood over there on the grass. I think it might be what he hit her with."

"He?"

"It's always a *He* in these cases, isn't it?" PC French surmised.

Layla's pretty face flashed before my eyes. "No. Not always. And maybe you should make a note of that."

The officer shuffled uncomfortably. "Yes, sir."

"Did anybody else see anything?"

"Not that I know of. It's secluded back here and people didn't start arriving for work until around eight."

I nodded before wandering off in the direction of the rock and found it within the cordoned off area. I prayed the killer had left a decent set of fingerprints, or trace evidence for us to find, but didn't hold out much hope. Everybody was aware of police procedures these days and wore gloves or wiped fingerprints, unless the attack was spontaneous. But I was certain the killer had lain in wait judging by the three roll-up cigarette butts behind the victim's car.

I waved over to one of the SOCOs and pointed out both the rock and the cigarette butts. He placed evidence markers beside them.

I took my time circling the entire area. SOCO would do a thorough fingertip search, but I just wanted to get a feel for the scene myself.

I headed back to PC French. "Make sure nobody gets near there and don't open those gates until you get the okay."

"Righto, sir."

Lauren was kneeling beside the woman's body quietly speaking into a *Dictaphone* as I made my approach. I couldn't make out what she was saying, but her brows were furrowed.

"Can I interrupt?"

"You already have," she snapped, lowering the recorder.

"Sorry."

"You look like shit, Dylan."

"Gee, thanks."

"I'm kind of up to my eyes, so what can I do for you?" She didn't have time for any form of banter with me. That much was clear.

"I wanted to check in, but it might be better if I come and find you at your office a little later?"

"I'd appreciate that." She turned and gestured to the crowds milling about, trying to sneak a look. "As you can see, I have an audience and the sooner we move the body somewhere more private, the better I'll like it."

"Are you planning on leaving her exposed like this, or do you want me to arrange for a tent to be erected?" I was concerned with the increasing throng of onlookers outside the gates.

"We're almost done, so there's little point. Like I've already said, I'll be much happier when we get her to the morgue."

"Looks like we're dealing with a sicko."

"Unfortunately, we're seeing this kind of thing more and more lately. I'm rarely surprised anymore by what I find when I arrive at a crime scene."

I nodded slowly. "Me neither."

Before leaving, I crouched down to take a closer look at the victim and almost vomited again. The killer had taken a lot of time and effort to display the body for maximum effect. Sickened, I stood up and backed away. "I'll see you later."

"You will." She turned, and continued speaking into the *Dictaphone*.

I wondered where Bella had disappeared to and spied her sneaking a cigarette in the smoking shelter across the car park.

"Bells," I shouted. All eyes turned to look at me. "Come on, we've got to go."

In between drags, she was chatting animatedly to a guy with curly hair and glasses. I watched as she took a final drag and threw the cigarette to the ground. She raced over. "Sorry, Dylan."

"Those things will kill you, you know?"

"Yeah. Don't remind me. I only smoke when I'm stressed, but I need to quit again."

"When did you start?"

"Last week. I guess I was worried about coming back and, after this morning's fiasco, I couldn't resist."

"Simon will go mad."

"What he doesn't know won't hurt him," she said with a grin.

I rolled my eyes. She often disregarded her long-suffering husband, who was away with the army. He was oblivious to most of the things she did. "I'm heading down to the hospital to speak to the security guard. Will you wait here until Lauren's done, then I'll swing by and pick you up?"

"Gotcha," she replied. "Whoever did this is one twisted bastard."

"Aren't they all?" I thought back to the brutal murders Layla had committed right under my nose. "Oh, while I think on, can you speak to somebody about the footage from the security cameras?"

"Bit of a problem there. That guy I was just talking to is the head of IT. I asked him for the footage, but it seems the security guard switched the cameras off."

"Why the fuck would he do that?" I asked, irritated.

"He's been sneaking his girlfriend into the building after hours for a game of hide the sausage, it seems."

"Shit! Couldn't he keep it in his pants till he got home?"

"Apparently, his family are deeply religious and don't approve of her. I've already called central to see if any street cameras picked anything up."

"Well done. Keep me informed, but link in with Will. He's the resident genius when it comes to scouring CCTV footage."

"Okay."

"Can I have my car keys?"

She reached into her pocket and threw the bunch of keys to me. I caught them, turned and walked toward my car.

I was exhausted and didn't know if I had the strength to go through this. Everything would be double checked – even triple checked now, to make sure we didn't miss anything ever again. We were all under the microscope because of Layla, yet I still found it hard to condemn her, despite what she'd done. I'd never understand what drove her to such horrific acts against innocent people, not when Maxwell – or Maxine as she now identified – was the source of her anger, but it wasn't my place to analyse her.

SIX

Ensconced in the dentist's chair, Oliver's jaw ached from the pressure of keeping his mouth wide open while his orthodontist, Dominic Walden, pushed and shoved his sausage-like fingers in and out of his mouth. The familiar, stomach-churning smell of latex gloves combined with clove oil and the unmistakable stench of the previous patients' drilled bone dust hung in the air.

Oliver fixed his eyes on the image taped to the ceiling directly above him, clearly meant for small children – a monkey dressed in a tutu, but apart from the stark white ceiling tiles, or staring up into the dentist's piercing brown eyes there was nothing else to focus on.

"You've broken one of your canine teeth, Oliver. Did you know?" Doctor Walden boomed.

Of course I fucking know, he wanted to say. Instead, he nodded and made a series of sounds confirming it.

"Yes, he did that last week while eating toffee," his mother piped up.

"I really don't want to extract it because it will undermine all the progress we've made, but it's too far gone to save."

Oliver shrugged. He knew they'd do what they wanted, regardless of what he said.

"Just do what you think, Dom. We trust you."

Oliver cringed at the gushing way his mother spoke – *slag*.

Half-an-hour later, the dentist had removed the tooth, and x-rayed his mouth again, and Oliver and his mother were sitting opposite him in the adjoining office.

"So, as you know, we wanted to examine you today with the intention of preparing you for the implants. However..."

"Here we go." Oliver stroked his numb cheek.

His mother swatted him in an attempt to shut him up.

"I know you're fed up with this, Oliver," Doctor Walden continued. "But the infection you suffered from the bone graft did a lot of damage, and now with the extraction, I'm not willing to compromise your future health until things have settled down. And, in my professional opinion, you're not ready for any further surgery at this stage—your mouth is still changing, and I advise you to wait for at least two more years."

Oliver groaned.

"That's not too bad, love," his mum said, placing her hand on his folded arms. "You've waited this long."

"This is only my opinion, of course," he continued. "You're more than within your rights to seek another."

"No point, Dom. We all know you're the best at what you do —but what will happen if he's still not ready in two years?"

"I'm pretty sure we'll be okay to proceed with the reconstruction by that time. We want to give him the very best possible chance, but he just needs to wait a while longer. That's all. We'll make a new impression of your teeth next time, if that's okay?"

"Whenever suits you, Dom," Emily gushed.

Oliver got to his feet. "Let's get outta here."

Oliver slouched in the car's passenger seat.

"See, it wasn't that bad, was it?" his mum asked.

"Hmph," he replied, holding onto the side of his jaw. "Easy for you to say—you've not had someone's hands in your mouth for the past couple of hours. And what for, eh? To be told they can't do anything for me."

"Come on, love, another two years won't kill you, then you'll have a lovely new set of teeth."

"I told you I didn't wanna go, so why did you make me?"

"You've been teased about your teeth for years, I thought you'd jump at the chance of getting them fixed. You should be pleased I'm willing to spend my inheritance on you."

"Did I ask you to spend your money on me?"

"You're an ungrateful little sod," she spat. "I could have had the new set of boobs I've always wanted, but as per usual, I put you first."

He flinched at the word boobs. "Why don't you then?"

"Because I want to do this for you instead."

"So, what d'you want, a medal?"

She ignored his sarcastic reply. "It's the first time I've seen you outside in daylight since your last appointment. It's not right, a lad your age staying holed up in the house, glued to that bloody *PlayStation* and only sneaking out at night."

"I've already told you—I don't sneak," he snapped, sick and tired of her trying to rule his life.

"Well, you're hardly up front about it, are you? What do you do? Wait until you hear me snoring before you go out?"

"Don't be stupid, Emily."

"It's Mum!" she hissed. "Listen to me—"

"Do I have a choice?"

She bit her lip and waited a few seconds before speaking. "You don't have to hide away in the day then wander about at night-time. You're a good-looking lad."

"Who are you trying to kid? I'm a fucking freak."

"No, you are not, and once you've got a new set of gnashers, any girl, or boy, will be glad to go out with you."

"I'm not gay." He glowered at her. "How many times do I have to tell you that?"

"I didn't say you were, but I wouldn't care either way. I dabbled a bit in my younger days."

"Oh, for fuck's sake." He cringed and looked away.

"Oi, foul mouth." She barked the words as she started the car. "Watch your language."

"Take me home, will ya? My mouth is sore, and I need to clean my teeth."

"Don't you want to go shopping for some new jeans while we're out?"

"No."

"You could have some new trainers too, if you want? Your black ones are caked in God knows what."

"I already said no. It's too bright out here and my eyes are hurting. Take me home. I need to get online, anyway. Sam's waiting for me."

"Bugger Sam and that sodding game. You need to get out and find a job if you don't intend to carry on with your education. I can't keep you forever."

"Nobody asked you to. But who's gonna give me a job looking like this, Emily?"

"Nobody gives a toss about stuff like that these days. Equal opportunities and all that. Besides, there's nothing wrong with you. I've seen people who look much worse than you, believe me. And you passed all your exams with A's, so sitting on that game is a waste of a good brain."

"Do you actually think before you speak?" He turned back to her, suddenly offended.

"What have I said now?"

"Just take me home, or I'll get out and flag a taxi."

"Fine," she replied. "But you need an attitude adjustment. Then maybe you'd feel a little better about yourself."

"And you need to get a job lecturing people—you'd be a multi-millionaire in no time."

He crossed his arms. The conversation was over.

She reversed out of the parking bay and headed home.

SEVEN

While on the road, heading for the hospital, I dialled Will's number.

"Hey boss." His voice blared from the loudspeaker. He sounded cheerier than he had earlier. "What's up?"

"I was just checking in to see if you'd spoken to Bella?"

"Yeah, just, and we're fine. She apologised and so did I."

"How were the others after we left?"

"Nothing was said."

"Thank God for that." I felt instantly relieved. "I can't be arsed with in-fighting, especially now we have another nutter on the loose."

"Bella mentioned the victim was a bit of a mess."

"Sickening stuff. Makes me wonder what society is coming to."

"It's nothing new for us. I'm working on the CCTV now."

"Great. I'm just getting to the hospital."

"Okay, boss, I'll catch up with you when you get back."

I grabbed a still orange drink from the hospital shop and

gulped it down before flashing my credentials and asking the receptionist where I would find Jay Chadha.

She pointed me in the right direction and, minutes later, I popped my head around the pale blue curtain with the brown hospital trust logo printed on it.

"Jay Chadha?" I asked.

"Yeah, that's me," the good-looking guy replied.

"Detective Inspector Dylan Monroe." I briefly held up my badge. "Are you okay to answer a few questions about Jane Cross?"

"I didn't see anything." He looked terrified.

"Well, tell me what you can, and we'll go from there."

"It was a quiet night. Most of the offices were empty by ten and, after doing the rounds, I settled down for the night. I was streaming Saturday's footie match onto the main screen when Jane left, so I didn't see very much."

I felt my nostrils flare and my top lip curl. "You mean you used the security screen to watch football?"

He had the good grace to hang his head in shame. "I still had the main corridors covered on the side monitors, but not the reception or car park."

"Why the hell would you do that?"

"By that time of night, the car park is usually empty. I'd arranged for a friend of mine to call in to see me, and I didn't want it picked up on the cameras."

"A friend?" I knew exactly what he was saying. He'd had a bootie call, but I wanted him to spell it out for me.

"You know, mate. My missus."

"Your wife?"

"Nah, man. My girlfriend."

"So, you were getting your end away while a woman you were supposed to be protecting was having her throat cut?"

He winced and shook his head rapidly. "No! My girlfriend had already left by then. I just forgot to turn the cameras back on."

"I'll need her details—she may have seen something."

I pulled the phone from my pocket and scrolled to Bella's number.

She answered on the first ring. "How'd it go with the security guard?"

"A total waste of time." I took a deep breath and exhaled. "Seems you were right. He'd turned off the cameras for a blow job."

"What a dickhead. I hope he gets the sack."

"I doubt it. He's related to the owner. Any news your end?"

"Lauren's finished here, and the body's being moved to the morgue as we speak. I can grab a lift with her, if you want to meet me there?"

"Yeah, do that. I'll leave now and pick up a latte on the way. Want anything?"

"I wouldn't mind a strong, black coffee. I have a feeling it's gonna be a long day."

"Here, he is—trouble," Lauren teased.

"Ha-ha, very funny." I plonked three takeaway coffee cups on the desk. I handed one to Bella and the other to Lauren. "White with two sugars, as usual?"

"Oh, thanks." Lauren accepted her coffee and took a sip.

"What have you got for me?" I asked.

"I've only completed preliminaries, but I have my lab technicians taking care of samples and other bits and bobs before I can get stuck in. It's fairly easy to see the cause of death, though."

"Go on," I encouraged, reaching for the remaining cup.

"Like I explained at the scene," Lauren said, "the victim had her throat slashed. No way she would've survived such trauma. There's also a deep puncture wound beneath her right ear, then we have the bite marks and the inscription on her chest."

I glanced at Bella, stumped. "What inscription, Bells? You never mentioned that." I'd seen the cuts on her chest, but I hadn't realised it spelled out an actual word.

"Sorry, but you'd gone by the time I found out," Bella said.

"If I had to guess, it was probably carved out with a cut-throat razor." Lauren pulled a picture from a file on her desk and passed it to me. "Stop whining and see for yourself."

I looked down at the image. "Lunatic," I read aloud, sickened by the bloody engraving in the victim's chest.

"Not quite," Lauren said, correcting me. "Luna-tic."

"That's what I just said."

"No, I don't mean that," Lauren replied. "Look at the image again."

"I don't see it. What am I missing?"

"Capital L for Luna and capital letters for TIC. See it now?"

I took a closer look. "And? Isn't that the same thing?"

"Lunatic is one word." She held her index finger up. "This looks like two separate words written closely together."

"Weird." I studied the image again. "I thought it was unintentional—I write like that sometimes. But I think you're correct. It's almost like a character-name."

"That was my first thought," Lauren confirmed. "Luna is Latin for moon, whilst the word lunatic largely means somebody who is mentally ill. I wonder if using the capital letters for TIC is his way of daring us to find out what makes him tick?"

"Do you think so?"

"Who knows how the mind of a killer works?" She tapped the image in front of her. "What I do question is whether our man, and I think I can safely say we're dealing with a man because of the ferocity of the attack, is leaving his mark in some sort of bid to become infamous, you know like the Zodiac Killer did in the 1960s?"

"He's playing games?" Bella added. "Taunting us perhaps?"

Lauren turned to her laptop. "The Oxford English Dictionary says the word lunatic originally referred to a kind of insanity supposedly dependent on the phases of the moon, though I'm not sure this is what we're really dealing with."

"So, this has less to do with our nutter pretending to be a werewolf, and more about his leaving some sort of calling card?"

"I have to say yes to the second point. But you're forgetting one more thing."

"And that is?" I suddenly felt stupid.

"Last night was a full moon."

"Oh, shit, so it was," I added.

"Could it be a coincidence that our killer strikes on a full moon, bites the victim like an animal would, and slashes her throat. Then he pisses all over her and carves into her chest?"

"You're kidding me," I said. "He pissed over her?"

"Yep, the dirty bastard." Bella answered for her. "As if he hadn't degraded her enough."

"Was she sexually assaulted or interfered with in any way?"

"No," Lauren said. "Maybe the fact that the poor woman soiled herself prior to death saved her from that. Every cloud, I guess. What she endured was bad enough."

I blew out, causing my lips to flap. "The press will have a field day with this—sounds like we have a modern-day wannabe werewolf on the loose."

"Wonderful," Bella added.

"This is the last thing we need. I was hoping we'd be able to keep a low profile for a while. At least until the Layla buzz dies down."

Lauren visibly flinched at the mention of her name. "Yeah, I read the papers at the weekend. How is everyone dealing with it?"

"Not the best, but we'll get there."

"I don't doubt you will, but it's good she's going to get the help she needs. That's the best we could've hoped for."

Bella shuffled uncomfortably. "Not another one," she muttered.

"You have something you wish to say, Bella?" Lauren wasn't one to take prisoners and would speak her mind.

"I just don't get why everyone's so bothered by what happens to her. Layla Monahan is a cold-blooded killer. But it seems I'm in the minority and I need to keep my opinions to myself."

"Good idea." I wanted to change the subject.

Bella sighed but ignored my suggestion. "I don't hate her, Lauren. I just don't understand why she felt justified to kill innocent people."

"Of course you know why. You're not stupid." Lauren was as cool as ice. "Her husband left her and told her he wanted to become a woman. It tipped her over the edge, and she took her rage out on the wrong people. End of."

It impressed me how she encapsulated what happened so succinctly.

Bella lowered her head and nodded.

Lauren turned to me. "So, are you planning on visiting her at Rampton anytime soon?"

"I've tried, but up to now she won't agree to see me."

"Don't rush into anything, but whatever you do, make sure you let Kerrigan know."

"Oh, don't worry. Everything we do will be above board. We don't need the powers-that-be breathing down any of our necks."

"Layla made us all look foolish," Lauren added unhelpfully. "But we move forward."

EIGHT

Jane Cross had lived in a modest semi in Allerton. The curtains were twitching as we pulled up outside the gate and the pillar-box red front door flew open before we'd even stepped from the car.

A distraught looking young woman in her early twenties, with short-cropped peroxide blonde hair, stood on the doorstep, her hand gripping the lower part of her face. I presumed she was the victim's daughter.

Apprehension washed over me. This part of the job never got easier, but I knew Bella would take control. She was far better at this kind of thing than I'd ever be.

The woman's high-pitched squeal reached my ears as I opened the car door.

A man, dressed in pyjamas and a housecoat, suddenly appeared and pulled her into his arms. He looked over the top of the woman's head at us, a look of dread across his face.

I headed down the narrow path, with Bella close behind.

"Mr Cross?"

The man nodded, forcing his lips into a tight line, as though trying to stop himself from blurting something out.

"DI Dylan Monroe, and this is my partner, DS Annabella Frost! Do you mind if we come in for a minute?"

The man ushered the young woman inside the house, leaving the door wide open. Bella and I entered and followed the sound of her anguished wails.

They had knocked the lounge through to the adjoining room, creating an impressively large open plan area with the modern kitchen at the far end.

"Is it Jane?" Mr Cross fired, before we were barely in the room.

"May we take a seat?" I asked.

He nodded, and they both sat down on the cream-coloured fabric sofa, leaving two matching armchairs free for us. Once we were all sitting, I turned to Bella and nodded.

"Mr Cross. I believe you called the station earlier this morning because your wife hadn't returned home from her late shift at work?" she said. "Is that correct?"

"Yes, that's right. Have you found her?" His voice sounded far calmer and in control than I thought it would.

Bella took a deep breath before continuing. "I'm sorry, sir. But I'm afraid the body of a woman has been found beside your wife's car. We have reason to believe it is your wife, but we will require a formal identification."

"What do you—?" He shook his head, placing trembling hands on either side of his face. "How did she—?"

"She was the victim of an attack."

The young woman's cries intensified as she buried her head in the man's chest once again. "I killed her, I killed her," she said over and over.

Bella and I exchanged a puzzled look before I cleared my throat. "I'm sorry. What do you mean?"

Mr Cross wrapped protective arms around his daughter. "Jess received a call from Jane last night asking if she'd pick her up from work. Someone had smashed her headlights in, but she dozed off to sleep again and didn't wake till this morning."

"I see. What time was that?"

"We checked her phone, and it was twelve-twenty-three. We've been calling her since we woke up, just after seven."

"I wanted to go over there as soon as I realised she hadn't made it home," Jess sobbed, eyeballing her father accusingly.

"I didn't think—" His voice cracked, and he swallowed hard. "I mean—why would someone want to hurt her?"

"At this stage, we just do not know. But her headlights *had been* smashed, so it looks like she was the killer's intended target. Are you aware if your wife has any enemies? At work maybe?"

He snorted, shaking his head. "Jane seemed able to make an enemy out of everyone she met lately. I don't know why. She's become very bitter and twisted over the past few years. Not a day goes by that she doesn't have a run-in with somebody or other at work."

"Or at home," Jessica snapped, eyeballing him again.

Mr Cross nodded. "Yes, I confess, we haven't been getting along recently. I sat up waiting for her last night because I was going to broach the subject of a separation. When she didn't come home, I presumed yesterday's fight had been the turning point for her, too. It was only when Jess told me about the phone call this morning that I panicked."

Jessica began wailing again.

Bella got to her feet and crouched beside the sofa. "Shall we go make a pot of tea?"

Jessica pushed herself to her feet, and they headed to the kitchen area. A good move as it gave me the opportunity to question Mr Cross freely.

"Do you mind telling me what you were arguing about, Mr Cross?"

"Jeremy, please."

I nodded.

"What didn't we argue about? As I said, my wife has been more difficult than usual of late. She hated her job, her colleagues, her hair, the neighbours, her car, the fact we couldn't afford a holiday this year, and of course, because my work has been sporadic since my accident, she blamed me for the lot."

"What do you do for a living, Jeremy?"

"I'm a self-employed painter-decorator. But I had a fall from a ladder this time last year and hurt my back. Now I can only do the odd job here and there."

"And your wife was angry about that?"

"She accused me of putting it on. Like I said, she's been a nightmare."

"I see. Can anyone vouch for your whereabouts last night?"

He jumped to his feet as though an electric volt had been shoved up his arse. "You think I did this?"

"We need to ask everyone connected to Jane for elimination purposes, you understand."

"Then no. I can't prove I was waiting up for her till 2am. Jessica came in and saw me at around eleven thirty, but then she went to her room. But I can assure you I had nothing to do with this."

"Okay, that's fine for now. Was there anyone at work Jane feared? Or had been threatened by?"

"Not that I know of. She didn't make friends easily and rubbed a lot of people up the wrong way, but I don't think she'd do anything bad enough for somebody to want to kill her. How did she die?"

"Your wife's body has been moved to the morgue where it's

undergoing a series of tests. However, I can tell you the cause of death appears to be a laceration to her throat."

He gasped and looked over his shoulder to check his daughter hadn't heard. She hadn't. Then he turned back to me. "Oh, my God."

"There's more, I'm afraid."

He gave his head a slight nod for me to continue.

"She had the word lunatic etched into her chest. Does that mean anything to you?"

His hands flew to his throat. "No. I have no—" A sob escaped him. He rubbed at his eyes.

"I'm sorry, Jeremy. I know this is a lot to take in. We'll leave you for now. As I already mentioned, your wife will need to be formally identified. A family liaison officer will be in touch with you before the end of the day and they will be your first point of contact, but in the meantime, if you need anything, please don't hesitate to call me directly." I handed him a card as I got to my feet. Then I signalled for Bella to wrap it up.

Bella held up a finger and turned back to Jessica.

I left her to it and headed back to the car to check my messages.

"How did you get on?" I asked when she slid into the car a few minutes later.

"I had a very interesting conversation with Jess. She told me her parents had regular slanging matches and the neighbours have called the police several times. However, the abusive party was Jane, not her husband. He's scared of her, apparently."

"Yeah, although he doesn't have an alibi, I don't think he's responsible. But we need to do everything by the book, regardless. I don't trust my judgement lately."

"Understandable. But I'd agree, he's not our man."

NINE

It was a relief to get back to the office, but the forthcoming task was a daunting one.

Steam rose from the mug of coffee. I took a sip, scalding my lip. "Shit," I said, wiping my mouth with the back of my hand. "If I could have your attention for a few minutes, please."

A sea of blank expressions greeted me.

"Thanks for being here, everyone." I still had no idea what I was going to say to them. "I wanted to touch base about a number of things. For one, the morale of the team of late."

I still struggled to process the last six months and couldn't be the only one. We needed to get everything out in the open, deal with it, then try to move on. It had cast a shadow over our personal and professional lives for far too long now.

Collectively, we were still reeling from the fallout of Layla's deception and subsequent incarceration. The hearing last week was supposed to have bought closure to that chapter of our lives. But she had been diagnosed with Dissociative Identity Disorder and was now a patient at Rampton Hospital in Nottinghamshire. She most likely would be for the rest of her life and this left everything wide open, for me at least. Would she ever be thought fit to re-join society? Our justice system was lax at the best of times, but mental health was a precarious subject – a panel of doctors would one day decide her future. I just hoped when and if that time came, they made the right decision.

The doors opened and Janine walked in. I hadn't expected her attendance. "Sorry for the intrusion—" She plonked herself down on the edge of a desk. "As you were, Dylan."

I cleared my throat before continuing. "I don't want to dwell on it, but following the outcome of Layla's hearing last week, I hoped we could talk about anything that is bothering us."

Pre-warned to keep any negative opinions to herself, Bella shuffled uncomfortably in her chair.

"What's the point of discussing any of it now?" Genevieve asked, her eyes shifting from Janine to other members of the team. "It won't change what she did."

"I'm not saying it will, but it seems we all have differing opinions, and I don't want any more friction going forward."

"She murdered innocent people right under our noses," Tommo added. "But she was one of us, that's the hard part to reconcile."

Janine watched with silent interest. I wondered when she would stick her oar in.

"I have the same problem, Tommo." I couldn't lie. To me, Layla was part devil and part angel. That was the cause of my inner turmoil. She was and still is mentally ill. Could we really condemn her actions when she wasn't responsible for them?

"I appreciate you caring enough to pull us all together but talking about it isn't gonna help." Pete suddenly joined the conversation.

I looked over at Heather and Will. "You two are unusually quiet."

"What is there to say?" Heather shrugged her shoulders.

"The damage is done. What more do you want us to do? Sit in a sharing circle and sing *Kumbaya, My Lord*."

Bella snorted a laugh.

I turned to glare at her, unappreciative of her finding any amusement in the situation.

"Sorry."

"So, you're all telling me you're okay with this?"

Joanna spoke up. "No, we're not okay with anything, boss, but we can't change the past, so we'll just get on with things as best we can."

"Sounds like a plan to me, Dylan." Janine clapped her hands together. "There really is no need to regurgitate any of this. The fact of the matter is, Layla is where she belongs. Let's leave her there, please."

It was a veiled instruction I had no choice but to follow.

"Fine," I snapped. "But my door is always open if any of you need to talk."

Janine got to her feet and straightened her skirt. "Dylan, can I see you in my office, please?"

"Sure." I placed the coffee cup on my desk and caught up with her.

"Come in and close the door."

I did as she asked and took my usual seat. "What have I done this time?"

She sat down and leaned forward, her hands clasped as if in prayer. "I wanted to talk to *you* about Layla."

"Why didn't you speak up during the meeting?"

"Because this involves you and has nothing to do with the others."

"I'm intrigued."

"Don't be." She leaned back in her chair. "You've made multiple requests to see Layla, and I wanted to know why?"

I wasn't the least bit surprised Janine knew. "I need answers."

"Layla will never give you what you crave, Dylan, no matter how hard you try."

"You don't know that."

"She's sick—very sick, and you forcing her to revisit everything for your own selfish needs could push her too far."

"Selfish needs?"

"Yes, you know what I mean. I get she was your friend as well as your partner, and you feel as though you let her down, but Layla was long on the path to crazy town before then. It wasn't your fault, and she is never going to absolve you of anything because you did nothing wrong. In fact, without you cracking the case, she could still be at it."

"She'd have slipped up long before then."

"Maybe, maybe not, but I'm asking you as a personal favour to leave it be."

"Why is it so important?"

"We have to play the game, Dylan."

"You haven't told me why. Be straight with me."

"Okay, fine, I will. The PSD is still watching us closely, and I don't want to give them any reason to come down on us like a ton of bricks."

"It's not entirely unexpected that they'd be watching me at the very least."

"We were all lucky to have escaped with our jobs, especially after the press reports slating us, so I'm asking you, do your job and leave Layla in the past, for all our sakes."

"Okay, I won't request another visit. However, if she asks to see me—"

"Focus on the Jane Cross murder—getting that solved will be a feather in all our caps."

"It might not be as easy as that."

"Why not?"

"Lauren Doyle thinks there's every chance the killer will strike again."

"Then it's imperative we're seen to be proactive."

"Got it!" I left her office and headed for my desk. I needed a drink to help clear my cluttered mind.

"Are you okay?" Bella asked.

"Yeah, but my head is wrecked."

"What did Janine want?"

"Let's grab a bottle of wine, then head back to mine. I'll fill you in then."

"What about Steve?"

"He's not coming around tonight."

She cocked her eyebrow at me in question.

"Long story. I'll tell you later."

"Okay, but let me call Penelope first and tell her I'm working late. She'll be expecting me for dinner."

"Won't she mind?"

"Oh, no, she won't care if she has prior warning, but she was planning on cooking—"

"Like you care about missing that."

"Exactly. I can only take so much of that plant-based muck she insists on feeding me."

"Seems to be all the rage lately. Maybe I need to try it."

"It's not too bad really in moderation, but the sooner my neighbour gets back from Cyprus, the sooner Lady Penelope can piss off back home and let me eat what I want."

"Bottle of wine and takeaway, then?"

"Sounds good to me."

I felt cheerier already and would fill Bella in on Janine's concerns once we were settled on the sofa, glass in hand. Despite our recent differences, I'd trust Bella with my life.

TEN

Oliver sat staring at the fifty-five-inch screen, champing at the bit to play *Wolven Army*. Since the beta copy crashed after its first release a year and a half ago, they'd been waiting for the bugs to be fixed. It seemed to be working perfectly the last few days and now, at a crucial part of the game, he couldn't believe Sam was late.

He got to his feet and stomped over to the window, angrily pulling the curtains together. He hated the way his mother insisted on opening them every single day. She knew he struggled with bright light. He longed for the winter months – the dull days and darker nights suited him better. In the height of summer, he needed to sit with the curtains tightly drawn to keep the daylight out. He returned to his desk in the corner of the bedroom.

Boredom took hold, and he tapped his index finger nervously on the side of the control pad he gripped tightly in his hands.

Suddenly an alert tone sounded as Liam, his internet buddy, who lived in America, came online.

Oliver clicked the audio button. "About time. I was beginning to think you and Sam were playing without me."

Liam's chuckle filtered down through Oliver's headphones. With the volume set to its lowest level – he could comfortably hear conversation without it irritating him. "Sorry I'm late, bud. I had to take my girlfriend to work—car trouble."

"What time is it in Colorado?"

"Nine forty-eight am. Have you heard from Sam today?"

"Not a thing."

"We could always start without him?"

Oliver bristled. He didn't like the way Liam always tried to come between them. "Erm—" He knew Liam would've said the same to Sam if he wasn't on. "No, we can't do that. He'll be here soon."

Sam suddenly appeared online. The sound of rustling, then his familiar voice could be heard.

"Sorry, guys. Had to grab a bite to eat if we're gonna be on this all night."

"I wondered if you were gonna give it a miss."

"Nah, mate."

"I texted you before. You could try answering," Oliver snapped.

"Sorry, Bro. My missus hates phones at the dining table – family time and all that."

"Whatever." Liam sounded disinterested in their chatter. "Can we get on with it? Some of us do have lives away from this game?"

"Hit it, mate," Sam replied.

"Fuck it, this is so shit," Sam screamed into his headset microphone. "I want my money back." He always mouthed off when he lost a fight with one of the other characters.

Despite the low volume selected on his headset, Oliver

winced, his hearing more sensitive than usual tonight. "I don't think it works that way, mate." They'd been at it for hours, but Sam seemed to be struggling.

Liam had been quiet the last few minutes, and Oliver wondered if he'd dozed off. "What do you think, Liam?"

"It's fuckin' sick, man. Like actually being in a horror movie."

"It's still not as good as I thought it was gonna be, even with all the fixes." Oliver was disappointed.

Liam barked out a laugh. "You're just like Sam. Give it a chance. As soon as somebody beats you, you have a bitch fit, and the next day, it's the best thing, like, ever."

"I don't have a choice, not after paying seventy-five quid for it."

"Total waste of money, if you ask me." Sam grumbled.

"We didn't." Liam replied.

"And what's all this I am lunatic, fear me shit you've started rattling on about, Olly?" Sam was still pissed off with his poor performance during the game.

"It's my character's new tagline."

"Well, it's fucking stupid." Sam grumbled.

Liam groaned. "Why don't you stop bitching at him and have a smoke. It might chill you out a bit."

"Yeah, whatever. I'll be back in five."

"Can't you just blow it out the window?" Liam asked.

"Nah, it stinks, and my missus would murder me if I smoked weed in the house."

Oliver laughed. "My mum goes fucking mental at me over it, too."

"I gave that shit up years ago." Liam seemed settled and had said many times that emigrating was the best move he'd ever made.

"Weed helps with my anxiety, so I usually go to Eastlake Woods at the back of my place and have it there."

"I'm out of here," Sam added, disconnecting himself from the chat.

"Doesn't your mum ever say anything about you being out late at night?" Liam asked.

"The next day, yeah, she moans about it. But that's only 'cos she thinks me being awake all night means I won't go out during the day. Had no choice today though. She dragged me to the dentist."

"That's a good thing, init? You're well paranoid about your teeth and once they're fixed, you won't be so worried that people are staring."

"Maybe, but there're bigger problems than my teeth to worry about. The scar on my lip, see-through skin..."

"Who gives a shit these days, man?"

Oliver looked at Liam's profile picture, then quickly glanced at Sam's. Jealousy took hold because he'd give anything to look like his friends. "I do, but my mum reckons I should get used to it."

"You'd make a cool looking character in *Wolven Army*."

Though I appreciated his support, Liam hadn't actually seen me. He only knew what I'd told him, and unlike them, I hadn't used a photograph of myself on my profile. "Do you think so?"

"Yeah, I do, so go easy on yourself."

"Maybe in a few years when I've had more work done, I'll feel better about myself, but right now, the thought of going outside during the day, having to work some poxy job and mix with people—I hate it."

"How did you manage when you were in school?"

"I went to a residential school on the Wirral until I was twelve."

"You went to a boarding school?"

"Kind of. I lived there from Monday to Friday but came home on weekends and holidays."

"Wow, that's a strange thing, you know, sending your child away. How come your mum did that?"

"She had a bad time with my dad shagging around, so I suppose dealing with my issues on top of everything after he left was too much."

"I bet that cost a pretty penny."

"Nah, some do-gooder charity funded my place."

"Where is your dad now? You never seem to talk about him."

"Probably fucked off back to Jamaica. Can't remember the last time I saw him."

"Don't you wanna see him?"

"As far as I'm concerned, he can stay away."

"Do you think he knew your mum had sent you to boarding school?"

"She didn't send me there 'cos she didn't want me."

"Then why didn't she keep you at home full-time?"

"My school was for kids that had all sorts wrong with 'em. Mum thought it was the best place for me at first."

"At first?" Liam queried.

"Yeah, but then we moved house, and she had me transferred to a mainstream high school close to where we live, but I hated it. Every single day was torture."

"Sounds rough, man."

"It was – she'd drive me to and from there just to make sure I went and stayed the whole day."

"What were the other students like?"

"At the residential school, okay, because they were used to what I looked like and the other things, like me hating bright lights and loud noises. It didn't seem to bother most of them 'cos there were some worse off than me."

"I don't mean to sound judgemental, but it sounds like a nightmare."

"It wasn't so bad. I'd been there since I was five and got used to only seeing mum on weekends. Mainstream high school was way worse."

"Why?"

"I was labelled a freak from my first day there—wherever I went, people laughed, pointed and stared. They didn't care—I was just the school weirdo."

"Was it really that bad?"

"If you think being alone every day and eating your packed lunch locked inside a toilet cubicle is normal, then no—."

"I'm sorry, man."

"Not your fault, but it was a shit time and I'm glad to be out of it."

"I'd have backed you up if I'd been there."

"Yeah? Would've been good to have had somebody on my side."

"Kids are cunts, Olly, but most of them only behave that way because it's what they learn at home."

"Probably, but nothing about my childhood was perfect. It's a shame you don't live in the UK now. I reckon we'd have a right laugh."

"I know, but at least you have Sam close by."

"Yeah, but he's a lot older than me."

"So am I. I'm twenty-two."

"Yeah, but he's twenty-five, and has kids. We don't have that much in common apart from gaming and weed."

"You see him though, in person, don't ya?"

"He calls round now and again, but we usually meet up for a smoke. He's really cool despite his mood swings."

"Your mum is right though. You should get out more."

"Maybe one day."

The *PlayStation* beeped as Sam re-entered the chat room.

"Are you two pussies ready to go again?" He seemed calmer and cheerier than minutes before. "I'm ready to whip your asses."

"Go for it, big man," Liam replied.

ELEVEN

The night bus exited the tunnel and pulled slowly to a stop.

"I'm getting off here," Mandy slurred, wobbling to her feet. She clutched a handful of her skirt and yanked it down. She'd drunk far too much.

"You're supposed to be staying at mine." Her friend, Debbie, screwed up her face in confusion.

"I'm too pissed. I just wanna go to sleep in my own bed and my house is only five minutes up the road. Do you mind?"

"No, but I'll be round yours for eleven. Don't forget we're meeting the girls in town at one o'clock."

Mandy's stomach churned. The thought of more alcohol didn't thrill her, but she knew by tomorrow, she'd be well up for another heavy session. "Okay." She leaned in and kissed her friend's cheek. "See you later, babe."

"Will you be alright walking from here on your own, or shall I come with you?" Debbie sounded concerned.

"I'll be fine. I'm only up that hill." She pointed directly opposite. "And I don't want you hogging the toilet all night in case I need it."

"Are you sure?"

"Yeah, I'll be okay. Besides, I have the house to myself for a few days. My dad and his cow of a wife have gone to their caravan. Bliss."

"Well, message me when you're home."

The bus had already stopped, and the passengers were talking loudly to one another.

"Are you getting off or what?" The bus driver shouted, his head poking out from behind the Perspex partition. "I haven't got all night you know. I've got to drop this lot off and go around again."

"Keep your wig on, gobbo," Mandy snapped. "I'm going."

She got off the bus, stuck her two fingers up at the driver and waited for it to pass before she staggered across the road.

The streets were deserted.

I could murder a kebab, she thought, looking around for somewhere still open.

Squinting at the time on her phone, she was out of luck. It had just gone 3:30am.

The night air hit her, and she suddenly felt more sloshed than she had on the bus. She needed to focus her vision, or she'd never make it up the dreaded hill.

Although it would add time onto her journey home, she decided it would be easier to cut through the park. She lurched through the wrought iron gates. Not seeing clearly, she almost fell face first onto the path.

After stumbling along for a few minutes, Mandy stopped and looked up at the monument plonked in the middle of the park circled by three rows of steps. It was something she'd taken little notice of before. "What's it supposed to be?" she asked herself.

The longer she looked up, the dizzier she felt, and that horrible smell that had just caught her attention was making her feel even worse.

"Want some?"

The voice startled her. She squinted and stepped backwards to focus on the dark shape of a person seated on the steps. Though his head and face were obscured by a dark hoodie his lips suddenly glowed orange as he took a deep drag on his cigarette.

"Some what?"

"Weed."

She shook her head. "No thanks. Smells like cat shit."

"Go on, it'll relax you."

"I'm already mullered, thank you very much. I don't think I need to relax anymore," she replied, haughtily.

"Suit yourself."

"Anyway, my step mum always told me never to speak to strangers." She wobbled past the man, the smell making her retch.

"Are you gonna throw up?" he asked. "Why don't you just sit down for a minute?" He patted the marble step beside him.

She turned and fell back, landing unceremoniously on her arse. "I think I'm gonna have to, but not too close—you stink, ya know?"

"Thanks."

Mandy could feel her phone buzzing and pulled it from her pocket. An envelope flashed, signalling a text, but she couldn't settle her vision long enough to read it. "Oi, stinky, what does this message say?" She shoved the phone toward his face.

He looked at it. "Are you home?" he said.

"Just reply for me, will ya, and say yes. She'll only start to worry."

He took the phone and did as she asked. "Done." He handed it back to her.

She noticed the skin on his wrist. "Bloody hell, you're pale. Don't you ever go out during the daytime?" She chuckled to herself. "Casper, the friendly ghost," she sing-spoke, mocking him.

He moved away from her and fidgeted in his pocket. "So, you fancy doing something?"

"Such as?" She slurred her words.

"What about a little game of hide and seek?"

She chuckled again. "Couldn't exactly miss you in the dark, could I? What's wrong with you, anyway?"

"I have an unfortunate condition, but most polite people try not to draw attention to it."

"I've never been accused of being polite."

"I wonder why?"

"Cheeky fucker."

"Well, do you wanna game or not?"

"Where am I supposed to hide? We're in the middle of a park."

"Come on. It'll be fun."

"Okay then, but what's your name?"

"My friends called me Lunatic."

"And mine call me Kim Kardashian," she replied with a sarcastic tone. "I wouldn't tell too many girls that name by the way, it might put 'em off you." She noticed him digging around in his coat pocket. "What're you looking for?"

"Just making sure I haven't dropped my phone."

She stood up, struggling to balance on the uneven concrete step then walked around the monument. Peeking her head around, she called out, "Come and find me then." But he'd already vanished. "Oi, Loony, or whatever your name is. Where are ya?"

"Behind you," he said.

She jumped and screamed, not expecting him to be so close. His hot breath warmed her ear. "Where'd you come from all of a sudden? You frightened the shite out of me."

"Don't turn around," he whispered.

"I wasn't going t—" Suddenly she bent over and vomited. It splashed at her feet.

"Dirty bitch," he growled.

Seconds later, she was thrust forwards and found herself face down on the grass surrounding the monument. "Eh, dick head..." she yelled, trying, but failing, to climb to her feet. "...that's not funny." She lost her balance and fell face down again.

He straddled her from behind, pressing her into the cold earth.

She was about to protest as he snarled into her ear.

"Don't move, bitch." He sounded a little different than he had before.

Her adrenaline kicked in and suddenly she felt more clear-headed than she had all night. Her instincts told her she was in danger. She managed to scramble out from underneath him, intending to run, but a well-aimed kick to the back of her knee sent her crashing to the ground with a thud.

"Look, I just wanna go home, okay." She tried to get up, then felt an almighty blow to her left side as he kicked her again.

"I told you not to move," he whispered. "Why won't you listen?"

Winded, she gasped for breath. "Please, I'll do whatever you want. Just let me go."

"Just let me go." He mimicked her in a whiny voice, then laughed.

"Please—"

"Shut the fuck up." With his foot on the back of her head, he pressed her face into the grass.

She closed her eyes, terrified, unable to speak.

He climbed back on top of her and sniffed at her, just like a dog would. Then he moved her hair out of the way, sniffing behind her ears. Without warning, he flicked his tongue over her ear lobe. He let out a low throaty growl, then sniffed at her again.

"P-p-please," she stammered. "I-I just w-want to g-g-go home."

He trailed his tongue along the nape of her neck and moaned in obvious pleasure before sinking his teeth in.

She screamed until he released her, and then her cries returned to a whimper. "Please, don't," she begged.

"Lie on your back," he demanded.

"I don't want to."

"Turn over," he snarled, grabbing a fistful of her hair.

"No—"

In a split second, he was on his feet. He kicked her ribs once again before repeatedly stamping his foot into the centre of her back.

"Okay, okay," she cried out. "I'll do whatever you want." She slowly pushed herself over and lay on her back.

"See, it's so much easier my way."

"Please, I just want to go home."

"And you will, bitch," he replied. "In a body bag."

I climbed back on top of her again and tore her pretty pink top, then I used both hands to tear it wide open, exposing the girl's bare breasts.

Power surged through my veins. I felt a stirring in my groin as the blood rushed to my cock, but screwing her wasn't what I was there for.

I pressed the tip of the razor blade to her skin, enjoying the sound of her cries, but I needed to be careful – I didn't want anybody to hear us. "If you make any more noise, it'll be much worse for you."

"Please, I'll do anything," she cried out. "Just stop."

"I'll stop when I'm ready." I looked down, thrilled to see tears running down her cheeks and into her ears. Then I let out another low growl and could feel her trembling beneath me. "Open your eyes," I said. "I want you to look at the moon."

"No, I don't want to." She squeezed her eyes tight shut, but the rapid breathing combined with the snot and tears coating her face contradicted the defiance of her words.

I'd grown bored with her whimpering and was aware the sun would soon rise. I needed to be home before then or my absence would be noticed.

With a sweeping motion, I slit her throat. Blood sprayed up at me and ran down my face. As it reached my lips, I licked at it, surprised how sweet it tasted.

I watched with silent interest as her hands flew up, instinctively trying to stem the flow. Nothing she did would save her now. I sank my teeth into her stomach.

The gurgling sounds excited me, and I wanted nothing more than to take my time and relish in her misery for a little while longer.

But time was ticking on, and I needed it to be over with.

After allowing myself another bite, this time to the meaty thigh, I picked up a rock, then knelt across the dying girl and brought it crashing down on the side of her head. This time, it only took one blow to silence her forever.

Blood gushed from the open wound.

Her dead eyes stared up toward the fading moon. Time had run away from me, and it was now or never.

I gouged into her chest and sat astride her to admire my handiwork;

I am
LunaTIC

FEAR ME

I felt proud seeing my name etched into her skin. I pulled down my zip and emptied my bladder all over her. The stench of my piss mixed with the heady scent of her blood almost pushed me over the edge.

I needed to get home before she noticed me gone, but I'd almost forgotten my trophy. Reaching down, I pulled at the ring on her finger, but it wouldn't budge. I had to have it. I tugged harder, hearing the bone in her finger break. Seconds later, it was mine.

One more quick glance and I could leave her.

The birds began to chirp high in the trees as I made a swift exit, bolting across the grass and down a bank into the bushes.

TWELVE

Oliver groaned as his mother charged into his bedroom just after 8am. She was fit to burst.

"Where the bloody hell were you until God knows what time this morning?"

Bothered by her loud voice, he covered his ears with his hands. "Out. I keep telling you the same thing. Just *out*." He groaned again. "Why?"

"What have I told you about sneaking around in the middle of the night? There's a bloody nutcase on the loose, and you're wandering the streets without a care in the world."

He didn't read the newspaper or watch it on the television, but he'd heard his mum talking to her sister about it. "Yeah, killing women, not young lads, Emily."

She dragged the duvet off the bed. "Call me Emily one more time, and I'll swing for you, d'ya hear me? Have some bloody respect. I'm your Mum, not one of those idiots from that chatroom you're so fond of."

"Respect? Yeah right, that's a laugh," he replied, "You've

gotta earn respect, and charging in here every morning screeching at me won't help."

"I'm worried about you, Olly." She sat down on the edge of the bed. "You've practically stopped going out during the day, unless I force you, you hardly speak to anybody but that reprobate, Sam, and that's usually over your headset. What's wrong with him coming around here more often? I don't like the lad, but at least you'd have somebody to talk to face to face."

"It's what guys *our* age do."

"But he isn't *your* age, is he?"

"What does that matter?"

"You told me Sam's twenty-five. Does he fancy you or something?"

"No, he doesn't. He's got a wife and kids."

"What about that other lad, Liam, is it? What's wrong with him coming over occasionally?"

"He lives in America. I keep telling you that."

She nodded, as though remembering their past conversations about it. "Then find yourself a friend you can spend proper time with."

"What for?"

"You're a young lad who's visually a shut-in. I don't like it, Oliver."

"It's my life."

"Some life," she hissed. "Stuck in this stinking bedroom night and day pretending to be some stupid character from a computer game."

He shook his head and sneered at her. "I don't do that."

"Then what's the big attraction?" She stared at the screen and screwed her nose up. "Playing bloody werewolves at your age."

"It's a game, that's all."

"And while you're glued to that screen, you're not living a real life in the real world."

"How has the real world worked out for me so far, *Emily*? Go on, answer that one."

"You can try a lot harder than you do—we're not living in the dark ages anymore. You look different from most, so what?"

"Do you know what it's like to be stared at, constantly? For kids to cry when they see you. Adults crossing the street when I walk towards them?"

"Stop exaggerating."

"It's happened in the past, and you know it."

"Ignore it. Simple as."

"It's not that simple, though. Far from it."

"If you don't try, you're gonna rot away in here and I want more for you than this, Olly." Tears filled her eyes.

"Get used to it. I have." He didn't like to see her upset, but she didn't understand and never would. He wouldn't allow her to bully him into something he couldn't handle, not when she seemed to control every other aspect of his life.

She wiped her eyes with the sleeve of her jumper. "I'm not having it anymore, and if you want to stay in this house, you'll act like a normal human being instead of sitting up all night playing that bloody thing then sleeping all day."

"You know I'm not normal."

"It's only you who thinks that. Nobody else does."

He sat up. "Look at me, Mum. There's nothing normal about me."

"I'm not listening to another round of your self-pity. I've told you before, get your arse out of bed at a reasonable hour and while you're at it, clean this pigsty up and get those cups into the dishwasher. And by the way, will you stop turning the bloody heating on full blast all night."

"But I get cold."

"If you were in bed at a reasonable time you wouldn't."

"You sound like a broken record."

"If you listened to me once in a while, I wouldn't have to keep repeating myself, would I?"

"I'm not a kid. You can't tell me what to do."

"You *are* still a kid, and yes, I can tell you what to do whilst you're under my roof. It's either my way or you can find a flat somewhere. Failing that, if you think you'd fare better, ask Sam to put you up. I mean it this time, son. If I have to tell you again, I'll put my foot through that TV and stamp on your *PlayStation*."

"You wouldn't dare."

"Don't test me, Oliver!" She stormed out of the bedroom.

THIRTEEN

I scraped the contents of last night's takeaway into the waste disposal unit and pressed the 'on' switch. The awful grinding noise made my temples throb. I felt a little worse for wear, and it was all Steve's fault. Because he hadn't come over, I'd foolishly finished a bottle of white wine on my own after Bella had left – bad idea. I thanked the lord I wasn't due at work until mid-morning. I'd squared it with Will to cover for me, as I'd suspected I might be a little delicate.

My phone flashed on the table and my stomach churned. It couldn't be good news if Will was calling me so early.

"Am I going to regret answering this call?" I asked, turning the tap on, wanting a glass of water.

"We've found another body."

This was all I needed. "Shit, where, when?"

"The obelisk at Eastlake Woods. An hour ago—a young female. Shall we go together? I can pick you up."

"Yeah, that would be great. I had a skinful last night and don't want to risk being over the limit."

"Do you want me to bring you a coffee?"

"If you wouldn't mind. Oh, and you'd best make it black. My head's banging like a shit house door in a gale."

"Gotcha, boss," he replied, chuckling. "See you soon."

The heavens opened as soon as I left the house, and I was drenched to the skin by the time I made it to Will's car. "Where did that come from?" I asked once I was in the passenger seat.

"Unfortunately, it's forecast for most of the day."

"Typical."

He handed me a super-sized black coffee.

"Thanks mate, you're a star." I removed the plastic lid, blew gently for a few seconds and took a sip. "I feel rough as hell."

"I can handle this for you if you're not up to it."

"Thanks, but it's better if I'm there. Two murders in forty-eight hours. If Janine found out I'd thrown a sickie because of a hangover I'd be hung, drawn and quartered."

"Yeah. She hasn't been in the best of moods lately."

"It's the fallout from Layla. Understandable, but things will settle down now she's been sentenced."

"Hope so, as it doesn't make for a pleasant working environment."

"So, tell me what happened?"

"Lauren's already at the scene, but I told you what I knew on the phone earlier."

"Thank God I didn't eat breakfast yet."

Will started the car, and we drove in silence while I finished the much-needed bucket of coffee.

He drove through the park gates and pulled up beside the police cordon.

They had placed crime scene tape around the area and members of the public and reporters were milling about, trying their best to get a good look at what was happening underneath the expanse of tarpaulins and the forensic tent.

As we approached the rear of the obelisk, the rain fell in sheets. I ducked underneath the tape and rushed for the cover of the closest tarpaulin, my jacket pulled up over my head. I spotted Lauren yelling at one of the uniformed officers at the base of the obelisk. After donning the relevant PPE, headed over to her. "Morning, Lauren, beautiful day for it," I yelled above the racket of the storm.

"You're having a laugh, aren't you? I got piss-wet through down to my flipping knickers before I had the chance to don my overalls this morning."

Lauren's soggy knickers weren't something I wanted to think about, but the pained expression plastered across her face made me want to laugh, but I wasn't brave enough. "I know, it's shocking. What have you got for me this time?"

She nodded up at the steps. "Look for yourself."

"Jesus Christ." My heart thumped in my chest. The girl was a mess. SOCO had made a decent attempt to cover the crime scene with tarps, but because of the size and shape of the obelisk, it had been impossible to conceal it entirely. Lying exposed on the steps, her throat had been cut from one side to the other. The smell reminded me of the stint I'd done as a teenager at the abattoir – the stench of recently slaughtered animals. I made an involuntary retching sound and stepped away, terrified of spilling my guts all over the murder scene.

"Exactly," Lauren replied.

"What the hell are we dealing with here?" I asked, my heart breaking for the young girl's family.

"A lunatic, that's what we're dealing with."

"Do we know who she is?" I directed the question to the uniformed officer in attendance.

"Yes, her driving licence was in her purse. Amanda Morris. She lived on Mount Pleasant."

"We'll go up there shortly." I scratched my head roughly with both hands. "Lauren, I'd like to sit in on the autopsy, if that's okay?"

"Sure."

"Phone me when you're ready and I'll come over."

"Got ya," she replied.

I spent another hour or so at the scene before searching for Will, who I eventually found shivering beside the SOCO team's van. "There you are."

"Yeah, sorry. I was just talking to Aiden. He tells me they've found a couple of cigarette butts again."

"Yes. And a rock that seems to have finished her off, just like before. He certainly enjoys staging the scene for us."

"Seems so."

I inhaled deeply. Cold and miserable, I wanted nothing more than a hot shower and to climb into my joggers, but the day had only just begun. "Can you drop me back off at my place to get my car?"

"Of course. Are you sure you're up to driving, though?"

"I'm still feeling a little ropey, but I should be fine now."

Will and I passed Joanna on the way back to the car. "Hi, Jo. Thanks for coming down. Keep an eye on the rabble over there, please. Nobody gets past that tape."

"No worries. I'll call you if anything crops up."

Reporters were already camped in the reception area wanting the scoop on Jane Cross by the time I got to the office. But after their less than flattering comments about my skills as a detective and the team as a whole, I decided the less said to them, the better.

I still hadn't spoken to Steve, which bothered me because going to bed on an argument wasn't my thing. I'd rather clear the air, but he was sulking. Nothing I could do about it, which made me see him in a different light. I needed a boyfriend that was mature and wanted to discuss problems rationally. His hiding behind his mobile phone infuriated me.

"Over here, Bells," I called out as she strode confidently into the incident room. "I need you for a minute."

Bella smiled and headed toward me. "Morning, Avaline." Mischief twinkled in her eyes.

I hadn't had a moment to think about my alter-ego of late, but I missed the buzz of performing and was eager to get back to it. I made a mental note to call Roy when I got home and invite him round for a meal tomorrow night. Sod Steve. I'd leave him to stew in his own juices. "Behave yourself," I hissed. "What do you have for me?"

"We got the CCTV footage back from central for around the time of Jane Cross' attack. Will and I had a look and we found something very interesting."

"Show me." I was keen to see what they'd come up with. Solving this case quickly would take the pressure off.

"Come over to my desk. I already have the footage loaded."

I followed her and took a seat beside her. Will joined us.

She hit play, and I spotted it immediately. "Ah," I said out loud, pressing the rewind button so I could watch it again. "The hooded figure dashing across the car park and down the bank before disappearing into the woods."

"That's the one," Will replied.

"What's he running from, I wonder?"

"No idea, but this could be our guy." He looked pleased with himself.

"Have you checked the other cameras to see if there was any commotion in the town centre he could be running from?"

"All checked and double checked. Aside from Jane Cross' murder, it was a quiet night. I've got uniform going in and out of all the fast-food outlets, bars, and shops surrounding the area asking if they have any footage they'd be willing to share with us. We might get lucky and find something from that. There's no trace of our runner after he disappears down the bank and into the woods."

"Damn."

"Don't worry too much, Dylan," Bella said, trying to stay positive. "He either lives close by or knows how to avoid CCTV."

Her words sent shivers down my spine. Layla knew our every move and planned her crimes meticulously. She knew where the street cameras were and avoided them adeptly.

"I'll pull up all the footage I can from last night," Will said. "And then cross check both nights. Hopefully, something will turn up."

"I have a feeling our man is fucking with us. All the crime shows on TV lately are playing havoc with real-life investigations. They give too many of our procedures away and so any would-be killer is always one step ahead of us."

"He'll mess up," Bella said. "You'll see."

"I hope so. Has anybody got hold of Amanda Morris's parents yet?"

"Still nothing. Pete's been over there twice already. The neighbour suggested they may have gone to their caravan."

"Okay. Keep trying that number for me, will you?"

FOURTEEN

As soon as I got the call from Lauren, I raced from the office. I didn't so much as want to be in on the autopsy, but I needed to get inside the mind of this killer. To do that, I felt I needed some kind of insight into what made him tick and why.

"Ah, Dylan. Just in time," Lauren said as I stepped into the examination room already covered from top to toe in surgical scrubs.

"You seem a little happier than you did earlier. Have you had your quota of caffeine for the day?"

"Sorry about that. The amount of people who try to access the crime scene nowadays just does my head in—nothing appears to be sacred."

"I hear you."

"My main priority is to get the body from point A to point B as efficiently as possible, with no contamination or loss of evidence along the way. I can come across as a bit of an ogre—I know that. But I promise, now I'm back here and in full control, I'll be much more accommodating."

"Hey, you don't need to preach to the converted. I'm with you on this. All unauthorised people at a crime scene should be shot!"

"Oh, don't say that—I have more than enough bodies piling up as it is." She laughed.

"Okay. Maybe not shot—just tortured to within an inch of their lives."

"Better. Much better. Now, I hope you've not eaten—this won't be pretty."

"No, but I must warn you, I'm already feeling a little queasy today. Please be gentle with me."

"I'll try."

I wished I hadn't mentioned it because Lauren took great pleasure seeing me retch into her sink. I was okay one minute, but the sight and sound of her unceremoniously dumping internal organs into a metal dish made me weak at the knees. It wasn't my finest display of manliness or professionalism.

I couldn't wait to get out of there.

Afterwards, once I was feeling a little more together, I called Bella.

"How was it?"

"Just awful."

"Rather you than me."

"So, it turns out there was no sexual assault on Amanda either. But he left his calling cards—the writing on the chest, bite marks and traces of urine, although the rain washed away a lot of it. Plus, he finished her off with a rock this time."

"What do you mean this time?"

"Oh sorry. I thought you knew—Jane Cross was already dead by the time he used the rock on her. Amanda wasn't."

"I see. Anything else?"

"She had a fracture to her finger and an indent in the skin

made by a ring. There was no ring recovered, so I'm guessing the killer took it. We need to ask her parents."

"Noted."

"Also, Lauren confirmed that there was no DNA found on Jane Cross."

"You're joking. Not even from the piss?"

"No. She said there's only a small chance of retrieving usable DNA from the epithelial cells in urine and there is a higher chance of finding these cells in a woman's urine than a man's."

"Fuck. We didn't get anything from the cigarette butts either."

"So, we're absolutely screwed?"

"Afraid so."

"How's Will getting on?"

"The same as us. He's logged all the cars approaching and leaving both crime scenes with a couple of hours' window either side, but nothing stands out unless our guy came in on foot, which is likely. Or he used a different car both nights."

"So, a complete dead end?"

"Yep. And if Lauren is right, and the murders coincide with the full moon cycle, we may have a third victim tonight."

"Please don't say that, Bells. We're already operating at full capacity without a third body, thank you very much."

The rest of the day was taken up with the inevitable paperwork that comes with any crime.

I still hadn't heard from Steve, which pissed me off no end, but I wasn't going to make the first move. So instead of going home to an empty house, I ordered a pizza and sat at my desk until well after midnight.

The mention of a third victim had bothered me. I had spent a good hour going over and over what we had, which was very little. I knew Janine would be baying for blood if we didn't come up with something, and fast.

FIFTEEN

Oliver's phone beeped at 2am. He quickly silenced it because he didn't want to wake his mum. She'd done nothing but moan at him for weeks now. The last few days had been particularly bad, the worst it had ever been. She couldn't understand that he preferred the darkness and quiet of early morning, no matter how many times he tried to explain it to her. He slipped his feet into his muddy trainers, grabbed his jacket from the hook and slunk from the room. At his mother's bedroom door he paused to check she'd made it up the stairs, pressed his ear closer, and exhaled when he heard her soft snores.

He would often imagine he was a superhero or a soldier of some sort especially where his mother was concerned – he needed to be soft on his feet and agile so as not to wake her. She was such a light sleeper and would have a fit if she caught him going out again. Taking his time to descend the stairs he hoped she'd had a few drinks – then she'd stay where she was until morning.

Oliver reached the kitchen in relative silence but almost screamed when a face appeared pressed up against the window.

He stopped himself just in time, unlocked the patio door and slid it open quietly. "Sssh," he said, putting his finger to his lips.

"Are we going out, or what?" Sam spoke in hushed whispers.

"Yeah, but I need to get back before the sun comes up or Emily will be on my case again."

"Don't worry, I've got things to do myself. I've got some good shit here." Sam waggled a little plastic bag in front of his face.

Once they were away from the house Oliver asked, "What happened to waiting at the usual spot? You shat me up peering in at me like that."

"I've been waiting there for ages. I couldn't get a signal, so I walked towards the house. I still wasn't able to connect till I was almost at your door."

Oliver glanced at his friend from the corner of his eye. He was a handsome man, their worlds couldn't be further apart. Dapper in his appearance and obviously well-bred, he didn't know why the older man had any time for him. Oliver had seen a photograph of Sam's wife and two small children, and he felt a little envious. *If I had a wife like that at home, I wouldn't be traipsing around at all hours of the night like this, not a chance.*

He suddenly realised Sam was looking at him with a strange expression on his face. "What's up?"

"Nothing." Oliver felt his cheeks flush. "I wasn't checking you out if that's what you're worried about." He knew he was overly touchy about his sexuality. But he was certain he wasn't gay, he was aroused too easily by the sight of a naked woman. But his mother always suggested he was, and then there had been that trouble at Oakleaf and, although that hadn't been his fault, he hadn't been opposed to it either. Maybe he was bisexual.

"I'm not," Sam said.

"You're not what?"

"Worried."

"Good. I was just thinking how great you are at choosing

clothes. When I buy stuff online I always end up looking like a twat. That's why Emily buys all my stuff for me. My only stipulation is it has to be black."

"Why black?"

Oliver shrugged. "I like it. Matches my mood."

"I keep meaning to ask. Why do you call your mum Emily?"

"'Cos it pisses her off."

"You shouldn't be so nasty to her. You've only got one mum."

"I don't really mean it but calling her by her first name is something I've done since she shoved me into that residential school. I felt like she didn't want me anymore."

Sam seemed bewildered and shook his head. "I've got a bag of clothes that no longer fit me that I was going to drop in at the charity shop—you're welcome to them if you want?"

"Really?"

"Yeah, of course. They should fit you. They're not black though."

"Thanks man. Not that dressing like you will make any difference to the way I look. But you never know."

"I wish you weren't so hard on yourself, mate. As soon as anybody gets to know you, your appearance pales into insignificance. Pardon the pun."

"That's a crock of shit, but I appreciate you saying it."

Sam rolled his eyes and shook his head. "I'll drop them off one night."

They fell into step and headed down the back streets until they came to a break in the fence between two houses that led into the wood.

"Tell me more about this shit you got," Oliver asked.

"Oh fuck, man. It's sweet. Costs a fair penny though, but I work hard enough. Cindy can piss off if she thinks she can get her greedy mitts on all of my wages."

"Doesn't she see what you've been spending, though?"

"Yeah. She controls the banking and gives me an allowance but what she doesn't know is that when I was given a pay rise a few months ago, I asked my boss to pay the extra into my savings account—one that Cindy doesn't have access to."

"How'd you wangle that one?"

"I'm the office manager for Prestige Real Estate, just off Edge Lane."

"Sounds decent."

"It was my dad's company, but now I'm a director too. I can do whatever I want, pretty much."

"Genius, man. I like your style."

"Needs must, mate. Don't get me wrong, I don't mind being married, but Cindy can be a control freak when given the chance, and tries to make me feel guilty if I have spare money. This way she's happy—thinks she has me under the thumb and I get a few extra quid to do what I want with. Win-win."

"Mum's the same. She's a control freak, too. I can't say I'd choose to be with someone who does that to me to be honest."

"It never starts out that way. Women are master manipulators, let me tell you. They're all sweetness and light and then suddenly, BAM! They have you trussed up like a chicken with a firm grip on your finances. I even have an app on my phone that tells her where I am."

"Really? Fuck, man. How do you get around that when you're coming here?"

"I leave it at home." His eyes twinkled in the moonlight. "She doesn't know about my burner phone either."

They reached the clearing where they usually met, and each took a seat on one of the flat topped rocks positioned beside each other.

Sam produced a massive spliff from his inside jacket pocket. "Here's one I prepared earlier." He grinned, eyes twinkling in the moonlight.

Oliver smiled and salivated in anticipation. He loved the way weed made him feel – he no longer cared about how he looked. Being stoned dulled his senses. Things that normally bothered him, like bright lights and loud music, were tolerable while under the influence and made him feel like any other teenager.

They spent another hour lying on the rocks looking up at the moon and smoked one more spliff between them.

"Right, I'm off. Things to do, people to see," Sam said.

"Okay, speak to you online later."

"Take it easy, mate." Sam jumped down and headed in the opposite direction they'd come from.

Once he was out of sight, Oliver lay back down enjoying the moonlight for a while longer.

There was something about the full moon that filled me with immense joy. Or was it rage?

Maybe it was the same thing in my case.

This was the third full moon in a row, but I was tired and had no intention of acting on it tonight.

Being out under the huge glowing orb was excitement enough.

SIXTEEN

Rhona made sure the young woman and her adorable baby girl were sound asleep before she prepared to leave for home.

It broke her heart the number of abused women she booked into the refuge every week, but the number she was forced to turn away upset her more. Technically, they'd been full today, but one of the residents had left a note that afternoon. She'd taken her twin babies and returned to her ex-husband, which didn't come as a surprise to Rhona. Although it was frustrating, they couldn't force the victims to stay away. The only thing they could do was to offer a shoulder to cry on, a warm meal and a safe bed for the night – well, several nights. And then, with the help of their social worker, they would be re-homed, if they got that far.

Unfortunately, that wasn't always the outcome. Nine times out of ten, the victim returned to her abuser, as had happened today. But who was she to judge? Statistics showed it takes seven attempts to leave before doing it for real. Rhona knew from personal experience why these women insisted on going back. Her own husband put her through years of cruelty and emotional abuse before she finally plucked up the courage to leave him. And even then, she had several wobbles.

The principal reason people stayed was because they believed in their heart of hearts that the person they'd fallen in love with would come back to them – but that was bullshit. They never did.

Then there was the thought of starting over, be it financially, romantically, or even geographically. Often it would be necessary to find a new job and avoid family and friends, and so they would decide staying put was the easier option.

Then there was the shame. Why a victim feels ashamed for being beaten puzzled Rhona the most, but it was definitely up there with the top reasons not to leave.

She closed the laptop and flicked the light switch off. Then she locked the office door and hid the key above the picture frame on the opposite wall. She left via the side door.

Once out on the street, she glanced about to make sure there was nobody hanging around. She never parked in the same place – paranoid someone might follow her and work out where the safe house was.

She looked at her watch – 4:17am – and yawned. She was used to her sleep being disturbed. A big part of her job involved being on call five nights a week, but most of those calls could be dealt with on the phone. It was only the odd one that meant she had to leave the warmth and safety of her house. She didn't mind too much. It wasn't as if she had anybody at home she needed to consider anymore.

A sound behind her put all her senses on high alert. She stopped and whirled around on the spot. The full moon made it easy to see up and down the street, but the woodland to the side of her appeared sinister and terrifying. She didn't see anybody – not out in the open anyway, but that didn't mean there was nobody there. The latest woman's husband sounded like a brute. Rhona hoped he hadn't found them.

Turning around again, she picked up her pace – relieved she could see her silver Peugeot a little further up on the other side of the street.

A guttural growl behind her made her stop once again. *What the hell was that?*

She froze.

Something was behind her.

Instinct pushed her forward with slow, determined steps. If it was a wild animal or a dog, then running could cause her more problems.

Another growl and the sound of something sniffing.

She held her breath. Terrified and with common sense now abandoned, she was just about to run when she was slammed to the pavement.

Something was on top of her.

The searing pain in her neck as the beast sunk his teeth in caused her to lose consciousness.

I hadn't expected the woman to pass out. It totally ruined my plans for her and brought about a rage I didn't know possible. I had decided I wouldn't look for another victim this month – I'd already done two in the small three day window, but when the woman rushed past me, I wasn't able to resist.

SEVENTEEN

I'd just finished rearranging my diary when Janine popped her head around the door. "Dylan, a word, please." Then she was gone.

I turned and looked at Will. "Here we go."

"Good luck," he said.

Grabbing the half-drunk mug of coffee from my desk, I sauntered down the corridor and walked through her open office door. "Sit," she ordered.

"What's wrong?"

"I've just had a phone call from Amanda Morris' father, demanding some information about his daughter's death."

"I'm heading over there with Bella in a few minutes. Apparently, the family have been at their caravan in Rhyl this past week."

"So why didn't you do the decent thing and head down there to speak with them?" She reclined in her chair, and I had the feeling she was about to go in for the kill.

"Do you have any idea how long that would take? We're in the middle of a murder investigation unless you've forgotten. I spent yesterday afternoon at their daughter's autopsy. Will tried to get hold of them several times, but there was nobody home. It took him a while to locate them and then, once we had, a colleague of mine in North Wales Police assured me he'd drive over to the holiday park and speak with them directly. I also left numerous messages on Mr Morris' phone, but—"

She wasn't going to allow me to defend myself, that much was obvious. Holding her hand up, she interrupted me. "Do I need to remind you what is at stake right now?"

"No, Janine, you really don't."

"Then do better because the last thing I need is for those idiots at *The Post* to write that we're a bunch of unsympathetic tossers. Do you hear me?"

"I'll grab my car keys and set off now." Mr Morris had already arranged an appointment with me for this morning, not that Janine was interested in the facts. I'd been thrown under the bus.

"Keep me informed, Dylan, every step of the way. We can't afford to screw this case up."

"I'm on it and focused."

"Words come easy, prove it, Detective Inspector."

I've never loathed her more than in that moment. "Got it, Ma'am."

"And before you go, DC Anita Khan—she's recently come over from uniform and will be starting on Monday morning. I don't want her walking into a shit storm."

"About time. It's only been six months since we lost Layla."

"Be thankful you're getting anyone."

"Do I get to know anything about the latest recruit to *my* team, or am I no longer deemed important enough?"

"I'll email the HR file to you. Look it over when you get the chance."

"Perhaps it would have been more professional for me to have seen that and sat in on the interview before they offered her the position?"

"Perhaps—" She raised her brows and, with a wave of her hand, dismissed me, though she already knew the reaction her attitude would bring. It was a fight best left for another day, but one I knew for a fact was coming.

Bella was at her desk when I returned to the incident room. "Don't get too comfy, Bells, we're off."

"Jesus, Dylan, I've not even had the chance to get a coffee yet."

"We'll stop at a Starbucks drive-thru on the way, but we need to go now. Janine's breathing fire."

"Fine," she snapped.

"Will, when Joanna arrives, can you ask her to make a start with the local dentists and see what you can find out for when we get back?"

"Yeah, can do," he replied.

"Right-o." With no clear place to begin with this part of the investigation, it came down to Lady Luck, so this idea was as good as any. "You ready, Bells?" I grabbed my car keys and other items before walking out toward the car park. "I'll drive."

She followed close behind.

I unlocked the car, and we both climbed in.

"What's Janine's problem now?" Bella buckled her seatbelt.

"She's on my back, but I shouldn't expect anything else. We've got this bloody nutter on the loose. The press are circling like vultures, but there's no motive or clue to who's killing these girls."

"We'll find him."

"I basically just promised Janine the same thing. But sometimes it feels like I'm just hovering on the perimeter, especially now."

"You're hyper-sensitive and need to calm down. Nothing is gonna get sorted this way."

"We're on the clock, Bella. The PSD are watching every move we make. How else am I gonna feel?"

"And they're looking for the first fuck up, and the way you're going, it's gonna be your balls on a plate."

"What are you saying?"

"You're still lost in what happened with Layla and obsessed with going by the book, but your focus needs to be on this case only—everything else should fall by the wayside."

"My career is on the line."

"Yeah, and so is a few of the other members of the team, but you don't see them wallowing. Instead, they're working their arses off to prove to themselves and others that they're good at their jobs. Let the past go, Dylan."

Her criticism was constructive and the kick up the arse I needed. "You're right."

"No shit, Sherlock. You got the job because you were the best candidate, okay."

"And because you were on maternity leave, Bells, let's be real."

"Crap! You cracked the Layla case, nobody else. Now take the credit and start doing what you're obviously brilliant at."

I reversed out of my parking space and drove slowly through the gates. Traffic was a nightmare because of the roadworks in the city centre. It was slow moving out of the tunnel too. We had an appointment to keep, so I used the blues and twos to push through it.

EIGHTEEN

Later than I'd have liked, we pulled up outside the house on Sanders Street where Amanda Morris had lived with her parents, James and Kathleen Morris. It was no more than five minutes away from where she met her untimely death.

"What an absolute shit hole." I was being judgemental, but looking around, called it for what it was. An abandoned car dumped in what used to be a garden and ripped rubbish bags strewn across patchy grass. "Why do people live like this?"

"It doesn't bode well for what's lurking inside." Bella grimaced.

We climbed out of the car and hopscotched towards the front door, bypassing piles of dog shit and God knows what else.

Bella turned to me. "Seems like, if they've called Janine already, they're pissed off with you, so why don't I take the lead on this one?"

"That's a good idea."

She pressed the doorbell.

We looked at each other as chimes rang out. There was no response, so she pressed it again.

"Get the friggin' door, will ya?" a female I presumed to be Mrs Morris called out from inside the property.

Bella rolled her eyes while I prepared myself for whatever was coming.

"The pigs are 'ere." This time it was a male voice we heard. "Get dressed and get your arse down these stairs."

"Charming," Bella says. "We're in for a rough ride with these two."

The door opened, and we were greeted by an unkempt guy wearing a filthy vest, dirty jeans, and a cap on his head. He obviously didn't want us there, but was left with little choice.

Bella held up her identification first. "Good morning, sir, I'm DS Annabella Frost, and this is DI Dylan Monroe." I showed my badge too, not that he even pretended to look.

"'Bout time," he barked as a woman looking not much better appeared behind him.

"Mr and Mrs Morris?"

"Yeah, that's us," he replied in a deep Scouse accent.

Trying to maintain the sympathy they deserved as grieving parents, I withheld further judgement and hoped they did not see us as a hostile presence. "May we come in?"

He pulled the door open slowly and I was reminded of Cruikshank from that old TV programme, The Munsters. "Go straight through to the kitchen, but mind the merchandise."

Bella stepped inside first, and we were guided down a long, dimly lit, hallway cluttered with boxes lining both walls. The carpet was covered in black marks, and sticky under foot. My first observations were correct. "Are you moving?" I asked, aware it could cause offence, but a perfectly reasonable question, regardless.

"No, bab," Mrs Morris replied. "We buy and sell stuff and shift it on eBay, you know how it is." Her dialect was a strange mix, though I detected a definite Black Country twang.

"You're not from Merseyside, I take it?" Bella said what I was thinking.

"Born and bred in Dudley, that's me, only moved up 'ere fifteen years ago when I met him."

Mr Morris glowered at us with suspicion in his eyes. We weren't going to get anything but the bare minimum from him, despite the harrowing circumstances of our visit. "Sit down if ya like," he added, though there was no way I intended to sit anywhere.

"We'll stand if you don't mind?" Bella knew what I was thinking and replied for the both of us.

"Suit yaselves," he replied, shrugging his shoulders.

We were in two distinct corners of the room. They stood shoulder to shoulder on one side, with Bella and me on the other.

"First, I want to say, on behalf of DI Monroe and myself, that we're sorry for your loss."

Mrs Morris was the first to speak up. "I warned her time and time again not to walk the streets alone in the dark, but I wasn't her real mom, so she took no notice of me." There was a hint of sadness weaved into her words.

"You did more for our Mandy than her real mother ever did. Lazy bitch she was."

"It wasn't her fault, Jim." Mrs Morris argued. "She was sick in the head and couldn't bring herself to bond with Mandy."

"Didn't stop her having more kids with that dickhead she's with now, though."

"Why bother bringing all this up again?" she asked.

"She never gave our Mandy anything apart from that cheap piece of tat she wore all the time."

"Are you talking about a ring, by any chance?" I asked.

"Yeah. A cheap gold ring with cubic zirconia stone. She never took it off, even after I offered to buy her something decent to replace it."

"It was the only reminder she had of her real mom, so just let it be," Mrs Morris snapped.

"According to the pathologist, Amanda had an indent where a ring had been, but there was no trace of one. Also, the finger was broken."

"But she never took it off," Mrs Morris added. "Ever."

"Would you happen to have any pictures of the ring, even if Amanda was wearing it at the time?"

"What difference does it make now?" Mr Morris cut in. "If it's gone, it's gone."

I swiftly replied. "Pardon me for saying so, but it's who took the ring that's important."

"So, they murdered her for a ring you could've got from a lucky bag? Is that what you're saying?"

"Right now, we're not sure if Amanda lost the ring or whether it was taken. I'd appreciate it if you would check and see if she left it in her room?"

"Kathleen already told ya... she never took it off."

Bella stepped in. "Mrs Morris, would you have any pictures of it, or perhaps you could find a likeness in a catalogue?"

"I'll try, but—"

I had a better idea and one that might yield faster results. "We will need to speak to Amanda's birth mother. Perhaps she could give us more information about the ring herself."

"Leave that bitch out of it." He slammed his fist down on the work surface.

"Enough, Jim." Mrs Morris rubbed the top of his arm, trying to calm him. "If that's what they have to do, so be it."

"I don't want her in this house." He raised his voice. "Do you hear me?"

"Just calm down. Nobody's said anything of the sort."

I wasn't in the mood to referee a family dispute. "Do you have any contact details for her?"

"Her name is Kirsty Lamb, and that's all I know," he replied.

"But you previously mentioned her being with somebody else and having other kids."

"Jungle drums beat fast round 'ere, mate," he replied. "That's all I know. Take it or leave it."

"I'll see what I can find out and call you," Mrs Morris volunteered. "No matter what Kirsty did, she was still Mandy's mom."

It was interesting to note the differences between how she considered the other woman compared to her husband. There seemed to be a touch of empathy from her, while there wasn't a shred of it from him.

"Thank you."

"Did she suffer?" Mr Morris asked.

It's always the question I dreaded the most, especially in a murder as brutal as Amanda's. I needed to be as honest as possible without sounding insensitive. "Your daughter would have been aware of what was happening for a time, then lost consciousness." It was true to a fashion, but as unlikeable as he was, I refused to be the one who broke his heart by revealing the extent of the viciousness his child had endured. That would all come out later.

"When can we bury her?"

"Lauren Doyle is the Forensic Pathologist assigned to your daughter's case. She performed the post-mortem yesterday afternoon, but I've not been told when Amanda's body can be released as yet. We also need to arrange for her formal identification before then."

"You mean to tell me it might not even be our Mandy in the morgue?"

"From ID recovered at the scene, we're fairly certain it is your daughter, but there are procedures we have to follow," Bella added. "The sooner we know for sure, the better."

"Fine, but just so *you* know, I've already been on the phone to a solicitor about making a criminal injury claim."

There was nothing I could say that wouldn't sound like condemnation, so I avoided it altogether. "I'll speak to Lauren as soon as we get back to the office. I'll find out when it would be suitable for you to view the body. Do you have a recent photograph of Amanda for our records?"

"Check her Facebook. They're all on there, but you'll be lucky to find one where she's not blind drunk," Mrs Morris added. "That girl lived for partying and died for it too, by the sound of things."

Where's the tears? I asked myself. *Where's the grief?* "Is there anybody you could think of that would want to hurt your daughter?"

"Everyone liked her," Mrs Morris replied, "She was too friendly, that was her problem... she'd talk to anyone, even the milkman who'd give her a lift on the back of his float when she was too smashed to walk up the hill."

"Are you sure?" Bella asked. "Even the smallest of connections could yield a breakthrough."

"She just said no, didn't she?" Mr Morris seemed so closed-off in not wanting to help us, I wondered if he actually cared at all. "Mandy did what she wanted and took no notice of anyone. She always thought she knew better..." His voice wobbled and for the first time the barriers came down and allowed us to witness genuine emotions. "... we had our ups and downs, but I loved her, ya know."

I sighed. "We understand, Mr Morris."

"Find the bastard that did this before I do, or I won't be responsible for my actions," he threatened. His voice had taken on a menacing tone. "We don't take too kindly to one of our own being hurt around 'ere."

I eyed him warily. "Respectfully, sir, I'd like to request that you do nothing to interfere with any stage of this investigation."

"Find him then, and I won't 'ave to."

"A Family Liaison Officer will be in touch shortly to assist you with anything you might need."

"Women should be safe walking the streets, so do your job and don't bother trying to send do-gooders 'ere 'cos we don't want or need 'em." It was obvious he would refuse the help of the FLO team for reasons only known to him. Right now, his anger was rising, but Mrs Morris took his hand and held it against her heart, diffusing what could have been a tense stand-off. "Sickos like that should be strung up."

"Just to reassure you both, we have an entire team working on solving your daughter's murder and we are doing our best to bring her killer to justice."

"How many more does he 'ave to kill before you stop him, eh?"

It was a fair question, but one nobody could answer truthfully. "We're doing all we can. If you think of any possible link, no matter how small, please call either one of us." I pulled a card from my wallet and left it on the grimy-looking table. Bella did the same, though neither of us would hold our breath for information. "Is there anything else you'd like to ask us?"

"Don't think so," he replied.

Mrs Morris picked the cards up. "Be good if you'd speak to that Lauren woman and ask when we can identify Mandy's body, that's all. Then we can start planning her funeral. We can't move on until that's out of the way."

I felt perplexed by her words. There was definitely no love lost between stepmother and stepdaughter, but I'd wager my career neither of them had anything to do with Amanda's death. "We'll leave you in peace for now, but before we go, would you know if Amanda had any connection to Jane Cross?"

Mrs Morris appeared confused by my question.

"The other one?" Mr Morris grunted.

"If you mean was Jane the first victim, then yes," Bella added. I could see by the disgruntled expression across her face that she'd had enough of his attitude, too.

Mrs Morris spoke up. "Mandy had a lot of friends and acquaintances, but I don't think they knew each other. If they did, we never saw her here."

"That's fine, thank you."

"Anything else?" Mr Morris edged closer to me.

"Not right now, but you have our cards if you need us, or if there's anything you think of that might help with the investigation."

"Kathleen'll show you out."

We were summarily dismissed. This was the second time it had happened to me today.

Bella followed Mrs Morris down the hallway.

I wasn't far behind them, eager to get outside into the fresh air.

Mrs Morris opened the door. "Well, tararabit."

"What did you make of that?" I asked Bella once we were back in the car.

"Family rows, a daughter that wanted to live her own life and listened to nobody, squalor, dodgy as fuck parents, but we weren't there to case the joint. Although I suspect if we opened those boxes, we'd find a few things they wouldn't want us to see."

"Can you run a check on both of them when you get back and see what it brings up?"

"Can do, yeah, but what about his threats?" She pulled out a small packet of baby wipes from the glove box and cleaned her hands, offering me one.

"Whatever he did or didn't say, he's still a grieving father. It's nothing we've never heard before."

"Something tells me he meant what he said, though."

"Oh, Christ, don't say that." I imagined the headlines and Janine's reaction. "Him roaming the streets with a pack of vigilantes in tow isn't something I wanna think about."

"He won't go that far."

"There's no guarantee of that." I started the car and checked the mirrors before pulling away. "Let's get back to the office so I can call Lauren for an update."

We drove back to the station.

Will was practically bouncing when we entered the incident room.

"What?" I asked, praying for a breakthrough.

"I found her. She got off the night bus, but we lost her when she entered the park. Come look."

Bella and I stood behind his chair and watched as Amanda got off the bus. The footage was from the main junction, but it was clear enough. She turned and made a hand gesture at somebody still on the bus. She appeared to be alone and once it had driven away, she staggered across the road.

"Bloody hell, she's pissed as the proverbial newt!" Bella said.

"At least we now know the exact time she arrived at the crime scene," I said. "Let's hope she's not the only person the street cameras pick up."

"Well, there are several cameras in this area covering most of the streets in and out, so hopefully we'll be in luck. I'll trawl through them all first thing." Will paused the footage once Amanda was out of shot.

"I'll contact the bus company and see what else we can find," I said. "Hopefully, somebody remembers seeing her. It's not as though there were droves of people about at that time of the morning."

"No need," Will said. "I've made an appointment for you to meet the driver on Thursday."

NINETEEN

I'd just walked through the door and slumped onto the sofa, exhausted, when my mobile phone rang.

Lauren was the last person I was in the mood to talk to, but I swiped the screen and answered the call, anyway. "Hi." I tried to feign interest. "What can I do for you?"

"I've got something I wanted to share with you about the killer."

"What is it?" She had never called me this late before to update me on a case.

"I've had a closer look at the bites on both victims and there's something very odd about them."

"In what way?"

"Well, from what I can see, our killer doesn't have the best smile in the world."

"I don't follow?"

"It means, once you see the impression, you're gonna be spending a lot of time speaking to dentists to find out if any of them have patients on their books with major dental issues."

"At least we have something to go on."

"Yes, you do. I'm surprised we didn't wake up to victim number three this morning, though. There was another full moon last night, and I honestly thought our killer was following the lunar cycle."

"I thought there was only one full moon per month?"

"Technically, you're right. The fact is, a full moon lasts mere moments in reality, but to the naked eye, it appears on three consecutive nights every single month. So, like I said, don't be surprised if body number three turns up soon."

I groaned, scratching my head roughly. "Don't say that. We don't want, or need, another serial killer on the streets."

"What you want and what I suspect you're going to get are two different things. Unfortunately, I have the feeling we haven't heard the last of Lunatic."

"Cheers, you've just ruined my evening."

"Well, I must go," she replied sardonically. "Have fun."

She rang off. I tossed my phone onto the other sofa and went into the kitchen to defrost tonight's meal. Roy was coming for dinner.

An hour later, I answered the doorbell to find Roy in full drag.

"What the hell?"

He looked flustered and waved his hand majestically. I caught sight of the black painted talons masquerading as fingernails and wondered how he had driven here wearing them. "Don't start me off, darling. I've just laddered my bloody tights on that overgrown bush out there." He took a deep breath and shook his head. "And I have a show in town later at the Cock-a-Doodle-Doo." He looked down to inspect the damage. "Don't you have a hedge trimmer?"

"No, I don't, but I might have a spare pair of tights somewhere. Come in." Everything about that sentence sounded wrong.

He stepped inside. "Oh, something smells divine."

"Beef stew and dumplings—not exactly fine dining I'm afraid."

"I don't care about that, darling, I'm more worried about the effects your rich food will have on my schoolgirl figure."

"You don't have to eat it. I can always rustle up a salad if you'd prefer that."

"Shut it, wench. If God intended me to eat leaves, he'd have given me a set of buck teeth."

I couldn't resist getting a dig in. "I thought he had."

He cocked a perfectly arched eyebrow. "Touché, you slack jawed mare."

We both erupted into laughter.

I loved the back and forth between us. It was one of the reasons Blanche, the manager of Dorothy's, had asked us to do a live spot together; not performing or lip-syncing this time, but a full-on comedy act. I'd flatly refused.

"Come on in and take the weight off your feet."

"What weight is this?" Roy protested. "I'm barely a hundred and forty pounds."

"What the hell does that mean?" I joked.

"I'm not far off ten stone, darling."

"Piss off! And the rest. Who are you trying to kid?"

He pointed a talon in my direction. "Listen here, Saddlebags, if you want any more help with costumes, I'm ten stone. Capiche?"

I rolled my eyes and stifled a grin. "Oh, whatever. Just come and take a seat in the kitchen. Food's almost ready."

"It does smell lovely. I'm positively salivating."

"Five minutes and you can get your chops round my dumplings."

"You can chomp on your own dumplings, darling."

He had the sharpest wit of any person I knew. "Stop making me laugh and sit."

He took his usual seat facing the window. "Thanks for inviting me over. It's been ages since I saw you last."

"I know. I've been working non-stop, but hopefully things will quieten down now."

"Blanche has been ringing me every week, asking when you're going back."

"I'm not sure I will be."

"Oh, bollocks to that," he said. "You know you want to, so why not get on with it?"

"I'd like to, but work—"

"Will always be there," he interrupted.

"I guess so." I wanted to shift the focus away from what I should or shouldn't be doing. "Who are you working with tonight?" I stirred the stew, ready to dish up.

"I've got a half-hour set with Rusty Pubes."

I thought I'd heard wrong, dropping the serving spoon. I snorted out a laugh. "Rusty what?"

"Pubes, darling. Pubes."

"Oh, my God. That's priceless."

"What's so funny?" Roy asked, looking confused.

"Who chooses these names?"

"Goodness knows." He poured himself a glass of wine, then added a dash of soda water. "She's a sour-faced old bitch, but I need the readies." He rubbed his thumb and fingers together. "These frocks cost me a fortune once you factor in material, time, and accessories. And don't get me started on sequins and crystals—"

"I've never heard of her. Is she new?"

"No, darling, she's been on the scene for years."

"I can't place her." I thought back to Polly Wanakracker's friend and tried to remember her name, but it eluded me.

"You won't know her because she got a lifetime ban from Dorothy's."

"What for?"

"She got caught giving Blanche's ex a gobble behind the wheelie bins."

"Classy."

"I know, filthy trollop. No way would I be getting down and dirty behind those bins."

"Don't you miss having a fella?"

"Where would I find the time? I'm always so busy."

"But you deserve to be with someone decent."

"I have my fun, but don't broadcast it like most queens do."

"Oh aye, do tell."

"This lady doesn't kiss and tell."

"You're no lady, Roy." I reminded him, ladling the red-hot stew into a deep bowl.

"Shut your faces, all twenty of 'em, and feed me. I'm wasting away here."

I sniggered. He was just the tonic I needed to cheer me up.

I hugged Roy at the door. "Thanks for coming. It was so good to see you."

"Anytime, darling." He gave me a tight squeeze. "Dinner was delightful as per, but I must return the favour one day."

"I don't mind cooking for you." I handed him a Tupperware dish full of leftovers.

"Thank you."

"You do enough for me, so leftover stew is the least I can do."

"We're friends, ducky."

"You know what I mean."

"I do, but before I forget, what do you want me to tell Blanche about us two doing a spot together?"

I wanted to go back, at least once more, but as a comedy act, definitely not. "I'm not convinced it's for me."

"Come on, Saddlebags, give it a go. That old trout Blanche knows a good thing, or she wouldn't keep harping on about it."

"What did you say to her when she asked?"

"I told her I'd speak to you."

"I really don't mind doing a few numbers on stage with you, but only lip-syncing, like I've been doing on my own, for the moment anyway."

"I can work with that and I'm sure Blanche will just be pleased to have you back."

"If she doesn't agree, tell her I've hung up my heels for good."

"Will do, but I've got to run—" He looked at his watch. "I don't want to be late for my adoring fans."

I laughed out loud. A few pissed and screeching gay guys in a crowd couldn't be classed as adoring fans, but I wouldn't shatter his delusions of grandeur. "Call me tomorrow and we can chat some more about what we're going to do together."

"I will do, darling, and don't worry, we'll knock their socks off."

"Nothing rude though, do you hear?"

"I'm a class act, thank you very much."

"If you say so, Betty Swallocks."

He pulled the door open and tapped the top of the Tupperware dish. "Right, wench, I'm off."

"Drive safely and remember to call me."

Air kisses abound to avoid smudging his makeup, Roy made his exit.

A couple of hours later, I was curled up on the sofa enjoying a new show on *Netflix* when the doorbell rang.

I'd already had a few glasses of wine and was comfy in my shorts. I didn't want to move but figured it might be important.

Jumping to my feet, I pulled open the door and was surprised to see Steve waiting there. He was the last person I'd expected. Usually, I was the one who had to do the legwork to make things right when he was in a sulk. *God, he looks fit.* "Hello, stranger."

"Hiya." He wore a sheepish grin.

I leaned against the door. "Why didn't you use your key?"

"I felt a bit funny..." His eyes swept over my naked torso.

"You're the one who had his knickers in a twist, Steve, not me."

"I haven't come here for a row."

"Then what have you come for?" I would not back down as I usually did. With drink came courage. "You've been ignoring my calls, so I assumed we were over and done with."

He shuffled uncomfortably. "I kind of miss you."

I arched my eyebrow. "Kind of?"

"For fuck's sake," he grunted, beaten. "I miss you, okay? And I'm sorry for being a moody twat. Is that what you want to hear?"

I couldn't help smiling at my small victory. I'd missed him too and was genuinely pleased to see him. "Then you better come in and start making it up to me."

He stepped inside. "What do you have in mind?"

"Surprise me."

TWENTY

I crawled through rush hour city centre traffic while fighting against roadworks. Not only that, the tailbacks were a nightmare. Glancing at my phone, it was already 9am and I'd achieved nothing.

Eager to get my day started, I thought back to the bust up with Janine yesterday and her demand to be kept in the loop at all times. I scrolled through my phone sitting on the docking station and called Will.

"Morning, boss."

"Yeah, hi, Will."

"Where are you? You're usually in by now."

"Stuck in traffic near the Adelphi Hotel."

"Is Bella with you?"

"No, and that's why I'm calling. My plan was to pick her up and swing by the bus company to speak with the driver. But I don't know what time we're gonna get there and back to the office, so can you let Janine know what's going on?"

"Yeah, sure. She was in here about half an hour ago looking for you."

"What did she have to say for herself?"

"Nothing much, but she asked about the CCTV and if I'd found anything more."

"And?"

"I told her we've yet to see the bus company's footage, but you're working on it this morning."

"What did she say to that?"

"Something along the lines of, it should've been done before now."

"Well, just let her know I'm en route to the bus depot, but traffic is backed up 'cos of these damned roadworks."

"Will do."

"Cheers. Would you also let the others know I'll catch up with them sometime later?"

"Got it. Oh, and before you go, a young girl called Deborah Fisher rang in late yesterday afternoon and said she was with Amanda Morris the night she died, apparently they'd been clubbing it and got the night bus together."

"Deborah Fisher, got it, thanks, mate. Can you send through her details?"

As soon as I hung up, my phone rang. It was Bella.

"Did you sleep in or something?" she asked.

"I wish."

"Where are you? I've been waiting for bloody ages."

"Stuck in traffic, but I've barely moved in the last ten minutes."

"Why don't I meet you at the depot, it'll be easier than you coming here then having to go back on yourself."

I was relieved she was so easy going. Nothing irritated me more than being kept waiting. "Would you mind?"

"Not at all. Put your lights on, that'll get you moving quicker."

"Okay, I'll be there as soon as I can."

"You took your time," Bella said as I pulled up next to her car.

"Sorry. It's a joke out there, I'm gonna have to start leaving for work at six just to get there for eight."

"Rather you than me."

"Let's get this out of the way."

"I've already been in and the driver, Gareth Mount, is due in at 10am to start his shift."

Glancing at my watch, I realised I'd just made it in time.

"I told the manager to make sure he's not sent out until we've spoken to him. He had a face like a slapped arse and grumbled about interruption to public services."

"Not another gobshite."

"That's precisely what he is, so I had the pleasure in telling him we'd be happy to have the conversation down at the station."

"What did he say to that?"

"He told me to wait in the car until Gareth arrived."

"Did you not tell him we have an appointment?"

"Yeah, but it seems he likes things his way or no way at all."

"Sod that," I said, getting out of the car. "Come on, let's go in."

She followed me.

"What's the manager's name?"

"Ernest Jones."

I wasn't in the mood to be messed about today and pushed the doors to the bus depot open. "Where's his office?"

She pointed towards the brown door with the gold plaque in place. "Over there."

Striding across the depot, his door suddenly opened. He'd obviously seen us coming. "What can I do for you?"

"DI Dylan Monroe." I held up my credentials. "And you are?"

"Ernest Jones, Depot Manager."

"Mr Jones, would you be kind enough to tell me if Gareth Mount has arrived for his shift yet?"

"A few minutes ago, yes."

"That's great. I'd appreciate it if you'd get him for me and find somewhere private where we can talk."

"Well, I don't know about that. He's got a bus to get out."

"Then find another driver. This is official police business. And we have an appointment, but as my colleague has already advised, we can do this at the station if there is a problem."

"There's no need for that."

"We'll wait here while you secure that private room and set up a screen so we can view the bus cam footage. How does that sound?"

"Give me a few minutes." He stormed across the floor and through a set of double doors.

"What an absolute wanker." Bella shook her head. "Why do these people want to make life so difficult? A young girl was killed, and this driver might be the last person to have spoken to her before she died, so it shouldn't be a surprise we'd want to find out more."

The manager reappeared. "Mr Monroe, this way," he called out.

"Don't move," I warned Bella. He was already trampling over my last nerve, so I purposely ignored him, making him walk over to us.

"Mr Monroe," he called out again.

"He's got a face like thunder, Dylan."

"Good."

He stomped towards us. "I was calling you."

"You were?"

"Yes!"

"Perhaps if you'd called out for Detective Inspector Monroe, I might have heard you."

Bella lowered her head. Clearly amused because I wasn't usually this difficult.

"Right, well, the room is ready, and Gareth is waiting for you. Now, if you wouldn't mind, I'd like to be there too."

"Suit yourself."

"This way, please." He'd changed tack entirely.

We were taken into a room with a large flat-screen TV attached to the wall. It was already switched on. The footage had been started and paused, hopefully in the right place. A weedy-looking guy in his early fifties, skinny with glasses and chewing his fingernails, was sitting waiting for us.

"Mr Mount?"

He stood up. "Yes, that's me." He seemed worried.

"Please sit down. My name is DI Dylan Monroe, and this is my partner, DS Annabella Frost."

He nodded.

Bella turned to the Depot Manager. "Mr Jones, do you have a coffee machine anywhere in the building?"

"Yes, in the canteen."

"Would you be a dear and grab my colleague and me a large coffee?"

"What, now?"

"Would you like one too, Mr Mount?"

"I like it milky with two sugars in mine please, Ern."

He looked fit to burst, but he was only going to be a hindrance, so the less we saw of him the better. "Fine."

"Thank you," I added. "Black. No sugar in ours."

Once he was gone, I turned to Gareth. "Don't look so worried, this is just a routine interview. You're not under arrest or anything like that. We just need to speak to you about Amanda Morris."

I slid into the chair opposite and Bella followed suit.

"Is that the girl that's been on the news?" he asked.

"Yes, that's her."

"There's really not that much I can tell you aside from the fact she got on at the stop just outside *Burger King* by the gyratory. I remember her clearly, and that's only because she gave me a mouthful, but that's nothing new with the piss-heads who use the night bus."

"Was she sitting alone?"

"No, she was with another girl."

"Did she get off the bus with this same girl?"

"When you look at the footage, you'll see. She got off on her own and stuck two fingers up at me." This confirmed what we'd already seen on the CCTV footage.

"And where did this other girl get off? Do you recall?"

"Two stops after."

"Let's have a look, shall we?" Bella picked up the TV remote and pointed it at the screen. The footage played and what he'd told us was exactly how the events unfolded. Amanda Morris could be seen chatting animatedly to another girl. She leaned in and kissed her goodbye, had a brief exchange with the driver, and got off. "It's a shame there's no audio."

"See, it's how I said it was, and if you keep watching, you'll see the other girl get off too. The pair of 'em were hammered. I don't know how anyone can drink so much and stay upright, but young girls are like that nowadays."

Mr Jones returned carrying three cups of coffee on a tray. "Sorry for the delay." He set the tray down in the middle of the table.

"Thanks," Bella and I said together.

She picked up one cup and took a sip.

"Is everything okay?" Mr Jones asked.

"Yes, it's fine, but, if you wouldn't mind, I'd like a copy of the footage of Gareth's entire shift." I wouldn't explain why, but there was the possibility our killer may have got on the bus at the same time as Amanda but got off at a different stop.

"That can be arranged."

I picked up one of the coffees and brought it to my lips. "We'll wait, thank you."

Once again, he walked out of the room.

"I won't have to go to court, will I?" Gareth asked.

Bella spoke up. "Unless we find it was one of the other passengers and you engaged with them beyond normal parameters, I wouldn't think so. It's pretty straight forward from what we can see."

"Was it really as bad as the papers made out?"

She placed her cup on the desk. "We're not at liberty to say, but the sooner we catch this person, the safer the streets will be."

"Good."

Mr Jones returned holding a flash drive. "I asked our IT guy to put what you need on this. Will that do?"

"Perfect," I replied, intending to pass it over for Will and Joanna to sift through. They'd confirm where Amanda's friend got off rather than us scrolling through it all here. "We appreciate your assistance and will be in touch if we need to speak with you again."

"Okay."

"Thank you, Mr Jones." Bella got to her feet.

I hadn't bothered finishing my coffee – it was no better than gnat's piss. "Have a good day, and thanks for being so accommodating." My comments were laced with sarcasm because Mr Jones had been anything but.

Once we were clear of the building, Bella giggled.

"What's amused you?"

"You're a sarky bastard at the best of times, Dylan, but since your drag persona was born, it's taken on a new level. And that's saying something, even for you."

"This job has changed me, Bells, and I'm not sure it's for the better."

"Sometimes you're too nice and we're all racing against the clock, so it's not gonna be plain sailing for a while."

"I don't want you or the rest of the team thinking I'm not approachable anymore."

"Nobody thinks that from what I've heard, we're just getting on with things right now."

"Let's get back to the station and give this flash drive to Will and Jo. Plus, I need to speak with the team 'cos we've got a new DC, Anita Khan, starting Monday morning."

"You never said."

"Janine told me, but it slipped my mind."

"Took them long enough to find someone."

"I said the same thing to Janine, but we don't have enough cover now, so anyone is better than nothing."

"Do you know anything about her?"

"Bugger all, aside from the fact she's just been promoted from uniform."

"Typical. We're searching for a potential serial killer, as well as dealing with other cases, and they send us a newbie."

"Her appointment had nothing to do with me, Bells. I'm obviously not important enough to be consulted, though I have my suspicions she's being placed here purposely."

"What, as a snitch?" She looked at me wide-eyed. "They wouldn't dare."

"Wouldn't they?"

"Slimy fuckers." She pressed her lips together until they almost disappeared. "Like we need to have that worry hanging over our heads. A member of our team reporting back everything we say and do."

"I don't think it's Janine's doing to be fair, but it wouldn't surprise me if the higher ups had a hand in forcing her to take Khan."

"If it's not bad enough having Lady Tanner on the team."

The lady reference made me laugh and was a little unfair, but I saw where she was coming from, as Genevieve Tanner wasn't your average officer. She spoke with what my mum would say a plum in her gob. Although she was nice enough, I knew very little about her personal life. "She's okay. She keeps herself to herself, but I've not had any issues with her work. She uses her initiative, and that's good enough for me."

Bella blew a raspberry, then scrunched her face up in disgust. "She's a stuck-up boot and trust me, she's another that sees everything."

"You're such a bitch, Bells, but it's so good to have you back."

TWENTY-ONE

Will hung up the phone to Dylan and turned back to his computer screen just as Joanna arrived.

"Where is everyone?" she asked.

"Dylan and Bella have gone to speak to the bus driver. Pete's chasing up the phone companies for both victims' call logs. Tommo and Heather are still out canvassing. Genevieve's rang in sick, so that leaves me and thee to work through this little lot. We've also got to contact a dentist, now we have the impression of the killer's gnashers."

"I've got a friend, Julia, who works for a dentist in Litherland. Shall I call her?"

"I guess it's a good place to start—she might be able to advise us where to go from here."

"Okay—I'll get onto it right away. Then what? Where are we up to with interviewing the witnesses that uniform took statements from?"

"Dylan followed up with the guy who discovered Jane Cross' body, but he didn't get hold of the businessman who found

Amanda. Apparently, he was too busy to hang around so, after his initial statement, he did one."

"Did one?"

"A runner."

"So that needs chasing up. Just to make sure we haven't missed anything. Then all the areas that have been canvassed need cross checking. But first things first, I'll call Julia and see if she can help with the dental side of things."

"Then maybe you should stick the kettle on. I think we're gonna have a mare of a day looking at this little lot."

"You are quite capable of making *me* a cuppa, you know?"

"I know, but yours tastes nicer than mine."

"For fuck's sake, Will, I've just told you how busy I am."

"Okay, okay, keep your hair on. I'll make the tea if it means that bloody much to you." Will toddled off to the kitchen and stood staring around him, embarrassed to admit he didn't know where anything was kept. But being a seasoned detective stood him in good stead and he soon found the tea bags. He filled the kettle and went back through to Joanna, who was talking animatedly on the phone. *Do you have sugar?* He mouthed at her.

She stuck two fingers up at him.

He goggled his eyes at her comically.

Joanna grinned and blushed, wafting him away like an annoying fly.

When he returned a few minutes later, she'd ended her call.

"Julia told me to send the images through to her and she'll get her boss to look at them straight away."

"Fab. A nice cup of char with two sugars just how madam likes it. Don't say I never give you nowt."

"Bloody Nora! That's the first brew I've had since working here that I haven't made myself."

"What can I say—can't get the staff these days."

They each returned to their desks. Will still had hours of footage to trawl through, and Joanna made a start on her list.

"I wish murder investigations were more like they are on telly," Joanna said after a couple of minutes.

"In what way?"

"You never see Cagney and Lacey stuck at their desks with reams and reams of evidence to cross reference."

"Cagney and Lacey! Bloody hell, that's a blast from the past. I doubt they even had computers back when they filmed that, never mind a forensic team."

"Well, you know what I mean. When I first decided to be a cop, it was because of the way the TV shows glamorised it—all high heels and designer suits catching the bad guys without breaking a nail. Little did I know I'd be stuck at my desk compiling hundreds of crime scene photographs and videotapes. Or documenting and collating trace evidence and then having to chase it up—"

"Stop complaining and get cracking otherwise we'll still be here at midnight." He winked at her.

Her phone vibrated alerting her of a call, saving Will from a blasting. She scowled at him before getting to her feet and answering. She stepped into Dylan's side office.

A few minutes later, she emerged. "Julia said someone with a bite that bad would be under an orthodontist or a specialist dental hospital, at least. Her boss agreed he shouldn't be too hard to find and has sent the images to all the local orthodontists on our behalf. Hopefully, we'll hear something soon."

"Good. Let's hope it's cut and dried." He turned back to the his screen, unable to believe how unlucky Amanda Morris must've been – there was absolutely nobody else on the streets that night.

He could feel his eyes getting heavier as he stared at one lot of footage after another. Suddenly, out of the corner of his eye, he noticed a slight movement at the edge of the screen. He gasped, rewound the film and zoomed in. "Got him!" he barked.

Joanna jumped to her feet and rushed over.

He replayed it once more.

An image of a male, average height and build, came into view dressed in what appeared to be a black boiler suit with a hood. The man turned briefly to face the motion detector camera at the park's entrance before ducking out of sight again.

Will hit pause and zoomed in once more, bringing the stark white face into the centre of the screen. Because of the zoom, the quality was impaired and so the actual features were obscured, but the white hair poking from the front of the hood was unmistakable.

"So, we're looking for someone with white hair?" Joanna asked.

"Or blond hair. The moonlight might make it appear lighter than it actually is because look at his face—how white that looks too."

"But it's something, at least."

"It certainly is. I'll send this to IT and see if they can clean it up at all."

TWENTY-TWO

The incident room appeared to be a hive of activity.

I'd already been informed that Will had discovered more footage of who we suspected was the killer, and Pete had also established the two victims had jewellery items missing. Jane Cross' watch was never found, nor was Amanda Morris's ring.

Whatever direction I looked in, the team was hard at work, but with cases coming out of our ears, we had little choice but to get on with things.

Bella slunk off to her desk in the corner, muttering something about needing to sort paperwork before it became a backlog. She had the right idea, but I had other, more pressing, matters to take care of first, though I knew I'd regret it down the line.

I turned to look at the glass wall partition acting as a bulletin board and noticed pictures of Jane Cross and Amanda Morris were now taped to it, along with corresponding information written underneath.

Will was deep in conversation with Pete and Tommo while Heather chatted on the phone. Joanna was sitting behind her own desk, seemingly engrossed in poring through more CCTV footage.

Dropping my files, car keys and phone onto my desk, I waited for Heather to finish her call, then I cleared my throat. "Afternoon, everyone."

All eyes focused on me.

"Hey, boss," Will added as the others murmured their own greetings.

"I know you're all crazy busy right now and won't keep you long, but I wanted to let you know we've got a new officer starting on Monday."

"Wonders will never cease," Heather said.

"About bleedin' time," Tommo added. "Who do we have to thank for that?"

"It's not been ideal lately, but with the arrival of DC Anita Khan, it should lessen the burden you're all feeling somewhat."

"Uniform?" Pete queried.

"Recently promoted." I knew the team would've preferred an experienced officer, but we had to take what we could get. "It'll be our job to help get her up to speed."

"Fuckin' wonderful," he replied. "We're up to our necks in shit and they send a rookie for us to babysit."

"We'd be better off with Noddy," Joanna butted in, unhelpfully.

Bella pushed herself to her feet and joined the conversation. "She hasn't even started and you're already tearing her to pieces."

Joanna was quick to reply. "We're not doing anything of the sort, Bella."

"Sounds like it to me," she argued.

I had to nip this in the bud before it escalated. "Regardless of your opinions, DC Khan *will* start on Monday morning and I expect *everyone* to make her welcome, and that's an order."

Despite my own suspicions regarding her appointment, I figured she deserved a chance. "Do I make myself clear?"

I was greeted by a series of grunts.

"Well—?"

"Fine," Tommo said.

"Whatever you say." Joanna headed back toward her desk.

"Gotcha," Pete added.

Heather said nothing.

Only Bella spoke up. "C'mon, you miserable lot, we've got eyes watching us from every direction and if we don't get this right, how's it gonna look to Janine and top brass?"

Without spelling it out, it was her way of telling the team we had to stick together.

"Bella is right." I looked around at them in turn. "Our backs are against the wall right now, and the last thing I want is for us to be seen as ineffective."

"We get what you're saying, boss, but why do I feel like we're being set up to fail?" Will voiced my thoughts exactly.

"I don't think that's the case, and even if it was, I don't intend to roll over and take it up the arse from anybody. We've all worked too hard and for too long and, as teams go, I'm lucky to have you at my side." I hoped my words encouraged them. "Now, enough of this mushy shit. Let's get back to work."

Well said, Bella mouthed.

I nodded my thanks and returned to my seat. "Heather, have you got a minute?"

She stood up, then made her way over to me. "Sure. What is it?"

"Are you busy?"

"Nothing I can't put off. Why?"

"I need to go and see Amanda's friend, Deborah Fisher. Do you fancy coming along?" It would usually be Bella accompanying me, but I needed to find a way to re-bond with the team, and for them to see me as a colleague, not just their superior.

"What about Bella?"

"Admin." I'd explain it to Bella later, but I doubted she'd care anyway.

"If you're sure."

"Yep, grab your coat and let's go."

It had been a while since I'd had conversations with the various members of my team about anything other than work, so it was nice to have this time with Heather. "How's Billy?"

"He's fine, but still hates the fact I'm in the force and wants me to find another job."

"You're not going to, are you?"

"No way. This is all I ever wanted to do and if he doesn't like it, sod him."

"Is he still driving for Eddie Stobart's?"

"Yeah, he loves the freedom of the open road, but that life isn't for me."

"What's his problem, then?"

"He wants kids."

"And you don't?"

"Yeah, I do. But I'm only thirty-one and have plenty of time to play wife and mother."

"Plenty of women have kids and maintain their careers. Look at Bells."

"From the outside in, she seems to balance it well, but as devoted to my career as I am, something tells me when the time comes, I'd wanna be a stay-at-home mum."

"I get it."

"But that's down the line and right now, I'm happy with things as they are."

As sheets of rain fell, I slowed the car to a stop at a newly built property on Millford Estate, one of the better housing estates in the area. "You ready?"

"Quick, before we get soaked." We dashed towards the front door.

"I'm happy for you to take the lead," I said.

She nodded and pressed the doorbell once.

Seconds later, a pretty young girl with porcelain skin and long, flowing red hair stood before us. It was obvious she'd been crying.

"Are you Deborah Fisher?" Heather asked, trying to shield herself from the elements.

"Who are you?"

We both held up our badges.

"DS Heather Stubbs, and this is DI Dylan Monroe. Are you Deborah?"

"Yeah."

"Do you mind if we come in?"

She stepped aside, then showed us into a sitting room. The kitchen was at the far end and beyond that, patio doors led toward the garden.

"Can I get either of you a tea or coffee?"

"Not for me, thanks," I replied.

"I'm fine too," Heather said.

"Please, take a seat."

Heather and I sat on the sofa and Deborah sat opposite, shifting uncomfortably in her chair. I spoke first. "We'd like to ask you about Amanda Morris, if that's okay?"

"It's all my fault." She dissolved into a stream of tears and buried her face in her hands.

"It wasn't your fault, Deborah." They were empty words to a

young girl who'd lost her friend in horrific circumstances.

Although sobbing, she carried on, but her words were muffled. "I should've gone with her. I did ask if she wanted me to, but she said no."

"You didn't know what would happen, sweetheart," Heather added in a calming tone.

I wasn't the best at dealing with displays of emotion, but I felt for her.

"Mandy was my best friend. She didn't deserve to die like that."

Heather glanced at me before turning back to face her. "You're right, and we're doing all we can to catch her killer."

"And when you do, hang the bastard." She buried her head in her hands again.

Although her grief was hard to see, it warmed me to know Amanda had somebody in her corner that cared, at least more than her parents seemed to. "We've got a whole team working on the case, Deborah, and I promise you, we'll find him."

"Excuse me a minute, I need a tissue." She jumped up and raced out of the room, returning a minute later, blowing her nose. "Sorry about that. It comes in waves."

"Are you okay?"

"Not really, but I'll do anything I can to help."

"Do you mind if we ask some questions?"

"Yeah, sure."

Heather opened her notebook, pen in hand. "The night in question, you and Amanda had been out drinking. Is that correct?"

"We'd been to Heebie Jeebies."

"Was it just the two of you, or did you meet up with other friends?"

"Just us."

"Okay. So, you left the club and took the night bus. Did you notice anybody hanging around, or taking a particular interest in Amanda, or yourself?"

"We were mullered, her more than me, so it took us all our time to walk for the bus, never mind focus on anyone else."

"I understand." Heather scribbled away.

"Mandy wouldn't harm a fly, so why would anyone wanna hurt her?"

"That is what we need to find out." Heather sighed.

"Now, while you were on the bus, did you interact with anyone?" I already knew the answer because we had viewed the footage, but I wanted her version of events.

"We were chattin', to be honest, and making plans for the next day."

I nodded. "What was happening the next day?"

"We'd planned to go into town again for one o'clock."

"Any reason in particular?"

"Nah, just to meet up with some other friends, have a bit of a laugh."

"Okay, so, back to the night bus. Neither of you interacted with any other passengers?"

"Not that I can remember."

"Who got off the bus first?"

"She did."

"And did you notice anybody getting off at the same time, or perhaps hanging around at the bus stop?"

"She got off on her own and I didn't notice anyone else." She took a breath, then continued. "It was dead late by that time anyway."

"Do you have any idea why Amanda would cut through the park when there was a faster way for her to get home?"

"She was hammered, so probably couldn't face hoofing up that hill. I told her loads of times it was too risky cutting through the park, but she didn't take any notice."

I smiled at her sadly. "Well, unless DS Stubbs has anything to add, I think that's all for now. But we may need to speak to you again."

Heather shook her head.

"I don't care if you come back here every day. Just find whoever it is and make sure he doesn't hurt anyone else."

"We're doing our best." I pushed myself to my feet. "Thank you for your time."

"I'll show you out."

We stepped out into the rain as Deborah closed the door behind us.

Once back in the car, I turned the engine on, then the heaters. Thankfully we'd avoided a complete soaking.

"That poor girl." Heather sniffed and dabbed her eyes with a tissue.

"Awful, isn't it?"

"How will she ever get over losing her friend like that?"

I shrugged. "She doesn't know the worst of it yet, either. Once the papers get wind, they'll report every horrible little detail."

"Vultures, the lot of 'em." She blew her nose. "They don't give a damn about those left behind or what the fallout will be."

I could see the interview had affected her, but it was part and parcel of our job, though one I hated the most. "Come on, let's have a drink somewhere, and a bite to eat. I think we've earned it."

"Don't we have to get back?" She glanced at me, hopeful.

"We're allowed a lunch break, and there's nothing back there that can't wait for an hour or so."

"Okay, boss."

"I fancy pizza, what about you?" Junk food is just what I needed right then.

"Sounds good to me."

TWENTY-THREE

After a heavy lunch, we returned to the office.

I approached Bella's desk. "Did you manage to run a check on Mr and Mrs Morris?"

"Just finished, funnily enough."

"And?"

"Like we thought, dodgy as fuck."

"Oh?"

"Mr Morris has a list of convictions for assault, theft, benefit fraud, driving while disqualified, speeding tickets, you name it."

"I still don't think he had anything to do with his daughter's death, though."

"Perhaps not."

"What about Mrs Morris?"

"Convicted of benefit fraud and fined, undeclared income. It was a joint claim with her husband, but that's it."

"Okay."

"I also ran checks on Jeremy Cross and his daughter, Jessica – both squeaky clean."

"Good! Heather and I have just been to see Deborah Fisher.

She seems like a decent girl and is devastated by Amanda's death, but her story checks out with what we already know."

"So, we're still no further along as to why—no motive, nothing concrete to go on aside from this lunatic calling card."

"We're coasting along on this case, and I don't like it one bit."

Bella glanced over my shoulder, "Sorry to say this, but your day is about to get a whole lot worse."

"Why?"

"Dylan, my office." Janine's voice filled the room.

Rolling my eyes, I followed like an obedient dog. "Coming, Ma'am."

I knew a bust up was brewing between us, and it seemed we'd reached a tipping point.

I closed the door behind myself and took a seat, ready for her to tell me what I'd done wrong this time.

"Why do I always seem to be chasing you for information?" she asked.

"Perhaps because I'm up the wall trying to solve two murders with a reduced number of staff."

She leaned forward, resting clasped hands on her desk. "I told you I wanted to be kept in the loop at all times."

"Yes, you did, and when I know something worth sharing, you'll be the first to know."

"I don't think I like your attitude, Detective Inspector Monroe."

"If we're speaking truths. I don't like yours either, Detective Chief Inspector Kerrigan." I was skating on thin ice, but at that very moment she could fire me and order me out of the building, and I wouldn't care. Being unemployed would be a lot easier than dealing with hostility from my boss day in and day out.

"I beg your pardon."

"You walk into *my* office, in front of *my* staff, and speak to me like something you've dragged in under your shoe and I don't like it."

"I've never done anything of the sort."

"I'm not imagining it, Janine, and nor are the rest of the team who see exactly what's going on."

"Rubbish."

"You're not happy with me, fine. I'll take whatever you have to dish out if it's justifiable, but I won't be your whipping boy." I paused to take a breath. "I'm working to the best of my ability, but if that's not good enough for you, fire me, it's that simple."

Janine clenched her jaw. I heard the grinding of her teeth. She was mulling over what to say without it escalating into a full on battle. "Do you have any leads?"

"Nothing, and before you remind me, I know it's not what you want to hear."

"Do I need to get somebody else to take over this case?"

Despite my earlier thoughts about her firing me, I wouldn't offer myself up as the sacrificial lamb. "As my superior, you can do whatever you want but I'll go straight to HR and raise an official grievance against you because from what I can see, based on the information we have so far, no other officer here, or anywhere, would be any further along in this investigation."

"Is that your excuse?"

"I don't need an excuse, Ma'am. What I'm saying is fact."

Clearly exasperated, she blew out a breath. "How many times do I have to say we're being watched?"

"I heard you loud and clear, every time, but what do we do? We didn't kill those girls, Layla did, and yeah, I get top brass took some shit for it, but what about what we were left to face—one of our own on a rampage right under our noses."

"You don't realise what I'm dealing with, Dylan."

"I'm not stupid. I know what's going on behind closed doors and that Anita Khan is being forced upon us to spy—"

"It's worse than that," she said, interrupting me.

"Why?"

"Khan is her married name."

"I don't follow."

"Her maiden name was Sharma."

Whatever she was trying to say flew right over my head. "What am I missing?"

"For goodness' sake, Dylan, her grandfather is Arjun Sharma."

My blood ran cold at the mention of his name. "Our Police and Crime Commissioner?"

"The very same."

"Oh, shit."

"Exactly. Self-righteous lover of the television camera, Arjun Sharma; gobshite and voice of the people, not to mention the one person with the power to hold police forces accountable, has manoeuvred his granddaughter into a position where she can observe everything that goes on in that incident room."

"We're not doing anything wrong, though."

"The families of Layla's victims are causing a ruckus and threatening to sue. Some are being paid tens of thousands to give interviews to the press and TV, then add the fact we've got a nutter running around butchering women and that's all Sharma cares about right now."

"Have you spoken to him personally about all of this?"

"Too many times for my liking, but shit rolls downhill fast, Dylan, and right now it's stinking up my office."

"He can't hold us responsible for what Layla did. There was an inquiry, and we were absolved."

"All of which was conveniently forgotten."

I was getting angrier by the second. "I was the one who stopped her and nearly died doing it."

"And as Phil Lyons testified, you went against his orders, which could have jeopardised the operation."

"He's a wanker." My blood boiled. "If it wasn't for me, Maxine would have bled to death, then what?"

"Another victim quickly forgotten, but this is politics, Dylan, plain and simple. This is what we're dealing with."

"It's a joke."

"After Lyons gave his testimony, some saw you as a rogue element, thought you'd been promoted too soon, but I argued we'd made the right call. You connected the dots and stopped her, so how could they see you as anything other than the hero?"

"I never wanted praise for doing my job, Janine."

"I know, but a certain Mr Sharma lost his fall guy, and he won't forget that in a hurry."

"Fuck him," I snapped. "He won't force me out for being good at my job."

"Add in Layla's mother threatening legal action against the force, saying we pushed her perfect daughter to snap. It's a storm that doesn't want to blow itself out."

"What can we do?"

She shrugged her shoulders. "Ride it out, but it doesn't allay my suspicions that Anita Khan will stir up trouble."

I hated politics in the workplace, especially if it had the potential to hinder an investigation. "Fuck this." I blurted out, forgetting my manners. "Sorry, but there's no way I'm going to let Anita Khan rock up and step on our toes, no matter who her granddaddy is."

"Well said." She picked up her telephone and I could see she was impressed with my determination. "Emma, cancel my appointments for the rest of the day—yes, that's fine—okay, I'm on my mobile if you need me." She replaced the receiver. "Up," she demanded with a wiggle of her finger.

I rushed to my feet. "What for?"

"We need a drink."

"Janine, I've only just got back from lunch. I've got a mountain of work to be getting on with."

"Delegate," she demanded. "Tell your team we're going for a well overdue pow wow, I really don't care, but we're going for a drink if only to clear the air."

"You do know I'm on your side, don't you?"

"I'd forgotten for a moment, which is to my detriment, and for which I apologise unreservedly."

"The rest of the team are on your side too, so why don't we forget the drink, walk into the incident room and tell them all what's really going on?"

"I'm not sure that's a good idea, Dylan."

"Secrets led us to where we are, and my bet is, you tell them the truth and they'll walk on water to back you. Lie to them and we're both screwed."

"You might be right!"

"It's been known to happen sometimes."

"Okay, let's do it your way before I change my mind."

"We're doing the right thing—what is that saying? Forewarned is forearmed?"

"In this case, most definitely," she replied.

"If I can make one request, though?"

"Go on."

"Can we not make Anita out to be the villain just yet?" It's important to my sense of right and wrong that we give her a chance. "I want her to get a fair crack on Monday—for all we know, she might be the best thing since sliced bread."

Her eyes narrowed. "And if she's what we fear?"

"Then we'll be prepared for it."

"Okay then, as long as we make them realise the thumbscrews are being tightened, that's good enough for me."

"You're going to be surprised how lucky we are to have the team that we do."

"Let's hope so."

"Give them the respect they deserve, and they'll stand by you, I promise."

She opened her office door. "Lead the way." As I strolled past, she grabbed my arm.

"What's wrong?"

"Thank you."

"We're on the same side again. That's all that matters."

TWENTY-FOUR

Pushing the door of the incident room open, I walked into a flurry of activity.

It had only just gone 9am, but seemingly, after Janine's heart-to-heart with them yesterday, the team were re-invigorated. It was good to see, and finally, I felt like we were all on the same page. Steve had come home as usual last night, too, so life was good, for now.

"Morning, everyone."

A chorus of hello's came back at me, but each carried on with whatever they were doing.

"Where've you been?" Bella called over from her desk.

"Stuck in friggin' traffic again—it's getting worse."

"Are you sure you didn't sleep in?"

"I wish." I strolled over to her. "What time did you get in?"

"Only about twenty minutes ago. The kids were an absolute nightmare to deal with this morning, and then Simon called me as I was doing my hair, which delayed me even more."

"How is Simon?"

"Looking forward to coming home in a few weeks, apparently."

"I bet you can't wait."

"I've missed him a lot—"

"I sense a 'but' coming on."

"He's thinking of leaving the Army."

"That's good news, isn't it?"

"Well, yeah, but we've never lived together like a proper man and wife all year round because he's been deployed here, there and everywhere."

"And you're worried how you'll rub along together when he's around permanently?"

"Yes, exactly. Him being there twenty-four-seven will be strange because I'm so used to counting down the days till he's back, then dreading him going away and leaving me again."

"See, you won't have to deal with any of that if he does come home for good."

"I know, but I'm conflicted. I tried to explain it to Penelope, but she didn't get it and accused me of being selfish."

"Having Simon home would mean more help with the kids and you having to rely less on others, namely your sister."

"Every cloud," she replied with a smile on her face.

"Just deal with it if it happens, and if it does, stop thinking the worst."

"Yeah, you're right. Cheers, Dylan."

"No problem. Now, what have I missed?"

"Nothing new. I'm just sorting the last of this paperwork."

Genevieve approached. "Good morning, Dylan."

"Are you feeling better?"

"Much, thank you."

I didn't bother to ask her what was wrong. She'd probably view it as an invasion of her privacy, anyway. "Good to hear. Do you need me for something?"

"I just took a phone call from a lady called Valerie Wiggins who reported finding a dead cat in her back garden."

"And?" I failed to see its importance, or why she had found any interest in a cat, considering the nature of our job.

"It had been decapitated."

Bella looked up from her paperwork. "Oh, that's horrible, but it's probably just a fox. They like to take the heads, apparently."

"From chickens, yeah, but not a cat," I replied. "Unless it was already dead by the time the fox came upon it."

"That's not the worst part of it, though," Genevieve added.

"I'm going to regret asking this, but what?" I hadn't eaten yet, but had been looking forward to a fried egg and brown sauce butty from the canteen.

"From what she says, the animal appears to have bite wounds over its body."

"That's not overly concerning, wildlife does what it does—"

Tommo walked toward us. "Sorry to interrupt, but I couldn't help overhearing your conversation."

"What's up?" I asked.

"I took a call late last month from an elderly man who reported his dog had been taken from his back garden and found dead in Eastlake Woods, which is just across the road from his property."

"What type of dog was it?"

"One of those yapping little things, I think."

"When was it exactly? Do you remember?" I prayed it wasn't a full moon.

"Not sure, but I'll double check and get back to you."

"I don't think I like where this is going." My stomach lurched for many reasons, one being hunger and the other the torture of animals. It didn't sit well with me at all.

"He said something had savaged the dog."

"You don't think—?" Bella was the first to say it.

"Bite marks on the bodies of our victims and now domestic pets are suddenly being killed and savaged." Genevieve said exactly what I was thinking.

"I really hope not. This could be a coincidence, but my gut instinct tells me otherwise."

"If he's hurting animals too, what's next on his list, kids?" Bella looked sickened.

"Tommo, can you look back over the last few months and see if any other animal deaths, aside from the ones just mentioned, have been called in? Also, link in with the local RSPCA office close to where both animals were found and ask if they've had any reports."

"On it, boss."

"Bella, Genevieve, can you go and speak to this Valerie Wiggins, and ask Tommo for the details of the old guy too. You may as well speak to him while you're at it."

"Together?" Bella and Genevieve replied.

"Yes, now, please, chop-chop."

Bella would throttle me for pushing her together with Genevieve, but we didn't have any time to piss about. "Find out all you can, and what they did with the bodies—if they've been buried, find out where. We'll need a qualified vet to look over them."

"Okay," Bella replied.

"Keep in touch with Tommo in case he finds any more, and if there are, while you're out there, you know what to do."

"I'll nip to the loo first and see you outside, Bella." Genevieve turned and grabbed her handbag from her desk, then left the room.

Bella cornered me and snarled. Her eyes narrowed. "You're going to pay for this, Avaline."

"We've all got a job to do."

"Whatever you say." She was miffed, but I couldn't afford to show favouritism, not that there was any. Not from my side of things, at least.

"Perhaps if you both dropped your preconceived ideas of one another, you might find common ground."

"Don't bank on it." She stormed from the room.

Will peered over his screen and chuckled. "You're a braver man than I am putting those two together."

"I can't be arsed with backstabbing or bitching—Bella needs to learn how to work as part of a team."

"In her defence, boss, Genevieve is just as bad. You just don't see it."

"I'm sure she is. They can hate one another as much as they like outside of work—I don't care, but here, I want harmony." Though I sounded hippy-dippyish, it was imperative we presented as a united front, especially with Anita Khan only days away from walking onto the team.

Will sat back down but I couldn't ignore the feeling gnawing away inside of me – these animal killings were linked. I was certain of it.

A couple of hours later, I found myself at the bulletin board trying to make sense of everything with Will, Pete, Tommo and Heather. This was something we often did, so we could make sure we were all on the same page.

"Surely there must be some connection to the two attacks, but the victims' lives couldn't be more different. We need to go back to the very beginning. Look at the two murders and try to see if there are any similarities we've missed. So, what do we know about Jane Cross?" I asked. "Heather?"

"Erm—she turned off her computer at 12:08am and left her office soon after. It wouldn't take her more than five minutes to get down to the car park. If she'd gone to the bathroom first, you could be looking at ten minutes, so twelve-fifteen-ish, give or take a few minutes. Then she called her daughter at twelve-twenty-three after discovering her car had been vandalised."

I nodded. "Yes. And the fact that he'd targeted her car and hung around smoking while he waited for her to come out makes me think he knew what time to expect her. So did he know her, do you think?"

"It was late and there weren't any other cars in the car park. That may have been the reason he targeted her," Tommo added.

"Yeah, but what if the owner of that car had been a strapping hulk—I can't see he would've attacked him. Can you?" I asked.

They all shook their heads.

"Unlikely," Will said.

"So we have to presume he knew exactly who to expect. He smashed her headlights and hung about, smoking several joints while he waited. What else do we know?" I asked Will.

"Sorry to interrupt, but I disagree," Heather added. "I don't think our guy had any idea who was coming, because, if you look at this picture—" She pointed to the bulletin board and the image of the interior of Jane's car. Aside from the pink steering wheel cover, hanging from the rear-view mirror were two fluffy pink love hearts. "I don't think it's out of the question for him to assume this was a woman's car."

"Yeah, you're right, Heather. Good call. What were you going to say, Will?"

"He attacked Jane Cross, then cut her throat. Once she'd died, he smashed her head in with a rock. He didn't subject her to a sexual assault, but the victim had soiled herself and from the report the smell was pretty ripe. We initially thought this could've been the reason he hadn't raped her. But saying that, the killer did get up close and personal—tearing her clothes, carving an inscription into her chest. Then he emptied his bladder all over her. Apart from one man dressed in black running away from the scene, there was little, or should I say nothing else picked up around that time on any of the cameras."

"Yes, that camera picking up anything at all was a fluke. The very next night Amanda Morris got off the bus alone at Manderley Bridge Road, and apart from a few cross words with the bus driver, nothing untoward took place. The streets were deserted, with only a handful of cars spotted over a three-hour period. This time, none of the street cameras picked up the killer, so we have to conclude he approached and left the obelisk via the adjacent woodland. He was briefly spotted on the motion detector camera at the entrance to the park." I turned back to face the room. "So, tell me about Amanda Morris's death, Pete."

Pete cleared his throat and glanced at his notepad. "Once again, he cut the victim's throat and bit her a few times, but he didn't wait until she'd taken her last breath—this time he smashed her brains in while she was still very much alive. Then, as with the previous victim, he etched his message into her chest."

I nodded. "And there were several cigarette butts left at the scene—the same blend of tobacco mixed with marijuana as before. But unfortunately, because of the torrential rain afterwards, we were unable to get any forensics. Again, no sexual assault, so it's clear to me these attacks aren't sexually motivated, at least, not in the usual way. Once again, considering it was in a public place, there were hardly any cars in the area and no witnesses. Her ring was taken, breaking her finger in the process. By the way, did we check with Mr Cross if any of his wife's possessions were missing?"

Will held up his hand. "Yes. He said her watch was missing, but he wasn't sure if it had been stolen or if his wife had pawned it because she'd told him she intended to."

"Okay great. My guess is he probably took it, but we should check the pawn shops in the area, just in case. Lauren predicted we would have a third victim on Tuesday night, considering it was another full moon, but it looks as though we were spared that—thank Christ."

"So, you think it's a serial killer then, boss?" Tommo asked. "Not just a couple of randoms?"

I held my palms up towards the ceiling. "As there is nothing connecting the victims, I've no choice but to believe they were selected randomly—which also leads me to believe that we are dealing with a serial killer in the making as opposed to someone with a score to settle. But I don't mind admitting, I'm stumped. I might go for a recce around the crime scenes—anyone want to tag along?"

"I'll come, boss," Pete said.

"Okay. Let's go then. The rest of you can get back to it."

We took my car and headed to the call centre – the scene of Jane Cross' murder.

Apart from a length of police tape, one end attached to the trunk of a tree and the other flapping in the wind, there was nothing to show what atrocities had occurred there just a few days before. But the details were burned into my memory.

We found the exact location Jane had parked her MG, but, in the cold light of day, murky and drizzly though it was, it still seemed like a bad dream.

"You know, Pete, I'd expected to see some sort of floral tribute to a fallen colleague, maybe a few candles... something—"

"Yeah, it's strange. It's like nothing happened here."

"Was she really that despised by those she worked with?"

"Looks like it—it's pretty sad that a person's life ends in the way hers did and people don't seem to care."

"I agree. But putting that aside, like I said earlier, the only thing that appears to connect the two cases as far as I can tell is this place." I pointed down the bank to the dense woodland running the entire width of the car park. "But that could just be a coincidence. It's four square miles in total. The park where Amanda Morris was murdered also borders it."

Pete nodded. "And don't forget the mutilated pets Genevieve was talking about, too."

"Yeah. I'm worried about who we're dealing with here."

"I know."

"Are you up for a trek in the woods?"

He looked down at his highly polished tan-leather brogues and suit pants. "I'm hardly dressed for it, but go on then, why not?"

"Don't you carry a spare pair of wellies in your car?"

"Yes. But we're in your car." He flashed me a smile.

I was under no illusion of how good looking he was, in an Idris Elba kind of way. His skin tone was the colour of melted milk chocolate, and his deep, sexy voice could charm the pants off anybody, man or woman. If we'd met in a bar, I would definitely approach him. But he was straight, and I was his boss, so I quickly shut down any inappropriate thoughts. "Oh, so we are." I laughed, feeling a little flustered. I'd always been a sucker for a handsome face.

Stepping off the concrete and down the bank, I ran the final few feet, and found myself surrounded by huge trees with only the odd glimmer of daylight breaking through here and there.

"Ugh!" Pete said, suddenly beside me. "Who turned the lights out?"

"I know, it's creepy, isn't it?"

"Yeah. It reminds me of a graveyard—gives me the willies."

After minutes of trudging through dense and muddy woodland, we stepped out into a break in the trees onto a path.

"Which way?" Pete asked.

"You choose."

Pete shrugged and turned right.

I followed.

A few moments later, the path opened up into a sunny clearing with three huge flat-topped rocks positioned side by side.

"What's this?"

"Some kind of place of worship for religious rituals and sacrificial slayings."

"You're joking, right?" Pete's eyes were almost out on stalks.

"No. It's for witches and warlocks to make and cast spells on."

"Stop shitting me. I'm already freaking out here. Are you serious?"

I laughed, amused by his fear, considering he was such a strapping hulk of a guy. "Of course not."

"What's it really for?"

"I have no idea. But I think it was probably something to do with Druids originally."

Pete bent and picked up a couple of roll-up cigarette butts. "Do you think this is just a coincidence?"

"Probably. I can't see how we can connect it to the murders—they're too far away. Judging by how well-worn the path is, I'm guessing this is a popular spot. There's probably loads of dog-walkers and randy teenagers passing through here every week. They could be from anybody."

Pete pulled a bag from his pocket and popped them inside. "I think I'll take them anyway, just in case."

We walked a few minutes more before retracing our steps back to the car park. Then we drove round to the monument. Once again, we headed into the woods and within twenty minutes, we arrived at the same set of stones.

"I think you're right—the murders are linked to this place," Pete said.

"Yeah, maybe they are, but it doesn't really give us anything to go on, does it? I mean, how many entrances and exits must border these woods? It's not like a fenced off park that only has one or two gated entrances. This area is vast, not to mention the hundreds of houses that are dotted along the perimeter. We're still no further on."

TWENTY-FIVE

It had only just gone 9am when I heard a hammering on the front door.

I assumed Steve had forgotten something and raced downstairs.

He'd been dealing with some last-minute problems on one of his client's accounts and had decided to go into the office. Which was rich considering he'd complained about my job taking over our lives, then he agrees to do overtime on my day off.

I opened the door and was surprised to see Roy standing there, loaded down with bags. His aluminium makeup case was on the ground beside him.

"What are you doing here?"

"Are you gonna stand there looking gormless or give me a hand?"

"Yeah, sorry." I took two of the bags from him, then bent down to pick up the makeup case. "Come in." I walked back down the hallway into the living room, dropped the bags on the sofa and balanced the makeup case on the arm, praying it didn't crash to the floor. "So, what brings you here so early?"

"I need you, darling."

"That sounds a tad dramatic, even for you."

He narrowed his tired and bloodshot eyes into tiny slits. I could tell by his cranky nature that he hadn't had his usual strong, black coffee. "Blanche called me at the crack of dawn in a blind panic."

I lifted my brows, trying to feign interest. "Why?"

"One of the queens pulled out of the line-up and she literally has nobody else and begged us to take the closing slot."

"Uh-uh, forget it. I'm not going onstage unprepared, not in front of that lot in Dorothy's."

"You barely had time to practice for your debut and smashed it."

"I know, but I want to give the crowd something better than my debut performance."

"You've become quite the entertainer, Avaline, worrying what a gaggle of gayers think."

"Caring isn't a crime, Roy."

"Look, Saddlebags, I've been up since six putting costume ideas together. I think with a bit of practice we can pull it off."

"Well, you've wasted your time because I'm not doing it."

"Come on, she's that desperate she's offered us two hundred quid, cash in hand."

It's quite the change from the few free drinks at the bar I'm used to. "I'm a police officer, Roy, remember?"

"So what?"

"Income Tax evasion isn't my thing."

"Then give your share of the wedge to me and let me work it out with my conscience—"

"And the taxman," I interrupted.

"Yeah, him too." He had no intention of declaring his earnings but that was for him to worry about, not me.

"So, shall I ring the old slapper and tell her we're doing it?"

"I'm not sure."

"It'll be a laugh, and you were only saying the other day how much you missed it. What's stopping you?"

"I don't want to look stupid, or amateurish."

"You won't. Avaline Saddlebags even without practice is better than most of the trollops that click-clack their way across that stage, and you know it."

"I'm on the fence, Roy."

"Well make your mind up 'cos my arse has splinters, and we have songs to choose."

I suddenly remembered something I'd thought of earlier in the week. It could work, if Roy was game. "Perhaps Adele's *When We Were Young* could be our first number?"

"Come off it, Saddlebags."

"What?"

"Do you want to put the audience into a coma?"

"That song's got a lot of meaning, if you listen to the words."

"Granted, darling, it's a nice little number for a matinee show at the bingo, but not for Dorothy's on a Saturday night, especially when we're the closing act. They expect the best so we need something that will blow their socks off and have 'em screeching for more."

"Blanche loves my slower numbers."

"You could squat on the stage and do a number two and she'd clap like the demented old bat she is, but I was thinking of something a little rockier, and then we could really let ourselves go."

"Such as?" I dreaded to think what he would conjure up as the ideal number.

"What about *Devil Gate Drive* by Suzi Quatro? I've always wanted to give it a whirl and we could really camp it up as Morticia and Wednesday Addams, you know, show the darker side of drag, use a bit of fake blood, white contacts, and go the whole hog."

Having never heard of the singer or song, nor approving of being dressed like a witch spewing fake blood, I shook my head. "Forget it, Roy."

"It's a seventies classic and will have the place jumping, you mark my words."

"You're crackers. Most of the audience will have never heard of it, I know I haven't."

"I know what gets a crowd going and this will set the place on fire."

"Okay, fine," I said, not wanting to argue. "We'll do a number you choose, and one I choose, that's fair."

"I'm not shuffling out from the wings to some miserable ballad, darling, not even for cash up front."

"Then I'll find something a little faster that wasn't recorded in the 1800's."

"Cheeky bitch." His lips were pursed together like he'd sucked on a lemon.

"You love me really."

"Yeah, I do, but don't think I won't give you a slap, after all you are my drag daughter."

I didn't subscribe to the malarky of drag mothers and daughters. "If you do, you're not getting any of my homemade chicken curry and rice for lunch."

He shrugged his shoulders. "I can't believe you'd consider the idea of feeding me curry, of all things, on the day of a performance. I'll be blowing off all over the place."

I knew I shouldn't laugh, but even when he wasn't performing, he had me in stitches. "Please don't do that because I'll end up a mess on the stage."

"That's the problem, darling. There *will* be a mess if you've loaded it up with spices."

"Don't worry, I'll water it down a bit."

"Best had," he agreed. "Now, fly that kettle on, will ya. My gob's as dry as a nun's crutch."

"You're so disgusting at times."

"Okay, Shirley Temple, keep your hair on."

"Who's she?"

He shook his head, his expression conveying one of disgust. "Does your knowledge of queer culture begin and end with Lady Gaga?"

"Who?" I was joking with him, however he could be right. I'd made a point of not embracing gay culture but stepping out onto the stage as a six-foot-something drag queen kind of defeats the purpose of trying.

"Sod off and get my coffee."

"Coming up, Your Highness."

"I think you mean, Your Majesty."

"Sit down and chill for a few minutes while I put the kettle on and shove some crumpets under the grill."

"Low fat spread for me, darling, or I'll never get that corset fastened otherwise."

After a bite to eat and copious mugs of coffee, I finally agreed to doing *Devil Gate Drive*. I had no idea what I was letting myself in for, but Roy assured me it was a glam rock anthem. I knew he was the expert, so I bowed to his wisdom.

"Are you ready, Saddlebags?"

"As ready as I'll ever be at 10am on a Saturday morning."

"Shove your feet into these heels and get used to them." He threw a pair of pointed black patent leather shoes at me.

The heels scared me and, as I suspected, slipping into them wasn't as easy as it sounded. "Shit, Roy, what size are these?"

"Size feminine," he replied.

Wedged into them, my feet throbbed due to lack of circulation. "You're taking the piss. I can't even feel my toes."

"I haven't felt mine since 2001. Now shut it, wench, and get in position."

"Alexa, play *Devil Gate Drive* by Suzi Quatro." Roy stood in the middle of my living room prepared.

I was dreading this and wished I hadn't opened the front door.

Playing Devil Gate Drive by Suzi Quatro, Alexa repeated.

The opening bars of the music filled the room and almost shattered the glass in my double glazed windows.

"What the hell...?"

"Just close your eyes and get a feel for the song first time round."

I did as he suggested, convinced the shoes should be re-classified as torture devices.

"COME ALIVE," he suddenly screeched, forgetting he was supposed to be lip-syncing. I'd never heard him sing before and wasn't in a rush to repeat the experience.

My eyes flew open. "Roy, keep it down for God's sake," I yelled over the ear-splitting racket. He was lost in the music while I wondered what my neighbours would think about this supposed glam rock anthem blaring out and disturbing their weekend.

He was in his element playing air guitar and using every inch of floor space he could find. His black skyscraper heels hammered across my wooden floors. "This is faaaaaabulous," he cried. "Come on, ducky, move your arse and follow my lead."

Rolling my eyes, I decided it was pointless arguing because I wouldn't win anyway. I steadied myself on heels far too high but imagined my less than graceful walk, more Tina Turner than Heidi Klum. I wasn't a novice to heels but I was going to struggle. "I'm gonna break my ankles in these damned things."

He reached out his hand. I caught hold and moved unsteadily. "Follow my lead, Saddlebags."

"And do what?"

"We'll both have long black wigs on, so I think a bit of headbanging is in order."

"Alexa, STOP!" I roared as the noise thankfully faded out.

"What did you do that for?"

"Headbanging at Dorothy's, we'll be burned at the stake."

"Good one, but once the routine comes together, it's gonna be bloody marvellous."

"We're on stage tonight. I'm not so sure this is gonna work, Roy."

"When have I ever let you down?"

"You haven't."

"So, I'm not gonna start now. Tell *her* to start it up again and we'll have a little shimmy for a bit, get you used to those shoes, and in no time, you'll be like Jayne Torvill."

"Jayne Torvill was on ice skates, not in crippling high heels."

"Can it," he snapped. "Fame costs. And right here is where you start paying."

"Alexa," I begrudgingly added, while wondering which TV show he stole that line from. "Play it again."

As the guitar kicked in, Roy bellowed at the top of his lungs. "Let's goooooo, Saddlebags."

To be fair, he was right, and despite not knowing the song, I could see its appeal. An hour later and after repeated plays, we had something resembling a routine that would get the punters going. Still, I was knackered and didn't know where Roy found the energy night after night. But I admired him wholeheartedly for it.

"You look ready for bed, ducky."

"I am tired and it's not even lunchtime yet."

"I thought you coppers were a fit, active lot."

"We are, but not in six inch stilettos and a wig that weighs a ton."

"You'll get used to Sally in no time."

"Who's Sally?"

"That's the name of the wig. They all have names, you know."

"You're kidding me?"

"I'm not."

"What's yours called?" Instantly I regretted asking.

"This is Judy. Ain't she lovely?" He stroked it like he would a fluffy kitten.

"Why do I feel like I've just been sucked into the twilight zone?" I was dying to laugh, but I knew he could throw a bitch fit like no other.

"You can skit all you like, Saddlebags, but these girls earn me a lot of money. The least they deserve is a name."

"I'm not laughing."

"Then tell your face that."

"I'm sorry, but this is still unfamiliar territory for me—I don't own any of this stuff, so I find it all a bit odd. I don't mean to be flippant. Forgive me?"

"Fire up that stove and heat the curry up, and I'll consider it."

"You're hungry already?"

"I'm sweating my false tits off under this gown. Do you know how many calories I'm losing?"

"Okay, do you want chips or rice with yours?"

"Both, and if you've got any naan bread going spare, I'll use that to mop up the sauce."

"Fine, but don't have a go at me when your gunt is on show."

"Gunt!" he screeched. "I have no such thing." He looked down and felt the space between his stomach and pubic area. "It's as flat as a pancake, thank you very much."

"You're so easy to wind up, Roy."

"Sorry, wench, I'm just a little stressed about tonight, and if truth be told, I don't like to be caught on the hop. Prepare,

prepare, prepare is my motto, so this has thrown me a touch off kilter."

"Don't worry. We can have some lunch, let it go down, then get cracking again."

"Thanks, ducky."

"Before I start, what do you think about us doing *Yes Sir, I Can Boogie* by Baccara?"

"That's not a bad idea."

"Finally." I breathed a sigh of relief, having gone through so many songs in my mind he might agree with. "It's not a firm favourite, but one I've seen other drag artists perform in that movie *Kinky Boots*."

"No, I think you've hit the nail on the head. It's an old classic and everyone knows it."

"Let me get lunch sorted, then we can get started."

Roy used the naan bread to mop up the last of the curry sauce. "That was heaven on a plate, Avaline."

"Glad you liked it. I've put some in a Tupperware container for you to take home."

"Why do you cook so much food?"

"Work keeps me busy, so it's easier than coming home and starting from scratch."

"Does Steve not cook?"

"He does, but we've had a few disagreements lately."

"Oh?"

Waving away his concerns, I was eager to get started again. "He thinks I'm too involved with my job and feels left out."

"We can't all sit in an office every day crunching numbers."

"True. Now, let's go and sit down for ten minutes, rest our bellies, and then we can get this routine nailed down."

A while later, the opening strings of *Yes Sir, I Can Boogie* caught me unaware and emotion swelled within me. "Oh, God," I said, teary-eyed.

"What's up with you?"

"Nothing," I said, trying to hide my face.

"You felt something in that music. I saw it." He looked like the cat who'd got the cream. "Don't hide it. Use it in your performance. I do."

"I'm not even keen on the bloody song, so why do I feel like I could burst into tears?"

"You've had a shitty time these last six months, darling, and music can get the better of any performer."

"Probably."

"Like I said, use your emotions to convey what you want to say to the audience. They'll get it too, mark my words."

Once we were happy with our routine, Roy made his excuses to leave and told me he'd return to pick me up and drive us to Dorothy's.

I hadn't heard a peep from Steve so I gave him a call. He didn't answer at first, then his voicemail clicked in. I tried again. This time, he picked up.

"Hi, babe."

"Hey."

"Are you still at the office?"

"Yeah, I've had loads to sort out and don't know what time I'm gonna finish."

"That's cool. I just wanted to let you know I won't be back home until late."

"Why?" he fired at me.

"Roy asked me to do him a favour and—"

"And what, put a sequinned frock on and parade around for a bunch of pissheads?"

"It's not like that."

"Sounds like it to me," he argued.

"I'm helping him out is all."

"Look, Dylan, when we met, I assumed this cross-dressing crap was only because of your job."

"It is—it was," I stammered, thrown by the confrontation.

"Which one is it?"

"I enjoy it."

"I wanna date a real man, Dylan."

"You are."

"Look, do whatever you like, but leave me out of it."

"Steve, don't be like that."

"Make a choice, Dylan—drag, or me."

"Don't give me ultimatums."

"If you love me, you'll consider my feelings."

"I do love you, but I won't be dictated to."

"Then we have nothing to say to one another."

He still hadn't said it back to me. "Steve, please—"

"Bye." He ended the call, leaving me feeling worthless.

TWENTY-SIX

Despite Steve putting a downer on my enthusiasm, I'd enjoyed spending the day with Roy, and rocking up to Dorothy's I felt as though I'd come home.

"You're back then?" The same burly security guard with the shaved head asked as I followed Roy through the door. I was already in full drag, still reluctant to be seen as Dylan Monroe.

"Looks like it," I replied, moving fast before he pulled his usual trick of caressing my arse. "Bye."

Strutting down the corridor toward the dressing room, I could smell cigarette smoke. "Jesus, we'll need oxygen masks if we're getting ready in there."

Roy pushed the door open. "Oof, it bloody reeks in 'ere. Have you lot never heard of passive smoking?"

They certainly didn't seem to care that it was illegal to smoke inside places of work.

All eyes turned to stare at us.

"Look who it is." Polly Wanakracker, my old drag mate, rushed over and hugged me. She'd gone up a few dress sizes since we last met, but still looked amazing. "I thought we'd seen the last of you."

"So did I until Betty decided she needed a partner."

"It's lovely to see you again, doll."

"You too. Let's catch up for a drink at the bar before I go on."

"Definitely," she replied.

"You're closing, again?" Another drag queen suddenly snapped, her words tinged with bitterness, as she sauntered past.

I didn't recognise her.

"True talent always closes the night," Roy hissed. "Which is why you're always the opening act."

A chorus of ooooh's filled the room.

"Cunt," the other queen bit back, while the rest of us watched open-mouthed. She slammed the door behind her.

"Slag!" Roy shouted after her.

"Who's that?"

"Ayeeta Lottapasta."

"You what?"

"That's the fat cow's name—Ayeeta Lottapasta. Suits her, don't you think?"

For some reason, I was amused and impressed by the ingenuity of the stage name and burst out laughing. "I love it."

"She's got two left feet, and I've seen a cat's arsehole lip sync better than her."

"Miaowwww," I teased. "Not bosom buddies then?"

"We were dating the same bouncer once upon a time, though she continues to deny it."

"You dated a doorman?" It wasn't often I got any juicy details from Roy about his personal life, so I needed to take whatever tasty morsel I could get.

"So?"

"I didn't peg you to fancy the big butch type."

"What type do you think I fancy then, somebody like you?"

He squeezed past the row of drag queens half in and half out of makeup.

"Ouch." I followed him and found my old seat at the end of the row, then shoved the bag with my day clothes underneath. I planned to get changed afterwards and take Roy out for a bit to eat. "It's like déjà vu being back in here." I thought of Kimberley and wished things had turned out differently. She had been such a lovely girl, and I deeply regretted putting her in harm's way.

"We're gonna bring the house down, darling."

"I'm still not sure about that first number."

"That lot out there will be pissed as farts by the time we hit the stage and won't care if we flap our gums to a rendition of Googie the Liverpool Duck."

"Googie? You're so random."

"Don't tell me you've never heard the song."

"Thankfully, no," I laughed.

"Well, remind me next time I pop over to bring a copy with me. In fact, it might work well as a comedy number."

"I'm not dressing up as a duck, no matter how you spin it."

"We'll see."

I finally caught up with Polly Wanakracker at eleven-thirty. We chatted for a while until I saw Roy waving his handkerchief at me from the stairs at the side of the stage. "I better go, but let's do this again."

"I'd love to." Air kisses seemed to be de rigueur with drag queens to avoid smudging their makeup. "Mwah, mwah, see you soon."

"Break a leg."

"I might do in these bloody heels."

Pushing through the crowd, I met Roy hovering on the stairs. He looked like a nervous wreck. "We're on soon, Saddlebags. Get your arse backstage and stop fraternising with the enemy."

"I know what time we're on and Polly's not the enemy."

"If you say so, now move it."

"You're so bossy." He was one of the nicest men I'd ever met, but with the false nails, wig and corset in place, Roy slipped away and out came Betty Swallocks, the demonic side to his personality.

We were behind the curtain as Blanche rushed over dressed as an aged Betty Boop. I think I preferred her Dusty Springfield look. "Avaline, there's somebody 'ere to see ya."

"Now?" Roy shrieked. "Tell whoever it is to piss off."

"Apparently it's important, life or death."

It had happened to me before. Somebody waiting at the stage door wanting to ask me out. But my gut instinct told me it was something different this time. "Can you delay the curtain while I see who it is?"

"Yes, but hurry up," Blanche added, "or this lot will kick off and wreck the place."

Roy was seething as Blanche waved to Kelvin, the sound engineer.

A familiar booming voice echoed in my ears. "Let's welcome back to Dorothy's, the incomparable Miss Betty Swallocks and the stunningly beautiful Miss Avaline Saddlebags." He'd mistaken her signal to stall and, ready or not, the show had to go on.

Turning to Roy, we both knew it was too late to back out. We had no choice but to go along for the ride.

The curtain opened as the music kicked in. A roar of approval filled the cavernous club. Blanche dashed off the stage, heading towards Kelvin.

Momentarily, I panicked but, seconds later, I got my groove on and found my lips moving while shimmying into position.

Despite my misgivings, Roy was right – we had the crowd eating from the palm of our hands. Even down to our outfits, and biting down on the capsule of fake blood, they cheered and egged us on, wanting more and more.

As the song drew to a close, we took our bows. It was a quick change at the side of the stage, wiping the blood off, a re-touch of makeup, then back for *Yes Sir, I Can Boogie*.

I was just about to pull the dress over my head when I heard my name being called. "Dylan."

I turned to look – terrified somebody else might have heard. My real identity was still shrouded in secrecy. Will was at the bottom of the stairs looking up at me. I met him halfway. "Sorry to bother you, boss, but another body has been found in Eastlake Woods. Looks like our guy has struck again."

"Oh, God, not now."

"Janine has been on the phone demanding to know where you are. I tried calling you earlier, then Bella suggested you might be here. I hope you don't mind, but I thought you'd wanna know."

"Thanks, mate. I feel a right twat dressed in this."

Will pressed his lips together in an obvious attempt to stifle a laugh. "I'll call Janine and tell her we're on our way—buy you time to get the slap off and change, if that's okay?"

"I owe you one."

Roy joined me on the stairs.

"I'm parked around the back." Will dashed off.

"Sorry, Roy, but I have to go."

"Of course, you do what you've gotta do, and I'll close the show."

"I'll make it up to you."

"I presumed you'd need this." He handed me my bag.

"Thanks, I'll get changed in the back of the car."

"I've shoved a pack of wipes in there. At least you'll be able to get that lot off your face."

"You're a star."

"Call me tomorrow."

I raced up the stairs and along the corridor.

The lech of a security guard held the door open for me. "Take care, *Avaline*." He winked as I slid past him. "Or should I say, *Dylan?*"

I didn't have time to converse with him right then, but I hoped he wouldn't make life difficult by revealing my real name.

TWENTY-SEVEN

I was in the backseat of Will's car, wiping caked-on makeup from my face using a small hand mirror. As he rounded the corner onto Lodge Lane, he almost sent me flying. "I shoulda put my belt on, really."

"Almost there, boss. Five minutes, tops."

"You're gonna have to stop off somewhere before we get to Eastlake Woods, so I can get out of this dress and into my normal gear."

"Okay." He indicated, then turned right down a dark alley and slowed to a stop. "This might look a bit dodgy but better than out in the open."

"I'm not attending a crime scene dressed as Morticia-fucking-Addams."

He burst out laughing. "That would make a great headline in the papers. *Detective Inspector Drag Queen—*"

"That would put the kibosh on any career advancement, especially if Arjun Sharma settled down for his bowl of corn-flakes, and that was what greeted him on the front page."

"Quite." He lit a cigarette, blowing smoke out of the window. "I'll look the other way while you strip off."

Certain I'd erased as much of the makeup as I could, I struggled out of the skin-tight black dress. The stockings would have to stay for now but, with my jeans over the top, nobody would be any the wiser. I pulled the long-sleeved jumper over my head and jammed my hands through, noticing the false nails. "Dammit, I hate this part."

"What?" Will asked, as a plume of smoke blew right back at me.

I coughed, wafting the smoke away, ready to say something about it, then I remembered it was his car. "Getting false nails off." I pried the first one off with my teeth, and the other nine in quick succession. My nail beds burned a little, but I didn't have time to soak them off as Roy always insisted, so needs must. "Done."

"Shall we go?"

"Yeah, all I've gotta do is slide my feet into these trainers and I'm all yours."

He reversed out of the alleyway and, minutes later, pulled up to a scene of carnage.

As I opened the car door, the cold cut right through me. It was blowing a gale and, not expecting to be called out to a crime scene, I'd not thought about a coat. "Christ, it's freezing."

"I've got a spare mac in the boot if you want it?" Will took one final drag, then dimped it out and put the cigarette back into his packet.

"Please."

He grabbed the coat and offered it to me.

"Cheers, I'll get it dry cleaned and have it back to you."

"Don't worry about that—it goes in the washing machine, anyway."

Blue flashing lights from emergency service vehicles lit up

the corner of the woods that led to the kids' play area. To the right was a shallow storm-water drain.

I donned a pair of booties and gloves, crouched underneath the crime scene tape, scrambled down the bank using the small stone bridge to steady myself, and spotted Lauren on the perimeter, kneeling on the ground. A tarpaulin had been erected around the scene, but, once again, it didn't stop reporters trying to get their pictures to sell to the highest bidder.

"Ah, Dylan, Will, thank goodness you're both here." Janine strolled toward me and looked like she'd been pulled into work from a hot date. It wasn't my place to say, but she looked amazing.

"What are you doing here?" I asked, surprised.

"I told Joanna to call me if anything out of the ordinary happened, so I thought I'd come down and check it out for myself."

"Is it as bad as I think it's gonna be?" I watched as crowds milled around the area and turned to a uniformed officer. "Keep that lot away from Lauren and the SOCOs," I ordered. "Arrest them and throw 'em in the back of a van if you have to."

"Yes, sir," he replied.

I turned back to Janine. "So, same guy?"

"Definitely—the poor woman had her head caved in. The rock he used to beat the living daylights out of her is over there." She pointed to it.

"Any bite marks?"

"She's a mess—I've never seen anything like it."

"I need to see for myself."

Stepping closer, I acknowledged Lauren, being extra careful where I placed my feet. Evidence markers littered the area. It was like playing hopscotch, but as an experienced officer, I knew my way around a crime scene. "What have we got?"

"See for yourself." She lifted the cover from the body.

I shook my head, appalled by the obvious ferocity of the attack. "Oh, my God."

The body of a woman lay splayed out, a gaping wound to the side of her head. I could see she was blonde from the artificial lights that had been set up to illuminate the area, but it was matted with congealed blood. One of her eyes was open, whilst the other was battered shut. Heavy bruising covered that side of her face. There were definitely more wounds than on the previous two victims.

"What did she ever do to deserve this?" I asked, my voice hardly a whisper.

"I don't think he cares," Lauren added.

"Do we have an ID?"

"There was no identification, none that we could find anyway," she confirmed.

"How long has she been here?"

"I'd say a few days at least, judging by the state of the body's lividity and secondary flaccidity."

"Is it possible she was killed on the last full moon of the month?"

She nodded her head. "Didn't I tell you there would be another?"

"I was really hoping you were wrong."

She shook her head, her lips in a tight, thin line. "This one won't stop until we force him to."

Janine joined me. "We have to catch him, Dylan, and fast."

"Her injuries, while similar to the other two victims, reveal an increased viciousness," Lauren added. "It's almost like he's getting bored and taking out his frustrations where he can."

"Any evidence of sexual assault?" Janine asked.

"Not that I can see, though I can't rule it out until I get her on the slab."

"Any urine this time?" Will asked as he approached.

Lauren shrugged her shoulders. "I've no reason to believe this will be any different, but it's been raining on and off the last few days and being in the drain—"

"Filthy bastard." Janine shuddered. "Like a dog marking his territory."

"Any messages this time?" I asked, hoping and praying it wouldn't be the case, though I knew it would be as I suspected.

"Exactly the same as Amanda Morris." She pulled the cover down to reveal the wounds to the victim's abdomen.

I am
LunaTIC
FEAR
ME

I didn't need to ask about injuries to her throat because I could see the gaping laceration.

"Okay, Will, you supervise here until the body is moved, then ensure uniform guard the perimeter until SOCO has finished."

"Sure thing, boss."

"Are you in your car, Janine?"

"Yes, why?"

"Do you mind playing chauffeur?"

"What for?"

"There's not that much around here, so, if she drives, I'm thinking she might have parked somewhere, and that if we can find any cars about, I can call them in and run a few checks."

"Okay, if you think it'll help."

"Our killer is an opportunist, Janine," Lauren added. "He's not choosing his victims unless he happens upon them, so Dylan might be right. Wherever she was taken from, it's pretty close."

Janine dug into her pocket for her keys. "Let's go then."

"Lauren, I'll call you tomorrow, and Will, thanks for picking me up."

"Not a problem, boss."

We removed the PPE when we left the scene.

"I'm over there." Janine gestured to the black Audi A3 parked behind a patrol car. Once we were in the car, she turned the heating on. "It's brass monkeys out there."

"Tell me about it." I rubbed my hands together for a little warmth.

"So, good show?"

"What?"

"Did you put on a good show tonight?"

"I don't know—"

"Don't bother bull-shitting me, Dylan. I know where Will picked you up from."

Panic suddenly engulfed me. "I was just helping a friend, it won't be a regular thing."

"Look, I don't care what you do in your own time, so you don't need to explain."

"It doesn't affect my job at all, and I don't get paid."

She held a finger up. "No explanations, but I wouldn't turn up in the office tomorrow with that mascara on, and certainly not when Khan starts Monday."

I flipped the mirror down. "Shite!"

She was clearly amused. "So, where to?"

"Let's start along the perimeter of the woods."

Driving around, it suddenly occurred to me that Pete and I had walked this area just the day before when we cut through from the obelisk.

"What is it?"

"Oh, nothing really. I just realised how close we actually are from where Amanda Morris was killed."

"Yeah. I did wonder about that myself."

We continued travelling around the perimeter, stopping to inspect any cars parked on the street and calling in their number plates. Each of the cars we checked were parked close to their owner's home addresses.

We passed a small silver Peugeot parked away from any houses and so close to the woods it caught my attention. "Back up a little, Janine."

"What did you see?"

"The car we just passed."

"The one with the couple leaning against it sucking the faces off one another? Won't it be their car?"

"Not necessarily. If they had the keys, why wouldn't they be inside it?"

"Good point." She slowed to a stop, carried out a turn in the road and headed back the way we came.

The couple was totally oblivious to our presence as we pulled up alongside.

I climbed out of the car. "Excuse me."

No response from either.

Janine joined me. "Oi, Romeo and Juliet," she barked.

They unlocked their lips and looked our way.

"What do you want?" the guy asked, clearly miffed he'd been interrupted.

She held up her badge. "DCI Janine Kerrigan. Is this your car?"

"Nah," he replied. "Nothing to do with us."

"Then I suggest you both move your arses before my colleague arrests you for public indecency."

"We're only snogging," the young girl bitched.

"I don't care if you're doing the *Y.M.C.A*, move it, *now*."

I was itching to laugh. Sarcasm and I were familiar bedfellows, but I had never heard Janine so openly snarky. "I'd listen to her if I were you." I stepped towards them, and they scarpered.

"You know. If that was my daughter playing the slut, I'd nail her to the door and beat her with a wet mop." Janine shook her head, bewildered.

I chuckled and pulled out my phone to call the station again. I hit redial and spelled out the number plate for the duty officer.

"Let's hope we strike lucky." Janine peered into the vehicle. "There's a folder on the back seat, but nothing else."

"Are you there?" the officer asked.

"Yep, still here."

Janine had her pen and notebook ready.

"The car is registered to a Rhona Jean Fraser, date of birth, 6th August 1970. Address is number 4 Washington Avenue, Tuebrook, L13."

"Do you have photo ID of her?"

"Yes. It's not the best photo, but she looks slim, blonde hair, nothing out of the ordinary. I'll screenshot what I see and send it over to you."

"Thanks, buddy." I ended the call.

My phone buzzed. I opened the message and passed the phone to Janine.

"It's hard to make out, especially in this light, but let's take this back to Lauren—she might have more of an idea."

We said nothing on the short drive back to the crime scene.

Will approached us. "I didn't expect to see you both back tonight."

"Thanks to Dylan, luck might be on our side for once."

Hearing appreciation from Janine felt good.

"Oh?" Will raised an eyebrow.

"We found a car parked up pretty close by, so we ran the plates, and it turns out it's registered to a Rhona Jean Fraser." I held the picture on my phone up for him to see.

"Couldn't say for sure from that."

"Me neither, but it's a start."

"Where's Lauren?" Janine asked.

"Back there still."

"Come on, Dylan, let's get this over to her and see if it helps."

We donned PPE again and then stepped carefully across the crime scene with SOCO working all around us.

Lauren was busy preparing the body for transport. I caught a quick glimpse of the victim's hands, bagged and tied at the wrists to preserve any trace evidence.

"Hey," I said.

"Hello, again."

"We've got something we'd like you to take a look at if you would?"

"Go on."

I handed her my phone. "Could this be our victim?"

She stared at the screen for a moment, then stretched the image with her fingers to a certain spot.

"What are you looking for?"

"This." She knelt next to the body and pointed to a small tattoo of a rose halfway down the side of the victim's neck.

"What about it?"

She indicated the screen. "See that?"

My eyes focused on the faint black line I hadn't noticed earlier. "Well, no, we didn't." I turned to look at Janine who was squinting to get a better view.

"Can't say with absolute certainty, but that looks like part of the tattoo I just showed you."

"I think she's right, Dylan." Janine appeared to be impressed.

"Don't quote me though, but it does look like it to me."

I didn't believe she was wrong. From what I could tell from the picture and the victim's neck, it was too much of a coincidence.

"We're not going to get any sleep tonight, Dylan." Janine

stared at the body again. "It's late, but let's drive to Washington Avenue and see what we can find out."

"Now?"

"Death waits for no-one—come on." She tugged me away from the scene.

"Thanks, Lauren," I called back.

"Good luck, you two."

"Are we really going there now?"

"If anybody at that address can confirm she has a tattoo of a rose on her neck, then we have the identity of our victim."

"God, I hate doing this."

"It's been a long time since I last dealt with victims' families at this point in an investigation, and my guess is, it's still awful."

"The worst, but you're right, we've touched on a bit of luck."

"Now we just need a motive and for our nutter to slip up."

"If only!"

We were back in the car. "Let me put the address in the sat nav because I don't have a clue where this place is."

I fastened my seatbelt as the sat nav plotted the journey. "Oh, I know where it is. It's not too far away from here."

TWENTY-EIGHT

There had been no answer at Rhona's address, so Janine and I headed to the station.

Upon further investigation, we discovered that Rhona Fraser had been reported missing by her boss just the day before.

At Janine's request, I called the team in early the next morning.

Joanna had already worked alongside me, Janine, and Will all night and was almost dead on her feet, so she had gone home.

Bella abstained for childcare reasons.

Tommo, Pete, Heather, Genevieve, and Will stood with Janine and me in front of the bulletin board.

Janine took the lead. "Sorry for ruining your weekend, but we need you all up to speed so we can hit the ground running in the morning."

"No problem," Pete said.

The others echoed him.

Janine nodded. "Well, thanks to Dylan, we may know who the victim found last night is."

"It was a joint effort." I wasn't one to steal glory from

anybody, let alone my boss. Pointing to the board, I stuck the picture to it. "We think the victim is Rhona Jean Fraser, aged fifty-one. She worked for a refuge that helped battered wives—"

"Oh, the irony," Genevieve added. "The poor woman worked her backside off to help others and look what happened to her."

"How did you ID her?" Pete asked.

"Well, we haven't yet, but her car was found close to the woods, and her boss reported her missing yesterday. We won't know for certain until we can get hold of her boss at the refuge tomorrow."

"Great effort," Janine said, nodding at me.

Feeling a little self-conscious, I turned away. "How did you get on with the guy who found her body, Will?"

He opened his notepad. "A guy named David Sharp had been out walking his two dogs. They went crazy and literally dragged him toward the body."

"Must have been a shock finding her like that," Tommo added.

"Yeah," Will replied. "The poor man was in a right state but there was nothing he could really tell me. He didn't see anyone hanging around, but she'd been there a few days, so I doubt our killer would still be hanging around."

While I was interested, it didn't escape my notice that this could be the break we've been hoping for. "Her murder does provide us with a possible motive—our killer could be connected to one of the women Rhona helped."

"That's a lot of interviews, boss." Will didn't look convinced.

"I know, but it's the only lead we have right now, and anything is better than nothing."

"Dylan's right," Janine added. "Sharma has already bombarded me with calls, wanting to know what's going on, plus Melling wants to see me tomorrow, and need I remind you all that DC Khan starts on Monday too?"

It was embedded in my mind. "So, we can utilise Anita pretty much right away."

"Who's she going to be partnered up with?"

I'd dreaded this question, but they'd find out eventually. "Genevieve has the honour." I wasn't going to apologise for making that call because it made sense. The relief on everyone else's faces was plain to see. I looked at the woman of the moment. "Are you okay with that?"

Genevieve shrugged her shoulders. "Somebody had to do it, and you're right, I'm going to give her a fair chance, and as she's my new partner, you'd all better do the same."

She didn't look at me as she issued her warning, but I was in no doubt I was very much included. "Well said."

The others were nodding their agreement, and I made a mental note to remind Bella. Will would take care of relaying it to Joanna.

Janine, unfazed by the petty threats of an officer at a lower grade than her, was not to be silenced and she pulled rank, "Keep an eye on her, Genevieve, and that's an order."

"Yes, Ma'am, I mean, Janine," she quickly corrected herself.

"Right, you lot. I appreciate your hard work and dedication, but there's nothing more we can do until the refuge office opens, and I want you looking fresh and alert tomorrow morning, so go home and spend time with your loved ones whilst you can."

"Sorry," I interrupted. "But before you all go, Genevieve, how did you and Bella get on with your enquiries into the dead animals?"

"We spoke to Valerie Wiggins. She was the one who reported the dead cat…" Her words trailed off as she scrolled through her notes. "… that's right, she took the remains to her local vet."

"Ah, and?"

"We spoke to him in person—Antony Pilgrim, quite a strange little man. He said he'd call as soon as he'd run some tests."

"Did he say anything else?"

"Only that the bite marks were unusual and while the flesh was torn, it didn't appear any chunks were missing."

"Weird," Pete added. "Another animal would consume the flesh, which leads me to believe our killer is behind it."

"Could be," I replied. "Certainly seems to fit."

Janine scrunched her face up in disgust. "So, this sicko is killing animals too? What for?"

I shrugged one shoulder. "Because he wants to, it seems."

Janine scratched her head. "I take it Lauren hasn't said anything about missing chunks of flesh on any of our *human* victims?"

"He's biting into them but not for any cannibalistic reasons—it must be linked to this lunatic thing he carves into them—a wolf bite if you will."

Janine turned to Genevieve. "I want you back on that first thing in the morning. Perhaps take DC Khan along with you and see how she fares."

"No problem," she replied.

I was curious about the other report. "What about the older guy Tommo mentioned, the one who called last month? Did you track him down?"

"Yeah." Genevieve flipped through her notes again. "Fred Granby. His dog was taken and found dead in the woods. We didn't get much from him. He buried it but wouldn't say where because he didn't want us to disturb its grave."

Though I understood why he didn't want his beloved pet exhumed, I rolled my eyes. "And what about the RSPCA? Any leads there?"

"A few dead rabbits were brought in over the past few weeks, mainly pets."

"Any bite marks?"

"Yes, but it was assumed to be caused by another animal."

"Did you tell them to inform us if anything else comes in?"

"Of course," Genevieve replied. "Bella and I gave the receptionist our cards."

"Good. Right, enjoy the rest of your day."

They moved fast, and less than a minute later, Janine and I were the only ones left in the incident room.

"Thanks for that," I said. "They're already worn out."

"Same goes for you, Dylan. You did well last night and need to get some shuteye."

"Sharma will still find fault, no matter what I do."

"That idiot can kiss my arse—I'll deal with him."

"You said so yourself—he can cause all sorts of trouble for us."

"Maybe, but I'm no pushover and will protect my team like a lioness would her cubs, and the quicker Sharma realises that, the better."

"Okay, I'll get going."

"I'll drive you home, but before we go, I want you to listen and remember what I'm about to say."

"What?"

"You got the DI job because you were the best candidate for it."

"Thanks for saying that, but I've always wondered what would have happened if Bella hadn't been on maternity leave—?"

"Let me say it another way, you were, and still are, the best person for the job, got it?"

"Yes."

"Good."

"Now, let's go, you're not the only one that needs to get some sleep."

I pushed the key in the lock and wearily stepped inside. Dropping the bag filled with the drag clothes behind the front door, all I wanted to do was climb up the stairs and slip under the duvet.

In the kitchen, I filled a glass with tap water and brought it to my lips.

"Where the hell have you been until now?"

The voice startled me. Jumping back, the glass shattered against the sink. "What the—?" I spun around – my heart hammering in my chest.

"Come on, I'm waiting for an answer." Steve stood in the doorway, glowering at me, his fists balled at his sides.

"You frightened the shite out of me. What are you playing at creeping around *my* house?"

"You gave me a key, remember? And you told me to use it. I've been here all night, waiting."

"You didn't text or call. How was I supposed to know?"

"Perhaps if you were where you should've been—"

"And where's that?" I asked, too shattered to argue.

"Home, Dylan. Here with me, but you obviously had a better offer."

"Where is it you think I've been?" He'd obviously been stewing all night and now had something he wanted to get off his chest.

"How the fuck do I know?" I could tell by his mood, he was itching for a fight.

"What exactly are you accusing me of?"

"Are you screwing Roy?"

I burst out laughing because I'd never heard anything so ridiculous. Roy wasn't my type, and I certainly wasn't his. Against all the odds, we'd become best friends and occasional performing partners. "You're way off the mark, Steve."

"Am I, really?" His voice was raised. "Or have I hit the nail on the head?"

I didn't like what I was hearing and instantly retaliated. "You're a dick!" I seethed. "And wrong to accuse me of anything."

"Doesn't seem that way to me, Dylan."

"Obviously not. But I can assure you of one thing, Roy or no Roy. I'm not a cheat. Got it?"

"Then where *have* you been?"

"Working, Steve. End of."

"All night? Don't treat me like a fool."

"You're certainly acting like one."

He crossed the floor in a few strides, his hand raised, but he stopped short of me, slamming his fist into the cupboard door beside my head.

"I think you should go."

"And then what, eh? Will you ask lover boy to come over for round two?" He cradled his hand in his other one and pressed it to his chest, obviously in pain.

I'd learned enough on the job not to engage when somebody was clearly beyond reason. This was one of those moments. "Go home, Steve. I'm not getting into this with you right now."

"Come on, tell me, you've got a thing for cock in a frock, is that it?"

"Grow up." I felt immense rage brewing inside me. "I was at work. Take it or leave it. I don't care either way."

"Working where?" he fumed.

"First at Dorothy's with Roy, then I got called to a crime scene."

"In full drag? What do you take me for?"

"I changed in the back of Will's car, then went straight to the scene."

"And all that took over twelve hours, I suppose?"

"Janine called the entire team into work—" I stopped and shook my head. I didn't know why I was justifying myself to him. If he didn't believe me, I wasn't going to beg him to.

"Yeah, yeah, so you say."

"Yes, I do."

"I bet Roy liked the feel of your cock up his saggy old arse." Contempt dripped from every word. "His type always does, and they don't care who gives it to them, either."

I'd never seen this ugly side of his personality before, and I'd heard enough. "Right, that's it. Get out of my house." This time I could feel my own temper wavering. Exhausted, I didn't want to say anything I'd regret.

"Or what?"

"Don't push me, Steve."

"Or what?" He repeated. "What ya gonna do, arrest me? Call the police?"

"No, I don't need them. I'm more than happy to throw you out of here myself if need be."

He stepped closer, shoulders raised, nostrils flared, but I stood my ground.

"Move away from me. Now."

"I'm not scared of you, DI Monroe," he snarled.

His words were designed to intimidate me, but I'd dealt with plenty of people like him during my years on the beat. My instinct was to talk him down, but his body language told me he wasn't about to retreat. "You've got this all wrong, so go home and think about your behaviour." I tried to change my tone to one that I hoped was less combative. "Maybe we can talk tomorrow, if you've calmed down."

"Who do you think you're talking to?" The vein in his temple popped. "I'm not a naughty fucking kid that will respond to your namby-pamby, baby voice."

I moved back and, for the first time, wondered what he might be capable of when he felt pushed. "This is the last time I'm going to tell you Steve—go home."

"Slut." His top lip curled, which only served to antagonise me more. "Banging him, you'll be riddled with all sorts."

My blood boiled at the insult to both myself and Roy. "Get—"

He spat in my face.

I stared at him, gobsmacked, unable to respond.

"Drop dead," he called over his shoulder as he stormed out of the kitchen. "And never call me again." He stomped down the hallway toward the front door, and I braced myself for the inevitable slam. He didn't disappoint.

My body shook uncontrollably once he'd left. I grabbed the kitchen roll from the countertop, tugged off a few sheets, and wiped my face. What the fuck had just happened?

Bending over the sink, I retched.

Tears came because, although I loved him, I knew it was over between us.

TWENTY-NINE

Oliver's mother emerged from the bathroom, a towel wrapped around her hair and a face full of makeup. "Our Carole wants to know if you're coming."

"Of course I'm not."

She shook her head and blew out noisily. "I'll never understand the youth of today if I live to be a hundred. All you wanna do is sit in your room and ferment. You're all crackpots." She stomped to her bedroom, and he heard her hairdryer fire up through the wall.

He couldn't wait to have the house to himself, even if it was only for a couple of hours.

A short while later, she suddenly appeared in his doorway again, dressed to the nines. "Okay, I'll be home around ten-thirty-ish. I'll bring us some chips back, if you fancy?"

"Okay. And say hey to Aunt Carole for me."

"Will do and get this bloody bedroom tidied and those dirty plates in the dishwasher—I'm sick of telling you." She ran downstairs and, moments later, the front door banged shut, rattling the windows throughout the house.

He put his hands to his ears and winced. "Shut the door, why don't you, Emily?" he muttered.

Emily paid the taxi driver and almost fell out the door onto the pavement. She grinned as she thought about the last few hours.

They'd had a fantastic night.

Although her sister Carole had always been great fun socially, she was a terrible wife to her long-suffering husband, Michael. She'd had multiple affairs over their twenty-year marriage, but the fool always forgave her and allowed her to slink back.

Tonight, Carole's raucous laughter and not too lady-like sense of humour had attracted a gang of young men who were on a stag do. Emily didn't know how, but her sister had convinced the guys to include them in their rounds, so every time drinks were ordered, they both got one too. What a scream they'd had, considering it was a Sunday. She'd not spent a bean apart from the taxi fare home.

The front gate squeaked as she shoved it open. She glanced around and spotted Mr *Always* Wright from across the street, nosing through his blinds. She stuck two fingers up at him, bent and took off her shoes, which were too high for her when she was sober but were lethal after a skinful. Then she tiptoed down the path.

Oliver was gonna have a fit. She'd told him she'd be home by ten-thirty. "Oh shit, I forgot the chips." She glanced at her watch – 12:05am. "Oops." She giggled, almost peeing herself. "Nowhere will be open now."

She unlocked the door, and it swung inwards. She waited, holding her breath, expecting Oliver to give her a mouthful. But it was quiet, apart from the TV in his room. Maybe he was asleep or engrossed in one of those zombie programmes he loved so much. If she played her cards right, she might be able to get into bed undetected and face the music in the morning. She closed the door with a click and considered heading into the kitchen to turn the heating off – Oliver always cranked it up on high when he got the chance – but she didn't want to alert him she was home.

She crept upstairs – bag and shoes still in her hands.

As she rounded the landing, she realised she didn't need to worry after all. Oliver's door was wide open, and he wasn't there. She stepped into her son's room, surprised he hadn't closed the door before he left, like he usually did. After finding the remote control under a jumble of bedding, she turned the TV off and the room filled with perfect silence

She flicked the light on and cringed. The sight before her resembled a squat she'd been to as a teenager with one of her mates – empty cups and plates crowded every spare surface, and one cup had some kind of funky green mould growing inside it. She was surprised they weren't overrun with rats. Gagging, she dropped her shoes and bag on the carpet and ran to the bathroom where she spewed up pints and pints of cider – *what a waste.*

She'd never been a good drinker – not like Carole, who wouldn't even have a headache the next day.

Feeling better, she ventured back to Oliver's room. *Where the hell is he?* She worried about him no end. She presumed he was sneaking about with that Sam bloke.

She suspected Sam had an ulterior motive for befriending her son. He was a lot older for starters, had a decent job, money, and was always well-turned-out. But Oliver insisted he was just another mate and had never tried anything untoward. Not like that lad at the residential school had.

It had horrified her when she found out another, much older, pupil had sexually assaulted her little boy. The headmaster had begged her not to press charges, saying it would ruin the school's reputation. And the parents of the other boy, Damien, had resorted to emotional blackmail and the temptation of money – a lot of it, in a lump sum as well as a monthly allowance. She didn't want them to get away with it, of course she didn't, but what would Oliver get out of the negative attention it would bring to the school or the lad being sent to a young offenders institution? By accepting the money, she could quit work and have his medical needs met privately. She'd never told Oliver where the money had come from, just that it was an inheritance from an elderly relative she hadn't seen in years. He believed her. Why wouldn't he? She didn't want him to find out the truth – it would hurt him. There was no way she would have allowed the snooty trustees and Damien's loaded parents to get away with hushing up her baby being abused without Oliver, and her, getting something positive out of it.

Tears spilled from her eyes and once again she made her way to the bathroom for a wad of tissue. She sat on the toilet, had a wee, and closed her eyes. The room began spinning.

"I need to get to bed."

Pushing upright, she steadied herself, using the wall and the door frame, then staggered to her room.

Booming music jolted Emily from a deep sleep, but she was so tired, she didn't want to move. Her head was pounding. *That bloody kid.*

She couldn't face another slanging match with him while she felt so rough.

Rolling over, she pulled the pillow over her head to drown out the terrible racket. Oliver usually detested loud noises. He was no doubt paying her back because she hadn't brought supper home when she said she would. His dad had been the same – a self-centred manipulator. In fact, Oliver was more like his father than he knew.

At the end of her tether, she threw off the bedsheets and ran from the room.

"I am lunatic! FEAR ME!" Oliver yelled at the top of his lungs, followed by a stream of laughter.

She kicked his door open, livid.

THIRTY

It was 6am when my phone alarm rang, jostling me from a deep sleep.

My first instinct was to launch it across the bedroom, but I couldn't afford to drift off again.

I kicked the duvet back and forced myself into a sitting position, rubbed my tired eyes and sighed.

Checking my phone, I saw the text and missed call alerts – all from Steve, but he was the last person I wanted to talk to. I opened my inbox but didn't bother to read any messages because there was nothing he could say or write that would make me change my mind. I hit delete on every single one consigning them to history. He wasn't the type to give in easily, but I'd made my mind up – we were over.

I pushed the block button. Steve wouldn't get through to me now even if he wanted to, unless he withheld his number or tried from another phone, of course.

Not wanting to second guess myself about Steve or sit and dwell, I got ready in record time and drove to the station.

I was sitting at my desk checking emails when the doors to

the incident room swung open and caught my attention. Just for a second or two, I thought I was hallucinating.

"I don't believe it," I said to Bella, who had just plonked her arse on the corner of my desk.

"What?"

I nodded toward the doors. "Look who it is."

"Bugger me," she replied. "He's got a bloody cheek."

"I should be surprised, but I'm not."

DC Anita Khan stood in between Janine and Arjun Sharma, her grandfather – the Police and Crime Commissioner.

His presence would do nothing to help settle his granddaughter onto the team. In fact, it would have the opposite effect because it was basically his way of saying he was watching us through her.

Janine clapped her hands together and brought the room to order. "Can I please have your attention?" Everyone stopped whatever they were doing and looked her way. "I'd like you all to offer a warm welcome to DC Anita Khan, the newest member of our team."

A round of applause rang out, but I was certain that it was more for Arjan's benefit than Anita's.

Looking around, the sea of faces told me all I needed to know. There was suspicion mixed with disinterest. She'd started off on the wrong foot, but I didn't know if it was her doing or at the insistence of the snake standing next to her.

"Thank you, everyone." She seemed affable enough, but what was hiding behind her smile? "I'm so happy to be here."

"Dylan, if you wouldn't mind?" Janine beckoned me over.

I rose out of my chair and approached.

"Anita, this is Detective Inspector Dylan Monroe," Janine added. "Your superior."

I extended my hand. "It's a pleasure to meet you, Anita." I felt a little self-conscious about how Janine had introduced me – I got it; she was just point scoring with Arjun, but I wished she'd leave me out of it.

"Your reputation precedes you, sir."

"Oh, I hope not." I grinned.

"Your work on the Layla Monahan case was fascinating to read about. I'd like to talk in detail to you about it at some point, if you wouldn't mind?"

The atmosphere in the room shifted to one of tension.

Arjan coughed into a handkerchief.

I didn't respond to Anita's request but focused my attention on Arjun. "And how are you, sir?" I didn't extend my hand.

"I'd be a lot better if you'd catch this full moon murderer."

"We're working on it."

"Work harder," he snapped, echoing Janine's sentiments from a few days ago.

I wasn't going to stand there and take shit from him, but nor would I engage with him in a public argument. He'd thrive on it. "Right, Anita, let me introduce you to the team, then we can throw you in at the deep end."

"Sounds good."

Genevieve stepped forward, her hand outstretched, not waiting for me to make the official introduction. "Good to meet you, Anita. I believe we're to be partnered up. I am Detective Sergeant Genevieve Tanner."

"Nice to meet you too, Genevieve."

"I'll catch up with you later, Janine." It was my way of dismissing her in the hope she would take Arjun with her.

She led him back toward the door. "Arjun, shall we go to my office and have coffee?"

"Yes, and you can fill me in on the progress Monroe is making."

He wasn't addressing me personally, but I'd answer anyway. I would not allow him to disregard my colleagues. "You'll find it is very much a team effort, sir." I carried on with introductions as Janine ushered him out.

Once the team were chatting amongst themselves, I turned to Bella. "I'm going outside for some fresh air."

"Are you okay?"

"I've got a banging headache and just need to get out of here for five minutes."

"Do you want two paracetamol?"

"Yeah, go on."

She handed me the tablets, and I nipped into the canteen and got a can of coke to wash them down with.

Once outside, I took a few cleansing breaths. The atmosphere in the incident room had been stifling, and it was all because of Anita Khan. Despite Janine's request for them to give her a chance, she'd walked into a minefield by asking for more information about Layla from the offset. Not to mention having her reviled grandfather hold her hand on her first day.

I was lost in my thoughts when I sensed somebody approaching.

"I've been calling you." Steve edged closer, looking dishevelled in jeans, tatty trainers, and an old T-shirt.

I'd only ever seen him suited and booted, especially on a workday.

My blood boiled at his audacity. Turning up at my workplace highlighted his need to control every aspect of his world.

"What are you doing here?"

"I've been texting and calling all morning, but—" He cradled his bruised fist in the other hand.

"I didn't respond, because…"

Stepping closer, he interrupted me. "Can we talk?"

I moved further back. "I didn't respond because there is nothing you can say that I want to hear, okay."

"Look, Dylan, I know I messed up, but please give me a chance to explain."

Aware my colleagues might be in the vicinity, I dropped my voice. "You spat in my face. There's no coming back from that."

"I lost my temper. It won't happen again."

"Too right it won't, because we're done."

"But I love you, Dylan, and want to make things right."

I was never sure he loved me but hearing him speak the words I've been wanting to hear confused me. No – I needed to stand my ground. "I'm sorry, Steve, but it's too late."

"Isn't there anything I can do?"

"Yeah, stay away from me."

"Maybe if I give it a few days, you'll calm down enough to listen."

"Don't make a show of yourself, Steve. We're done." Even when speaking the words, I didn't believe them because aside from his outbursts and what happened yesterday, things between us had been going well.

"Please, Dylan—"

"Go home before I ask one of my officers to remove you." Though I felt I'd regained the upper hand, it devastated me to see him walk away with his head bowed. A part of me wanted to call him back, but in my job, I'd witnessed the fallout from too many abusive relationships to allow it to happen to me.

"Dylan, what's going on?" Bella was suddenly beside me.

"Nothing."

"Was that your Steve I saw you talking to?"

"He's not *my* Steve anymore. We've split up."

"Hang on—when was this?"

"Yesterday."

"And you're only just telling me now."

"It's not a big deal—we just want different things."

"But you really liked him."

"I loved him, Bells, and still do." I'd never suffered a broken heart and if this is what it felt like, I never wanted to experience another.

"Can't you fix it?"

"I don't think so."

"Can you try?"

"I don't know."

"Do you want to?"

"Ask me something I know the answer to."

"That bad, huh?"

"We're different people and it got in the way of any future we might've had."

"Is this anything to do with you performing as Avaline?"

"He wasn't keen on me dragging up or spending time with Roy."

"Don't tell me he's jealous of Roy?"

"Kind of."

"That's stupid—you and him are just good mates and that's it."

"Try telling Steve that."

"I will if you need me to."

"You know what? It's best to let it lie."

"If you love the guy, fight for what you have."

I didn't want to tell her the full extent of our problems, but a part of me wondered if I was giving in too easily. Maybe with a heart to heart, we could sort out the mess our relationship had become. "Maybe it's not for me?"

"What isn't?"

"Being with somebody full-time. Our kind of work can be brutal, you know that."

"Rubbish, you're just making excuses and perhaps if you think of it another way, you might be more willing to hear Steve out."

"What do you mean?"

"Like you said, our job is brutal and sometimes, even when we don't realise it, we push our partners to the side—it's the only way we can process things, you know, make sense of the horrors we see day in, day out."

"Why do you have to be so rational?"

"'Cos, you're a drama queen, and in your feelings right now."

"Shit, Bells, I don't want you to talk me round, not when my instincts are screaming at me to walk away."

"If you don't hear him out, you'll always regret it."

"I don't know if I have the strength to deal with his issues while trying to catch this nutter."

"There has to be some separation, Dylan, or you'll never have a private life. And besides, what makes you think all the issues are his?"

"Whose side are you on?"

"I can't help it if I like the guy, can I?"

I rubbed my temples. Although now wasn't the right time, I felt a little less bombastic about it than I had minutes earlier. Maybe Bella was right. I'd pushed some of my issues onto Steve and they'd manifested themselves as jealousy? "I'll see how I feel tomorrow."

"Don't leave it too long. A hottie like him won't be single forever."

"If you say so."

"I do."

I wanted to move the conversation from my personal life on to work. "Janine and I had zero luck when calling at Rhona Fraser's last night. Do you fancy coming with me to the refuge first and then we can check her place out again afterwards?"

"Yeah, sure, just let me run back in for my stuff."

"Is Sharma still here?"

"Nah, he toddled off a few minutes ago."

"Don't tell me, he used the front entrance."

"How did you guess?"

"'Cos the press is out there in force. Smarmy bastard loves the cameras."

"Yeah, forgot about that," she replied with a smirk. "Give me a few minutes."

"Okay, and do me a favour, tell Janine where we're going and that I'll pop in and see her as soon as we're back."

She headed back inside.

I walked to my car. Once there I unlocked my phone.

Scrolling through my contacts, I found Steve's details and hit unblock. Perhaps Bella had a point, and I should hear him out. It wouldn't happen today, but I'd think about it.

I tried the number I had for Rhona's boss, but it went to voicemail. Calling the refuge, I spoke to a member of the crisis team who didn't know Rhona and had no clue what I was calling about, so I gave up.

Five minutes later, Bella dashed toward the car.

"Sorry, mate, call of nature." She slid into the passenger seat. "Shall we go?"

"Yeah, and I spoke to Janine—she said fine."

"Did she mention Sharma?"

"Not to me, but I suppose she'll fill you in later."

"Come on, I can't get through to anybody at the refuge, so let's just get to Washington Avenue and see if we can find out anything about her there."

A few minutes into the drive, we hit a long queue of traffic. "Fucking roadworks," I snapped. "This is a right pain in the arse."

"We'll clear them soon enough."

"Yeah." I spotted a service station, hit my indicators and turned left onto the empty forecourt. "Do you want a drink?"

"Bottle of water for me—not fizzy though."

"Anything else?"

"A bag of cheese and onion crisps."

"Okay." I stepped out into the humid air, crossed the forecourt and reached to push the door open. A sign told me they were closed. "Dammit," I said, turning on my heel and walking back to the car.

"Forget something?"

"It's closed—no fuel."

"Then the owners should put the cones up to stop people driving onto the forecourt."

"I know." Pulling away, I turned left onto the main road. "We'll do Washington first, then go for coffee."

"Sounds good to me."

"Have you given any more thought to Steve?"

"Kind of."

"And?"

"I'll give him a chance to explain, but I'm still not sure it'll work out the way I'd like it to."

"If you go in with that negative attitude, nothing will get fixed."

"Yeah, you're right."

"Listen, it's been a while since you've seen the kids—why don't I get rid of Penelope tomorrow night and invite Roy round? We can have a bite to eat and a few drinks?"

"That's a good idea."

"I'll call Roy now." Bella grabbed her phone from her handbag and found his number. She pressed the speakerphone so I could hear their conversation.

"Hey, doll," he said. "How are you?"

"Good, hun. Listen, I'm having a little get-together tomorrow night at my place with Dylan – I fancy a curry, a few drinks and loads of gossip, are you up for it?"

"Well, yes, but nothing too spicy for me because I still haven't recovered from Slack Alice's food last week—I've been playing concerto's from my back passage ever since."

Bella burst out laughing and pointed at me.

I rolled my eyes and stifled a grin. "Slack Alice can hear every word you say, dog breath."

"Oh, hello, Avaline, love, what are you up to?"

"Listening to you slate my cooking, that's what." I wasn't really offended, but I liked the fact I had caught him on the hop although he wouldn't really care.

"You know I'm only joking, Saddlebags. Now, I'm halfway through sewing diamantes onto this frock and don't have time to flap my gums with you two—what time?"

"Say about seven," Bella added.

"Swing by and pick me up, will you, Avaline? It's bloody murder getting taxis lately."

"Do I have to?"

"If you want the joy of my company, wench, then yes."

"Fine, I'll see you about half-six tomorrow night."

"Right, Bella, love, can't stop, see you then—ttfn."

Roy ended the call.

"What does ttfn mean?" I tried to work it out, but the answer wouldn't come to me.

"Ta-ta for now." She tutted. "Don't tell me you've never heard of that?"

"Somewhere along the line, yeah, but I completely forgot what it meant." I took a right turn onto George Street that led onto Washington Avenue. A minute later, I slowed to a stop outside Rhona Fraser's semi-detached house.

Walking up the short path from the pavement to her front door, I pressed the bell. "This place doesn't look any different than it did last night." Peeking in the front window, I noticed the place was spotless, aside from a few files left strewn across the sofa.

"Shall I check around the back?"

"I'll go with you." I followed Bella down the side of the house when an elderly lady with curlers in her hair appeared over the top of the rickety-looking fence.

"She's not in."

"Do you know the person who lives here?" Bella asked.

"Rhona, yes, she's lived here for about ten years. Why?"

I held up my badge. "DI Monroe and this is DS Frost, would you mind if we asked you a few questions, Mrs, erm…?"

"Mabel O'Connor, and it's Miss, I never was stupid enough to get married." Suddenly she stared and appeared to recognise me. "You're that copper from the news, aren't you?"

This was another side of my job I loathed. Since the Layla case, my face had been plastered everywhere. "Yes, but that's not important right now."

"Rhona's not in any trouble, is she?"

"Do you know who she lives with, husband, children, perhaps?"

"She doesn't have any kids and threw her husband out a few years ago."

"Would you know his name?"

"Ricky, something or other, ooh, let me think for a minute—he had a different surname from her."

"It really would help us out if you could remember."

"Woods, that's it, Ricky Woods, right nasty bastard he was too."

I caught Bella's expression and wondered if the ex-husband had been the violent type and the reason she worked at the refuge. "Would you happen to know where he lives now?"

"Not a clue, but I know he used to drink in that Irish bar on Mathew Street. Now what was it called?"

"Flanagan's Apple?" Bella suggested.

"Yep, that's the one—Rhona had to drag him out of there

many times over the years. Gave her a few black eyes for her trouble, too."

"You don't happen to remember what he looked like do you?"

"Scrawny looking, like a good bath would kill him—face like a bulldog chewing a wasp and, like I said, a right nasty bastard—handy with his fists too."

"When did you last see Rhona?" Bella asked.

"I don't see that much of her. She works nights and so I'm always tucked up in bed when she's up and about.

"Well, thank you for your time."

"She's okay, ain't she?" The woman's eyebrows furrowed. "Right lovely girl she is—tell me nothing's happened to her."

"We're just making enquiries right now, Miss O'Connor." Although we were certain our latest victim was Rhona, we needed to speak to her next of kin and arrange a formal identification before we spoke to anybody else about it.

"If you say so, but a word of advice—if you go hunting that shitehawk down, make sure you've got a paddy wagon on standby 'cos he'll go in fists first, and that's the truth."

"Thank you, Miss O'Connor. Good day to you."

Back in the car, Bella appeared troubled. "What now?"

"Mathew Street, here we come."

"What if the old girl is right and he'll swing first and ask questions later?"

"I'm more than ready for him. Can you ring the office and ask one of them to keep trying to contact the manager of the refuge? Catching up with Rhona's ex is more important."

THIRTY-ONE

Bella made the call, and soon after we were heading in the direction of the city centre.

Walking the hallowed pavements of Mathew Street, it wasn't hard to remember its history – tributes to the Beatles and Cilla Black were set in place for the thousands of tourists trekking in from all over the world, not realising the infamous Cavern Club closed its doors and relocated to another site in 1973, well before I was born.

"It's years since I've been here," Bella said to me as we stepped inside Flanagan's Apple. "I thought it'd be a right dive now, but I kinda like it."

"I can't remember the last time I was here," I said, looking around. The place was empty aside from a few customers seated at random tables. "I'm not sure our guy is in here, not if the neighbour's description is anything to go by."

"Let's ask the barman."

We approached the bar as a handsome younger guy called Niall, according to his badge, finished serving a customer. He took the money and turned his focus on Bella and me. "What can I get for you?" His accent took me by surprise – cockney born and bred.

"Some information would be good, Niall," I answered.

We flashed our badges.

"What do you want to know?"

"We're looking for a man by the name of Ricky Woods. Does he drink here?"

He rolled his eyes, nodding his head at me. "I'm sorry to say he does."

"Any sign of him today?"

"It's a bit early yet—he'll be sleeping off the skinful of ale he had last night."

"What time is he usually in?"

"About four and he stays right through until we sling him out."

I looked at my watch. It was a few hours away, time I wouldn't waste sitting at the bar. "Thanks for that."

"What's he done now, if you don't mind me askin'?"

"We just need to speak to him — routine enquiries is all."

"Yeah, and a pig just flew past that window." He grinned. "Ricky's always causing trouble, so whatever it is you want him for, go easy because I don't want him smashing up the place if you come to arrest him."

"We'll do our best, but if you don't mind, if he does come in, can you please give him my card and ask him to call me? He's not in any trouble, we just need his help with something regarding his ex-wife."

"Things must be bad if you need his help."

I wouldn't go into any further detail. "Pass it on to Ricky if you would."

He looked down and read the card. "Sure thing... erm... Dylan."

"Cheers."

As soon as we stepped outside, Bella giggled. "He was flirting with you."

"You always say that."

"Well, he was."

"No, he wasn't."

"Don't say you didn't notice."

I actually had picked up those vibes from him, but I wasn't going to encourage her, not that she needed much. "He was kinda cute, but way too young for me."

"You're hardly an old crock, Dylan."

"I know, but he was—"

"Fit as, but you have a boyfriend, remember?"

She was wrong. I didn't have a boyfriend, even though he wasn't far from my mind. As tasty as Niall looked, my heart belonged to Steve, even though I wished it wasn't the case.

We'd just arrived back at the station and pulled into my parking space when my mobile phone rang. I didn't recognise the number.

"DI Dylan Monroe," I said, after hitting the speakerphone.

"This is Ricky Woods. I hear you've been looking for me."

I gave Bella the thumbs up. "Ah, yes, Mr Woods, thank you for calling me."

"I ain't done anything to Rhona, no matter what she says."

"Mr Woods, that isn't why I need to speak with you."

"What is it then?"

"It's rather delicate, so would you mind if we spoke face to face?"

"I'm not gettin' arrested, am I?"

"No, sir, I promise. It's nothing like that—if you would agree to meet me, I can explain everything."

"Rhona's okay, ain't she?"

I found it hard to believe that he cared one way or the other. "That's what we need to talk to you about. Could you meet my partner and me?"

"Where?"

I gave him the address for Lauren Doyle's office. "Shall we say half an hour?"

"I'll get there as soon as I can."

"Thank you, Mr Woods. We'll be waiting at the main entrance."

After meeting with Ricky Woods, we returned to the station. I finally felt we were getting somewhere.

"Okay, guys, listen up. We've had a positive ID on Rhona Fraser."

"Great," Will said. "How'd you manage that?"

"The ex-husband met us at Lauren's office and confirmed it was her."

"That wouldn't have been a pretty sight to be confronted with."

"Thankfully, Rhona had another tattoo around her ankle, a daisy chain, he ID'd her from that. Apparently, she got it done over in Birkenhead not long after they first met."

"How did he take the news?" Genevieve asked.

"He was quiet and didn't say much after that, but what could he say? He used to knock her around, apparently."

"Bastard," she added. Hearing profanity from her wasn't the norm. "I called the manager of the refuge earlier, like you asked. She pretty much said the same thing about Rhona's ex. Now we have confirmation that she's our victim, Anita and I need to drive over there and ask if there have been any threats from disgruntled exes directed towards Rhona specifically."

"Thanks for picking that up. Where is Anita?"

"In with Janine at the minute."

"How did it go with her this morning?"

"Fine, she just wants to do well, I think."

"Did she ask any more questions about Layla?"

"She tried, but I told her that talk of Monahan was off-limits and not to rock the boat with it."

"Well done, Genevieve," Bella joined in.

I turned to look at Bella. Even she appeared to be impressed.

"Anything about Sharma?" I asked.

"Apparently, they don't get along very well—she's too westernised for his liking and I'd quite believe it from that misogynistic prick."

Another profanity from her, but totally accurate.

"So why escort her to work on day one?"

"Anita reckons she tried to talk him out of it."

"Hmm." I didn't know whether or not I was buying it, but I'd keep my cards close to my chest. He was responsible for her promotion; I'd stake my life on it. "Well, it'll all come out in the wash, as my mum says." Thinking about my mum, a visit was long overdue.

"Yeah, but up to now, I get the feeling she just wants to fit in, and yes, Sharma might grill her, but Anita can only tell him the truth."

"You're right, and thanks."

Anita walked into the room just as we'd finished the conversation.

Genevieve grabbed her bag and headed for the door. "Gotta go, Anita. You ready?"

She nodded and smiled at me from across the room.

"You okay?" I asked.

"I'm great. But I'd better—" she pointed at the swinging door Genevieve had just walked through.

"Go. We can catch up when you get back."

THIRTY-TWO

An hour later, Genevieve and Anita returned.

"How did it go?" I asked.

Genevieve sat at her desk.

I motioned to Anita to sit in the spare chair beside me, which she did.

Genevieve swivelled around in the chair to face us. "Susan Prentis, the manager of the place, said Rhona was an unassuming woman who rarely socialised. Her husband was definitely out of the picture though—had been for years."

"I see. Was she able to give us anything?"

"Late Tuesday night, Rhona took a call from a woman via the helpline number. She picked up said woman and her two youngsters and booked them into the safe house, which is a secure location, one we now know to be located on Crowther Street. It was early hours of the morning before she'd finished the paperwork. Her car had been found a few hundred yards away."

"What time was this, exactly?"

Anita flipped through her notepad. "4:15am."

"And how can this Susan Prentis be so precise?" I asked Anita.

"Rhona closed down the computer and then set the alarm before leaving. They're both time stamped."

"Good." I turned back to Genevieve. "Tell Will, he's been going through the CCTV in the area, so at least he'll be able to narrow the search down now."

"Will do." Genevieve turned back to her computer and began tapping away.

"So, how was your first morning?" I asked Anita. "How are you finding things so far?"

"Oh, just fantastic. Everyone is so friendly and welcoming. I needn't have worried at all."

"Worried? Why were you worried?"

Her cheeks reddened. "Whose grandad escorts them to their first day at work?"

I laughed. "Yeah, but he has a vested interest in us. He's not just a random grandad holding your hand."

"I asked him not to, though. But the stubborn bugger insisted."

"No harm done," I said. "Just so long as you know nepotism has no place in this office. You'll work as hard as the rest of us, no exceptions. And if you're okay with that, then we'll have no problems—understood?"

"Perfectly, thanks, boss."

"Dylan is fine, unless you piss me off and then I'll insist on my full title—comprende?" I grinned, but hoped I'd got my point across.

"Totally." She smiled. And, although she seemed amiable enough, I wasn't about to be taken in by her kind eyes and jolly disposition. Maybe she was just a talented actress.

Joanna suddenly burst through the door, breathless. "Have you checked your email?"

I shook my head. "No, why?"

"There's been a match on the dental impressions. *Hollywood Smile Dental* in Halewood."

"You're kidding?"

"I'm not."

"Are they sending the file through?"

"I just called them, and the receptionist said she's too busy and won't get around to it until tomorrow, so I suggest we head over there and demand it now."

I was out of my seat in a shot. "Fine by me. What are we waiting for?"

"Shall I come too?"

"Well, this is your result, so yes."

Joanna drove, and what should've taken thirty minutes took over an hour in stop-start traffic because we'd timed it just right to get caught up in the school run.

Hollywood Smile Dental had converted a large, double-fronted Victorian house into business premises and, from the quality of the renovations and the expensive line of cars parked up outside, it was clear to see this wasn't your average NHS dentist.

"If our guy is registered here, he must be loaded," I said, getting out of the car.

"Yeah. Julia told me this practice is classed as one of the best in the country."

I pressed the doorbell and moments later a petite Middle Eastern woman answered it with a smile that would put Simon Cowell's to shame.

"Can I help you?"

We held up our badges.

"We spoke on the phone earlier," Joanna said. "We're here to pick up the file in person."

"Oh, I don't know about that. I'm not authorised to release

any information without the practice manager's consent, or a court order."

"Then may we speak to the practice manager, please?"

"I'm sorry, Mr Boyd isn't in the office today. Doctor Walden might be able to help you, but he's in with a patient at the moment, so you'll have to wait." She led us through to a flashy seating area and disappeared behind the counter.

Twenty minutes later, a tall, good-looking man appeared from a side room escorting a teenage girl. He had one hand on her arm, and she had both her hands pressed tightly to her right cheek. "Are you sure you're okay? Amelia can call your mother if you like?"

A mouthful of cotton wool muffled her words. "I'm fine."

Once he'd shown her out, he returned and introduced himself.

Joanna told him who we were and what we wanted.

"Ah, yes. I've been expecting you. I recognised the dental impression you've been searching for, but I can't help thinking you're mistaken. Although Oliver isn't the most likeable of boys, he's no killer. In fact, scratch beneath the surface and ignore his stand-offish exterior and you'll find an insecure young man."

"Oliver?" I asked.

"Yes. Oliver Leyland. He's been coming here for a while now and I've always found him to be respectful."

The doorbell rang and Doctor Walden stepped forward, allowing an elderly man inside. "Ah, good afternoon, Bill. I won't be long." Then he turned back to us. "Look, I wish I could be of more help, but one of our dentists didn't turn up today, no word—nothing, and I'm trying to juggle two sets of clients in different practices. Is it okay if Amelia takes over from here?"

"I guess so. Thanks for your help."

"Amelia, I'll leave these officers in your capable hands. Give them anything they need."

A few minutes later, we left with a copy of Oliver Leyland's dental file.

Once back in the car, I opened the file and began reading aloud. "So, this lad is just sixteen years old. And, according to this, he has several health issues."

"Where does he live?"

"Oddly enough, Eastlake Estate."

"Are we going there now?"

"As much as I'd love to, I feel maybe we need to run everything by Janine and go from there."

"So, back to the station then?"

I nodded. On the one hand, I was excited to think we had the name and address of the prime suspect in our possession, but on the other, I didn't want to count my chickens before they hatched.

I rang Will from the car. "Hey, are you still at the station?"

"I am. We're all here waiting to see if you fancy a pint. It's been ages since we chewed the fat after work."

"Hmm. That might not be possible—not yet anyway, but don't tell the others. We'll be back in twenty minutes."

"Sounds ominous. See you soon."

"Oh, and Will, can you tell Janine to wait for us too?"

"No problem."

I hung up and glanced at Joanna.

She took her eyes off the road momentarily and eyed me curiously. "Why didn't you tell him?"

"I'd rather tell them all together. I doubt Janine will do anything tonight—she's a procrastinator, but you never know. We need to put forward a powerful argument and hope she listens."

THIRTY-THREE

Oliver logged on to the *PlayStation* app on his phone and was immediately alerted that Liam and Sam were online.

"Hey, where've you been?" Liam asked. "I thought we were supposed to be on ages ago."

"Sorry, man." Oliver yawned. "I'm out tonight with my Aunt Carole, but I should be back tomorrow."

"An all nighter?" Sam sounded confused; he knew Oliver didn't like to stay away from home.

He shrugged. "Emily won't take no for an answer."

"Okay, dude. Have a good day—I mean night," Liam said.

"Will do—you too." He closed the app down and then uninstalled it. One thing he hated more than lying was being found out.

A hammering on the front door a short while later wound him up. He trudged down the stairs to open it.

He rolled his eyes at another rat-a-tat on the door. "Alright, alright, I'm comin'—" As he opened it he was immediately shoved backwards, his head smacking against the wall behind him. He screamed out in pain.

"Police!" A loud, authoritative voice boomed, hurting his ears.

He drowned out a lot of the noise pressing his hands tightly to either side of his head, but he couldn't believe his eyes. The front garden swarmed with people, both uniformed cops and plain-clothes officers. Blue lights flashed in the twilight up and down the road. It was like something he would watch on *YouTube*.

Oliver froze – unable to react – terrified by the scene playing out before him. How did they know what he'd done?

"Oliver Leyland?" A stylish man stepped forward and thrust a badge in his face.

Although his words were muffled, Oliver read his lips and nodded.

"I'm arresting you on suspicion of murder. You do not have to say anything, but it may harm your defence if you do not mention when questioned something which you later rely on in court. Anything you do say may be given in evidence. Do you understand?"

Oliver nodded rapidly, feeling his legs were about to give way on him any second.

It was only when his hands were roughly pulled from his ears and the handcuffs were slapped on him that he realised it wasn't a joke.

The satisfaction of making a crucial arrest – that feeling of getting a perpetrator off the streets was second to none, usually. But this time, something about it didn't feel right.

"I know that look." Bella eyed me suspiciously. "You don't think he did it, do you?"

I gave a half-hearted shrug.

"It has to be him, Dylan. We have his dental records, don't we? It doesn't get more cut and dried than that."

"I know, but—"

"But nothing. The team deserves a pat on the back for another great result."

"Did you see him, though? The poor lad doesn't seem to have it in him. He was petrified and even peed his pants in the car."

"That doesn't prove he's innocent." Will pulled a chair up and straddled it.

"I know. But did you see him, Will? He's just a kid."

Will sighed heavily. "He's not just any kid, boss. He's a very different—probably very confused and angry kid. His hormones will be raging, yet when he looks in the mirror, what does he see? I felt bad enough with a face-full of spots at sixteen—imagine having to deal with his issues."

I leaned back in my chair, crossed my ankles on top of the desk and stared at the ceiling. I knew both their arguments were valid, but I couldn't help but think we were totally wrong on this, regardless of what the dental records seemed to indicate.

Janine entered the room, rubbing her hands together, a stupid grin across her face. "Well, what a result, thank you team. Our Mr Leyland is settled in for the night and you lot can get yourselves off home—unless you still want a drink—this time on me. You've played a blinder."

"I'm not in the mood." I sighed and got to my feet. "But don't let me stop you guys."

"Yeah, me neither," Bella said. "I need to get back to the kids but thank you."

"What's the plan for tomorrow?" Will asked.

"Bella and I will begin questioning him in the morning. He's adamant we're not to contact his mother, and he won't give us her number. He said she's gone away for a few days. However, he's only sixteen, so we've arranged for *Appropriate Adult Services* to send someone over first thing. Regardless of what he says, because of his age, we need to contact his mother anyway."

Bella and I left together and headed for the car park.

"Don't forget, we've asked Roy if he wants to catch up tomorrow night," Bella said. "Is that still alright with you?"

"Yeah, up to now, but we may have to see what tomorrow brings."

She gave me a thumbs up and walked towards her car.

It was almost ten o'clock and I was starving but didn't have the energy to queue for a takeaway. I would have to take my chances with the contents of my fridge, although whatever that may be was anybody's guess.

It turned out I was in luck. Although I usually did the bulk of the food shopping online, Steve would often bring home all kinds of goodies, and I found a sizeable chunk of Roquefort cheese in the fridge door and half a packet of digestives – just the ticket.

After devouring every crumb, I climbed into bed utterly exhausted without even taking time to shower the day off me.

Just as my eyes closed, my phone vibrated on the nightstand. It took all my effort to reach out and check who was messaging me at that time of night. My stomach flipped to see Steve's name across the front of the screen – a text message.

Just heard the news.
An arrest! Go you!

"What the..." How did he know? Had the media found out about Oliver's arrest already?

Who told you?

It was on the ten o'clock news.
Don't tell me it's wrong?

> **No, not wrong.**
> **Just a little premature.**

Oh, sorry. I hope
they haven't fucked it
up for you.

I shrugged, realising Steve had wheedled his way in and I'd fallen for it.

> **I'm still not talking to you.**

I know. I just wanted to
congratulate you,
that's all. I'm sorry.

I shoved the phone underneath the pillow and closed my eyes.

Five minutes later, I turned over and punched the mattress beside me. "Fuck you, Steve," I shouted out in sheer frustration.

I knew sleep was a million miles away from me. And tonight, of all nights, when I needed to have my wits about me tomorrow.

I scrambled about under the pillow for my phone.

> **Arsehole!**

???

> **You, of all people, know how**
> **I struggle to sleep and that**
> **tomorrow's a big day for me**
> **yet you had to inch your way into**

> **my brain and knowingly fuck me over.**

Sorry.

> **You're not sorry. And if you are, you're only sorry for yourself, not for me. Now leave me the fuck alone.**

If that's what you really want...

> **Yes, it's what I really want. Leave me ALONE!**

THIRTY-FOUR

Excitement coursed through my veins. Everything had been building to this one moment, and I wanted to savour every second.

The plan had been to wait until the next full moon, make two fresh sacrifices before – BOOM! Ending in a blaze of glory.

But it didn't matter that it wasn't a full moon, not really. I'd made my point with the other deaths and doing it now gave me the element of surprise. The papers were already calling me the full-moon killer, so this would throw their theories off.

I glanced down at Emily's supine body and reached into my pocket for the blade – shop bought but adapted and sharpened for maximum effect.

I leaned over and plunged the blade into her throat. The jet of blood that began spurting like a fountain from her carotid artery delighted me. It was far more impressive than all the others put together and it gutted me I hadn't researched it sooner. The bright red blood had even sprayed the ceiling. Impressive.

It didn't take long for the flow to subside to an ooze, which didn't hold my attention for long. I climbed beside her on the bed and slit her nightie from top to bottom, thrilled to see she was stark naked underneath.

I set about making my mark, taking my time to etch the message into her exposed skin.

Twenty minutes later, after placing a surprise package in Oliver's bedside drawer, I exited through the back patio door and along the alleyway towards the woods. Apart from startling a cat, I saw nothing or nobody.

Once I had the shelter of the trees to hide me, I slipped off my overalls and shoved them into a plastic bag.

I reached my car in the layby on the other side of the woods in record time and climbed behind the wheel. Then I made one final stop at the back of the supermarket and threw the bag in the bin amongst the huge pile of rubbish.

THIRTY-FIVE

As I'd known it would, sleep eluded me for the best part of the night. When my alarm sounded, I dragged myself out of bed and straight under the high-pressure jets of the shower. Oliver's face flashed before my eyes as I massaged shampoo into my hair.

Why the hell did I do this? No other detective I knew would question such damning evidence, and yet I couldn't help but feel we had the wrong suspect in the cells. The sight of the poor young lad sobbing, while curled into the foetal position on the hard mattress, tore at my heartstrings.

But how could I go into the station today and tell the team what I thought? I needed to get more evidence. Even though we had the grainy image showing someone with white skin and hair matching Oliver's colouring fleeing one of the scenes, I still doubted he was our killer.

The way he'd reacted when we turned up at his house – not just surprised we had caught him out, but totally shocked like he hadn't got the foggiest clue what was happening.

I believed him.

Was I losing my touch?

"Morning, boss." Will was first to greet me as I entered the incident room.

"Good morning. Don't you ever go home?"

"It certainly feels as though I live here sometimes."

"Hopefully after today things will calm down."

"Yeah right. Anyway, Leyland is already in the interview room with an appropriate adult. Got time for a cuppa?"

"Already on it," Bella said, appearing at my side with two steaming mugs.

"Oh, good. Sit down, we need to discuss our plan of action."

Once we'd drained our cups, I got to my feet. "You ready?"

The interview room was the bog-standard square room that was empty apart from a table and four chairs plonked in the centre. Oliver sat on the far side of it, opposite the door. He was still crying and wiped his nose on his sleeve as we entered. Seated beside him was a middle-aged woman with lank blonde hair and sallow skin. She was the appropriate adult provided by the agency.

"Good morning, Oliver. Sorry to keep you."

He snivelled and grunted something I didn't understand.

"I hope the rest of the answers you give are clearer than that or this is gonna be a long day indeed."

"Sorry."

"That's better. Before we start, can I get you anything? Water? Soft drink?"

"Don't want anything."

"Let me know if you change your mind. Now, I need to inform you this interview is being recorded. For the purpose of the recording, the time is 9:05am and my name is Detective Inspector Dylan Monroe. The other officer present is…"

Bella cleared her throat. "Detective Sergeant Annabella Frost."

Oliver glanced up at Bella and nodded.

"As Oliver is under seventeen-years-old, there is a responsible adult also present. Could you please introduce yourself for the purposes of the recording?"

"Erm, Faye Grant."

"Oliver, can you give me your full name, address and date of birth, please?"

He confirmed his details, and I double checked it with the information we had on file.

"Okay, Oliver, thanks for that. Now, can you tell me why you think you're here?"

"You said something about a murder last night. But I—" His breath was coming out in heavy gasps, and I was concerned he would pass out if it continued.

"Take your time, Oliver. Just be honest, tell us what you know and if you've done nothing wrong, you don't need to worry. Okay?"

He nodded.

"Now, for the record, can you confirm that you've declined a duty solicitor at this stage?"

"Yes, I don't need one. I'm innocent."

"For the record," Ms Grant said. "I advised him to accept one."

"I'm innocent," Oliver repeated, directed at her this time.

She raised her eyebrows in disapproval.

I didn't want him getting agitated. "It's okay, Oliver. If you change your mind, just say."

"I won't. I'm innocent."

"Oliver, who do you currently live with?"

"My mum, Emily—Emily Leyland."

"Just your mum?"

"Yes."

"Where is your dad?"

He shrugged. "I dunno. Long gone."

"I see. Can I ask you about your condition? Do we need to arrange any medication to be brought from home?"

He shook his head.

"Do you mind telling me what you suffer from?"

"Albinism, which is why I don't have much pigment in my eyes or skin, and my hair is white, plus I have an increased sensitivity to light and noise. I also have ectodermal dysplasia that affects my nails, teeth, skin and glands. Basically, I'm a fucked-up mess."

I glanced at Bella who, judging by her expression, felt as sorry for him as I did.

"Yes, Oliver, I won't lie, you certainly seem to have your fair share of problems, but you seem a gentle and respectable young man, but you wouldn't be the first person to try to deceive us."

"I'm not doing that."

"Can I ask you, is there another side to you that isn't so gentle and respectful?"

He nodded. "At times, yes."

"Okay." I was impressed with his candour. "Tell me about that?"

"I'm nasty sometimes." His voice cracked.

I flashed a glance at Bella, who was leaning forward in her chair.

"What do you mean, Oliver?" Could I be totally off the mark? Was he about to confess to murder?

"I'm not very nice to my mum sometimes. I lose my temper and swear at her."

"Anything else?"

"No. Not that I can think of."

"Do you know Jane Cross?"

"No."

"Have you ever been to the car park at Eastlake Call Centre?"

"No. But I can see the top of that building from the woods."

My ears pricked up. "You go to Eastlake Woods, then?"

He nodded. "Most nights, yeah. I like it there. Nobody bothers me. I can't go out in the daylight looking like this. People stare and laugh at me."

"I understand. What about the obelisk at the park on the other side of the woods? Have you been there recently?"

"No. Never."

"What about Crowther Street?"

"What about it?"

"Have you ever been there?"

"Yes. I walk that way to the woods from my house. There's a shortcut through a broken fence."

"Do you know Rhona Fraser?"

He shook his head. "I don't know any of these people or why you'd even think I do." Understandably, he was a nervous wreck. Tears flowed freely down his face and off the end of his chin.

"I'll level with you, Oliver. We have the killer's dental records which are a match with yours, so it's pointless denying it. Tell me the truth, for your own sake."

He jumped to his feet, his chair crashing to the concrete floor. "What? How the fuck can it be me?" He shook his head repeatedly, as though trying to make some sense of my words. "I want my mum."

THIRTY-SIX

Walking into the incident room, I blew out a breath and while I should feel relieved; I was anything but.

"How did it go in there?" Tommo asked.

"Reckons it wasn't him."

"They all say that at first, but what do you think?"

"I don't think it's him either, but what can I do when every piece of evidence points his way?"

"Shouldn't say this, but I kinda feel sorry for him," Tommo said.

"Me too, but he's finally given me his mum's telephone number and agreed to speak with a duty solicitor."

"Imagine what the press are gonna say—somebody that looks like him, murdering those women on a full moon…"

"Doesn't bear thinking about." I picked up the phone on my desk. "I need to sort that solicitor."

"I can do it if you've got other stuff to do?"

"Cheers, Tommo." I looked around the near-empty incident room for Bella, but she was nowhere to be seen. "I really need to speak to Emily Leyland as a matter of urgency and find out what she knows."

"It won't be easy for any parent to hear what he's done."

The way he was speaking, Oliver was already tried and found guilty. "Where's Bella?"

"She's popped outside with Heather for some fresh air."

I rolled my eyes. She'd probably gone for a cigarette. "I'll find her on my way to the car—if you could sort the solicitor out in the meantime, and let the others know when they get back what's going on, that'd be great."

"No problem, boss."

I grabbed Bella's handbag and phone before leaving. It didn't take long to spot her, but she was deep in conversation with Heather when I shouted over. "Oi, Frost, when you've quite finished, we've got places to be."

"Coming."

"Sorry, Heather." I called out, feeling rude for interrupting.

Heather waved at me. "No worries."

Bella raced across the car park.

I held up her bag and phone. "I've got your stuff."

"I need to pee before we go anywhere," she replied, crossing her legs at the ankles.

"Bloody hell, hurry up."

"Two minutes," she said. "Promise."

I looked at my watch. "Time starts now."

She darted off.

I started the car and, while waiting, called Emily Leyland. She didn't answer, so I left a voicemail with my name and contact details.

A few minutes later, Bella slid into the passenger seat. "You know, since I had the kids, I've got no control over my bladder."

"Lovely," I added, pulling away and out onto the road.

"Where are we going?"

"To see Emily Leyland."

"She doesn't seem all that concerned that her sixteen-year-old hasn't been home all night."

"Reading between the lines, mum and son don't get on all that well."

"Are you still in two minds about him?"

"Call it instinct, but there's more to this than meets the eye."

"He bit his victims, and by the looks of his teeth, no dentist is going to make a mistake like that."

"Perhaps not, but something is off."

"Do you think you're being overly cautious because of what happened with Layla?"

"Maybe, but I've been a copper a long time and nothing about this adds up."

"If I'm being honest, I don't see what you do—sometimes it's cut and dry."

"You've seen him, and aside from his physicality, does he seem the type?"

"Did Layla seem the type?"

She had a point, and I couldn't argue with it. "You got me there."

"Wait and see what today brings, Dylan. People wear masks to hide their true selves, and this kid might be a bloody good actor."

I couldn't help comparing him to a wounded animal–something so damaged, it was impossible for them to inflict pain upon others. "Well, let's see what the mother has to say." I indicated right and pulled up outside the Leyland house. I noted the curtains were partially drawn and two bottles of milk sat on the doorstep. The warm sun would curdle it in no time. "Maybe she's not been home yet?"

"There's ten other houses in this street, and his arrest wasn't exactly low key, so you'd think one of them would've told her what happened."

We exited the vehicle and walked up to the front door. I knocked twice and listened for any noise from inside the property. "I don't hear anything."

"Try again."

I did as she suggested, but there was no sound from inside. Peering through the gap in the curtains in the front window, nothing seemed out of place.

"She is in there." An elderly man approached from the opposite side of the street. "Are you the police?"

"We are." Bella and I flashed our badges. "Are you talking about Emily Leyland?"

"Yes."

"How do you know she's inside?"

"Because her car is right there."

"But have you seen her?"

"Not since I saw her falling out of a taxi on Sunday night."

"Falling out?"

"Drunk as a skunk—she could barely walk in a straight line or get her key in the front door to open it."

"Was she alone?"

"Yeah, from what I could tell."

"And you've not seen anything of her since?"

"I don't spend all my time spying on my neighbours, you know."

"I'm sure you don't," I replied. "But you saw us take Oliver away last night, I assume?"

"The entire street did. You weren't exactly undercover."

"You didn't think to pop over and check on her?"

"Nothing to do with me," he replied. "I'm not a busybody and, to be honest, we don't see eye to eye. As for that weird-looking lad of hers, it doesn't surprise me he's in bother with you lot."

I didn't want to get into the reasons right now or listen to his opinions because I was positive they'd only come from a place of malice. "Well, thank you, Mr…?"

"Wright," he replied. "If Emily ain't answering the door, try round the back. She never usually locks her side gate."

For somebody who isn't a busybody, he seemed to know an awful lot about the goings on in his neighbour's house.

"Thank you, Mr Wright," Bella added.

We waited for him to leave. "Let's go," I said.

"We're not going to try around the back?"

"There's no need. I've left her a voicemail, and nothing looks out-of-place inside there. She'll call when she picks it up."

"What now then?"

"I'll drop you back at the station, then I need to visit my mum. It's usually her day off."

"Aw, how is she?"

"I haven't been for weeks, and as I'm anticipating working late, I might as well take an early lunch and get it outta the way."

"You're gonna get your arse slapped when she sees you."

"I feel guilty."

"So, you should. I wish my parents were still around."

"Yeah, I know, and I'm going to make more of an effort from now on."

"You should – you are their only child, after all."

"I don't need reminding of that fact."

"I wasn't meaning anything like that, mate, sorry."

Her words pricked my conscience. "Yeah, I know, I get it."

THIRTY-SEVEN

Oliver's duty solicitor still hadn't arrived by the time I dropped Bella back at the station, so I continued with my plan to drop in on my mum. I stopped at a florist to buy a bunch of flowers on the way.

"Well, look what the cat dragged in." She was sitting at the kitchen table when I walked through the back door.

"Hi, Mum. I got these for you." I set them down, then swooped in to kiss her cheek and give her a hug.

She wrapped her arms around me, kissed my cheek in return, and patted my back. "Thank you, they're lovely."

"My pleasure."

"Your dad and I saw you on the news the other day." She stood up, then got a vase from under the sink. "My baby, the celebrity."

"Ugh, don't remind me."

"You seem busier than ever, son."

"I am, but that's no excuse for me not visiting sooner." It's been well over a month since I'd last been there. "I'll make more of an effort in future."

"We totally understand. You've got a job to do." She'd always been respectful when it came to my career choice and never asked for details about cases I was working on.

I looked at my watch. "How's Dad?"

"Fine. He's just popped out to B&Q."

"Oh, I thought he was at work."

"No, he's taken a few days off."

"What's he gone there for?"

"Undercoat and gloss for the spare bedroom."

"Are you having visitors?"

"Your Aunt Cynthia is coming the weekend after next, and you know what she's like."

"Yeah, I do." She reminded me of Bella's sister, Penelope. Both were from working-class backgrounds but had elevated themselves beyond their upbringings. "It'd be nice to see her." She lives in Worthing, on the Southeast coast of England and had done so since she met Jason in her early twenties. "Is Uncle Jay coming with her?"

"Not this time—he's still in Dubai working on that big contract."

"Lucky for some, what I wouldn't give for a fortnight in the sun."

"He's there for another few months, apparently."

"Why didn't Cynthia go with him? It's not like they can't afford it, and she's never worked a day in her married life."

"Doesn't like the sun." My mum and her sister were as different as chalk and cheese. "And she'd starve rather than eat foreign food."

I chuckled, but I had a genuine fondness for my aunt. "She's such a snob."

"Tell me about it—I sometimes feel she looks down her nose at me."

"You're down to Earth, Mum, and there's nothing wrong with that."

"Our Cynthia wouldn't see it that way."

"You'll have to call me when she arrives, and I'll swing by and see her."

"Bring Steve with you—she's always asking when you're going to settle down and get married."

"Yeah, I'll see if he's free." I didn't want to discuss what was happening with Steve because she'd only worry.

"Cup of tea?" She pushed herself to her feet. Still raring to go, she looked at least a decade younger than her fifty-eight years.

"I'd love one, Mum."

"Sit down if you're staying." I didn't have long and sat at the table while she pottered about. "Cake?"

"Oh, go on, twist my arm."

She cut into the cake and placed a slab on a plate before setting it down in front of me. "Are you still going to the gym?"

I eyed up the cake, terrified of the calorie content. "Yeah, but not as much as I'd like."

"Don't get fat, sweetheart, or you'll never be able to run after those criminals."

"I won't. In fact, I'll probably go when I leave here." I wouldn't because I'd be too busy. I bit into the moist sponge and chewed carefully.

"Good idea." She pulled a tin from the cupboard nearest to her and removed the lid. "I'll give you some to take home for later. You'll be famished after a workout." Typical mother worries about my weight, then sends me home with enough cake to add two inches to my waistline.

"So, how are things with Steve?"

"To be honest, I've been so busy with this latest case, we haven't seen much of one another."

"Now, that's not good, Dylan, you know we all need that special somebody to go home to at night."

I was so lucky I could talk openly to my parents. My sexuality never fazed them. But some things were off-limits and if I told them the extent of my worries, Steve would become persona non grata, which wouldn't be fair because I still didn't know how I truly felt about our relationship. "I'm not sure he's the right one for me, you know."

"Every pot has a lid, and from what I could see, you two seem perfectly matched."

"We've had a few arguments lately."

"Crikey, Dylan, your dad and I bicker over the slightest thing, but we still adore one another."

"Yeah, I know, but—"

"Don't get too lost in your thoughts." She approached and ruffled my hair, something I hated. "You always did think too much, which is probably why you're so good at your job."

I fixed my hair as best I could. "I'll try not to." It was one of my worst failings. If something went wrong in my personal life, I'd run the opposite way rather than deal with the issue.

"Right, eat your cake and drink your tea before it goes cold."

"I'm thirty-two, Mum, not a child."

"Thirty-two or not, you're still my little boy."

"If you say so." It was my go-to phrase when I knew I wouldn't win an argument.

"I do." She took the seat opposite and tilted her head from side to side, scrutinising me. "You don't seem yourself."

"This latest case has me tied in knots, but I don't wanna talk about it."

"Well, as soon as it's sorted, book yourself and Steve a break somewhere. You don't want to burn yourself out."

"I will." It wasn't a lie, but whether or not Steve was with me was another matter entirely. "How long did Dad say he'd be?"

"You know what he's like—he goes out for one thing and comes back with a boot full of stuff that sits in the shed until he finds a use for it."

"How's work going for him?"

"I think he's fed up with it to be honest."

"Working for the council is a thankless task."

"He says he regrets accepting the promotion, but it was a lot more money than he was earning before."

"I imagine it takes over his life a bit?"

"It's certainly done that, but we're only in our late fifties and retirement is still a while off for both of us."

Mum worked part time in a local bakery and had done since me and my late brother, Scott, were toddlers. "Is the shop busy?"

"Chocka, and no matter what state the world is in, people always want fresh bread, pies, and cakes."

"So, you're off-loading a shop bought cake onto me, hmm?"

Playfully, she clipped me around the ear. "Cheeky sod, I baked that myself."

"Just messing, I'm grateful."

"It really is lovely to see you, Dylan."

"I miss you, Mum, and how things used to be."

"There's no point dwelling in the past. It won't solve anything." As a family, we're open with one another, but some topics were uncomfortable for her.

You are their only child. Bella's words echoed in my mind. "I still miss him, you know."

It wasn't often I allowed myself to think about Scott, and how he'd died. He'd been the reason I'd joined the police force.

I remembered it like it was yesterday. Scott, aged fifteen, was out doing his paper round in the dead of winter when he was hit by a car. The driver had left him to die in the gutter, which was something me and my parents had never recovered from. He or she never handed themselves in or took responsibility in any way.

His death had left me with a definitive sense of right and wrong and the overwhelming need for justice.

Scott's death had moulded me into that man I'd become. I thought about him every day and would try to focus on the good times we had growing up, rather than how he'd died. It had taken a while, but I could actually look back and smile now.

However, it hadn't been so easy when it came to processing my sexuality.

Aside from the grief of losing my only brother, his death had left me with feelings of guilt for being the one who lived – the gay son. The one who might never give my parents the grandchildren I knew both craved. I'd voiced it to Mum once. Her reaction wasn't something I'd expected, nor had I ever seen things from her perspective, not until she spelled it out for me. *"Your dad and I have never, ever thought like that, Dylan. We loved you both equally, so losing you would have hurt just as much as it did losing Scott."* When it came down to it, I worried I was a disappointment, but that had been my insecurity. *"We're blessed to have you, so never feel you're not good enough. To us, you are perfect."*

"So do I, but let's not go there." Talk of Scott usually reduced her to tears. Neither she nor my father had forgiven themselves for not insisting on lights for his bike or reflective gear.

"Okay, Mum, sorry."

She patted my hand. "So, how are Bella and the kids?"

"Bella's her usual self and the kids are adorable."

"Does it make you broody?"

"Sometimes, but then I remember my job and question whether it would be fair bringing kids into my world."

"You've a lot of love to give, Dylan."

"And a lot of baggage that comes with it."

"What am I going to do with you?"

"Maybe we can talk about it after you make me another cup of tea?"

"And I suppose you'd like another slice of cake to go with that?"

"One of your cheese and tomato sandwiches with a bit of mustard wouldn't go amiss."

She chucked me under the chin, then walked to the fridge. "It's a good job I love you, Dylan Monroe."

"Love you too, Mum."

Back at the station, the incident room was busier than it had been earlier. I made my way over to Bella. "Mum told me to say hello."

"Aw, I must take the kids to see her."

"She'd like that."

"How was your dad?"

"I only saw him for a few minutes, but we've promised to go out for a pint when things settle down here."

"Oliver's just gone in with the duty solicitor."

"Who is it?" I asked.

"Fiona McCall."

"Ugh, I can't stand her."

"She's ruthless, but if what you suspect is true, she won't leave any stone unturned."

"Good," I replied, suddenly feeling better about her presence.

"Anything from the mother?"

I looked at my phone. "Nothing yet."

"Oliver is adamant he wants her in the room while he's being interviewed."

"Well, if she doesn't call soon, we're gonna have to go back round there."

"I've already called Penelope to let her know I'll be late home tonight and messaged Roy to postpone our catch up."

"How did Penelope take that?"

"Fine, but it won't be for much longer because my neighbour will be home soon and besides, Simon is pretty sure he's leaving the Army."

"Wow, I knew he was thinking about it, but I didn't realise it was all agreed. When did that happen?"

"Last night, he called and told me he'd had enough and wanted to come home."

"And how do you feel about it?"

"Excited to see him, but still not convinced it's the right decision."

"Give it a chance, Bells."

"Don't get me wrong, I worship him, but it's uncharted territory for us and our marriage."

"It'll be fine."

"Yeah, I guess you're right."

"I'm gonna go and see Janine." I turned to leave.

"I'll put the kettle on," she called out.

"Not for me, thanks. I've had two cuppas at my mum's."

Walking along the corridor, I spotted Oliver through the interview room window in conversation with Fiona McCall. He was sobbing while she scribbled notes on a pad. He looked up and saw me watching. Quickly, I moved out of sight and continued towards Janine's office.

I knocked on her door.

"Ah, Dylan, come in."

I stepped inside and took a seat. "You look pleased with yourself."

"I'm thrilled to be honest. We've got our guy, which also means that wanker Arjun Sharma is off my back."

"Hold your horses a little," I warned. "I really don't think we do."

"What do you mean?" Her shoulders sagged.

"Oliver is definitely involved, but not in the way we think."

"Look at the lad, Dylan—it's plain to see."

"On the outside, it might seem a done deal, but I'm not convinced."

"About what? Do you think he had an accomplice?"

"I don't know, it's just a gut feeling we're celebrating too early."

"Keep that to yourself."

"He's in with Fiona McCall now."

"Shit." She massaged her temples with her fingertips.

"Exactly. This case is high profile enough and she likes nothing better than to make us look foolish."

"Yes, exactly, so let's not give her any reason to hang us out to dry."

"Look, sorry to cut this short, but Oliver wants his mother in the room while I'm interviewing him, so I better get back round there and find out what she's playing at."

"I want everything done by the book, Dylan—no surprises and certainly no cause for the CPS to backheel prosecution."

"Got it. I'll let McCall know what I'm doing—she can continue briefing her client until we return."

"I know I keep saying this, but keep me in the loop."

"Will do."

After speaking with Fiona McCall, I stepped into the incident room. "Bells, let's go." I walked back down the corridor with her following close behind.

"Where to now?"

"We really need to speak to Emily Leyland."

THIRTY-EIGHT

Pushing open the front gate, I heard a familiar voice.

"Are you back again?" Mr Wright called from across the street.

"Looks like it," I replied.

"The lazy madam still hasn't shown her face." He edged closer to the road, seemingly eager to involve himself in something that wasn't his business.

"Right, thank you," I called out, not requiring his attendance.

"Nosy twat," Bella mumbled.

I rapped on the front door while Bella peeked in through the window. "Anything?"

"Not that I can see."

"Try the side gate," he yelled from across the street.

I ignored him.

We made our way down the side of the property. As he'd predicted, the gate was unlocked. "Smart arse," I grumbled, stepping into the well-maintained back garden.

"This is lovely," Bella said, eyeing up the array of plants in full bloom.

"Yeah, it is, but we don't have time to admire the flowers—"

"Okay, moody arse." Bella eyeballed him. "She's definitely in there."

"How do you know?"

"The patio door is open."

Something seemed off. The place was wide open, yet we couldn't get any response from her. I stepped closer to the patio door and peered inside. "Mrs Leyland," I called out. "Police, are you home?"

I slid the door open as far as it would go, pushed the curtains back, and crossed the threshold. I almost tripped over an enormous bag of clothes just inside the door. "Watch out," I said, pointing to the bag. I couldn't get over how hot it was in there. I touched the radiator and it almost took the skin off my fingers. Why would they need the heating on in the height of summer? My instincts were screaming that something was amiss.

I walked in a little further and that was when the unmistakable stench hit my nostrils. "Do you smell that?"

She lifted her arm to her nose. "Yeah. I think it's coming from upstairs."

There was no sign of anybody on the ground floor. "Mrs Leyland, my colleague and I are coming up the stairs, so if you can hear us, please respond."

We were standing in the hallway, the front door behind us, when I noticed the white painted banister had a smear of something that looked like blood on it. I pointed it out to Bella. "Don't touch anything. Come on." Treading slowly but cautiously up the stairs, all sorts of scenarios flew through my mind, but we had a job to do. I led the way, with Bella close behind.

At the top of the stairs was the bathroom. Nothing seemed out of place.

Then I popped my head into what I assumed was a spare bedroom.

Bella passed me and walked to the end of the landing. Suddenly, she froze. "Dylan—" She gagged. Her hands flew up to cover her mouth.

I rushed to her side. Emily's room was a bloodbath. "Oh, God, no."

My first instinct was to help her, but I wasn't about to step into the room for fear of contaminating a crime scene. Whatever I felt the need to do was pointless because nothing I did would change the fact that Emily Leyland was dead. Her mutilated corpse lay on top of the double bed. Blood soaked the sheets underneath her. Completely naked and wide-eyed, the heel of a stiletto shoe embedded into her forehead.

Bella continued to retch into her hand.

I pushed her towards the stairs. "Go outside and calm yourself down, then call it in."

"I'm—" She tried to answer but heaved violently.

"Go, and that's an order." I was fighting the urge to vomit, and with her gagging so close to me, I was in danger of throwing up. Once Bella had gone, I took a deep breath, trying to ignore the stench of death and the fact that Emily had obviously evacuated her bowels. The unpleasant aroma was so much the worse for the heating being left on high. "I'm so sorry," I whispered, deeply affected by what must have been an agonising death. I prayed that she hadn't suffered the indignity of sexual assault. From what I could see, her throat had been cut, just like the others, and bite marks covered the tops of her thighs. But it was the angry wounds on her torso that drew my attention.

I am
LunaTIC
REVENGE
IS
SWEET.

As gruesome as it was, there was something I couldn't quite put my finger on. Aside from the words carved into her, their positioning seemed to indicate he'd had more time to leave this particular calling card. The word sweet was just above her pubic line, with the other words above the belly button.

Emily Leyland's property was sealed off with crime scene tape while access to the street was restricted to residents and emergency services only.

Uniformed officers milled about, and my more experienced team of officers canvassed neighbouring houses for information. Will and Joanna were taking Mr Wright's statement.

I was standing at the front gate when Lauren pulled up. Bella stood beside me, smoking a cigarette. I'd never seen a crime scene affect her this way, and it worried me. I wafted the cigarette smoke away. "Are you okay, Bells?"

"I'm sorry, Dylan, but seeing the heel of that shoe—" She held her hand up, unable to carry on for a moment.

"What have you got for me?" Lauren approached us, then focused on Bella. "You look like you've seen a ghost."

"It's worse than that," I replied.

"I've never seen anything like it," Bella added.

"Well, I'd best get on then. I'll catch up with you both later." She left us and briefly spoke to the uniformed officer guarding the front door, before stepping inside.

"How could he have done that to his own mother, then made a big deal about wanting her with him at the station?" Bella asked, shaking her head.

"I don't know," I replied, cursing myself for getting it so wrong. I'd spotted the *PlayStation* on his bedroom floor with a heel through it. Thinking of the words etched into Emily's skin, was that Oliver's revenge? She'd stamped on his console and had to die for it. It sickened me beyond belief, and I was eager to return to the station to question him.

Before speaking to Oliver, I reported to Janine.

"Is the mother here yet?"

"Afraid not."

"Why?"

"Bella and I found Emily Leyland's body a couple of hours ago."

"Where?"

"In her bedroom. By the looks of it, Oliver killed her."

"How bad was it?"

"Heel of a shoe through her forehead, bite marks, throat cut, and revenge is sweet carved into her torso."

She shook her head, her longevity on the force had clearly desensitised her to this kind of thing . "Have you told McCall what you've discovered?"

"Not yet—I wanted you to know first."

"Get her in a room on her own and let her know what's what."

"Will do." I jumped to my feet. "Wish me luck."

"While you're doing that, I'll go upstairs and see the Chief. He's eager to know how the case is progressing.

"Rather you than me." Kenneth Melling was Chief Constable and Janine's boss. He wasn't the most patient of men, but more approachable than Arjun Sharma. "I'll come and find you later, but I don't know what time that will be."

"I've a feeling I'll be here until late anyway, so don't worry."

I glanced through the window of the dimly lit interview room and could see Fiona McCall still sitting with Oliver, scribbling into her notepad. The appropriate adult was also still present. I knocked on the door and pushed it open. "Do you have a few minutes, Fiona?"

"Now?"

"Yes."

"Hang on." She turned to her client. "Excuse me, Oliver."

I hadn't intended to speak to him, but I noticed he didn't have anything to drink, nor did I know if he had eaten. "Would you like a drink and a sandwich, Oliver?"

"No thanks," he replied in a meek tone.

"Are you sure?"

"Yeah, and call me Olly, for fuck's sake."

I guided Fiona along the corridor and into an empty room. She leaned against the table as I closed the door.

"What can I do for you?"

"We found Emily Leyland's body a little while ago."

The colour drained from her cheeks. "Where?"

"The family home, and this is strictly between us, similar injuries to his mother's body as with the other victims."

"That puts quite the spin on things."

"How?" I asked.

"My client is adamant he's not responsible for any of the murders I've discussed with him and told me in no uncertain terms that he wouldn't say anything on record until his mother got here."

"Did you mention to him the true extent of the wounds on the victims—the bite marks matching his dental records?"

"I do not lie to my clients, Detective."

"I was just asking."

"Regardless, Oliver is insistent he had nothing to do with those deaths."

I didn't vocalise my confusion because Fiona was, in essence, working against us and shouldn't be trusted. "I need to go in there and tell him what we've found."

"Okay."

"Just give me a few minutes to grab one of my colleagues and I'll be right in."

"Got it."

"I'm advising you to say nothing until we get there because I don't know how he'll react," I warned.

"You have my word."

Walking into the incident room, Tommo greeted me. "Hey, boss."

"Hey."

"Is it true then?"

"About Oliver's mum, yep."

"Bella said she was a mess."

"That's putting it mildly. Where is Bella anyway?"

"Toilet," he replied.

Genevieve and Anita appeared, chatting with one another. "Where have you two been?"

"I took a call from Mr Pilgrim, the vet – he's given me photographs and x-rays of the dead cat's bite wounds." Genevieve held a plastic bag in her hand with the images in.

"And?"

"Anita and I need to compare it to the dental records we have on file for Oliver and see if we can match it."

"Great, I'm going in there now to tell him we've found his mum's body, so if I'm not here when you leave for the day, email me or leave a voicemail."

"His mum's dead?" Anita gasped. "Did he kill her?"

"Tommo will fill you both in while I wait for Bella."

THIRTY-NINE

When Bella returned a few minutes later, she still looked peaky.

"Are you okay?"

"I'm sorry, Dylan. I can't stop thinking about that poor woman." Her hands were shaking uncontrollably.

"You should go home."

"I can't. You need me."

"I'm not being funny, but you're no use to anybody in this state. I'll get one of the others to drop you home, if you like?"

"Don't be silly. I can drive myself. But I feel awful leaving you to interview him on your own."

"I won't be on my own, don't worry. Go home and get yourself right."

"Are you sure?"

"Go!" I put my arm around her shoulder and walked her to the stairs just as Pete and Joanna arrived.

Once Bella had left, I quickly filled them both in with what had happened.

"Pete, are you free to interview Oliver with me?"

"Sure thing, boss."

A few minutes later, Pete and I entered the room.

"Hello, Olly. How are you doing?" I said once we were seated.

"I'm not saying anything until my mum gets here."

"That's not going to be possible, is it, Olly?"

"What are you on about?" He looked at me and then Pete before turning to Fiona. "What's going on?"

Fiona looked flustered and began to say something to him.

I butted in. "This conversation won't be recorded, Oliver, but I need to inform you we discovered the body of Emily Leyland a few hours ago."

"Fuck off." His body stiffened. "I'm not speaking to you until she gets here, so try again, knob head."

"Olly, your mum is dead."

"You're lying."

"No, I'm not."

He looked at Fiona for confirmation.

"DI Monroe is telling the truth, Oliver."

From nowhere, a guttural, anguished wail filled the room. Then carnage broke out.

Fiona jumped back as Oliver upended the table and kicked his chair across the room, all the while screaming at the top of his lungs.

I opened the door and pointed to the appropriate adult, who was cowering and terrified in the corner. "Out. NOW."

She dashed past me while Pete edged closer toward Oliver.

Fiona followed her out of the room.

I slammed the door shut.

"Calm down, Olly." Knowing he was sensitive to loud noises, I spoke in gentle, hushed tones.

But he was too far gone. He couldn't or wouldn't listen.

He picked up another chair and threw it at me. I dodged it as he ran at Pete.

I grabbed him from behind and tried to hold on to him.

Stronger than he appeared to be, he freed himself and rushed back into the corner nearest to the recording equipment.

"I want my mum," he screamed like a child.

"Come on, Olly, this won't solve anything. Let's sit down and talk."

"I want her here, now." With the fingernails on his right hand, he scratched at his left wrist, splitting the skin and drawing blood.

Had his rage been as terrifying as this when he attacked and killed his victims? I really didn't know what to think. Then, when I least expected it, another sliver of doubt crept in. If he'd killed his mother, why put on such a powerful performance? Is he a good actor, or were my first instincts correct?

As he scratched at his skin, I saw spots of blood dripping onto the floor. "We need to get your wrist looked at."

"I didn't kill her," he cried, when suddenly all energy seemed to leave him as he crashed to his knees. "I didn't, I swear it." He fell onto his side and curled into a foetal position. "She was alive the last time I saw her."

Maybe I was stupid for doubting his involvement, but he seemed so convincing. "It's okay, Olly, take deep breaths. I'm going to get you some help."

I noticed the gathering of officers outside the interview room and held my hand up to keep them from entering. The last thing Oliver needed was a barrage of noise. It would only set him off again.

"Be careful, boss," Pete warned. "His fingernails look sharp."

"Dim those lights right down." I ordered as I knelt beside him. "And get the on-call doctor here now."

He rushed out of the room and Fiona re-entered and stood with her back against the wall. "Is he okay?"

"I don't know, but for your own safety, please stay where you are."

FORTY

I grabbed a coffee from the canteen, then took a few minutes to compose myself in the car park. This case had twisted me in knots and, despite the nature of the crimes, seeing Oliver in such a distressed state bothered me more than it should. Something still niggled at me, but I couldn't put my finger on what it was.

Rather than linger with my own doubts I walked back into the station, saying a quick hello to the desk sergeant on duty as I passed.

Back in the incident room, Genevieve approached. "What happened in there?"

"The on-call doctor said Oliver wasn't in a fit state to be interviewed, so we have moved him to the Royal for observation."

"I've never seen a meltdown like that before. But, with that level of rage, it's easy to see how he killed those women."

"I'm not so sure of anything right now." I heard a phone ringing in the background.

"That's mine, excuse me." She rushed toward her desk and picked up her mobile phone.

I spotted Anita sitting at her desk. Upon approaching, I could see she was reading through the autopsy report on Jane Cross. "This doesn't make for pleasant reading, sir."

"It never does."

"Thank goodness the boy is locked up and can't harm anyone else."

"Quite." I didn't trust her, so had no desire to share any doubts about us having the wrong suspect in custody. "How are you getting on?"

"Very well. The team couldn't be friendlier."

"They're the best."

"I know they'll be wary of me because of my grandad but I won't let him use me to cause trouble."

"Admirable," was all I had to say. I was aware I was being harsh, but she could be lulling me into a false sense of security. "Keep that attitude and you'll have no problem."

Genevieve approached and rested her hand on Anita's shoulder. "Sorry to interrupt, boss, but I've just taken a phone call from Dominic Walden."

"Oliver's dentist?"

"Yes."

"What did he want?"

"He said there was a discrepancy with the information he'd previously provided."

"Such as?"

"Apparently, the mouldings and x-rays we have for Oliver are wrong."

"How?"

"He asked if I could go in and talk to him face to face. There was some reluctance to discuss it over the telephone."

"Right..." I glanced around the room. Most of the team were out. "... Anita, if you could link in with Will and ask him to show you why he's the resident genius when it comes to CCTV, that will give you something to do."

"Sure."

"Is that okay, Will?"

"Fine," he replied, not bothering to look up from whatever he was working on.

"Genevieve, you're with me."

Minutes later, we were in the car and on our way.

I put my foot down, not in the mood to be stuck in traffic again.

"Something bothering you, boss?"

"Yes. But until now, I thought I might have been overthinking things."

"In what way?"

"I've never been entirely convinced Oliver was responsible, and seeing his meltdown earlier, he seems far too fragile to have butchered those women."

"He was pretty scary, by all accounts."

"The poor lad had only just been told his mum was dead. How would you have taken that news?"

"We've been fooled before, boss."

"Yeah, I know, which is why I'll leave no stone unturned this time. And if it is Oliver, I'll take it on the chin, but if there's the slightest possibility he's innocent—I won't stand by and see him sent away for it."

We chatted during the journey, more so than we ever had before. It felt good getting to know more about my team and who they were behind their respective badges.

I parked up outside *Hollywood Smile Dental* and got out, stretching my legs. "That didn't take too long."

"No, not at all."

I pressed the bell. When the door opened, I recognised Amelia and hoped she wouldn't be as difficult as she'd been the last time I was there. We held up our badges. "Hello again. We're here to see Doctor Walden."

"Certainly." She gestured for us to step inside and follow her. "Dominic is expecting you. This way please."

She led us to Doctor Walden's office.

He was sitting behind his desk. "Ah, Detectives, thank you for coming so soon." He motioned for us to take the two seats opposite him.

"What is it you wanted to talk to us about?"

"I've seen the news about Oliver Leyland's arrest."

"Yes, it's quite sad."

"And his mother's death—shocking."

"We think so too, but what was so urgent you had to see us face to face?"

"Ah, yes, Oliver—it's my fault entirely, but you don't have up-to-date information."

"We don't?"

"No." Doctor Walden pressed a few buttons on his keyboard and images suddenly flashed up on the two view screens on the wall behind his desk. He stood and pointed to the screen on the left. "These are the images you already have..." Then he reached into a drawer in his desk and retrieved a pink mould. "... and this is the impression taken at the same time as the x-rays I am pointing to—they match."

"And?"

He signalled we looked at the screen on the right. "This is the last x-ray taken of Oliver's mouth, right after the extraction of a canine tooth last Monday to be exact—do you see it?" He pointed to the spot on the left screen where a tooth could clearly be seen, then to the x-ray on the right where the tooth was obviously missing.

"Monday last week you say?"

"Yes."

"I knew it."

Wide-eyed, Genevieve looked at me. It was the first time I'd ever known her to be lost for words. I was certain she'd made the same links as I had.

"So, whoever is killing these women, I can say for certain, it's definitely *not* Oliver Leyland."

My mind raced with possibilities and begged the question, if it wasn't Oliver, who was it and how does the killer manage to have near-identical dental issues? "Do you have the latest impression of his mouth?"

"No, because I removed the tooth and wanted to give his jaw time to settle. I fully intended to take one on his next visit."

Genevieve stood and leaned in to get a closer look at the x-rays. "All this treatment, I assume it's funded by the NHS?"

"Gosh, no, Detective, we are purely a private practice."

"Then who is paying for it all?" I asked.

"Let me just look into that..." He sat at his desk and tapped away at his keyboard. "Yes, as I thought, my records show Emily Leyland pays for the treatment after every visit."

"By what means, credit card, finance, perhaps?"

"Debit card, if my accounts are correct."

"And how much has been paid for Oliver's treatment so far?"

"Erm, one moment..." He used his finger to find the column he was looking for. "Well, over twenty-thousand pounds as of his last visit."

"And you're certain Emily Leyland pays for the treatment herself."

"Absolutely." He turned the screen toward me so I could see the payments made and on what date. In the right-hand column on the spreadsheet, the person billed is listed as Mrs E Leyland. I could see the treatment date and payment date always matched.

"Not many people have that amount of money just lying around." I thought about her house, and while it was in a pleasant area, there was nothing grand about it.

"There is no error, Detective. Mrs Leyland paid for every

treatment—the instruction was to do all I could to give Oliver a perfect smile. From what I recall, money was no object."

"Would you please give us a copy of the before and after x-rays so I can send them to the pathologist working on these particular cases?"

He pulled a large envelope from his drawer and held it out for me. "Already done, and please take this impression with you too. If you need the x-rays emailed over or another impression made, call Amelia and she will sort whatever you need."

I took them from him. "Thank you, Doctor Walden. This is most helpful."

"Before you both leave—" He looked at the images on the screen again. "My patient did *not* kill those women. I'd stake my reputation on it."

Genevieve sat back down and was staring at the screens. "Doctor, if I may, what are the chances of another individual having the same problems Oliver does?"

"There is no chance whatsoever that a random individual would have such identical issues as my patient, with or without that missing tooth."

I didn't comment further. "Well, you've been very helpful."

"Yes, thank you, Doctor," Genevieve added, standing and making her way out of the room.

"If you need anything else, please call me."

I followed and nodded to Amelia as we sailed past her desk.

FORTY-ONE

Once back in the car, I turned to Genevieve. "I bloody knew it."

"So, it's not Oliver?" she replied. "I'm stumped because everything leads to him."

"How can it be him? You've just heard what Walden said."

"I don't know, but if it's not him, how do we explain the bite marks?"

"He's being set up."

"Do you think?"

"Yes, but why would anybody go to those lengths?" I couldn't think of any reason, but I'd learned to discount nothing in this job. "What did Oliver ever do for somebody to want to see him locked away for murders he's not responsible for?"

"I don't know, but it's interesting to discover Emily Leyland paid for Oliver's treatment."

"Agreed."

"I don't know if she worked, but even if she did, that's a lot of money to shell out, and with no end in sight, something tells me she wouldn't have started treatments she couldn't continue to pay for."

"As soon as we're back at the station, I want you to check to see if she was employed or self-employed, then get a magistrate to approve access to her bank account."

"Got it, but that could take a while, then the bank could object. We'll have to make our case ironclad."

"Women are being killed, Genevieve, and a kid is being set up, I think they are reason enough to justify looking into her financial history."

On the drive back to the station, a thought occurred to me. "I have an idea."

"What?"

"Let's take a minor detour to Emily Leyland's house."

"For?"

"Bank statements. She could have some lying around, which could save us waiting to access her accounts."

"Good idea."

At the Leyland house. Uniformed police still guarded the property, but we had no problem getting inside.

Pulling on protective gloves and covering our feet with plastic booties, we made our way into the kitchen.

"This is as good a place to start as any." I opened the kitchen drawers, surprised to see them so tidy and organised. They weren't like mine at home. "There's nothing in here."

We continued to search the most obvious places but didn't go in Emily's bedroom as Lauren and two members of the SOCO team were still busy in there.

"Oh, well. We'll have to come back when they've finished." I felt deflated.

"It was worth a shot."

"Yeah. It was just an idea and had she been anything like me and left things stuffed in drawers, we might have found a few answers."

"Men..." She tutted and smiled.

"Before we leave, I want to tell Lauren about these x-rays and the dental impression. I think she'll be very interested in the latest findings."

"I'll wait for you in the car. I've got some calls to make."

"Afternoon," I said, popping my head in the doorway.

Lauren looked up. She was kneeling on the floor beside the bed. "Ah, Dylan, just the man."

"Sorry to disturb you, but I have something pretty important to show you."

"What is it?"

"Before and after x-rays?"

"From who?"

"Oliver Leyland."

"He's still in custody, isn't he?"

"At the hospital under observation at the moment."

"Hang on a minute." She got to her feet, removed her bloody gloves, and stepped out into the hallway. She took the envelope from me, opened it and held both x-rays up to the light that was streaming in from the window at the top of the stairs. "When were these taken?"

"Do you see the one with the missing canine? That tooth was extracted last Monday." I handed her the impression, and she studied it carefully. "And the bite marks on this latest victim don't show a missing tooth—so what are your thoughts?"

"You tell me."

"I'd say somebody has an impression of Oliver's teeth and has had a prosthetic made."

"I thought the same thing, but he's just a young lad. Why would anybody want to frame him?"

"That's your job, Dylan."

"I've got Genevieve trying to gain access to Emily's bank accounts. Apparently, she pays for Oliver's treatment herself."

"None of that will come cheap. Not if a private practice is doing the treatment."

"I know—according to Doctor Walden, twenty-odd grand has already been spent, and I'm hoping that, if we discover where the money is coming from, it will shed some light on who might be behind this. I'm wondering if Oliver has an accomplice, but even that doesn't sit right with me."

"Did Emily work?"

"I don't know for sure, but even if she did, she'd have to be earning a good salary to pay for treatment outright with no form of finance or putting it on credit cards, which isn't the case."

"So, what do you need from me?"

"Well, we know Oliver had the tooth removed last Monday, so how many deaths have there been since then?"

"Jane Cross was killed Sunday night, so I'd expect to see different bite marks on the subsequent three victims."

"So, that throws the accomplice theory out of the window. Whoever is trying to fit Oliver up wasn't aware the tooth had been removed and they were using an old impression of his mouth."

A smirk settled on her lips. "The clever little bastard almost had it all sewn up." She almost appeared impressed by the ingenuity of the sick plan. "Did SOCO tell you they've found a ring, watch, and locket in Oliver's bedside drawer?"

"No, but it doesn't surprise me. This whole thing is calculated and has been planned meticulously and I wonder about the message cut into Emily—Revenge is sweet—had she always been the killer's intended last victim?"

"Who knows?"

"I don't have any idea who's behind this, Lauren."

"Be sure your sin will find you out," she added, unhelpfully. "He'll slip up soon enough."

"But how many more have to die before we catch him?"

"None, I hope—I have every faith in you."

"Thanks, but I don't share your optimism."

"Perhaps speak to Oliver and ask him what his mother did for a living." She turned and placed her hand on Emily's bedroom door, an indication my time was up.

"If he's fit enough to talk that is."

"Only one way to find out."

"You're right. I'll get out of your hair."

"Something's bothering me about this latest victim, but I'm still working on a theory and will call you once I have something concrete."

"Such as?"

"Time of death, mainly."

"Okay, right."

Back in the car, I waited for Genevieve to finish her call. "Everything okay?"

"We need to speak to Oliver."

We headed back to the station and told Will about the dental impressions.

"You're kidding!"

"Nope."

"Shit, this case is more convoluted than a *Netflix* original."

"Tell me about it." I pinched the spot between my eyes and knew I was heading for a migraine if I wasn't careful.

"I just had a call from one of Emily's neighbours who said they saw Oliver leave the house last night through the back gate, wearing dark clothes. She'd seen him arrested earlier on and just presumed he'd been released."

"What time was that?"

He looked at his notepad. "She wasn't certain because she'd

been in bed and had just got up to use the toilet, but she said it was well after midnight."

"What the hell." I sighed.

"Exactly. I presumed she was mistaken at first, but with you saying that about the dental records, I don't know now. Oh, and I contacted Emily Leyland's sister, Carole McCloud. She's kicking off—demanding to see her nephew. I've appeased her for now, but she said she'll be here first thing tomorrow and won't be leaving until she sees Oliver. I didn't tell her he was in the hospital because I thought she might head over there and cause a fuss."

"Okay, thanks for the heads-up. I've got a few things to deal with here and then I was going to find out if Oliver is up for a visit yet."

Will shook his head. "The doctor said he's not to be disturbed until tomorrow. We have an officer guarding his room and he's been told to let us know if anything changes."

"Okay. I may as well head home soon then. I feel a stinking headache coming on."

I tidied up a few details at my desk before leaving. Once in the car, I dialled Bella's number.

"Hi, Dylan. Sorry about today."

"That's okay. How are you feeling now?"

"A little under the weather. I might not come in tomorrow."

Instantly, I was suspicious because Bella wasn't the type to take sick days. "What's wrong?"

"I think I might be coming down with something."

"Come off it." I'd heard the tremor in her voice and knew there was more to it. "Tell me the truth—what's going on?"

"Every time I close my eyes, my mind goes into overdrive."

"Sorry, but I don't follow."

"I keep seeing flashes of Emily with the heel of that shoe embedded into her forehead. Her eyes just staring up like that—

and knowing her own child did it to her. His face was the last thing she saw before he beat her to death." She sobbed.

This bothered me because Bella was usually hard as nails. I didn't want to burden her with our latest findings. She had enough going on in her head. "Listen, you need to get a good night's sleep and we can talk about it tomorrow."

"If only it was that easy."

"Would talking to a counsellor help?" My heart went out to her, and to anybody who had to deal with what we did on a daily basis. "I can organise it for you." I'd done my homework after Layla's arrest in an attempt to understand, or even justify, why she'd done what she had. Latest research showed one in five police officers and staff in the UK had symptoms consistent with either post-traumatic stress disorder or what's known as complex PTSD, however many people remained unaware.

"I don't know how to get past it and no matter how many conversations I have with myself, it's still there."

"Look, Bells, I get it. I know it was traumatic finding her like that, I just don't want you to fall into some pit of depression you can't crawl out of."

"I just can't seem to settle myself, and feel nervous, anxious even."

"That's not like you. Do you want me to come over?"

"No, there's no need. Penelope's here so I'm gonna try to get some shut eye. I'm sure I'll feel much better afterwards."

"Okay but call me later and let me know how you are, and if you need to take time off, I'll sort it."

"Thanks, Dylan."

"Don't forget, we still have a night planned with Roy." I wanted her to have something to look forward to.

"Yeah, I know, but I can't face it right now. Is that okay?"

"Just let me know when and I'll be there."

"Will do."

"I love you, Bells, and I know as your boss I'm not supposed to say that, but you're my best friend and I'll always have your back."

"You're gonna make me cry."

"Well don't, 'cos you'll only set me off."

"I'll call you in the morning."

I felt awful because I should have voiced my concerns. I'd let her down, just like I had with Layla. This time, though, I wouldn't allow somebody else I cared about to slip through the cracks.

I arrived home later that evening and dashed straight into the kitchen, needing painkillers.

A telltale blind spot in my vision told me a migraine was coming on, but with an early night, hopefully I'd avoid the full onset of symptoms.

Filling a glass with cold water from the fridge, I settled on the sofa and placed a migraine melt on my tongue.

I glanced at my phone and, even though I'd told him to leave me alone, there was still nothing from Steve.

Should I text him? I quickly argued with myself and decided otherwise. He'd caused the problems in our relationship and would have to work hard to put things right.

My phone began ringing, startling me. It was Lauren. "You're working late."

"Story of my life," she said.

"Yeah, I've just walked in the door myself. What can I do for you?"

"Are you sitting down?"

"Oh fuck, what now?"

"Emily Leyland was killed on Monday night."

"But Oliver was in custody then! So, I was right? He isn't the killer?"

"Unless he's working with somebody, then no, it appears he isn't."

I pinched the skin between my eyes again, desperately needing sleep.

FORTY-TWO

The next morning, I woke feeling refreshed even before the alarm sounded. It clearly paid to have an early night occasionally. And, instead of lying awake, I'd slept soundly for a change and had no sign of the migraine that had been threatening.

The situation with Oliver still puzzled me. At least I knew he wasn't our killer. However, it was clear that there was a link between him and the murders in some way. But how? I had no idea, and I didn't relish telling Janine. I knew she wouldn't be happy; but I wouldn't allow an innocent person to take the rap for something they hadn't done.

I dialled Bella's number, and she answered, sounding flustered. The baby was screaming in the background.

"You okay?"

"Peachy!" Sarcasm oozed from her words, giving me hope that she was feeling a little better.

"Did you get any sleep last night?"

"A little. It helped to talk to you."

"Good."

The baby continued to scream.

"Is baby Dylan ill?"

"Nope, just teething. And he's just shit through the eye of a needle. It's up his back and everything."

"I'll let you go and sort yourself out, but I just wondered if you had decided whether you were coming in today?"

"Yes, I'm coming in, and please don't go. Penelope's taken over nappy duty now I'm on the phone."

"Oh, you're bad."

"I know. Arrest me."

"I didn't wanna say anything last night, but Oliver's not our killer."

"Oh, don't start this again."

"It's true. His dentist confirmed yesterday that the records were incorrect. He'd had a tooth removed the day we found Jane Cross' body."

"What the hell?"

"I know."

"I don't get it. It must be him. What are the chances of two people having exactly the same bite? Well, not natural teeth anyway. The dentist must be mistaken."

"That's what I thought initially. I couldn't get my head around it. But then Lauren confirmed that when Emily was murdered Oliver had been in custody."

"Well, you could've led with that snippet of information."

"Sorry. Anyway, I need a word with Oliver. He's in hospital, by the way."

"What's he doing there? What did I miss? I only left a couple of hours early yesterday, for goodness' sake."

"I'll fill you in when I get there. I'll pick you up in twenty minutes."

True to my word, I arrived at Bella's house a while later. I sounded the horn, and she came bounding down the path with her daughter, Lily, at her heels. She flew through the gate and closed it promptly behind her.

"See you tonight, baby girl." She stroked her daughter's hair over the top of the gate and waited for Penelope to reach them.

Penelope picked up a now tearful child and made an enormous display of waving us off.

"Lily doesn't usually cry, does she?" I asked once Bella was in the car.

"She's just started it. I don't think she enjoys being left with Penny. One more week and my neighbour will be back."

"I thought she loved Penny?"

"Not anymore. She won't let her have any sweets. My sister is like the Gestapo where food is concerned. Anyway, come on, tell me what I missed yesterday."

Once I'd brought Bella up to speed, we were practically at the hospital.

We headed to the ward, and I caught up with the doctor before finding Oliver. As expected, the private room had a uniformed officer guarding the door.

"How has he been?" I asked.

"Quiet," the officer said, getting to his feet.

"We've released him from custody, but I think we need to monitor him for a while longer, so if you wouldn't mind?"

"Yeah, I'm going nowhere until I'm told otherwise."

I placed a hand on the door and glanced at Bella. "Ready?"

She nodded.

Oliver was lying back on the bed staring up at the ceiling. The curtains were closed, shutting out any daylight. He didn't so much as flinch as we entered.

"Hey, Olly. How are you today?"

The boy shrugged without blinking or tearing his eyes from the ceiling.

"Listen, I know you're not feeling too good at the moment, but I just wanted to ask you a few questions. It's important."

"I didn't mean it. She just winds me up."

"Sorry, Olly. I don't understand. We know you didn't kill your mum."

He suddenly sat up, staring at me. "You do?"

"Yes, we do. But right now, we need your help to find out who did."

His frantic eyes darted between me and Bella, as though searching for some kind of reason to believe me. "This isn't a trick?"

"No trick." Bella smiled and reached for Oliver's hand. "But somebody has gone to a lot of trouble to make it look like you were responsible for a string of murders, and we need to work out why. Do you have any idea who it could be?"

Deep furrows appeared between his brows. "Why would somebody want to do that?"

"We don't know, mate," I said. "But we'll get to the bottom of it, trust me. Now, are you okay to answer a few questions?"

"Don't I need my solicitor?"

"No. You're no longer a suspect."

"Okay then."

"Can you confirm the last time you had any dental work done?"

"Last Monday. I had a broken tooth removed by Doctor Walden." He eyed me warily. "Why are you asking about my teeth if you don't think it was me?"

"Because whoever killed these women used the impression of your teeth from before your tooth was removed."

"So having that tooth out saved me?"

"Yes. That and the fact your mother was killed the night you were in custody."

"Really?"

I nodded.

"So, I definitely didn't kill her?"

"No. Did you think you had?"

"I didn't know what to think. I thought I must be losing my mind."

"I can assure you; your mother was killed while you were in a police cell. Now, if it's okay, I need to ask you a few more questions."

"Go on then."

"Can you tell me if your mother ever worked?"

He nodded. "Yes. She used to be a dinner lady at some school, but I don't remember what it was called."

"And what has she done for money since then? Did she claim a benefit that you know of?"

"No. She got an inheritance from an elderly relative a few years ago and she quit her job straight away."

"Nice. Do you know how much she received?"

"No, she didn't like to talk about it."

The fact she'd inherited a large amount certainly explained quite a lot, but something still bothered me. "Do you know where your mum kept her bank statements by any chance?"

"I presume they're in that box file under her bed. She once told me if anything ever happens to her that's where she keeps everything."

"Oh good. At least that will save us some time because banks can drag their heels with releasing this information."

"No problem."

"Now, I wonder if you can tell me what the words, *I am lunatic – fear me,* mean to you."

"It's what my character says in the game I play on *PlayStation.*"

"Tell me more about that."

"*Wolven Army*. It's a game I play with my friends."

"I see." I glanced at Bella, suddenly excited. "Who else besides you knew about this?"

"My mum, and my friends, Sam and Liam. That's it."

My pulse quickened. "I'd like to speak with Sam and Liam. Any idea where I'd be able to find them?"

"Sam told me he worked at Prestige Real Estate just off Edge Lane. It's his dad's firm, I think. I'm not exactly sure where he lives though."

"And Liam?" I asked.

"He lives in Colorado—in America."

"You sure about that?"

"Yeah. We have a map on the screen showing where each of the players are located. Liam's in Colorado, in a place called Cripple Creek. It's obvious why I remembered that name, isn't it?"

"No," we both said.

"Because look at me—I'd be right at home in a town called Cripple Creek."

"You're not a cripple, Oliver," Bella said, close to tears.

I cleared my throat, suddenly moved by the show of emotion. "So, I have a feeling the doctor will discharge you soon, but I need to advise you not to go home. Your house is still a crime scene, and the Scenes of Crime Officers haven't released it yet."

"Okay."

"Do you have anywhere else you could go to?"

"Aside from my dad, who I haven't seen for years, Aunt Carole is the only relative I have left but she probably won't want anything to do with me now Mum's gone." Tears trickled down his cheeks.

"That's not true." My voice sounded croaky, and I cleared my throat. "Your aunt was informed of her sister's death and has already been into the station demanding your release and insisting you're taken to her house, if that's where you want to go?"

"Really?" Oliver's sad eyes filled with hope.

"Yes," I replied. "For now, I'll make sure the police officer stays with you but once you leave the hospital, I suggest you keep a low profile. The doctor told us he was discharging you this afternoon, so, once I get the go ahead, I'll drive you to your aunt's. Remember, somebody is out to get you, and whoever it is may be pretty angry to find out you've been released without charge."

"Yes, sir. I understand." He smiled sadly. He was such an odd-looking man-child, yet I couldn't help being drawn to his aura.

"Just by chance, you don't happen to have an old mould of your teeth, do you?"

"Yeah. I have it in my room somewhere. Why?"

"Have Sam or Liam ever been to your house?"

"Well. Liam obviously hasn't but Sam has, a few times."

"Before we go, do you happen to know their surnames?"

"Erm, I don't think so. It's not something we ever talk about but if I looked on their profile page it might be there."

I very much doubted that information would be willingly displayed but with some digging we would find Liam's IP address and trace him that way. Sam would be easy to find if he'd told Oliver the truth about where he worked. "That's fine, but for now, I'd rather you didn't go on the game or tell anyone what's happened, okay?"

"Yeah, I get it, but do you think this has something to do with Sam or Liam?"

"I don't know anything for sure right now, Olly, but it's my job to find out."

"Sam's my friend, he wouldn't do anything to harm me."

"That might be so, but what about Liam?"

"He's just some lad I chat to."

"Well, right now, we don't know what either are capable of, but I have stuff to get on with, so I'll be back later on to take you to your aunt's house. Is that okay?"

"Yeah, thanks."

FORTY-THREE

I could sense Bella's apprehension as we approached Emily Leyland's house. "We know where we need to look, so won't have to be here for long."

"Good."

"Do you want to wait here, and I can grab what we need and go through it in the car?"

"Would you mind?" She wrung her hands together, clearly distressed.

"No," I replied, seeing how agitated she was becoming. "I'll go and grab the file and I'll be out soon."

"Thanks, Dylan."

Once inside the house, I was glad she'd stayed in the car. The stench of death still hung in the air.

I took two stairs at a time to the next floor. Walking into Emily's bedroom, I navigated around the room and dropped to my knees to peer under the bed. I couldn't help noticing how clean the carpet was, the only thing I could see was a box file. Reaching under, I grabbed hold and pulled it out. I wasted no time in getting out of there.

A minute later, I slipped into the driver's seat and detected the stench of cigarette smoke coming from Bella. "Have you been smoking in my car?"

"Can we get out of here?" She skilfully avoided my question.

"Sure." I pulled away slowly, aware Mr Wright was nosing out of his front window. I took a left turn, knowing there was a small cafe close by. "Let's go for a coffee and we can go through the box in there."

"Okay."

I ordered our drinks while Bella found a seat in the corner, away from prying eyes.

She'd already started rifling through the file when I sat down with the coffees.

"Any luck?"

"Copy of her Last Will and Testament leaving everything to Oliver in the event of her death, but if he couldn't inherit, then her estate would go to Carole McCloud."

"That's the sister."

"Yeah, figured as much."

"Anything else?" I took a sip of my coffee.

"A marriage certificate between Emily and Winston Leyland. There is also a decree nisi, but no decree absolute."

"That means nothing to me." I shook my head, confused.

"Decree nisi is what you get when you start divorce proceedings. It's when the judge agrees there is no reason the two parties shouldn't divorce, and the decree absolute is when the divorce is final."

"So, they could be still married?"

Bella nodded. "Unless she's just misplaced it, but she has everything else in meticulous order, it doesn't seem likely." Deep wrinkles appeared in her forehead. "This is very interesting."

"What?"

"This statement shows the payments to *Hollywood Smile*

Dental, but there are credits to her account from Fawkes Technologies and Oakleaf Residential School on the same day."

"What month is that from?"

"June."

"Is there anything from prior months?"

Bella rifled through the file again and pulled out more sheets of paper. "May. The same payments received from the same recipients." She scanned another sheet of paper. "Here again for April..." More searching. "... and March."

"So, she didn't work, we know that, but Oliver mentioned she had received an inheritance from an elderly relative."

"Yeah, but there's nothing in here that reflects that unless these payments are something to do with the relative's estate."

"Unlikely," I replied. "How much are we talking about?"

"Five thousand a month in total, so that's sixty grand a year being paid into this account."

We went through other statements that dated back the last twelve months, but all showed the same thing.

"She has the title deeds for the property, too. So, it doesn't look like she's paying a mortgage either, she owns the house outright. That means everything in this account is disposable income."

Bella pulled out another sheet of paper. "And this is a tidy sum that never seems to be touched or dipped into but gains a hefty amount of interest annually. Have a look."

I took the statement from her. "That's half a million quid—why would somebody who didn't work have that amount of money?"

"The inheritance perhaps."

"I don't think there was one, Bells."

"You don't?"

"I think that's what Emily told Oliver, so he wouldn't ask questions about how she could afford to pay for everything."

"Maybe she was into something dodgy?"

"My instincts tell me that's not the case either."

"Then what?"

"I don't know, but we need to speak with Oliver again."

"He'll be discharged soon—we can ask him then."

"Let's go through this file thoroughly and see what else there is. I pulled out a brown envelope, opened it, and read the contents. I couldn't believe what I was seeing. "Christ—"

"What?"

"This is a non-disclosure agreement between Emily Leyland and Oakleaf Residential School and..." There were multiple pages stapled together. I flipped through them. "...there is another NDA between Emily Leyland and Fawkes Technologies. Both effectively ban her from talking about Oliver's time at the school."

"So, she was being paid off?"

"Yes, looks like it, but what for?"

"That's what we need to find out. Drink up and let's get back to the hospital and see if Olly is ready."

On the way to the hospital, I called Janine to let her know what was happening. She was as intrigued as we were and asked me to fill her in properly once we were back at the station.

"Do you think Oliver knows anything?" Bella asked.

"He must know something, even if he doesn't understand it, because everything seems to revolve around him."

"Well, take it easy where ehe's concerned. You don't want another meltdown."

"I won't tell him about my suspicions for now, not until we've spoken to the school and whoever is in charge of Fawkes Technologies." I parked outside the hospital's main entrance. "Bells, will you wait here and deal with any traffic wardens?"

"Yeah, and I'll search Companies House for the directors of Fawkes Technologies. Hopefully, we'll find an address and can pay whoever they are a visit."

"Good idea." I left her to it, rushed through the doors and into a waiting lift. I made my way to Oliver's room and knocked before I walked in. He was sitting at the end of the bed fully clothed, seemingly staring into space. "Hi, Olly. Are you ready?"

"Yeah. The doctor said I'm free to go."

"How long have you been waiting for?"

"Only about fifteen minutes."

"Sorry about that."

"Don't be. But I do wanna get outta here."

"Before we go, would you mind if I asked you a few questions?"

"No."

"Have you ever heard of Fawkes Technologies?"

"Nope, never."

"And what about Oakleaf Residential School?"

His shocked expression told me I'd hit the nail on the head.

"Yeah, I used to go there when I was younger, but then switched to a normal high school."

"Why was that?"

He was hesitant to answer, and I could see the lie formulating as he spoke. "My mum couldn't afford it any longer."

"Even with the inheritance you told me about?"

"Nah, it was quite a posh place, and expensive. But my funding was stopped for some reason and keeping me there meant she would have no money to pay the bills, so I agreed to go to one closer to where we lived."

"And how was it there?"

"Boring. But I didn't mind it that much."

It was obvious everything he'd just said was a lie. But I didn't want to force the truth from him yet. He was still too fragile and pressing him could risk another episode. Instead, I decided I would drive over to the Wirral and speak to the headmaster. Hopefully Bella had made progress with Fawkes Technologies and its directors. I was so close to cracking this case, I could feel it, but some pieces of the puzzle still wouldn't slot into place.

"Right, come on, your aunt will be waiting for you."

There had been an emotional display when we first arrived. Oliver's aunt and uncle flew from the house and the three of them formed a huddle, all sobbing.

It was hard to watch, and I had to force my own tears back.

Bella didn't seem to care and let her tears flow freely.

Afterwards, we got him settled and accepted a cup of tea, answering as many questions as we could without jeopardising the investigation.

"Thanks for taking him," I said when Carole showed us to the door a while later.

"I love him, always have and somebody's gotta look after him now Emily is—" She covered her mouth with her hand as fresh tears fell.

"I'm sorry, Carole." Bella rubbed the other woman's shoulder.

"Just catch the bastard," she said in between sobs. "That's all I ask."

"We will. And please remember, somebody has it in for Oliver so, until we find out who, keep him inside and don't answer the door to anybody you don't know. Any problems, dial 999 immediately."

She nodded.

"And you have my number. Call if you need me for anything at all." I shook her hand warmly.

We got back in the car.

"That was heart-breaking," Bella said.

"I know, but at least Olly is being taken care of."

"Poor kid."

We were now free to talk openly. "Did you find anything on Fawkes Technologies earlier?"

"I did—Leonard and Marjorie Fawkes are the owners, and both are listed at Companies House."

"Any address for them?"

"Yes, somewhere in Alderley Edge."

"That's a bloody hike. We can go there in the morning."

"Probably better tomorrow."

"So, what about this Sam guy?"

"Prestige Estate Agents on Edge Lane—Malcolm Curtis is listed as Managing Director and there is a Samuel Curtis listed as Director."

"That must be our guy."

"Yep, I think so."

"Let's go."

Once again, we were stuck in traffic, so when we pulled up at the estate agency, I was in a filthy mood.

Upon first impressions, the agency seemed to represent high-end properties going by the window display.

"Hello, can I help you?" a middle-aged lady in a black skirt and white blouse asked. *Louisa*, it said on her gold-coloured name badge, just above her title as Sales Manager.

"Detective Inspector Monroe and Detective Sergeant Frost." We showed our badges. "I'd like to speak to Samuel Curtis if he's available."

"May I ask what it is about?"

"No," I replied a little more brusquely than I'd intended to. "Is he in the office?"

"Yes, but—"

My mood was worsening by the second at her reluctance to

help. "If you could lead the way, Louisa, that would be most helpful."

She glanced nervously around as other members of staff took an interest as she led us towards a small central staircase at the back of the building... "This way, please."

Two rooms sat on the mezzanine level. I followed Louisa, then waited as she knocked on the door to the right. I could see from the nameplate that this was Samuel Curtis' office.

"Come in," a voice called out.

She pushed the door open. "There are two police officers here to see you, Sam."

"What for?" I could hear the panic in his voice.

"Do you mind?" Bella and I sidestepped Louisa and flashed our identification. "We'd like a word with you, Mr Curtis."

"I haven't done anything wrong."

I wasn't expecting him to be as handsome and well groomed, or as immaculately dressed as he was. "We never said you had."

"Louisa, can you please call my solicitor and tell them the police are here."

"Yes, of course." She turned on her heel and rushed back down the stairs.

Bella glanced my way.

I knew what she was thinking.

"For somebody that has done nothing wrong, you seem to be a little flustered," she said.

"I know how you lot fit people up."

"What could we possibly fit you up for? Is there anything you need to tell us?"

"No, and I'm not saying anything until my solicitor gets here." He folded his arms like a petulant child.

"Do you know a young man by the name of Oliver Leyland?" I asked.

"I ain't saying a word."

Bella took over this time. "It's a simple question, Sam. Do you know Oliver Leyland?"

"What if I do?"

"Did you ever meet his mum, Emily Leyland?"

"No, and I never hurt her either."

"So, you're aware Mrs Leyland was attacked and killed?"

"I saw it on the news, but I had nothing to do with it."

"When were you last at the property?"

Louisa appeared at the door and interrupted us. "Sam, I spoke to your solicitor, and he's on his way. He advised you to do as they ask, but don't say anything else until he gets here."

"You heard her; I'm not saying any more."

"Then I am arresting you on suspicion of murder. You do not have to say anything, but it may harm your defence if you do not mention when questioned something which you later rely on in court."

"I didn't touch her, I swear it," Sam yelled. "Olly is just some kid I felt sorry for, but I never hurt his mum."

"Turn around please and put your hands behind your back."

Surprisingly, he did as he was told. I snapped the handcuffs closed.

Bella turned to Louisa. "I'd suggest calling Mr Curtis' solicitor back to tell him we've arrested his client and are taking him to the station." She gave the woman her card. "The details are on there."

We led Sam out of the office and settled him into the back of the car.

I didn't know what to think, but for now, at least, I had twenty-four hours to hold him and, if I needed to, I'd apply for an extension.

FORTY-FOUR

Sam's solicitor was a first-rate, jumped-up tosser who thought he was shit hot. However, we soon established that, although Sam had been to Emily's property on the evening in question to drop off a bag of clothes for Oliver, he wasn't our killer. He had an alibi; his wife and kids had been in the car with him. But I intended to keep him in the cells for a while longer, just because he'd wasted two hours of our time when he could've just cooperated from the outset.

"That was a massive waste of time," I said to Bella as we left the interview room. "I need a strong coffee before I go any further."

We fell in step beside each other.

"I'll make you one. In fact, I'll grab you a flat white from the canteen just as soon as you tell me what Janine said earlier."

"What could she say? She wasn't jumping for joy, put it that way."

"I'll bet she wasn't. So, what do you think about Sam?"

"It's not him."

"I agree. But we'll need to dot all the i's, etcetera, just

in case."

"Yes, I know." I felt I was getting bogged down with all the procedures and they were getting in the way of us doing our job.

"Are you hungry? I'll grab us a sandwich too, shall I? My stomach was growling in there."

"Was that your stomach? I thought it was the plumbing."

She batted my arm. "Cheeky sod." She turned off as we reached the main corridor and took the stairs.

"I'll have egg mayo," I called after her.

"Hey, boss," Will said as I entered the incident room. "I finally got hold of Kirsty Lamb, Amanda Morris's mother. She's apparently been in Turkey sunning herself while her daughter's been in the morgue."

"You can't blame her for that."

"No, maybe not, but she'd heard on the grapevine and still refused to cut her holiday short. She said she wouldn't be any help to her daughter now, so what was the point?"

"What a bitch."

"She couldn't wait for the phone call to end, as she had an appointment at the nail salon."

"I'll never understand some people. Poor Amanda never stood a chance with parents like that."

"She probably won't even bother attending her own daughter's funeral."

"Wouldn't surprise me. But she provided me with some information about the missing ring. And I sent her the photos through of the one found in Oliver's drawer, and she has identified it as the same one."

"That's something at least."

"Yeah. Did you have any luck locating that Liam bloke?"

"Not much. He's definitely been using a VPN, but that's not unusual in this day and age. My home computer keeps reminding me to set one up for security purposes. I contacted *Sony*, but they said it will be up to twenty-four hours before they get back to me. I applied for a court order in the meantime, as I don't think they will give me any information without one."

I exhaled noisily between pursed lips. "Do you ever get sick of all this red tape?"

"Every single day."

"Without it, our job would be a doddle."

"You can say that again. What are you doing this afternoon?"

"We need to pay a visit to Oakleaf Residential School," I said the name in my poshest voice.

"Shall I call ahead? Make an appointment."

"No thanks. I don't want to give them any warning. Something huge must've gone down for them to agree to pay out so much every single month."

"What do you think it could be?"

"I have no idea. But could you run a check on the Fawkes' for me? Bella checked out the company in Manchester, but I need you to dig up what you can. I'm intending to pay them a visit in the morning."

"Do you think it might be connected to the murders?"

"Who knows? But my gut tells me it is, and I intend to find out one way or another."

Bella returned laden down with Styrofoam cups and sandwiches. "I got enough to sink a battleship and there's nobody here!" she complained.

"I'm sure they'll all be back before too long. If not, I'll eat their share." Will laughed.

We drove along the sweeping driveway of Oakleaf Residential School, a stunning red brick building situated in picturesque, manicured grounds. The hulking, great 18th century structure, with its beautiful arched windows and impressive turrets, would have made a wonderful movie setting.

I parked out front and we jogged up the steps to the main entrance.

"Can I help you?" The Scottish woman at reception wore a high-necked blouse. She had a pointed pale face topped with too-dark black hair scraped into a severe bun. Deep grooves surrounded her disapproving lips.

"I'm looking for Professor Etherington." I held out my badge for her inspection.

She sneered at me and then turned to eye Bella who entered behind me. "Do you have an appointment?"

"No, but it's important, so I suggest you let him know we're here."

"This isn't a drop-in centre, detective. The Professor is a very busy man."

"Well, either he comes out here and meets me of his own accord, or else I'll march through that door and take my chances. Then I'll arrest him, and possibly you too, for wasting police time." I couldn't legally do what I'd threatened, but I hoped she didn't know that.

Her left eye twitched. "Take a seat."

I winked at Bella who was watching me with her mouth agape. "I'm impressed," she said as we sat down on the row of red leather seats opposite reception.

An equally po-faced man approached us soon after. "How may I help you, detectives?"

"And you are?"

"Professor Walter Etherington—headmaster. I believe you asked to see me."

"Yes. Is there somewhere we can speak privately?"

"Certainly. Follow me."

I could tell he wasn't thrilled with us being there, but tough. I was sick and tired of dancing to everybody else's tune.

He led us through the door at the back of reception and along the dark, panelled corridor to a vast room that was as pompous as I'd expected. The smell of aged books, old leather and furniture polish filled the space. "Now what is it? I'm a busy man."

"Oh, that's funny. We're not busy in the slightest. We only have a psycho serial killer to get off the streets, but I best not keep *you* any longer than necessary." I was being facetious, but I didn't care.

"What does any of that have to do with me?"

"Emily Leyland." I dropped the bomb and watched his reaction with amusement.

The colour drained from his face and his head suddenly resembled a blinking, nodding dog. "Sorry?"

"You heard. Now I'm not in the mood for lies, Professor, so please tell me why this establishment has been making payments in excess of two-and-a-half grand, every month, into Emily Leyland's account for the past four years?"

"Maybe she's a member of staff?"

"You know damn well she isn't."

He shook his head, clearly flustered. "I don't know what you are talking about."

I reached into my pocket and pulled out a copy of the non-disclosure agreement. "Take a look at this and see if it jogs your memory."

His face took on a greyish tinge. "I am not permitted to discuss this with you until I speak to my solicitor."

"I'll be back by 10am tomorrow and I don't intend to leave here without answers, even if it means taking you in for questioning." I stormed from the room, along the corridor, through reception and out the door with the sound of Bella's heels clacking close behind.

"Bloody hell, Dylan. Who pissed on your pizza?"

I laughed, her turn of phrases never failed to amuse me, but I knew what she meant this time. I usually had a more laid-back approach to my policing, but I was sick and tired of getting nowhere fast. "He knows exactly who Emily is. Did you see the look on his face when I mentioned her name?"

"I did. I thought he was about to have a coronary. And I bet he could make the *Guinness Book of Records* for the most blinks in one minute."

"I know, I saw that too." I unlocked the car with the fob.

"So where to now?" Bella asked once we were back on the road.

"I'll drop you home. We'll need to leave bright and early in the morning. I intend to pounce on the Fawkes' first thing, so I'll be at yours at the crack of dawn."

"Yay!" she said sarcastically.

"If you don't want to come, I can always take someone else on the team."

"Would you pull your head in, Dylan, for Christ's sake? I don't like this ratty version of you. Maybe you need to go home, grab a bottle of wine, and have a long soak in the bath."

"Maybe I do."

"And maybe you should call Steve and suggest he join you?"

"Maybe you should mind your own business and let me deal with my own failed love-life the way I see fit."

"Maybe I don't want to—while I'm trying to help you out, it's deflecting from the fact my hubby is planning on making huge life-changing decisions without even consulting me." She smiled at me sadly.

"Maybe he's the one you need to focus your attention on then and leave me and Steve alone."

"Maybe I will."

"Good."

"Good."

FORTY-FIVE

The next morning, the traffic was a breeze, and I pulled up outside Bella's house shortly after 6am. We hadn't spoken much after our childish spat in the car and from the look on her face, she still intended to carry it on.
"Morning," I said, brightly.
"Morning."
We drove, not speaking, the entire journey – the radio filling the silence between us.
The lavish tree-lined streets and stunning houses of Alderley Edge were a far cry from where we'd come from.
I pulled into a parking space minutes away from our destination, and Bella eyed me questioningly.
"Can we clear the air before we go any further?" I asked.
"I don't know what you're on about."
"Really?"
"Mm-hmm."
"So, you're not sulking?"
"Nope."
"I'm sorry I was crotchety yesterday. Does that help?"

She shrugged. "A little."

"Good. Then stop moping around. I need you firing on all cylinders today if we have any chance of solving this case."

She gave me a half-smile and nodded. "Okay."

The GPS directed us to a pair of elegant wrought-iron gates that were wide open. I drove through them along a driveway flanked by established trees.

"Nice," Bella said.

"Yeah. This is how the other half live. Premier-league footballers' territory around here, you know."

The stunning period farmhouse suddenly came into view. As did a man who appeared to be in his fifties walking towards a silver Tesla, his arms filled with files and a briefcase. He placed the case at his feet and popped the boot.

I pulled the car to a stop beside him and cut the engine.

"Who are you and what are you doing on my property?"

"Mr Fawkes?" I asked, climbing from the car, my back already up because of his attitude.

"Whoever you are, I've not got the time. I'm about to leave for an important business trip."

I groaned. Why was it that everybody I met recently presumed they had bigger fish to fry than me? "Detective Inspector Dylan Monroe, and this is my colleague DS Annabella Frost. Are you Leonard Fawkes?"

"Yes. What's this all about?"

"We need a word with you about Emily Leyland."

The man stiffened and slowly turned to face me.

"Who?"

"Let's cut the bullshit, Leonard."

If looks could kill, I'd have been dead as a dodo right then, but he nodded.

"I know you're in a hurry but I can assure you it won't do you any good to give us the run-around."

He slammed the boot and stepped towards us. His eyes bulged, and nostrils flared. "You'd better come inside."

A middle-aged woman dressed in a trendy silver-grey trouser suit and lime green silk blouse was descending the stairs as we stepped into the entrance hall. "Is everything okay, Leonard?"

"You'd best join us, Marjorie. They're here about Emily Leyland."

"Emily?" Marjorie ran down the last few stairs, her heels clattering on the wood sounded like a racehorse tap-dancing. "What has that bloody woman come up with this time?"

"These people are detectives, Marjorie."

She suddenly stopped clopping towards me, smoothed down her blouse and exhaled. "What can we do for you detectives?" Her smile didn't reach her cold, hard eyes.

"We have a few questions for you and your husband. Can we sit down, please?"

She followed her husband into a room to the left of the hallway. The huge, bright space wasn't at all what I expected of the ancient farmhouse. It was modern and vulgar, done out in several shades of white from the walls to the carpet, the sofas to the furniture, even the ornaments and artwork were bland and colourless.

Once we were all seated, Marjorie prompted me to begin.

"Can you tell us about your relationship with Emily Leyland?"

"There is no relationship. Why do you ask?" she snapped.

"Okay. Let me start from the beginning. We are investigating the murder of Emily Leyland."

Marjorie suddenly leapt to her feet. "She's dead?"

Leonard reached for his wife's hand and pulled her back down beside him. They both looked at me.

"We have reason to believe she was blackmailing you. Is this correct?"

"Her death has nothing to do with us—tell them, Lenny. We've not spoken to the woman in years."

"Okay. Now we've established you did actually know Emily." I eyed them both in turn. "Could you please fill me in on why you're paying her thousands of pounds every single month—the exact amount also being paid to her from Oakleaf Residential School, might I add."

"Detective, we don't—"

"Marjorie. It's time we came clean." Leonard said.

"But... but..."

"I'd listen to your husband if I were you, Marjorie. This is a serious situation and right now you're both looking like prime suspects in a murder investigation."

"Us? You think we killed her?"

"It doesn't look good, does it?"

She wrung her hands together on her lap. "You're not going to arrest us, are you? Oh, the shame."

"I suggest you tell us everything. If you've not broken the law, then I'm sure you'll be okay," Bella said.

"That crazy woman accused my Damien of sexually assaulting her son while they were both at that terrible school."

"I see," I said. "And instead of going to the police, she demanded payments?"

"Not quite," Leonard said.

"Go on."

"It was Etherington's idea. He didn't want an accusation like this getting out and neither did we. She needed money, and we had plenty, so it was a no-brainer."

"Quite."

"So, you see, we didn't do anything wrong. Not really."

I shook my head, disgusted. "You don't think so? You covered up an alleged crime and paid someone off rather than having it investigated—"

Marjorie glared at her husband, clearly terrified.

"We were just trying to protect our son. He was innocent, but you know what those types of accusations can do to a person's reputation," Leonard said.

"How do you know he was innocent?" Bella asked.

"Because Damien isn't like that. He's gentle and loving. This entire episode totally devastated him."

"Then why not fight it?" I asked.

"People are always so quick to believe the worst in someone, that's why," Marjorie snapped.

"Where is your son now?" I asked. "We need to speak to him."

"He doesn't live here," she said. "He left home and moved abroad years ago. He's settled at long last, and I'd prefer to keep it that way."

"Do you have a recent photograph of him, by any chance?" I asked.

She nodded and reached into her jacket pocket for her phone. "He sent me a lovely photo of him last year. I keep it as my screensaver."

I took the phone from her and froze. Then I turned the screen for Bella to see. "Do you have a phone number and address for Damien, should we need to contact him?" I asked, as though an after-thought.

Marjorie took the phone from me. "We don't have a physical address, just his email, but we communicate over *WhatsApp* linked to his old UK number."

"If we can take that number and also his email address, that will do for now." I got to my feet. "Oh, and can we have a copy of that photograph for our records?"

"Of course. Is that it? Aren't you going to arrest us for the other thing?" Marjorie sounded relieved.

"We'll need to speak to Oliver and ask if he intends to press charges, but for now that will be all."

She recited Damien's phone number and email address.

Bella wrote it down.

"I'll send the photograph to your email," she said.

"Thanks." Bella put the pad away.

"Just out of interest. Where is Damien living now?"

"Colorado. A little place called Cripple Creek."

FORTY-SIX

"What are you playing at?" Bella reached for her seatbelt as I manoeuvred the car and headed away from the house. "Why didn't you say something to them?"

"Because I don't want them giving their son the heads up."

"Are we on the same page here? Do you think Liam and Damien are one and the same?"

"Without a doubt."

"But if he's in Colorado, how can he be our killer?"

I eyed her in disbelief. "Do you still have baby-brain?"

"Why? What am I not getting?"

"He's obviously not in Colorado."

"But the computer game Oliver told us about shows that he is."

"Because he's using a VPN, Bella."

"And that means?"

"Virtual Private Network. You can set them to show you're anywhere in the world at the click of a switch."

"Oh, I get you. Sorry, I'm a bit behind the eight-ball where technology is concerned. So, you think Damien is pissed off with Oliver for blackmailing his parents?"

"Definitely." I signalled and turned onto the main road, which was back-to-back traffic as far as the eye could see. I hit redial on my phone and called the station.

"Hey, boss," Will answered.

"I need you to search for a Damien Fawkes. Bella will send you all the info we have on him shortly."

"Is that the guy you went to see this morning in Cheshire?"

"No, we went to see Mr and Mrs Fawkes. Damien is their son, and if I'm not mistaken, you'll find he's also masquerading as Liam from Colorado."

"You're shitting me!"

"Nope. Turns out the Fawkes' and Oakleaf school were paying Emily hush money to cover the accusation that Damien, AKA Liam, sexually abused Oliver when they were both enrolled as pupils."

"Shit! Poor Oliver."

"Bella will send you a photograph of him..." I nodded at Bella. "... you'll see why we thought it was Oliver on the CCTV that night. Damien is also albino."

"Wow! You have had a productive morning—it's only just turned eight-thirty."

"I know. I didn't alert the Fawkes' that anything was happening—figured it was best if we fly under the radar until we're in a position to pounce."

"Okay. So, are you on your way back?"

"Yeah, but this bloody traffic is a nightmare now, so don't hold your breath."

I sat staring at the TV screen, open-mouthed. Why the hell had they released Oliver? I'd given them everything they could need to lock the fucker away for life. I rewound the news item and hit play again.

> ... *police say they have released the sixteen-year-old male they'd previously arrested, pending enquiries. The boy, who can't be named for legal reasons, will stay with family...*

Family?

I knew he didn't have any family apart from his mother and her sister, so it wasn't difficult to figure out where he'd gone. But, apart from knowing she lived somewhere close to Bootle, and her first name was Carole, I had no other details.

Enraged, I launched an attack on the wastepaper basket.

"Why would they release him?" I yelled, the sound bouncing off the walls of my apartment. I couldn't believe they'd let him go but figured if the cops were too stupid to lock him up, then I had no choice but to sort it myself.

I reached for my phone and texted my boss.

Sick. Won't be in today.

He wouldn't like it, but I didn't care. I needed to work out where Oliver was, and fast. Opening my tablet, I logged on as my alter-ego – Liam Greenwood. Then I scrolled through Oliver's Facebook friends. Nobody called Carole was listed. Of course not – nothing is ever that easy.

I wouldn't let that stop me. My parents owned an IT company and I'd taken advantage of their expertise and any training on offer over the years. I knew how to find people – it would just take a bit of time, that's all.

We were barely moving. But it was no surprise as we'd hit the traffic slap-bang in the middle of rush-hour. I turned to Bella. "Could you find the number for Oakleaf Residential School for me, please?"

She did a search and then typed the number in for me.

"Hellooo, Oakleaf Residential School, Aileen speaking." The unmistakable deep Scottish tones of yesterday's receptionist filled the speakers.

"Professor Etherington, please," I said.

"I'm afraid the professor is on another call. Can I take a message?"

"It's DI Monroe. I'll wait—"

Classical music suddenly replaced her voice.

"Rude!" Bella screwed her face up, as though angry.

"Don't worry about it. People in these positions always seem to think they're better than the average Joe. She won't be so cocky once I've spoken to her boss."

"Professor Etherington speaking."

"Hello Professor. It's DI Monroe here. I'm calling to cancel our ten-o'clock meeting and also to inform you, I know exactly what the NDA was for."

"Would we be better having this conversation in my office?"

"It's merely a courtesy call to inform you I shall be advising Oliver Leyland to press charges, and for him to go public with everything that happened to him during his stay at your school."

"He can't—the NDA!"

"His mother who is sadly deceased signed the NDA. Oliver signed nothing. In fact, I don't even think he was even aware of its existence."

"But... But..."

"One of my officers will be in touch, Professor." I nodded at Bella, and she ended the call.

"Do you think Oliver will press charges?"

I shrugged. "Who knows, but at least I will have ruined that arsehole's weekend. The pompous prick."

"Stick that in your pipe and smoke it, Professor!" she laughed.

It took the best part of three hours to get back to the station.

My phone rang as I pulled into my parking spot. It was Will. "Where are you?"

"Downstairs, why?"

"Hurry up and get back here. I've found something."

"Coming now."

We practically flew from the car and into the building, taking the stairs two at a time.

"What is it?" I barked, barely through the door.

"I've found Damien Fawkes, and you're right, he is in the UK. In fact, he owns an apartment at the Marina close to the Albert Dock."

"I knew it." Adrenaline pumped through my veins.

"There's more." Will looked as though he was about to spontaneously combust.

"Go on."

"Once I found him, I was able to do a more detailed search on his employment status and you'll never guess what."

"Spit it out!" I snapped.

"He only bloody works as a technician for *Hollywood Smile Dental*. Same company Oliver goes to for treatment, but a different branch on James Street. Apparently, it's where all the moulds are made."

"You're kidding."

"Well, I never!" Bella shook her head, clearly floored.

"Send both addresses to my mobile. I'm going over there now. Coming Bells? We've got a killer to catch!"

"Right behind you."

It wasn't long before I'd discovered Emily and Carole's maiden name was Bertram. A further search showed that Carole Bertram married Michael McCloud twenty years ago. He was a self-employed mechanic who owned a chain of garages. His home address was registered with Companies House as 45 Innes Drive, Bootle.

Bingo!

I grabbed my keys and rushed from the apartment.

FORTY-SEVEN

The *Hollywood Smile Dental* practice on James Street was even more impressive than its counterpart.

"And how may I help you?" The receptionist, a twenty-something blonde woman with an equally fake smile as Amelia had, greeted us warmly.

I glanced at her name badge. "Hi, Kate. We'd like to speak with Damien Fawkes." I showed her my badge and waited while Bella did the same.

"Oh, sorry, lovely. Damien didn't come in today. Would I be able to help you instead?"

Disappointed, though not surprised, I smiled. "No, thanks. It's nothing that can't wait. Although I'd appreciate it if you didn't tell him we were here. If he gets in touch, that is."

"Oh, don't worry—I won't tell him a thing. Are you sure there's nothing else I can do for you?" She fluttered her eyelashes and pouted her over-filled glossy lips at me.

I smiled, taking advantage of her full attention. "Maybe. How well do you know Damien?"

She shook her head, a look of distaste on her face. "Not much, really. I mean, I've worked with him for almost two years, but he keeps himself to himself. All I can say is, I'm surprised you guys haven't been around to pick him up long before now."

"Really?" I glanced at Bella who was also hanging off the woman's every word. "Why do you say that?"

"Because he's creepy. Not just because he's different—I couldn't care less about that, but it's just the way he looks at me. He makes my skin crawl. I don't know how he's kept his job either—he's forever calling in sick."

"I see. Do you know if he has a partner?"

"A girlfriend, I think. Not that anyone here has met her, but he's mentioned her a few times. Liza or Lisa, I think she's called."

"Do they live together?" Bella asked.

She shook her head. "I wouldn't have a clue, sorry."

"Well, thanks for your help, and don't forget..." I put a finger to my lips.

"Mum's the word." She winked conspiratorially.

I followed Bella from the building.

"Did you notice her flirting with you?" she asked once we were far enough away.

"I did."

"Poor girl has no gaydar whatsoever."

"Come off it. You can't tell me you'd think I was gay if you saw me in the street. You didn't know till I told you."

"Au contraire, Mon Ami. I knew as soon as I first laid eyes on you."

"Liar."

"Okay then, maybe not, but I had you going there for a second."

"Rubbish. And anyway, I couldn't care less. I am who I am, and I make no apology for that."

"Good, I should hope not. But I do think you enjoy people flirting with you—men *and* women."

I grinned. "You're only jealous."

We climbed back into the car.

"Where to now?" Bella asked.

"The Marina. We need to see if Damien's home."

"Don't you think we need backup?"

"No. He won't be expecting us, so we should have the element of surprise with a bit of luck."

"Okay. If you're sure." She fastened her seatbelt, a frown on her face.

"You don't agree?"

She exhaled noisily. "To be honest with you, I've got no idea. All I know is, he's one sick individual and I really don't think we'd be smart to underestimate him."

"I can drop you off at the station if you'd prefer?"

"I didn't say that."

"Stop whining then."

I slammed the car into reverse and backed out of the parking spot. "Put the address into the GPS, please. The dock area is like a maze to me."

"Okay, but it's not far from here."

"If you know where you're going, you can give me directions."

The apartment blocks on the marina were roughly a five-minute walk from the dental practice.

"I wouldn't have thought a dental technician would make enough to fund a place like this," Bella said, taking in the stunning position with views across the water.

"Mummy and Daddy probably give him an allowance."

She nodded. "Ah, yeah. You must be right."

I glanced at the address. "He must live on the top floor. Apartment 12."

"Let's hope they have a working lift."

"These buildings have all mod cons. Not like the dilapidated council flats we were used to growing up."

We parked the car and headed for the entrance.

I rang the bell of an apartment situated on the first floor, and nobody answered. I tried another and a man's hoarse voice came over the intercom. "Who is it?"

"Detective Inspector Dylan Monroe. I need access to the building. Could you buzz me in please?"

"Sod off." The line went dead.

"Charming." I shook my head, then tried another apartment.

"Yes?" A woman's voice this time.

"Hello. I'm Detective Inspector Dylan Monroe. I need access to the building, could you buzz me in please?"

No response.

Just as I was thinking she'd also hung up, the door clicked open.

"Thank you," I called out, reaching for the door handle.

The large open entranceway was modern and painted in varying shades of purple, with bold artwork mounted on every wall.

I called for the lift and the door opened instantly.

We stepped inside and I hit the button for the 3rd floor. Moments later, we stepped out into a mirror image of the entrance hall below.

Apartment 12 was to the right and at the furthest end of the corridor.

I knocked on the door and noticed Bella's face. She wasn't coping very well, and I was worried that, with the reaction to the crime scene at Emily Leyland's, and recently giving birth, she'd come back to work too soon. "Stand back," I said.

Nobody answered.

I knocked again, harder this time.

"Can I help you?"

Startled, I spun around, searching for where the voice had come from. The neighbour's door was open a crack and a woman's face was barely visible.

"Oh, hello. I'm DI Monroe and my colleague DS Frost. We're looking for Damien. Have you seen him today?"

"Yes. He went out about thirty minutes ago. I told the cop on the phone you needed to come over sooner."

I scratched my head and glanced at Bella before returning my attention to the woman. "I don't understand. You've spoken to a police officer today?"

"Yes."

"About Damien?"

"Yes."

"Can you tell me what that was about?"

The woman opened the door fully and took a step towards us. "My friend, Liza. I've not seen her in days, and I think something's happened to her."

"I see. What makes you think that?"

"She was planning on leaving him. She told me. Then they had an awful fight, and I haven't seen her since."

"When was this?"

"A few nights ago. I've been going out of my mind with worry."

"Maybe she just left, like she'd told you she intended to do?" Bella suggested.

"I thought that too. But she's not answering her phone either. Something's wrong. I know it."

"Do you happen to know Liza's surname?" I asked.

"Roper."

"Thank you. Could she be at work?"

"She works at the Co-op on Dunstable Street. I went over there this morning, but her boss told me she's not been in for a few days and hasn't rung in sick either. That's why I called the police to report her missing. I didn't really want to get involved—he scares the bejesus out of me, but I couldn't just leave it."

I nodded. "You did the right thing. Sorry, what's your name?"

"Sandra. Sandra Jones."

"Thanks, Ms Jones. Now, do you know the number of the maintenance manager or anybody who might hold a set of keys for next door?"

"Yeah. Andy Lewis. Should I call him?"

I nodded. "If you don't mind. Tell him it's urgent."

On the other side of town, I drove past the address and then parked the car a little further along the road outside a row of shops.

I positioned my mirror so I could see the front of the property. I wouldn't be able to see anything happening inside the house from that distance, but I was certain nobody could arrive or leave without me knowing.

All I needed to do was wait.

FORTY-EIGHT

The property manager arrived at the same time as the uniformed officers. He was in his mid-thirties with ginger hair and covered in freckles.

"Don't you need a warrant before I open the door?" he asked.

I shook my head. "No. After speaking to the neighbour, we have reason to believe the occupant of the apartment may be hurt."

"So, I can open it?"

"Yes." I smiled and took a deep breath to control my bubbling annoyance at the idiot.

He unlocked the door and pushed it open.

Bella gagged instantly.

The stench was unmistakable.

"God, what is that smell?" Andy said.

"Wait!" I barked, making the man jump. "Don't go inside. We need to seal this place off."

"Eh?"

"This is now a crime scene."

The penny seemed to drop, and he backed away.

"Call it in," I said to Bella. "Then guard the door. I'm going inside."

Blackout curtains dressed the huge floor to ceiling windows leaving the apartment in total darkness. Not wanting to contaminate a potential crime scene, I reached for the light switch with my elbow. I pressed my other arm firmly to my nose.

Tentatively, I entered.

Although lavish, the apartment seemed excessively minimalistic. There was absolutely nothing out of place in the massive, open-plan room, which didn't fit in with the unmistakable stench of death.

There were three doors off the open-plan living area.

I checked the first room. It was totally empty – even the wide-open wardrobe had nothing inside.

The next door led to a large bathroom which was also empty. I checked inside the wall cupboard and found several everyday toiletry items stored.

The third door was up a couple of steps and as I approached it, I caught another whiff of the rank odour. Taking the steps one by one, I knew what I was going to find before I reached the top. Still, I braced myself before entering.

A huge super-king bed dominated the bulk of the space and appeared to be made at first glance, but once I'd stepped closer, I noticed a small lump underneath the sumptuous duvet.

I lifted the corner of the duvet, flicked it backwards, then I stepped away with my eyes closed. I needed to force myself to look, knowing exactly what I would see.

A small woman with dark curly hair lay on her back, staring up at the ceiling. She'd been there for days judging by the tinge to her skin and the lividity. And, although no expert, dark purple bruising on her neck told me she'd been strangled.

I quickly retraced my steps and left the apartment.

It was nice to be out of hospital, but Oliver longed to be at home in his room and in his own bed. Not that he wanted to offend his Aunt Carole by telling her any of that. But he intended to leave as soon as he got the okay from the police.

"You okay, love?" His aunt startled him standing in the doorway of the darkened living room.

"I'm fine. Do you want to watch TV? I can go into my room." His uncle Mike had given up his office on the ground floor and converted it to a bedroom for Oliver.

"No, don't be silly. If Mike wants to watch anything, we have a TV in our bedroom, so don't be worrying. Can I get you anything?"

"No, thanks."

"Maybe we need to have a chat about your mum's funeral. It's something we need to prepare for and make sure we're on the same page."

"Okay." He couldn't think of anything worse than planning his own mother's funeral, but he was her only child, and the responsibility fell squarely at his feet.

"I've got hundreds of photos of her from over the years, but maybe we need something more recent—what do you think?" She perched on the arm of the sofa.

"Whatever." He jumped to his feet. "I need to get some air." He headed for the back door.

Once he was outside, he filled his lungs and exhaled several times. Just as he got his breathing back into a regular pattern, the tears he'd been suppressing began to fall. Thoughts of browsing through photo albums showing his mum happy and smiling tore at his heart. *Why was I so mean to her? She was the only person who loved me unconditionally and, despite her faults, I loved her, too.*

"Can I get you anything?" Once again, Aunt Carole was at his side, like a stalker. She handed him his sunglasses.

"Thanks." He put them on and then looked up at her. "I just need a few minutes, if that's alright?"

"Of course, it's alright. Just remember what that detective said—don't venture too far from the house. You never know who's watching."

"I'll be in in a minute."

She nodded and re-entered the house.

He felt sorry for her. She'd lost her only sister, but he didn't have the emotional strength to deal with her grief as well as his own. At least she had her husband.

He missed his friends, especially Sam. He really didn't think he could be the killer, but he'd promised the detectives that he wouldn't contact them for now. But despite the fact his aunt was on his case constantly, he felt totally alone.

"Hey," his uncle Michael said, stepping outside. "Carole asked me to have a word."

"What about?"

"This guy that's out there. She's worried you might take off."

"And where does she think I'll go?"

He shrugged. "Don't ask me."

"I'm not intending to go anywhere. I can't even trust my closest friends yet, not until the detectives give me the nod."

"Do you think your friends could be the killers?"

"No. Not both of them. But the detectives think one of them may be."

"Which one?"

"That's the multi-million-pound question, isn't it?

"Why though? What would make someone kill people and try to set you up for it? It doesn't make sense."

Oliver removed the glasses and rubbed his eyes. "I've no idea, Uncle Mike."

"Sorry. I didn't mean to make you..."

"You didn't. It's okay."

His uncle wrung his hands together. "I've got to level with you, son. This has given me the creeps. Thinking someone might try to hurt my family under my own roof."

"Do you want me to leave?"

"God, no. I wasn't meaning that. I'm worried about you, too. You're family, aren't you? But I just wanted to put a plan together, just in case."

"What do you suggest?"

"So, what I was thinking is this—"

FORTY-NINE

Most of the afternoon was taken up at the apartment. I knew I needed to speak with Oliver, so, after dropping Bella off at home, I headed back to Carole's place.

Michael answered the door, holding a poker.

"Oh, Jesus. I thought you were about to brain me with that," I said.

"Sorry, detective. Come on in." He took a step backwards and allowed me to enter.

I followed him through to the living room, where Oliver and Carole were sitting side by side on the sofa flicking through photograph albums.

Carole slammed the album shut when she saw me and jumped to her feet.

"Don't get up," I said. "Sorry to disturb you both."

"Not at all. Take a seat," Carole said. "What happened out there just then?"

I grinned. "Michael almost coshed me over the head with a poker."

"Oh, gosh. We're all so wired, waiting for the killer to strike. Are you here to tell us you've caught him?"

I shook my head. "I wish that was the case, but no. I have some information for you, though."

"Do you know who killed my mum?"

"We think it was someone called Damien Fawkes."

Oliver gasped. "Damien?"

I nodded but couldn't fail to notice the furtive look shared between Carole and Michael. It was obvious they knew something. "Do you remember him, Olly?"

"Yeah, I knew him at Oakleaf. He was my friend."

"I see."

"Why would Damien want to hurt my mum? Or do any of this to me?"

I quickly glanced at Carole and Michael before continuing. "Can you tell me a bit about what happened back then?"

"Like I said, we were friends. But he was older than me, like, six years older. We were close, because he has a similar condition to me."

"Was there ever anything more between you?" I asked.

He shrugged. "I'm not gay."

"I never said you were, and even if you had feelings for him then, you were far too young to understand them."

"We had a connection, but, like I said, I think it was because we looked alike—we got each other, you know?"

"Yes. Although, apparently, your mother was of the opinion he took advantage of you. That he abused you."

Oliver shook his head – his usually white face flushed pink. "We had a moment which one of the other pupils saw. Nothing really happened. I'm not gay."

"Okay, Olly. Please don't upset yourself. But, just in case, let me tell you, there's nothing wrong with being gay. I'm gay myself and so

I do understand the fear of opening up. It's really nobody else's business but yours. My only concern is that he may have been grooming you and it was covered up. And now all this has stemmed from it."

"How? Because my mum said he'd abused me?"

"Yes. But that's not all. Your mum negotiated a monthly payment from both the school and Damien's parents."

I noticed another glance pass between Carole and Michael.

"The inheritance?"

I nodded. "Yes. She thought she was doing right by you."

Tears ran freely down his face. "He didn't hurt me. We were just friends."

"I understand. But whatever the reason, Damien, Liam, or whatever he calls himself, has it in for you now."

"Liam?" he stared at me, mouth open. "Liam?" he finally uttered.

"Oh, yes. Sorry. I should have told you first off that Liam is Damien Fawkes and he actually lives in Liverpool."

Oliver appeared totally deflated, beaten. He was clearly struggling to process the information.

I turned to Carole and Michael. Now was as good a time as any to ask. "Did either of you know about this arrangement?"

Michael nodded at Carole, giving her permission to reveal what she knew.

Carole inhaled deeply. "Emily made me swear not to tell a soul, but I've never kept secrets from Mike, so I told him."

"The whole thing made me feel uneasy," Michael said.

I nodded and turned back to Carole. "And what exactly did your sister tell you?"

"That some older lad had been fiddling with Oliver, but she didn't want to bring in the police because of the stress it would cause him."

"Come off it, Ca," Michael blurted. "Emily was friggin'

loaded. Face it, they offered her hush money, and she grabbed it with both hands."

"It wasn't like that, Mike, and you know it."

I silently observed their disagreement.

Michael was determined to reveal his thoughts on the matter. "I'm sorry to speak ill of your mum, son, but if she suspected something like that had gone on, she should have called the police."

Oliver wasn't saying a word either way.

"She only did it so Oliver could have a better life."

"Yeah, and conveniently it also meant she could sit on her arse all day, or trudge around shops in Liverpool One spending what she never should have accepted in the first place."

"You make it sound like she was only interested in the money, and not her son."

"I'm not saying she didn't love Oliver, but before all this happened, they were living in that hovel of a council house, and struggling to make ends meet, because your sister thought she was above working full time."

"Our Emily did work," Carole hissed.

"As a dinner lady, yeah, and how many hours a week was that?"

Carole crossed her arms. Her lips disappeared into a thin line. She was angry and no doubt her husband would pay for opening his mouth once I was out of the way.

"I don't care about any of that," Oliver suddenly piped up, breaking the tension slightly. "What does it matter anyway? Mum's dead and nothing will change that."

"You're right, son," Michael said. "And I'm sorry. I was very fond of your mum."

Carole put her arms around Oliver and rubbed his shoulders roughly. "Don't worry, we won't let him get anywhere near you."

"Yeah, I can vouch for that," I smiled. "Your uncle just

showed me how he wields that poker." I got to my feet. "Right, I need to get off, but call me if you have any concerns—about anything at all, you hear?"

Oliver nodded.

I signalled to Michael to follow me out. Once out of earshot, I said, "I didn't want to tell you in front of Oliver, but it appears Damien has gone AWOL. We found his girlfriend dead at his apartment this afternoon, and I'm worried Olly is his next target."

"Oh, my God—so you really think Damien is coming here?"

"Nothing is certain but if he does, call me right away. Keep all your doors locked and make sure Olly doesn't leave this house—"

"Don't worry, I will."

"Good. I'll make sure we post a patrol car outside as soon as possible."

FIFTY

"Are you okay?" Aunt Carole asked for what seemed like the hundredth time that day.

Oliver could still hear the detective chatting to his uncle in the hallway. He shrugged one shoulder, not really wanting to go into it with her. Not that he didn't think she'd understand, but because he honestly didn't know how he felt.

He'd often thought about Damien over the years. Wondered what he was doing and where he was living. He'd hoped the older boy had thought about him too. He'd never held any malice in his heart, just a feeling of love and loyalty. What had happened between them had felt natural at the time, and although he didn't think either of them was gay, there had been a connection. But he had only been twelve-years-old, and he understood how that must have looked to his mother. He had caused trouble for his friend without knowing it. That had clearly pushed him over the edge.

But why blame me?

Whatever had gone on had been between the adults and nothing to do with either of them. If anybody had asked him,

Oliver would've told them the truth – nothing untoward had gone on, not really. Unless you counted the one kiss and that had been innocent and not sleazy in any way.

Oliver had felt flutters in his belly. He thought back on that time as special and missed their friendship. He even hoped they'd eventually meet up again as adults.

"Penny for them?"

He shook his head, ignored his aunt's question, and went back to the photo album.

"Would you know what he looks like, if he comes here?"

"Like me."

"Oh, you mean..."

"Yeah. White hair, pale skin—a freak."

Uncle Mike returned, patting at his arms. "Jeez, it's getting ready to throw it down out there. I think we're in for a storm."

"That's all we bloody need," his aunt said.

His uncle threw a pile of menus on the coffee table. "I'm starving. What do you fancy to eat?"

"I don't mind, anything," Oliver said.

"Shall we order a curry?" his aunt suggested looking at Oliver.

"I'm easy."

"Good. Curry it is then. And don't forget to order lots of nibbly bits too. I could eat a horse." Her stomach growled as she spoke, and they all laughed.

By the time the food arrived, the rain was coming down in sheets. It felt more like a winter's day than the height of summer.

They ate at the dining table, sharing several different dishes between them.

Oliver had no appetite and spent the majority of the time pushing his food around the plate. Afterwards, he helped wash the dishes.

"I might just have an early night," he said to his aunt and

uncle who were preparing to settle down in front of the TV to watch a movie.

"Aw, you sure you don't want to join us?"

He shook his head. "I'm tired. I've hardly slept in days."

"Understandable, hun. Let's hope you get a good night's sleep." She jumped to her feet and gave him a kiss on the cheek.

"Hope so. Goodnight. Goodnight, Uncle Mike."

"Goodnight, buddy."

Oliver used the bathroom and as he crossed the hallway to his room, he could hear his aunt's sobs coming from the other end of the house. He had suspected she'd been putting on a brave face for him and her heart-breaking wails proved it.

He entered his room, flicked on the light switch and froze.

"Hello, again, Olly," Damien said.

FIFTY-ONE

Rush hour traffic in Bootle was a nightmare, so I stopped to have something to eat and then went back to the station. I had so much to do, and it wasn't as if I had anybody waiting for me at home like Bella did.

I was surprised to find Will was still hard at work. "Hey, boss. I was just about to call you. I've had the information back on Damien's phone, and I think I might have located him."

"Really?"

"Yeah. His phone has been static for several hours on a street in Bootle. But he could've left it in the car."

My blood ran ice cold. "Where abouts in Bootle?"

"On the corner of Buckland Street and Innes Drive."

"Fuck! He's found Oliver. Get an armed response unit out at once. I'm heading over there now—hopefully we're not too late."

I raced from the station and back to my car. Then I dialled Carole's number. She answered.

"Hi, Dylan." She sounded as though I'd just interrupted her crying.

"Carole. He's on your street. Stay inside the house and do not open the door to anyone except me—do you hear me? I'm on my way to you now."

"Oh, shit. Hang on."

"Mike here, Dylan. What's happening?"

"Damien's phone has pinged on your street. He knows Olly's there. I need you to make sure everywhere is locked up tight, and do not answer the door whatever you do. I'll be there soon."

"Roger that."

FIFTY-TWO

Oliver couldn't believe his eyes. His first instinct had been to run, but the blade Damien held up in front of him looked frightening. "You... you need to go. My aunt and uncle are just through there."

"Shut the fuck up and sit down," he snarled.

His aunt's mobile phone began ringing in the kitchen and he heard her answer it. "I'm serious, man. The police are on their way over."

"Liar. I saw that detective bloke leave earlier—he won't be back tonight. Now sit down."

The bedroom door suddenly flew open and banged into Oliver. It sent him careening forwards.

Damien grabbed Oliver, spun him around, and shoved the blade to his throat.

Crying out in terror, Oliver realised his aunt and uncle were both in the room.

Carole screamed.

"Hey, hey, calm down," his uncle said, holding his hands out as though trying to diffuse the situation. "The police are on their way. They know you're here, Damien. I suggest you scarper while you still can."

"And who the fuck are you to tell me what to do?"

Oliver could sense how unhinged his old friend was by his voice and the way the blade pushed deeper into the delicate skin of his neck. The expression on his aunt's face told him all he needed to know; he was close to death. But at that moment, he didn't care.

"Get off him!" his aunt screeched.

"Tell her to shut the fuck up or else you're gonna get it."

It was all too much for Oliver. The shouting and screaming, the lights, the situation. He took a deep breath and balled his fists tight. He dropped his arm and, with all the strength he could muster, hit Damien in the crotch as hard as he could.

Damien cried out and bent double, dropping his guard temporarily.

"Go!" Uncle Mike shouted, stepping in between him and Damien.

Oliver wasted no time, aware that his actions could have proved fatal for his uncle. He ran through the door and along the hallway and tried not to be distracted by what was happening in the room behind him – hoping his uncle had got the upper hand and was giving Damien what for.

I couldn't believe Oliver had bettered me. I almost threw up my balls.

When he ran from the room all hell broke loose. The dickhead uncle went for me, but he was fat and clumsy – no match for me. One swift motion rendered him helpless, pumping his life's blood all over the carpet.

The aunt screamed and fell to her knees, sobbing uncontrollably beside him as he was clutching at his throat, wheezing and spluttering.

She was next. I grabbed a fistful of hair and with one swipe with the knife, slashed her throat, deeper than I'd meant too – I almost decapitated her. But it had the desired effect and shut her up instantly.

Blood gushed out of the wound and pooled underneath her. I stood and watched as she died within seconds. It was a pity I wouldn't need to kill any more after tonight. Especially now that I was becoming so good at it.

But I didn't have time to admire my handiwork.

I needed to find Oliver.

Oliver had done what his Uncle Mike had told him to – they had equipped the secret space under the stairs with anything he could possibly need in the event of an attack.

He felt bad for deserting his aunt and uncle, but it was him Damien wanted, not them. So he figured the best way to protect them was to get out of there, and fast.

Holding his breath, he waited.

Terrified.

But with adrenaline coursing through his veins, he felt more alive than ever before.

Hearing his aunt's cries and then nothing, he prayed she would be okay. He couldn't bear for someone else to be hurt because of him.

When Uncle Mike had first told him of his plan, Oliver had questioned what would happen to them, but the older man had assured him they would be okay. Now he wasn't so sure they were.

"Ol-iv-er?" Damien called in a song-song voice that sounded

as though he was right next to the false panel. *Does he know where I am?* Surely that wasn't possible.

Footsteps going up the stairs confirmed he didn't.

Oliver wondered if there was any chance of him escaping, but he couldn't move – fused in place with fear.

"Come out, come out, Oliver," Damien called. "Whatever happened to the brave boy that's forever chanting, *I am lunatic— fear me?* Come and see your pathetic aunt and uncle bleeding like stuck pigs all over your bedroom carpet."

Oliver pressed his hands to his mouth to try to stop himself from sobbing. He couldn't allow the crazy bastard to find out where he was.

He turned on the torch his uncle had provided. Amongst the other items in there was a knife. When he'd seen it earlier, he'd wondered what on earth he'd expected him to do with that – now he knew.

Taking several deep breaths, he picked up the knife and bounced it off his palm, trying to get a feel for it in his hand.

FIFTY-THREE

The armed response team was already in situ by the time I arrived. Much to my dismay, I recognised DS Philip Lyons was in charge of the scene.

I filled them in on everything as quickly as I could.

"Make sure you keep well back this time, Monroe," Lyons said. "I'm not in the mood for fucking heroics."

I wanted more than anything to race down the path and kick my way inside, but after what happened with Layla, I knew I had to do everything by the book. "Whatever." I rolled my eyes at him and walked away, trying to calm my temper. There had never been any love lost between us since he'd testified against me at the inquiry.

I'd tried to call Carole several times, but it was just ringing out. The same with the land line. I tried once again, but nothing. Then I tried Oliver's number. I had a terrible feeling.

"He's inside," I said to Lyons when I returned.

He nodded. "Are you sure?"

"Damien's Audi has been located by an officer along the street. Plus, the occupants of the house knew I was on my way and were awaiting instructions, so they would answer if they could."

"Do you have Damien's number?" Lyons asked.

"Yes. Should I try it?"

"Worth a go."

I rang the number we had on record for Damien once everyone was in place, but nobody answered that either. I sent a text.

... We have the property surrounded. Come out with your hands up...

No response.

Eventually, Lyons produced a loudspeaker and barked the same line into it.

All the houses on the street suddenly lit up, people filling the windows and doors for a better look. All except for the house we were interested in.

"Come out, come out, Oliver." I was pretty sure he was still inside the house, as I'd removed the key from the back door when I entered. The front door was locked with the mortice and although the key was inside, it was still locked tight. But where was he?

I went through every room again, calling his name, carefully examining underneath, behind and inside of everything large enough to accommodate a gangly teenager, but I couldn't find him for the life of me.

My phone rang. It was a number I didn't recognise, so I ignored it.

"Olly? Come on out, buddy. I have so much to tell you."

The only sound I could hear was the thrumming of my heartbeat

"You're not mad at me, are you? Surely you know why I had to do it."

I waited a few seconds for him to answer, but nothing. "You know I'm gonna find you."

Anger bubbled inside me. I upended the coffee table with a roar, then struggled to control my breathing.

"She told everyone I was a nonce. You know the truth. I really liked you. In fact, I thought we had something special between us. But it was all about the money for you and your greedy whore of a mother."

I picked up a photo frame from the fireplace showing Oliver and Emily smiling. I smashed it to the floor and stamped on it.

"My parents never looked at me the same way again. Oh, they said and did all the right things, but I could see it in my dad's eyes – I disgusted him. He couldn't wait to send me away to Colorado to a friend of his who owned that shitty dental practice in the middle of nowhere."

I looked behind the door of the living room, suddenly certain that's where he was hiding, but I was wrong. I slammed the door shut and kicked it several times.

"That's where I trained to become a technician. I didn't tell anyone I'd come home. What was the point? But I couldn't believe my luck when your dental records were sent to me. Of all the dentists in all the world, you had to walk into mine." I said the last line using my best Humphrey Bogart impersonation.

I was clutching at straws, but I checked behind the sofa, running out of ideas.

"You should've seen your mum lying back on the bed, gagging for it. You'll be pleased to know I took my time. In fact, I sliced through her carotid artery with a precision I didn't know possible—it was beautiful. You would've been proud of me."

A text came through.

"Fuck!" I launched my phone across the room, and it smashed against the far wall. Then I made my way to the front window, taking care not to expose myself.

The street was swarming with armed police.

It was over.

I wouldn't mind as much if I'd been able to get Oliver. If I'd made him pay for everything. But he'd somehow got out – that much was obvious.

"Damien Fawkes, we have the property surrounded. Please come out with your hands up."

The nasally, tinny-sounding words reverberated throughout the entire house.

"Fuck-fuck-fuck!" I'd come so close to ruining Oliver's life.

I slumped onto the sofa and buried my head in my hands.

"Damien Fawkes, we have the property surrounded. Please come out with your hands up."

They said again. I had no chance of escape, and I didn't want to die. My only hope would be to do as they said.

Oliver stayed hidden under the stairs, trying to judge where Damien was in relation to him.

When he heard the police demanding Damien was to go outside, he knew he needed to act fast, or his opportunity would be gone forever.

Rain was teeming down, and it soaked me to my skin.

"Monroe, there's somebody at the door," Lyons shouted, his weapon raised.

With my heart hammering in my chest, I fixed my eyes on the door as it slowly opened.

Damien suddenly appeared; his arms raised high above his head.

Lyons ran along the path towards him, yelling something at Damien I couldn't decipher.

I followed close behind, although I knew Lyons would have something to say about it.

Another sudden movement caused a flurry of excitement. Something glinted in Damien's hand.

"He's got a knife!" one officer shouted.

Damien suddenly darted forwards towards Lyons, then all hell broke loose.

The armed officers flanking Lyons opened fire, riddling Damien's torso with bullets.

I could see the surprise on Damien's face as he looked down at his blood-soaked hoodie. Time seemed to stand still. Then he stumbled backwards and hit the ground with a thud, eyes wide open.

He was dead.

A river of bloody rain ran down the path towards my feet.

I jumped aside in total shock. The fact the killer had

appeared to go for one of our officers had been terrifying enough, but it was the blade sticking up through his chest that confused me more than anything. I couldn't comprehend what had happened.

That is, until Oliver stepped from the house with his hands raised.

FIFTY-FOUR

"Get on your knees and put your hands behind your back," Lyons ordered.

I watched the drama unfold, terrified the armed response unit would see his reluctance to obey their commands as means to shoot.

"Okay, okay," Oliver shouted, covering his hands with his ears. "Please don't shoot." He dropped to his knees.

"Hands behind your back, now." Lyons said once more.

Oliver closed his eyes and kept his hands pressed tight against his ears.

In panic mode, I rushed forward, determined to protect him. "Don't shoot," I roared. "It's the noise. He can't cope with the noise."

"Get back, Monroe," Lyons demanded.

There was nothing he could say that would make me move. "Listen to me, please." I looked over at Oliver, still kneeling. "He has hyper-sensitivity to noise and bright lights. Look at him for fuck's sake—he's scared, and not armed."

My words seemed to have registered with Lyons, but I was

under no illusion he would make a formal complaint about me to my superiors in due course. "Stand down, now, and get those flashing lights turned off."

"Thank you, thank you," I said.

Immediately all weapons were lowered, the lights stopped flashing, and a calm descended.

"It's okay, Olly, you can open your eyes now." He did so slowly, then looked right at me. Finally, he lowered his hands as I breathed a huge sigh of relief. "Do as you're told; they won't hurt you."

"He was gonna kill me, I swear it," Oliver said through tears. "He killed my aunt and uncle. I-I didn't wanna hurt anyone, it just happened."

I was terrified of what was to come. I know how it would look to the outside world.

"Hands behind your back, Oliver, I won't ask you again," Lyons called out, but this time in a gentler tone.

Oliver followed Lyons' command.

"Cuff him."

"Go easy with him. He's been to hell and back."

"You do your job, and I'll do mine," Lyons snapped.

Swarms of police officers and paramedics entered the property.

I watched as Oliver was bundled into the back of the waiting car. As it drove away, I followed close behind. I used the handsfree to call Janine and fill her in on what had just happened. Will had already warned her what was going down, and she had been awaiting my call.

"We're on our way back to the station now."

"Just to warn you, the press is still camped outside. They're gonna think all their Christmases have come at once."

"We stopped the killer—"

"Well, technically, Oliver did, but that's beside the point."

"What will happen to him, Janine?"

"With a good barrister, he'll walk."

"Do you think so?" I didn't dare get my hopes up, but it was obvious why he'd killed Damien.

"After what he's been through, if he claims temporary insanity, I'd be surprised if the CPS even pushed for a trial."

"I'm not so sure."

"Would it be in the public's best interest to vilify a young man for killing the person who butchered various women, including his mother, aunt, and uncle? And let's not forget, Fawkes was framing Oliver to take the fall for the murders."

"The kid deserves a break."

"I know it's easier said than done, but take a step back from this, Dylan. You've done your job, let everyone else do theirs now."

She'd echoed Lyon's sentiments almost word for word. Maybe they both had a point.

"I'm gonna try."

She chuckled. "Yeah, right."

Self-doubt crept in once more. "Maybe I'm not cut out for this job."

"Oh, here we go again," she muttered. "You put everything together and a vicious murderer is off the streets."

"Not just me, Janine, but the entire team."

"Fine, I'll pat them all on the back in the morning, but job well done regardless."

"You might not say that once DS Lyons has submitted his report."

"Oh, no, what have you done to upset him now?"

"Not that much."

She tutted. "Look, forget about it for now."

"He hates me and thinks I'm unprofessional."

"I've known Phil a long time, so don't worry, I'll square it with him."

"If you think I deserve a disciplinary hearing I'll take it, but for the record, I'd do it all again."

"Whatever you did or didn't do this time, Dylan, I'll pretend to slap you on the wrist, so it doesn't go on your record, then it's over and done with, okay?"

"Thank you."

"I'll see you when you get back to the station. Try not to upset anyone else along the way."

"Two minutes and I'll be there. I want to be with Oliver when he's booked in."

"So much for stepping back."

"After I sort this mess out, I'm gonna take a few weeks' leave, if that's okay with you?"

"You've certainly earned some time off."

"Yeah, I think a holiday somewhere tropical is just what the doctor ordered."

"With your man?"

"Hopefully." I wondered if taking a break with Steve would help iron out our problems, or even if he'd agree to go with me. It wouldn't hurt to ask, and perhaps this was the only way to see if we had a future together. "Right, pulling in now. I'll pop my head in once I've checked on Oliver."

Despite Janine's reassuring words, I still wasn't sure which way the axe would swing for Oliver.

Hearing his side of the story, the only side we'd ever hear, there was still a valid argument that he'd planned the attack on Damien. But I couldn't discount the fact he firmly believed his life was in danger.

It upset me closing the cell door on him, but I'd watch out for him as much as I could do.

I didn't want to go home and stare at the four walls so called in at Bella's. Thankfully, Penelope was out visiting a friend, so we could talk openly.

"He picked up a knife and stabbed him in the back, Dylan. That's premeditated, plain and simple."

"With mitigating circumstances, Bells."

"Yeah, I get it, but Fawkes was surrendering, and Oliver ran up behind him and shanked him."

"He was terrified and had just seen his aunt and uncle slaughtered." I was desperate for her to see it from my point of view. "Unless we're put in that situation, we can't know what we'd do."

"Diminished responsibility, maybe?"

"Janine reckons he'll walk."

"Do you think it's right if he does?"

"How would we react under those circumstances?"

"I don't know, mate, but thankfully, we're not gonna be his judge and jury if it goes to court."

"If there's any justice, he'll be left to live his life in peace now, though I have no idea how he'll ever come back from this."

"Oliver *isn't* your responsibility."

"I know but—"

"But nothing. Your job is to catch criminals, not to babysit those affected by crime."

"Tell me honestly, do you think he should go to jail?"

"The mother in me says no, that he's suffered enough, but another part of me questions why he went to such extreme lengths, and if pushed again, what would he truly be capable of?"

"He thought he was in danger. Isn't that enough of a reason?"

"Like I said, diminished responsibility, and for all I know, he could have been out of his mind at the time. In fact, he probably was. What do I know about anything these days?"

"I bet you're glad this case is over with."

"The less I have to think about it, the better."

"Yeah, I understand that, but I want you to promise you'll be honest with me."

"What about?"

"Just stuff..." I didn't feel the need to spell it out. "... if you need time off, or if you want to talk to a counsellor, whatever, I'm here for you."

"Cheers mate. I'll see how I feel."

"Okay." I heard the key in the lock.

"Yoo-hoo, it's only me," Penelope called out, obviously forgetting the sleeping children upstairs.

Bella rolled her eyes. "Lady muck is home."

I wasn't in the mood to deal with Penelope so decided to make a swift exit. "I'm gonna get out of your hair."

"You don't have to."

"I think I'll call Steve, see if he wants to meet up."

"About time," she replied.

I didn't want Steve turning up at my place, nor did I want to go to his. Thinking on my feet, I decided a neutral venue was the best option. In the end I chose a bar on Lime Street – I'd texted him to let him know to meet me at 10pm.

There was a lot to think about, but I wanted to be mature about our issues and make the first move.

I looked at my phone. 10:10pm. He was late, and for a moment, I wondered if he'd decided against it. I'd give him another few minutes and, if he still hadn't shown, I'd be outta there.

Bella had sent me a link to a *TikTok* video. I was watching it while trying to pass the time.

"Hey, stranger. Sorry I'm late. I couldn't find a parking space."

"Hey to you too." I placed my phone down on the table and looked up at him. There was that familiar fluttering in my stomach. "Sit down. I've already got you a pint."

He slid into the seat opposite me. "Thanks." He took a sip of his beer, then wiped his mouth with the back of his hand. "I've had a heck of a day."

"How come?"

"Work stuff—a junior ballsed up on one of our big accounts, so it came down to me to fix it."

"That doesn't sound good."

"It was a nightmare to sort, but it's done now."

"Thank God."

"How's things with you?" he asked.

"Work is manic, but you'll probably have seen the news."

"I heard it on the radio on the drive over. That's some scary shit to have to deal with."

"My back's been up against the wall lately., Even now the killer is dead, I don't feel settled."

"Me being a tit doesn't help, right?"

"You said it."

We both laughed.

"I'm sorry, Dylan."

"So am I."

"I really want to sort things out with you, but I'm not gonna lie and say you working at Dorothy's makes me happy, because it doesn't."

"It's just a hobby. And before you say anything else, Roy is just a good friend."

"From your point of view, maybe."

I shook my head, not wanting to get into this again. "Trust me, Roy is not interested in me at all sexually."

"So he tells you."

"Steve, I'm not a Detective Inspector because I'm stupid. I can see people's motives, but where he's concerned, it's simply a friendship, and a good one."

"I'm still wary of him."

"That's fine, but if you're hinting at me cutting Roy or anyone else out of my life, it's never going to happen."

"I didn't ask you to do that, did I?"

"Good, because no matter how much I love you, if you ever force me to choose, you'll lose every time."

"Charming." He picked up the glass and drained half the pint in seconds.

"Take it any way you like, Steve, but my friends are important and if you care for me—"

"I don't just care for you, Dylan, I love you."

"Then don't ask me to pick sides. Respect my choices. Remember that you're the one I want to be with, and things will be fine."

"I've never felt this way about another guy before."

His honesty was refreshing, and I thought perhaps with that said, he might feel more secure in our relationship. "You're the only person I've ever considered a future with, but while we're being honest, this is your very last chance—any more outbursts and we're done." I didn't have to mention him spitting in my face because his expression revealed to me how he felt about it.

"I'm ashamed of what I did." He sheepishly looked down at his bruised knuckles.

"Don't be. Just learn a lesson and make sure it never happens again."

"It won't, ever."

"Things will settle down, but no matter who I'm friends with, or what my hobbies are, I'm never going to betray you because you're the man I want to be with." I wanted to draw a line under the past and move forward.

"Are you sure?"

"Positive."

"I think I can live with that."

"Good, now we've got that out of the way, what do you think about us jetting off into the sunshine for a few weeks?"

"I like the sound of that."

FIFTY-FIVE

The last few weeks had been a whirlwind both personally and professionally.

While Steve and I were almost back on track, I still had lingering doubts. But unless I was fully committed to trying again, we didn't stand a chance. So, we did what we'd spoken about and booked two weeks in Phuket, just off the coast of Thailand. We were due to leave at the end of September.

I still had a list of stuff I needed to buy for the trip, but as I was buried under a mass of paperwork I'd put off for too long, I had no time or inclination to nip out to the shops. I was just wondering if it would be cheeky to offload my list onto my mum and ask her to pick it all up for me when I was interrupted.

"Do you fancy coming for a bite to eat at the pub, boss?" Pete asked.

"I wish I could, but this mess needs to be sorted, or Janine will boil my arse for breakfast."

"Anything I can help with?"

"No, but thanks anyway."

"Well, if you change your mind, we're not going until four."

"Okay, mate." He seemed to linger a little longer than usual and obviously had something to say. "What's up?"

"I just wanted to ask if you'd heard anything from Bella?"

"Not too much." I'd spoken to Bella daily since she'd gone back on leave, but she didn't want her private business airing at work. The team were an understanding lot and would know to an extent what she was going through, and they wouldn't push her by calling or dropping in uninvited. "But she's doing as well as can be expected."

"Tell her we're all thinking about her."

"Will do." I smiled as he walked away, feeling a little helpless. Bella still hadn't got over finding Emily Leyland's body, which had led to a decline in her mental health. On the advice of her doctor, and gentle persuasion from me, she'd decided to take the rest of her maternity leave. It was easier to arrange than to sign her off on the sick, and I hoped the time away as well as counselling would help her come to terms with what she'd seen that day.

Normally, I'd be concerned how she'd manage at home, but thankfully, the Army gave her husband, Simon, compassionate leave and, for the moment, he'd sent Penelope packing and was taking care of her and the kids.

My stomach rumbled. Pete had mentioned food. I was starving, but preferred to stay inside, rather than deal with the continued onslaught from the press camped outside the station. They had been relentless in their pursuit of me since Damien's death and Oliver's arrest. Speaking to them was the last thing I'd be inclined to do, but it hadn't stopped them from trying.

Whenever I stepped outside, cameras flashed in my face. I'd become some sort of poster boy for the police, an unwilling celebrity uncomfortable at being hounded simply for doing my job.

The only positive thing about it was that I knew it would

rankle Arjun Sharma. He gladly paraded himself in front of the TV cameras and salivating members of the press, complimenting the team as a whole, but never referring to me specifically. It seemed no matter what I did, my card was marked where he was concerned. Not that I'd lose any sleep over it.

Anita had slotted into the team well, but the suspicious side of me still erred on the side of caution where she was concerned. I wasn't sure I was being entirely fair, but I'd been burned by her grandfather too many times.

"Right," I said to myself, intending to get stuck back into the mountain of paperwork littering my desk. "Move yourself, Dylan..." But it wasn't to be.

Janine popped her head around the door. "Dylan, my office."

"Two minutes, please." I moved a stack of papers into the pending pile, then walked to her office. I took my usual seat. "What can I do for you?"

"I had a call from the CPS about half an hour ago and they've decided not to pursue charges against Oliver Leyland."

"You're kidding me?"

"No. He is a very lucky boy."

It wasn't the news I was expecting, but it was welcome, nonetheless. "I wouldn't say Olly has ever been lucky in his life, but thank God somebody had sense and saw it for what it was."

"I told you, didn't I?"

"Does he know yet?"

"I imagine Fiona McCall will contact him to relay the news."

It was a weight off my mind. "I wonder if public opinion swayed their decision?"

"You know how it goes when the press latch onto what they see as a lost cause. And we all know the British public love nothing more than a sob story."

"You don't sound too happy about the decision."

"Makes no difference to me, Dylan. The kid did what he did, and something a lot of us might have done in that same situation."

"He really believed his life was in danger."

"If Fawkes had his way, Oliver would have been gutted like a fish. The public won't care, they'll see it for what it is too, a cold-blooded killer is off the streets, and the taxpayer won't have to foot the bill."

"What did Sharma have to say?"

"I've fielded his calls all morning to be honest. I rang upstairs to my boss about the CPS's decision. Let him deal with Sharma."

"He won't be happy with that."

"Right now, I really don't care. The case is closed, and I need a large G&T."

"Do you mind if I tell the team?"

"No, go and celebrate."

I took a deep breath and pushed the doors to the incident room open. Aside from Bella, the entire team was present. "If I can have your attention for a moment..."

"What is it, boss?" Joanna asked, looking worried.

"The CPS aren't pursuing charges against Oliver Leyland."

A cheer rang out, and while it might appear we were celebrating somebody's death, we weren't, more the liberty of an innocent. Damien's actions had led to his own demise and, right or wrong, some form of justice was served.

"That's fantastic," Will said, grabbing his coat from the back of his chair. "Shall we all go to the pub now?"

"Common sense prevails," Pete added.

"Bloody brilliant news, boss." Joanna clapped me on the back as the rest of the team followed Will out of the door.

I stood back for a moment, needing time to think.

The last time I'd seen Oliver, I'd given him my mobile number and although I didn't want to invade his life, I felt a phone call after today's news was in order.

I decided to abandon my paperwork and followed the rest of the team to the pub for a quick drink.

Afterwards, I got back to my car and, before heading to Bella's, I dialled Oliver's number.

"Hello?"

"Hey, buddy, how are you?"

"Good."

"Are you sure? You don't sound it." In actual fact, he sounded like a lost soul, but I omitted to say that.

He sighed. "I'm sure."

"I was only calling because I've just heard the fantastic news and wanted to know how you were feeling. You *have* heard their decision, haven't you?"

"Yes. I've just got off the phone from Fiona."

"It must be such a relief. I know it is for me. We can never tell how these things will go. It would've been awful if they'd prosecuted you on top of everything you've been through. The newspapers would've had a field day."

"Yeah, don't talk to me about the newspapers."

"Why? Are they being a nuisance?"

"Someone called Martine won't stop calling me practically begging for an interview."

"Yeah. She's been hounding me, too."

"I told her to fuck off when she last called."

"Serves her right. I can't stand it when the press gets their claws into a story. But in this instance, it might not be a bad idea to get your version of events out there."

"Is that because people online are saying I got away with murder?"

"There are only a few keyboard warriors saying that."

"I'm trying not to read any of it, but—"

"People online have nothing better to do and will have you tried, convicted and sentenced to death in the *Facebook* court as soon as look at you. But they don't count. Most people know what you went through and your state of mind at that time."

"Yeah. And it wasn't as if Damien was an innocent victim. He killed all those women, not to mention my aunt and uncle. Plus, he would've knifed me if he'd realised I was hiding behind that false wall panel."

"I wouldn't worry about any of it now, Olly. Most of the papers are hailing you as a hero and this time next week, they'll have moved onto something else. So, now it's all over do you have any plans?"

"Not really. Sam has invited me to dinner tonight, to meet his wife and kids."

"That's nice. You need your friends around you right now."

"He's the only friend I have. And I've got no family left—unless you count my waste-of-space father who has been sniffing around since the papers let it slip I'd inherited a wedge of money. It doesn't take a rocket scientist to work out what he wants, and it's not me."

"Well, I'd be honoured if you would consider me a friend too. If you need anything, please don't hesitate to get in touch."

"Thanks. It means a lot."

FIFTY-SIX

With his chin resting on folded hands, Roy fixed his gaze upon me. It always made me nervous when he looked at me like that. It felt as though he was peering into my soul. "Something's up, Avaline, spill."

"There's nothing to tell, really. I'm just a little tired."

"You can't fool me."

"Honestly, it's just work stuff, isn't it, Bells?" Roy wasn't overly keen on hearing about crime scenes, so I hoped he would take my word for it and talk about himself instead.

Bella pottered around in the background, pulling plates from the cupboard and cutlery from the drawers before setting them down on the table. "Whatever you say."

"I'm not falling for that old chestnut. Fess up, wench," Roy demanded.

"You're not gonna give up, are you?"

"Not likely, so you might as well get whatever it is off your chest. Is it that man of yours?"

"No, not really, although I've had a few problems with him recently."

"What sort of problems?"

"He's jealous," Bella jumped in.

"Bloody hell, Bells, you couldn't wait to spit that out…" I'd barely had a chance to speak when Roy interrupted me.

"Oooh, sod that malarkey." He drummed his fingers on the kitchen table. "Walk away, Saddlebags, walk a-way."

"Hang on, Roy," Bella protested. "You haven't heard the whole story yet."

He held both hands up. "When jealousy is involved, I don't need to."

"He said he's sorry."

"They always are, Saddlebags, but if you want my advice, bin him, and fast."

"Shut up, Roy," Bella demanded. "It's not as easy as that."

"Is he hitting you?"

I hadn't anticipated anybody asking, but Roy wasn't the type to shy away from the harsh realities of dysfunctional relationships. "God, no, whatever gave you that impression?"

"Just wondered." He swept his eyes over me, obviously looking for signs of bruising.

"He wouldn't ever raise his hand to me." If I'd revealed he'd spat in my face, there would be a negative shift in both their moods, and now Steve and I were back on track, I didn't want to cause any further issues.

"Good, 'cos I'd wallop the lanky streak of piss with my best knock-off Gucci handbag." Roy pursed his lips together.

The mental image of Roy swinging any handbag at Steve tickled me.

"He's lovely, really." Bella placed containers of food down in front of us.

"They all are until they get their feet under the table." He pulled a lid off one container of Thai Green Curry. Screwing up his face, he delivered his verdict. "Ooft, smells like a dirty nappy that—not for me, thanks."

"Do you have to?" Bella pulled a face while I laughed.

He ignored her protests. "So, what's he jealous of?"

"You," I replied, though I hadn't meant to be so blunt in my delivery.

"Me?" he bellowed, then remembered the two sleeping cherubs upstairs. He lowered his voice and spoke. "What's there to be jealous about?"

"He thinks you and Dylan are playing doctors and nurses." Bella could barely keep a straight face.

"Don't be so dis-gusssting," he replied, stretching the last word for effect.

"Actually, no he didn't say that," I added, not wanting Steve slammed for something inaccurate.

"It's what he thinks though—that you and Roy are playing dress up and the occasional session of ring raider." She couldn't keep a straight face.

"You are vile, Annabella Frost," I added.

By his expression, Roy seemed to agree. "The very thought of Avaline's willy anywhere near my delicate flower makes me ill."

"Oh, cheers," I exclaimed as Bella tittered. "Am I that bad?"

"No, not at all, but you're not my type—I like my men big and butch."

"Who am I, Dame Edna Everage?"

"You wish you had half her talent. But no, you're far too pretty and particular for me, Saddlebags. I like a bit of meat on my man's bones and somebody that will give me a good rogering behind a skip, wipe his knob on the hem of my frock, then bugger off while I finish my kebab."

Bella squealed with delight.

"So classy," I replied, sounding every bit as sarcastic as I'd meant to.

"But you'll make somebody a fine wife, I'm sure of that."

"Husband," I corrected.

"Whatever," he replied, lifting the lid off the Chicken Kung Po, leaning in and inhaling the spicy aroma wafting up from the Chinese dish. "Now, this is more like it. Pile it on, Bells."

"Do you want boiled rice?"

"Just layer it on," he barked.

"Like he does with his makeup, Bells."

Roy was quick off the mark. "Shut your pie hole, Avaline."

Bella loaded his plate, then took a seat.

We chatted as we tucked into the moreish dishes and ate far too much, but the night wasn't over.

"I'm stuffed." I rubbed my stomach, trying not to belch.

Bella stood up. "Come on, let's sit in the living room. It's comfier there."

"I'm not getting hammered," Roy informed us, scooping up the bottle of red wine and a glass from the table.

"Yeah, right," Bella joked. "That'll be a first."

I took my seat nearest to the French doors next to Bella. Roy sat on the sofa opposite.

"So, what's kept you so busy lately?" I asked Roy.

"Work is flying in. I can barely keep up with the demand."

"That's good, isn't it?" Bella asked.

"Oh, yes, doll, but it means pulling all-nighters sewing new outfits—I can't be seen in the same thing too often, you know what the gays are like"

"I'm really pleased for you, mate." I was telling the truth, and there wasn't an ounce of jealousy inside me.

Roy swung his legs up onto the sofa. "Actually, I've got a gig tomorrow night with Fanny Zitchin and Yoko Oh-No."

Choking on my drink while laughing caused my eyes to stream with tears. I almost hacked up my lungs, coughing so much. "With who?" I spluttered.

Bella doubled over in fits of laughter next to me. "Oh, God, I'm gonna wet myself," she squawked.

"You heard, Avaline, and I don't know what you find so funny, Bella."

I tried to keep a straight face while Bella continued to chuckle next to me. "You're doing an act with two other drag queens, and you didn't ask me?" I feigned offence, but there was no way I'd have agreed to do it, anyway. "I'm hurt."

"You'll get over it, but yeah, I've signed up as part of a Bananarama tribute act at the Hokey Cokey Bar just off Duke Street."

I watched as Bella chugged down a full glass of wine. I'd worry about how much she was drinking another time, but right then I was thankful he hadn't bothered to ask me. "I've got to see that."

"Me too. I love their songs," she added.

"It's not the real Bananarama, Bella."

"I know that, Roy, but—"

"It's gonna be a great night though," he replied.

"Yeah, sounds like it," I agreed. "Eh, Bells, maybe Simon would babysit, and we can go and witness the birth of Liverpool's newest girl group?" I was joking, of course. "Atomic Mutton is kinda catchy, don't you think?"

"Isn't he joining us, by the way?"

"No, he wants to binge watch The Walking Dead, so he can stay up there."

"Ask him then, if he'll mind the kids while I take you out on the town."

"I will do. It should be a good night."

We laughed.

It was clear Roy wasn't amused. He pointed at us, then

wagged his finger. "I don't want to see either of you down there, you'll put me off, capiche?"

"Which one are you, if you don't mind me asking?" I didn't really know or care who they were, anyway. There were three of them and that's all I knew.

"Does that matter?"

"Well, not really. I was just curious."

"That gig is paying a fair bit of wedge and if all goes well, it might become a regular thing. I could certainly do with the cash 'cos I've spent the budget of a small African nation on crystals to sew onto my new frock— it's a bit plain Jane, so I've got to zhuzh it up a bit."

Now Bella had stopped laughing, she chimed in. "Eh, Roy, what was that song of theirs used in the advert?"

"Venus." There wasn't time for him to take a breath. "It was always on TV just before the six-o'clock news."

"Those adverts always are."

"Revolting, darling. Every single time I sat down for dinner —" He screwed his face up. "For a smoother vagina..." Suddenly, his voice dropped to a sultry whisper. "... why not try the new Venus formula. Out now," he purred. "Put me right off my liver and onions."

I was roaring with laughter at his attempt at a voiceover and quite disturbed there was actually an advert promoting products for a smoother fanny. "Don't exaggerate, Roy."

"I'm not. Don't you remember it?"

"No," I replied. "And I'm quite happy about that."

"I do, and Roy is right, it was something to do with fannies," Bella said, tittering. "Wasn't keen on the advert, but what a tune."

"They were the best girl-band ever!" Roy decreed. "I had to take a week off work when Siobhan left and joined Shakespears Sister."

"Gosh, the shock must have been overwhelming." With a

straight face, I teased him. "How did you ever get over such a tragedy?"

He turned and shot me his most withering stare. "Piss off, Saddlebags."

"I mean it. What a terrible shock." My tongue was planted firmly in my cheek.

"I was a mess, and don't get me started on the time Geri Halliwell left the Spice Girls." His eyes glazed over. He pulled out a handkerchief from his pocket and dabbed at his eyes. "I even rang that helpline number—"

"I've heard it all now," I muttered.

"I just couldn't believe Ginger would up and leave the other girls like that."

"Oh, God." I hoped he wasn't about to burst into tears.

"Ah, that's it!" Bella interrupted. "Goddess in a sequined frock..." she sing-songed out of tune. "... wasn't that how it went?"

Roy's eyebrows almost met his receding hairline. "You know damn well they're the wrong lyrics, smart arse."

"Oooh, sorry," she snipped.

Their banter always amused me. "Can't say it's one I know."

"That's because we've already established that you're a heathen, Saddlebags."

My tastes in music were a little more varied: Steps, Kylie and Madonna were definitely not for me even though I liked the odd song or two. I was more the Coldplay or Ed Sheeran type. "Give us a little taster," I asked, silently hoping he would refuse.

"Bugger off."

"Go on, please, Roy," Bella was speaking in a cutesy, baby-ish voice. "Sing a few bars for us."

"Every Showgirl needs a night off from the spotlight, so forget it." He poured the last of the red wine into his glass, then drained the contents.

"Booooooo," Bella crowed.

"Shut your face and get me another bottle."

"Your wish is my command." She jumped up, bowed in his direction, and raced into the kitchen.

Between us, we polished off two more bottles of wine and, before long, the conversation turned back to work.

"So, come on, I need to know why you're back on maternity leave, Bells," Roy said.

Bella took a deep gulp of wine before eyeballing me.

I cleared my throat. "She just wasn't ready. I should never have agreed to her coming back so early."

"The case you were working on was pretty terrible. I applaud that young man for his bravery—knowing it could've backfired on him. When will he hear if he's going to do time?"

"We got confirmation today he won't be prosecuted."

"Oh, thank God for that. I said my prayers for him."

"You don't pray," I laughed.

"I do. I often have a good old one-sided natter to the powers that be when I feel it's needed. That poor little boy broke my heart when I saw him on the news. What he's had to contend with all his life doesn't bear thinking about."

"Yes. He's a pleasant lad really. But I don't know how he'll come through this unscathed. I spoke to him today and he sounded so down." My earlier conversation with Oliver had bothered me and I intended to call him again tomorrow.

"It's so sad, I can't imagine how he feels," Bella said, her eyes brimming with tears. "I just want to bring him home here and mother him."

Shaking my head, I rolled my eyes at her. "I can imagine you working in a dog's home, you'd be adopting every stray."

"You can't tell me you don't feel for him." She wiped her eyes roughly.

"Of course I do, but I try to remain desensitised to it.

Granted, it sometimes doesn't work, but we can't afford to be soft in the line of duty."

"Maybe I'm not cut out for this." Bella necked the contents of her glass before reaching for another bottle.

This statement had been something I'd feared and yet I'd been expecting. "You'll be fine once you've rested, properly. Having a baby leaves you vulnerable and hormonal. You'll be back kicking our arses before too long, mark my words."

"We'll see."

Soon afterwards, I ordered a taxi and dropped Roy off on my way. I'd left my car at home, knowing two drinks wouldn't cut it tonight.

"You think she'll be alright?" Roy asked as we approached his building.

"I hope so."

"That poor boy could break the heart of the toughest cop, I bet. I mean, he's had his mother butchered and then his aunt and uncle—how would you get over something like that?"

I shrugged. Something he'd said niggled at me, although I was too drunk to work out what it was.

The car pulled up and Roy jumped out. "Thanks for the lift, Avaline. I've had a great night, as always."

"Me too," I said, kissing his cheek. Spending time with friends had been just the thing I'd needed to lift myself out of my funk. And, although I still had several professional and personal issues plaguing me, I was in no doubt I'd work through them with time.

FIFTY-SEVEN

Once again, I had a disturbed sleep. Something about Oliver had been niggling me all night, though I couldn't put my finger on what.

A little after 9am, I rang his number, and it went straight to voicemail. I tried several more times, before jumping in my car and heading over there – no doubt still over the limit.

After I banged on the front door, I waited, but there was no answer.

"*He* is in there." Mr Wright called over from the end of his driveway.

"Thanks."

He crossed the street and stood at the gatepost. "Yeah, he came home last night after dark, and I haven't seen him leaving today. Not that I blame him. If I were him, I wouldn't dare show my face to the general public, not after stabbing that poor lad in the back."

I exhaled. "Thank you, Mr Wright." I didn't want to get into a debate with him.

"How you lot could allow a killer to walk the streets is beyond me." The elderly man was obviously trying to provoke a reaction, but he'd be disappointed. "I mean, how are we supposed to feel safe with him living here?"

"Oliver is not a danger to you or anyone."

"Come off it, you only let him go 'cos he's a freak. I won't be convinced otherwise."

I wanted to smack him in the mouth and really give him something to complain about. "If you wouldn't mind, I'm busy and have little time to listen to your assumptions."

"It's a bit more than that, detective. The lad is a nutcase and shoving a knife in the back of a defenceless man proves it in my eyes." He stepped onto the path and took several strides towards me.

"You know nothing."

"Excuse me."

"Mr Wright, I am on official police business and unless you want to be arrested for obstruction, I suggest you return to your own property and keep your nose out."

"I'll be complaining about you," he huffed, charging back across the road.

"Feel free." I turned my back on him and knocked again. "Oliver, it's DI Dylan Monroe. Open the door."

Once again, I walked around the back of the property and found the patio door unlocked. I slid it open and poked my head inside. "Oliver? I'm coming in."

Remembering Emily, a feeling of dread descended upon me and almost rendered me useless. But I forged on.

Upstairs, I saw an envelope with a message written on the front pinned to the bathroom door. It was addressed to me.

TO DYLAN.
THE DOOR IS LOCKED.
FOR YOUR OWN SAKE

PLEASE DON'T COME IN.
CALL AN AMBULANCE.
I'M SORRY!

Through tears, I pulled the envelope from the door and stared at it, struggling to read Oliver's scrawl, only picking out the odd word in my panic. I could hear the dripping of a tap. I dropped the envelope and braced myself before shouldering the door.

I was too late.

Oliver lay submerged under the water of the blood-filled bath; his jaw was slack, and his milky eyes stared up at the ceiling.

Once I'd called the station, I returned to the landing, picked up the envelope and, with trembling fingers, opened it and pulled out the note.

Why hadn't I listened to my instincts?

To Dylan,
I hope you're the one who finds me.
I really like you and was made up when you called me your friend.
You were kind to me, so I need to tell you the truth.
I hope you can understand how it happened.
Mum was always on my back about stuff and was constantly
shouting at me, even though she knew I couldn't stand the noise.
That night, she was worse than she'd ever been because she'd been
out drinking with my Aunt Carole.
We had a massive row, and she put the heel of her shoe through my
PlayStation. I just lost it and lashed out.
I didn't kill her. I swear to you. But she banged her head and I

*think that was the reason she couldn't fight Damien off.
I loved her and can't live with what I've done.
I'm so sorry.
Please don't hate me.
Olly*

Seeing his body, and knowing there was nothing I could do, left me distraught.

My emotions were all over the place. Oliver had attacked Emily, after all! Why hadn't we considered that?

She must've been lying on her bed when we came to arrest Oliver that first night.

Why hadn't we searched the house?

I didn't know why I felt so bad. We'd done everything by the book. But, by all accounts, that poor woman had lain there, incapacitated for God only knows how long. In the letter, Oliver said she'd had a head injury – not a fucking stiletto heel smashed through her skull. Had he been capable of doing that to his own mother?

Or had Damien discovered Emily unconscious and used the shoe as another way to frame Oliver? He didn't know Oliver had been arrested at that point. And the blood spatter from the wounds we know Damien had inflicted proved she was still alive whilst Oliver was in custody.

What a mess.

I couldn't get my head around it. At first, we'd been convinced Oliver was the killer – but then we all believed he wasn't. Now, with this half-arsed confession, maybe he was the killer after all. The whole thing was a tragic farce, and one I didn't relish telling Janine about, never mind the shit-storm that would come our way once the media got involved.

I slid the letter into my pocket, not ready to share it with anybody yet. If ever.

EPILOGUE

Steve and I had planned a day at Chester Racecourse. I'd been looking forward to it for over a week and, dressed in my finest suit, I walked down the stairs, noticing the postman had been.

I swept the letter off the floor, turned it over, and read the sender's address.

"I don't believe it." I stepped into the kitchen, still staring at the envelope, filled with a mix of fear and dread. It wasn't how I thought I'd feel – after all, I'd tried countless occasions to get her to agree to see me and met a brick wall every single time.

"What is it?"

I tore open the envelope and pulled out the letter and scanned the contents. "Layla has agreed to see me." I wondered what had changed her mind, but I wasn't dealing with the most logical or level-headed of women, so I decided not to dwell on it too much.

"When?"

"Next Monday."

"Are you gonna go?"

"I have to."

"No, Dylan, you don't."

Would this be the catalyst to another argument? I hoped not, today of all days, but I needed to stand my ground. "Don't you see? Only Layla can give me the peace of mind I need to move forward."

"She's locked up for a reason," he replied. "Please don't let this obsession with her be the start of your own journey into madness."

"It won't be."

"Are you sure?"

"Once I've seen her, that's that."

"And if she wants to see you again?"

"It took me long enough to get this visit." With a trembling hand, I held the letter up. "Something tells me this will be my only chance."

"You don't know that."

Regardless of Layla's state of mind, I still believe she calculated her every move. There was a reason she'd requested to see me, and I doubted it was for a simple catch up. "I do."

"You're scared to face her, aren't you?"

"A little."

"For what reason?"

"She was my friend, my partner, and now she's locked up indefinitely. A part of me feels responsible for that."

"You didn't stand over her shoulder while she massacred those girls."

We'd had this argument more times than I cared to remember and now the opportunity was there, I'd grab it with both hands, no matter the consequences. "I know that."

"Will you tell Bella?"

"No way."

"Can I ask why?"

"You know why."

"In case she tries to talk you out of it?"

"Nothing she says would convince me not to see this through. But it'll only cause friction between us, and she has enough going on right now."

"Can *I* say anything that would convince you to change your mind?"

"I love you, Steve, but I'd much prefer you supported me on this. Perhaps you could drive down to Rampton and we could do something after the visit."

"I love you too, Dylan, but I won't aid you in this, this…" He seemed to be lost for words. "…no, I'm sorry, but you're on your own with this one."

"That's fine, but I hope it won't cause a rift between us."

"If you believe you're making the right decision, I'll be waiting here when you get back, but I don't wanna know anything about it, okay?"

"Agreed." Perhaps keeping it to myself would be the better choice. Though I should heed Lauren's advice and tell Janine.

"Right, are you ready to place some bets on the horses?"

"Yep."

The two and a half-hour journey from Liverpool to Nottingham left me with too much time to dwell on the horrors of the past few weeks and despite blasting the new Adele album for the entire journey, I was a nervous wreck when I turned into the car park.

Imagining Layla waiting for me behind thickened glass like Hannibal Lecter in Silence of the Lambs was my overactive mind trying to process a meeting I'd yearned for, but now that it was here, left me shaken and unsure of what I'd face.

Rampton Hospital wasn't what I expected at all, and while there were bars on every window, it was the mystery it held from within the high walls and its uncompromising security that occupied my mind.

Though I was an accredited visitor, I was still obliged to report to reception and present my driving licence as identification and proof of address. My position within Merseyside Police meant little because this was a social visit, and one I couldn't have attended without Layla first agreeing and applying for. Receiving the form to complete and return was the start of what Steve worried would be my journey into madness, but it was the only way I could see of leaving a painful part of my past behind. They took my photograph and biometric fingerprint and searched me before I entered through the security doors. I'd left all of my personal items, including my mobile phone, in the car. I only had my car keys and approved ID with me, which they took to be held in a safe place until my visit was over with.

The Visitors' Centre was touted as a home-from-home style daytime facility, enabling visiting friends or relatives to have a relaxing base. In actuality, it was a four bedroomed house five minutes' walk away from the main hospital. Stepping inside, I wasn't sure if it provided a safe enough environment, especially for the visitors of patients with Layla's complex issues.

Regardless, I took my seat at the table in a room that could be in any household up and down the country and waited.

"Well, well, well…"

Hearing her familiar voice pulled me from a world of regret and wishing I'd done things differently. I turned as two male members of staff escorted her into the room.

Layla Monahan was still an imposing presence, but she was far removed from the glamorous woman I used to know. Her once lustrous hair was peppered with grey strands and tied back into a messy ponytail. There wasn't a scrap of makeup on her pale face or anything to conceal the bags and dark circles under her bloodshot eyes. Wearing grey leggings and a black T-shirt, aesthetically she was a world away from the person I knew. I wondered what, if anything, was left of the Layla of old.

"... if it isn't Detective Inspector Dylan Monroe, Merseyside Police's latest celebrity." Her eyes swept over me as she approached.

I stood up to greet her. "Hello Layla, how are you?"

The staff sat her in a chair opposite me and remained close by. I returned to my seat and noticed her once manicured fingernails were chewed down to stumps, and the torn, bloody, angry-looking skin around them.

"Having a ball, and you?" Her expression was unreadable.

"Thank you for agreeing to see me."

"What do you want, Dylan?"

"First of all, for you to know that I still care about you."

"Aw, I'm touched. Try again."

"We, I mean, I, let you down."

"And you've driven all this way for me to soothe your conscience, is that it?"

"I'm your friend and should have known you were falling apart."

She let out a childlike giggle that sent shivers running down my spine. "Let's be real, Dylan. You were never my friend. I was just the stand-in until Saint Bella came back to hold your hand."

"No matter what you think, we were friends and still are."

"Do you lock all of your friends up with murdering scum like Beverley Allitt and Ian Huntley?"

She'd mentioned two of the most heinous, reviled criminals in recent history, and it wasn't lost on me that somewhere within the walls of the main building, not too far from here, they roamed about. But her tone was perplexing. They were detained indefinitely at Rampton for murdering babies and young children. Like her, they took innocent lives, but she appeared to view them as lesser beings than herself. "This isn't a prison, Layla—you're here to get better."

"There's nothing wrong with me."

"How is it here, are they treating you well?"

"Just wonderful," she hissed. "Locked up with the dregs of society, murderers, crazies who should have been put out of their misery a long time ago..." Her words trailed off.

"You killed people too, Layla. Many innocent women died at your hands."

"No, Dylan, you're wrong, they weren't women, not even close."

Her reaction did not surprise me because her hatred for the transgender community was personal and ran deep. "They didn't deserve to die."

"Freaks of nature that weren't fit to walk the streets," she hissed.

"Then why kill Darren Wilkes?" We'd found his body. He was Layla's final victim though I found it hard to feel any sympathy for him, or how he'd died.

"Wrong place, wrong time."

"Was it really as simple as that?"

"I can invent a reason if you'd prefer, Detective Inspector?"

There was little point arguing about something I couldn't change, nor did I want to piss her off. Still, I needed answers. "And what about Maxine?"

I wondered if mentioning her ex-husband was wise, but the words came out before I could stop myself. Instantly, I noticed the change in her demeanour and the warped, twisted side that had so far remained hidden emerged, fighting to reassert its dominance.

"Max-*well* had a lucky escape." Layla obviously felt it her duty to give me an unneeded reminder of who Maxine was pre-transition. "After I sliced off his useless cock, I should have choked him with it, but you got in the way and ruined everything."

"Max-*ine*," I corrected, remembering what she'd done that day, and how we'd both nearly died as a result.

"If you insist, boss." She didn't argue as I would've expected but hummed a tune, softly, just under her breath. "La-la-la-la," she crooned softly, accompanying it with the drumming of her fingers on the table, tapping out a rhythm that was familiar to me. I couldn't place it because my nerves were in danger of overriding any sense of calm I felt.

"How are your sessions with the psychologist going?"

"I talk, he listens."

"That's progress, isn't it?"

"The more I talk, the more he writes, and the more he writes, the less I feel inclined to say."

"Why?"

"He's trying to get in here." She tapped the side of her head, blinking rapidly. "But we won't let him, will we?"

We. Her use of the word wasn't lost on me. It's a symptom of her Dissociative Identity Disorder diagnosis and one I'd been warned to expect. "I know you don't believe me, but you're in the best place, and who knows, maybe one day—"

She rubbed her hands together as though pleased with herself, then cut across me as I was speaking. "Maybe one day I can turn back time and be there for the most important moments of my kids' lives." She flashed me a look filled with pure hatred. "Could I really do that, Dylan, could I?"

It was the one part that truly niggled at me on those nights I couldn't sleep. Layla's children were the innocents but are serving their own sentence too. "Have your kids been to visit?"

"Not as much as she'd like."

"She?"

"Monahan, the whining bitch." Whichever personality flitted in now eyed me curiously.

Unnerved, I looked over at the two members of staff standing guard. They seemed to pick up on the rising tension and edged closer. With a finger I stalled their approach, believing this personality, whoever it was, wouldn't attack.

"And that stupid whore, Pixie, how I'd love to wipe the silly grin from her face."

"Your mum loves you very much, Layla." I can still remember seeing Pixie's face from across the courtroom. Hers was a look of disbelief and anguish because she could do nothing to help her daughter. Tear-stained and grief-stricken, she'd pushed me away as I tried to comfort her before she jumped into a waiting taxi.

"*I* don't have a mother."

"You remember Pixie, don't you, Layla?"

She blinked a few times. "Yeah, she brings the kids to see me."

I was genuinely confused because I didn't know which personality I was talking to. "I've been thinking about popping in, but I wanted to give them time to acclimatise."

"Acclimatise to what exactly—their mother, *The Trannie Murderer...*" The words brought a smile to her lips, "... Isn't that what the press called me?"

The tabloids actually dubbed her *The Trannie Butcher*, but I refused to massage her ego by correcting her. She'd seemingly forgotten what brought us to this line of conversation. "I wanted to give your family time to adjust to you being here."

"I miss my babies." Her eyes filled with tears as a calmness seemed to befall her. But as quickly as it came, there was a switch and the atmosphere in the room crackled with tension.

My heart melted. I could only imagine how it would feel for a mother to be forcibly wrenched away from her beloved children. "Layla, are you okay?"

Her eyes locked onto mine. It was obvious she was calculating her next move.

I'm in danger. While my instincts yelled at me to move back, something rooted me to the spot, aware that showing fear would give her power she didn't deserve. *Don't break eye contact.*

A quick side-eyed glance, noting the proximity of those guarding her and me, warned her not to carry out the plan I was now certain she was formulating. Instead, she leaned in and with a menacing tone, spoke. "One day, Dylan..." Then, without warning, she pushed her chair out from under the table. It made a screeching sound against the floor. She rose to her full height and balled her fists as the staff moved quickly to intercept her.

I jumped back, furious at myself for allowing her to see any sign of weakness. I'd told myself no matter what, that I'd display strength, but I hadn't factored how seeing and speaking with her again would make me feel.

"Let's get you back to your room, Layla," one of the staff said, guiding her by the elbow. "Your favourite programme is on soon."

Acting upon his instruction, she stood with her back to me as both guards flanked her. After taking a few steps, she stopped.

I felt sick and my heart pounded in my chest. I'd never know what she was about to say. Eager to get out of there and onto the open road to put as much distance between us as possible, I opened my mouth to say goodbye, but the words wouldn't come.

Looking over her shoulder, she uttered a final chilling warning. "You'll pay for what you've done to me."

THE END

Troll Under the Bridge -
DI Dylan Monroe Investigates: Three

ABOUT THE AUTHORS

Netta Newbound lives between The Lake District and New Zealand with her husband, and their adorable grandson.

Marcus Brown lives in North Wales with his partner, Jon, their cat Tobias & three adorable dogs, Susie, Sally and Sammy.

For more information or just to touch base with Netta & Marcus you will find them on:

Facebook
Twitter
Instagram

ALSO BY NETTA & MARCUS

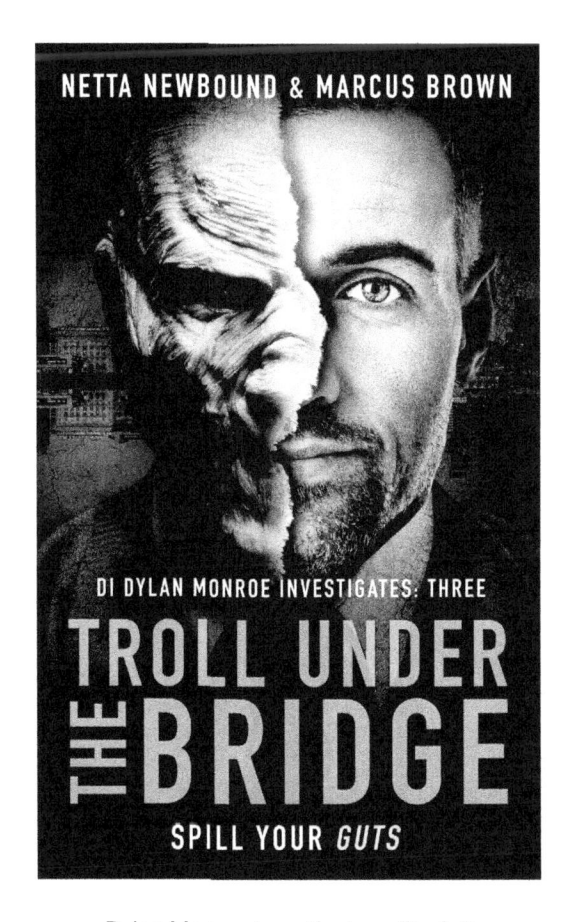

Dylan Monroe Investigates - Book 3

NETTA NEWBOUND
&
MARCUS BROWN

LORI VALLOW

DOOMSDAY CULT MOM: ONE - THE MISSING CHILDREN

True Crime -Lori Vallow

NETTA NEWBOUND
&
MARCUS BROWN

IN COLD BLOOD

DISCOVERING CHRIS WATTS - PART ONE - THE FACTS

True Crime - In Cold Blood

ALSO BY NETTA NEWBOUND

Rage: A Gripping Psychological Thriller

The Watcher: A terrifying psychological thriller

ALSO BY MARCUS BROWN

The Crockworthy Sisters - Parts 1-3

The Nightwalker Mysteries Series: The Complete Series

Copyright © 2022 Netta Newbound & Marcus Brown
All rights reserved.

Printed in Great Britain
by Amazon